About The Author

Marilyn Pemberton h... still a full-time project manager. However, at the age of 40 she decided she wanted to exercise the right side of her brain and so commenced a part-time BA in English literature. This progressed to an MA and then to a PhD on the utopian & dystopian aspects of Victorian fairy tales. After giving a paper at a conference she was approached by a publisher who suggested she gather together some lesser known fairy tales and as a result *Enchanted Ideologies: A Collection of Rediscovered Nineteenth-Century English Moral Fairy Tales* was published by The True Bill Press in 2010.

During her research Marilyn "discovered" Mary De Morgan, a Victorian writer of fairy tales, amongst many other things. She became somewhat obsessed with De Morgan and as she wanted to share her research she wrote *Out of the Shadows: The Life and Works of Mary De Morgan*, which was published by Cambridge Scholars Publishing in 2012. Despite her intensive research there were still many gaps in her knowledge and because she just could not let De Morgan, or the act of writing, go she decided to write a fictional novel based on De Morgan's life – the result being *The Jewel Garden*. This novel is a labour of love and she is thrilled that it has been published by William & Whiting.

Marilyn is a member of the Society of Women Writers & Journalists, the Historical Novel Society and The Society of Authors.

Marilyn is currently working on a new historical novel, set in 18th century Italy that tells of two young boys who are bought from their families, castrated and then trained to be singers. This was something that was actually done at the time, though this story is purely fictional. It follows the boys' careers, one who becomes a successful singer and the other who does not.

ISBN 9781912582037

Williams & Whiting (Publishers)

15 Chestnut Grove, Hurstpierpoint,

West Sussex, BN6 9SS

To Sasha and Hattie,

my own two jewels

THE
JEWEL
GARDEN

Marilyn Pemberton

Williams and Whiting

Prologue

1916

Last night I spoke with Mary. I had not seen her for over twenty years; not since the day she died.

It had been too real to be just a dream but as in a dream I found myself walking in a garden that was unknown to me and yet seemed somehow familiar. I was not following a path, but was chasing the sound of bells whose tinkling chimes always seemed to be tantalisingly just round the corner. I walked on damp grass, enjoying the sensation of each blade tickling my bare feet. A light breeze played over my face and danced around my body, caressing my bare arms. I was only wearing a shift of a material so light and sheer I might as well have been naked.

The path was flanked by the most beautiful shrubs, shimmering with flowers that sparkled in the sunlight and filled the air with an exquisite fragrance. When I went to pluck a rose I was amazed, and yet somehow not surprised, to find that each petal was translucent mother of pearl, and the raindrop nestling inside was a diamond. I inspected other flowers and discovered that they were of sapphire, pearl, turquoise and coral.

As I wandered on, still chasing those elusive bells, each step I took was lighter and faster than the last and a feeling of peace and well-being flowed through me, as if my veins carried an elixir. My body felt young and supple again, my flesh had the plumpness of a youth long past and my joints no longer tormented me with the pain of rheumatism.

Out of the corner of my eye I kept seeing slivers of light flitting between the undergrowth but no matter how quickly I turned, there was never anything there. I came to an enormous tree, and I saw that the leaves were emeralds and the fruit it bore were rubies. As I stood in wonder a voice came from the other side.

"Hullo, Hannah. I've been waiting for you."

I knew that voice, how could I ever forget it?

I walked round and there was Mary. She was leaning nonchalantly against the great gnarled trunk. She was as beautiful as when I had first met her, as when I had fallen in love with her. Gone were the grey hairs, the lines of pain that had etched her face during her last illness, the consumptive pallor. I felt confused. I wanted both to slap and kiss her. Most of all I wanted to know why she had been so treacherous.

Before I could ask her she danced away, her laughter like a shower of musical blossom fluttering in the breeze. She was decked in an incandescent light that glittered and rippled like a kaleidoscope of mist as she darted away.

"Mary, wait for me!" I ran after her, delighting in the stretching of my muscles, the working of my lungs, the beating of my heart. "Wait for me!"

She did eventually stop just in front of a golden arch. I could not see through it clearly, but could only discern movement and hear sounds that could have been voices or bird song or the wind. Mary smiled at me and tilted her head as she was wont to do. "It is not your time yet,

Hannah. Not today. It soon will be and I'll see you then. We all will." She kissed me on the cheek and then walked through the arch and disappeared.

"Mary, wait. I want to know why..." I went to go after her but my body felt heavy and cumbersome and I had no energy to move. I felt a great sadness and yearning for something I could not name. I lay down on the grass and the dew wet my cheeks like tears.

When I woke this morning, I knew it had not been real, but my cheeks were still wet, my feet cold and damp and my body ached as if I had truly been running. I felt restless and unsettled. Why had I dreamed of Mary after all these years? Why were the jewelled flowers so familiar? It was when I was sitting in front of my easel, ready to put the finishing touches to a water colour I was doing for a friend that I suddenly remembered. Of course, it was the jewel garden! The garden Mary had told me she had dreamed of when she was just six years old; where she had played with her dead sister.

It had been 1882, when I was twenty two and Mary ten years older. By then I had known Mary for two years and had already fallen in love with her. I had wanted to give her something special for her birthday. Over a week of dreary, wet winter days, when Mary had been out of town visiting some distant relations, I created a watercolour garden for her. The flowers were all based on real ones, but I let my imagination run free and mixed winter jasmine with spring cherry blossom; summer delphiniums with autumn roses. The blooms ranged from alabaster to deep purple, and I added even more colour by painting exotic butterflies that balanced on the edge of the petals, looking as if the slightest breeze would blow them off the paper. I had the painting framed and I was pleased with the end result.

On the day of her birthday, February 24th, I invited her around to my house for tea. She arrived promptly at three o'clock and we chatted happily over bite-sized sandwiches, dainty cakes, an assortment of pastries and numerous cups of tea. She asked me what I had been doing whilst she was away and I suddenly felt rather shy. I handed her the painting, which I had wrapped in brown paper and waited nervously for her to open it. Mary, impatient as ever, tore off the paper, giggling excitedly like a small child rather than a thirty-two year old woman, but when the picture was revealed she suddenly went silent and her face paled.

"Oh, Mary. You don't like it! I know it is not absolutely accurate, but I wanted to create you a garden you could enjoy all through the year." I went to take the picture from her, but she hugged it to her breast. There were tears in her eyes.

"Hannah, how did you know?"

"How did I know what?"

"How did you know about this garden?"

"It is not a *real* garden. I made it up. I just picked flowers out of a book and put them all together. Mary, what is wrong with you?"

Mary continued to look askance at me. "Would you come to our house tomorrow? I'm sorry, I cannot explain

4

now. I need to show you something. But Hannah, it is a beautiful painting; thank you so much."

Despite her belated thanks the mood was ruined and Mary left soon after, leaving me to wonder why my present had caused such a strange reaction.

The next day I duly arrived at the De Morgan household, and having paid my respects to Mrs De Morgan I went up to Mary's bedroom and waited patiently for her to explain.

"You know my mother is a keen spiritualist, and has been for many years. She believes absolutely that there are such things as spirit guides who appear to certain people in visions or dreams and who pass on messages."

Mary stopped talking, as if waiting for me to argue or even laugh, but I stayed silent. She bit her bottom lip, her whole body tensed and then she blurted out,

"When I was six years old, two years after my sister Alice died, I began to have very vivid dreams. I woke my mother once because I laughed so loud, and when she asked me the reason I told her that I had been playing in a garden with Alice."

Mary looked intently at me and repeated "In a garden. It was the garden you painted, Hannah."

"In my garden. In my garden? The one I painted for you?"

"The very same. Let me show you something." She took a small leather-bound notebook from the table and flicked through the pages until she found the one she wanted, and then handed it over to me to read. The writing was that of an adult, small and precise. The page was headed "Mary's walk in the jewel garden" and it was dated November 1856.

The narrative covered three pages and was obviously Mary's mother's interpretation of her young daughter's dream, rather than Mary's own words. When I came to the description of the flowers in the garden I read it out aloud.

"First of all there were violets of a rich blue sapphire and green emeralds for the leaves; the lilies grew among them made of white pearl with emerald leaves also. The roses were some of red ruby and some of red ruby with pearl. The chrysanthemums were made of many coloured stones. The periwinkles were of turquoise and some of a beautiful white pearl. The geraniums were of ruby and coral and the buds were so transparent that they shewed the colour of the flowers' buds through. The breezes smelt so sweet without your trying to smell them the scent comes to you. The jasmines were inside and outside the crystal water and shewed through."

I stopped reading.

"And you think this is the garden I painted? Mary, honestly, I made it up. It came straight out of my imagination. I don't even know what a periwinkle looks like."

"I don't know where it came from, Hannah, but what you painted is the jewel garden that I visited when I was six years old."

The jewel garden, where Mary had played with her dead sister.

The jewel garden, where I had talked to a dead Mary. When she had told me that it was not yet my time.

What did it all mean?

I didn't want to dwell on the possibilities.

I don't know what happened to the painting I had done for Mary but I remembered that I had made preparatory sketches. I had kept all my art work, from the very first one I had done when I was about four years old to the one I had finished the previous week. They were all rolled up and put into two cupboards in no particular order. I realised I was not going to find what I was looking for quickly, so I dragged a chair across and settled myself down for a trip down memory lane.

The first bundle I took out were sketches that I had found secreted away in my father's bureau on the day of his funeral. Only now did the tears flow, tears I had never been able to shed for him before.

Chapter 1 – The Toy Princess

1860 - 1880

Soon afterwards a little Princess was born, and the Queen died. Of course all the courtiers were sorry for the poor Queen's death, but it would have been rude to say so. So, although there was a grand funeral, and the court put on mourning, everything else went on as it had done before.

The little baby was christened Ursula, and given to some court ladies to be taken charge of. Poor little Princess! She cried hard enough, and nothing could stop her.

All her ladies were frightened, and said that they had not heard such a dreadful noise for a long time. But, till she was about two years old, nothing could stop her crying when she was cold or hungry, or crowing when she was pleased ... She was not allowed to play with other children, lest she might learn bad manners; and she was not taught any games ...

... she passed most of her time, when she was not at her lessons, looking out of the window at the birds flying against the clear blue sky; and sometimes she would give a sad little sigh when her ladies were not listening ...

"This is your father!" the fairy godmother said to Ursula, pointing to the King; and on this, Ursula, needing no other bidding, ran at once to him, and putting her arms around his neck, gave him a sounding kiss.

His Majesty almost swooned, and all the courtiers shut their eyes and shivered.

("The Toy Princess," in *On a Pincushion* by Mary De Morgan)

My father never forgave me for killing his wife.

He hadn't blamed the frailties of the human body, God or even Mother Fate. No, the blame was mine alone; it was evident in my father's silences; in his inability to hug me or even look me in the eye; in the emotional void that separated us all of our lives.

It was 1880 and I had just had my twentieth birthday. One day my father was there for our customary evening stilted tête-à-tête and the next he was lying in a coffin. The doctor said that his heart had finally given up the battle, having suffered from a weakness all of his life. I agreed that it was his heart, but I knew that it had been my mother's death that had eventually broken it.

The funeral was simple, as he had requested; his coffin, draped with a black satin cloth and adorned with roses from the garden, was carried to the village church by six of his tenants, with the mourners, led by myself, following in a straggling line. It was early August and by the time we had walked the short distance from the house to the church, the heat had given me a headache, and I could feel the sweat trickling from my brow. Propriety insisted that I wear full mourning but my hands were clammy inside the black lace gloves, and I felt as if my body had been squeezed into a too-small metal tube.

All the staff from the Hall were there, along with the rest of the tenants and their families, who offered their condolences and told me that he had been a fair landlord and had looked after them well. What surprised me was the number of my father's business colleagues who took the time to travel from London; what surprised me even more was that they all said what a well-respected and well-liked man he was. It was if they were talking of a stranger.

The service was overly long, with too many slow dirges and mumbled Bible readings, but an excellent eulogy by the vicar, who knew far more about my father than I did. In my opinion funerals should be happy occasions that celebrate life, not the depressing, morbid affairs that they are. I felt quite detached throughout; after a life-time of emotional coldness from him I could not manage to force even one tear for him.

Even though we were wealthy we didn't have a family crypt. My father's wish was finally granted and he was laid next to his beloved wife in the simple grave at the edge of the cemetery overlooking the rolling hop fields of Kent. As I watched the coffin being slowly lowered into the hole I realised with absolute clarity that the words of reassurance that had been said during the service were merely words. I did not have the necessary faith to believe that my parents were now both with God and that their spirits were blissfully reunited for all eternity; I knew instead that it was just their bones that would lay in the same piece of earth for all eternity. Mistaking my shuddering to be from grief, the lady next to me took my hand and squeezed it hard, repeating the trite reassurances I knew to be false.

After everyone had had a surfeit of sherry, cake and reminiscences I was left with just Mr Wilkes, the solicitor. I had sometimes accompanied my father when he had had to pay Mr Wilkes a visit at the London office. I had always been treated with great kindness and a handful of mint humbugs. We sat now in companionable silence for a while whilst the maids cleared the room, then he took a parchment from his inner pocket. I knew the contents of my father's will but listened anyway as Mr Wilkes read it out to me.

"So, Mr Wilkes, I am not to be like the young innocent female in a novel who finds out that her father has gambled all the family money away, and the only way she can survive is by marrying the horrid Lord Whatsit, or by going into service? So she goes into service, is seduced by the young master, begets a child and throws herself off the nearest bridge? That, I take it, is not to be my sorry lot?"

"Oh, Miss Hannah, you have such an imagination. No, yours is a much happier tale and would doubtless make a very dull novel. You get to keep everything, although you will have to wait until you are twenty five before you have total control of your inheritance. You have no need to work and you can marry for love alone, although I would suggest, if I may be so bold, that you make sure that he has enough money of his own and has no need of yours. Your father does stipulate, however, that Mr Black remains as estate manager as long as he is willing and able. I see no reason, though, why you would want to

11

remove him from the position in which he has served so loyally and so competently?"

I nodded my agreement.

"Your father has made it very clear that you are to inherit everything, and that no-one else from the family can take it away from you, despite you being a daughter and not a son. You have no right to the title, of course, that has died with your father, but apart from that you are able, if you so wish, to be an independent woman of means. He must have had a lot of respect and love for you, Miss Hannah."

I did not disillusion him.

That evening I went into the study and sat in my father's chair for the first time. Although I had never seen very much of my father during the day, I had gone to his study to say "goodnight" every evening for as long as I could remember. He would sometimes ask desultory questions about my day, which I answered with the minimum of detail because I knew him to be totally uninterested. He always asked if I needed anything but my wants were few. As long as I had enough paper, paints and pencils I was happy.

My love of sketching had started from an early age when Bessy, my nursery maid, had noticed that it was always the pictures in the fairy tale books that fascinated me, never the words. Even when I learned to read I ignored the written story and made up my own, based purely on the illustrations. I would sit with an open book on my outstretched legs, head bent in concentration, tracing the outlines of the characters with my plump

12

fingers, mumbling as I told myself their stories. Bessy saw me like this one day and asked if I wanted to draw. I wasn't sure why I would want to but said "yes" anyway, and from the moment she handed me a pile of blank, white paper and a box of coloured pencils, I felt an excitement surge through me, an excitement that has never left me. It was as if all my thoughts and dreams travelled from my head, down my arms, through my fingers and out of the end of the pencils. I started by copying my favourite pictures from the volumes of fairy tales, myths and legends that filled most of the bottom shelves in the library, but before long I was creating my own scenes, with the characters doing what *I* wanted them to do.

One day, when still a novice artist, I was so pleased with one of my sketches that I suddenly wanted to show someone other than Bessy or Cook, so I ran into the house and straight into my father's study, without knocking and without thinking about the likely outcome. "Father, Father, look what I have done!" I thrust the now crumpled paper onto his desk and jumped up and down in my excitement.

Not the hint of a smile touched his lips and his eyes remained dull. But he spoke to me kindly enough. "Be still, child. What is so important that you forgot your manners?" He studied the drawing. "What is this exactly?"

I was a bit disappointed that he could not tell what it was, but I patiently explained that it was a princess fighting a giant.

"Ah, I see now. A princess fighting a giant. Yes, very good, Hannah. Very good. Isn't it usually the prince who fights the giant?"

I snorted derisively. "The prince is locked in the tower and the princess has to save him." Did I imagine that his lips twitched? He made no further comment and bade me go back outside, but a few days later a parcel arrived for me containing reams and reams of paper and the most beautiful wooden box which, when opened out, was full of pencils, crayons, inks, paints, paintbrushes and India rubbers of various sizes, one so large that my small hands could hardly hold it.

He never asked to see any more of my sketches and I never proffered them again.

Each evening we followed the same dry ritual. He would sit stock still in his chair - the same chair I was sitting in now - and I would bend to give a brief, loveless kiss on his bearded cheek. I could still feel the sharpness of the bristles and the smell of his cologne. Once, before I knew better, I had tried to hug him but he had sat stock still, his back ramrod straight, his face motionless, as if it was carved out of marble. I never tried to hug him again.

Each evening as I left the study I would blow a secret kiss to Mama. She sat serenely in an emerald gown, her hair perfectly constrained, her hands demurely folded on her lap, imprisoned by an ornate gilt frame. Only I could see the twinkle in her eyes; only I could sense the weight of her hair, just minutes away from release; only I could hear her sweet voice wishing me a peaceful night and sweet dreams.

14

I looked nothing like Mama. Whilst she had been short but shapely, I was, as Bessy laughingly told me, as long and thin as one of my pencils. Mama's hair had been long, wavy and almost black; mine was light brown, straight and, since the age of seven when I decided to save brushing time, unfashionably short. My one saving grace was that I had Mama's warm, brown eyes rather than my father's cold grey ones.

I not only lacked Mama's looks, I also lacked her poise and would often stumble over nothing on the carpet, or bump into the corner of some furniture for no reason other than that it was there. Each evening I was a constant reminder to my father of what he had lost. No wonder he had never loved me.

I studied the picture as I sat in father's chair. As a child I had often imagined her stepping out of the frame and waltzing around the ballroom, her gown glowing in the candlelight. Her hair would finally escape from the pins and cascade down her back like a stream of black molasses. In my mind's eye I saw her laughing and out of breath, collapsing into one of the chairs and hugging me close to her bosom, her tresses wrapped around me like a blanket.

I never had imagination enough for my father to be present.

Mama didn't seem to resent my presence and looked down on me with her kindly, forgiving gaze. Without my father being there I felt as relaxed as I have ever done in that room. I nonchalantly opened a few of the drawers in the table, finding nothing of any interest to me, apart from a silver hip flask, engraved in fine gothic characters with "To my darling Albert, from your loving wife Anne, on the occasion of our wedding, April 11th 1855." I shook it and found that it was half full. I opened the stopper, thinking to taste the liquor, but the astringent smell was sufficiently repellent for me to put the bung back in as quickly as possible. I had never smelt anything other than his cologne when I had kissed his cheek each evening; I wondered whether he had tried to drown his sorrows once I was abed. I got up then and wandered around the room, studying and straightening each hunting print, fondling each china vase, stroking the smooth back of a galloping bronze horse. All these had been my father's and now belonged to me, but I felt no sense of connection. There was a rather beautiful oak roll-top bureau which I supposed held more of my father's documents that he had spent his working life writing and reading and were now probably just so much fuel for a fire. On opening the clever curved top, I was surprised to find a large leather binder, inside of which was a selection of my own sketches and paintings. I had never missed them; I did so many and he must have just picked them up from one of the various locations around the house where I tended to leave them. On the back of each one, in the top right hand corner he had written a title of his own choosing, the date and the words "by Hannah Anne Russell" in his neat hand. I felt angry that he had shown more care for my pictures than he ever had for me.

In the following days, although there was only one person less, the house seemed unbearably large. I wandered the rooms aimlessly and speculated on the amount of time and effort required to keep each one clean and aired for the benefit of no-one. The Hall gave no real pleasure to anyone other than myself, but I knew that the upkeep of the house and gardens meant that a large number of the villagers were in regular work. I would never want to be the one to change that.

I could not settle. I strode around the gardens; I sat for hours with an unread book on my lap; I rode around the country lanes but cannot recall where I went; I could not even sketch. I did not miss my father but my life suddenly seemed pointless. It was Bessy, now a lady's maid rather than a nursery maid, who suggested that I went to London for a change of scenery, and so it was that three weeks after the death of my father I left the country house and holdings in the capable hands of the estate manager, Mr Black, and Bessy and I moved into the London house.

It took only a few days to settle into a routine, very similar to the one we had always followed when staying in London, but this time the dining table was not even blessed with a man's presence. I loved London and we spent as much time as we could exploring, especially its parks. It was late September when we moved into the town house and I spent many a contented hour sketching and painting the trees with their stunning autumn coats; the lakes with their feathered visitors; the toy boats that sailed haphazardly along their edges; once, a dog that could not resist the temptation to chase anything that moved therein; the nurses with their huge prams containing their tiny, precious charges; the small girls and boys running after missed balls or uncontrolled hoops; the older boys and girls sitting more sedately reading or conversing politely with their nannies and wishing that they were younger; the young lovers strolling along the paths, wishing that they were older.

I had no friends or acquaintances in London whom I sought out; in fact I felt no need of social contact. I had always been alone and knew no different. I hadn't been allowed to play with the children on the estate and it had never occurred to my father that I might need playmates. Alone, yes, but never lonely, for I was happy in the enchanted worlds I created with my crayons and paints, where motherless princesses were brave, overcame evil and were loved. I did, however, have one person I considered to be a true friend, but she was on the other side of the world. It was my father, ironically, who had made our friendship possible.

It was when I was nearly eleven. We were in London for a few weeks and father told me at breakfast that he had to attend the funeral of an Augustus De Morgan the following day and that it would do me no harm to accompany him. Bessy was to come too and so that day was spent purchasing the required apparel for us both, this being the first time either of us had attended a funeral. I had never heard of the man but decided I should know something about him if I were to pretend to mourn his passing. So, I found Mr De Morgan's obituary in *The Times* and read that he was an eminent Professor of Mathematics at University College London. I skimmed

18

over the details of his academic career and his interest in spiritualism. I read that his end was hastened by the death of his daughter, Helena Christiana, and that he would be greatly missed by his wife Sophia Elizabeth and his children, William, Edward, Anne and Mary.

The following day, suitably attired, we were driven to the church and even though we were not late, we had to sit right at the back because the pews were filled to capacity. The account of the funeral that I read a few days later reported that the congregation was made up not only of academics, but also fellow spiritualists and business people whom the Professor had charmed during his life. Knowing that my father was neither an academic nor a spiritualist, I assumed that he was one of the charmed business men, although I never found out under what circumstances the two had met. As we sat waiting for the proceedings to begin I tried to distinguish the family members sitting at the front to see if I could discern whose back of the head looked like a Sophia, a William, an Edward, an Anne or a Mary. I was not, however, yet tall enough to see over all the hats that separated me from the front row and one glare from my father was enough for me to stop my fidgeting and concentrate instead on the order of service.

I was sitting between my father and Bessy, and next to my father was a couple whom I did not know, but the woman smiled kindly at me and surreptitiously passed me a mint behind my father's back. There was still some time before the service began and suddenly the woman turned to my father and whispered very loudly.

"Did you know Professor De Morgan well? He was a very dear friend to us; it is so sad that he has gone. My husband works at the Embassy and met him at a soiree; we both have nothing but respect for the very dear man."

My father was not a rude man and answered her politely enough, although he was not very informative. "I knew him from business. I am Lord Russell of Kent." He held his hand out and awkwardly shook their hands whilst the woman exclaimed so loudly that quite a few people turned around in their seats to stare.

"Oh goodness, what a coincidence. We are Russells too! Sheriden dear, is your family connected with Kent at all?"

At this point the man put a hand on his wife's arm to silence her and said, "We are very pleased to make your acquaintance, Lord Russell. I am Sheriden Russell and this is my wife, Sarah. The service is about to begin but perhaps we could meet up afterwards and see if we are indeed related?"

I was surprised when my father nodded his assent. The service was long and very boring. I was momentarily relieved when the monotonous bible readings, tuneless hymns and sycophantic anecdotes were over, only to find to my horror that we still had to bury the man, with due and lengthy ceremony. It was only afterwards, when we were all standing around admiring the many wreaths that I was able to study the family group. Mrs De Morgan was a woman well into old age, although she looked sprightly enough and had a good posture. I was not sure, of course, but I assumed that the two men and two women who

20

stood close to her, shaking the hands of all those who gave their respects, were her offspring. Luckily my father said I did not have to offer my insincere condolences, so I watched from behind a pillar. To my eleven year old eyes the younger De Morgans all looked very grown up and I came to the rather sweeping conclusion that the brothers were not at all handsome but the sisters were quite pretty, though not beautiful.

My father was rounding Bessy and I up, like a pair of recalcitrant sheep, when the other Russells approached us and continued the conversation regarding our possible common ancestry. It was when both my father and Mr Sheriden Russell admitted to having a distant relation called Walter that Mrs Russell clapped her hands with glee. "Oh, how marvellous! Hannah, you and I shall do further research and draw our respective family trees to see if we are indeed related. Wouldn't that be wonderful, to find we are all the same family?"

My father did not look as if he thought it was wonderful, but I was quite excited. I had never heard of any living family members and the thought that I may have someone else to call my kin was thrilling to me.

"Lord Russell, you will let me and Hannah write to each other won't you? We have only recently moved to London from Manchester and I know very few people here yet. I would so enjoy writing to your daughter and finding out about the Russell family together. You won't forbid it, will you, dear Lord Russell?"

How could any man, even one such as my father, resist such a plea? So, Mrs Russell promised to write to me and instructed me to search through all our family documents to see if I could find a family tree, and she promised to do the same.

Just six days later I received my first letter from Mrs Russell. Since the age of ten I had been allowed to join my father at the breakfast table and I was thrilled when the envelope addressed to me, along with my father's correspondence, was brought to us on the silver platter. I didn't open it then, but waited until I was excused and read it in my bedroom, hugging myself in delight. Mrs Russell, forgoing any epistolic correctness, wrote to me as if I was ten years older than I actually was. She told me something of her childhood in Manchester, her meeting with Mr Sheridan Russell, her marriage, the birth of Maurice, her first-born, the previous year and her feelings of loneliness in London. I wrote back to her immediately, admitting how excited I was at receiving her letter and that it was the first I had ever been sent. I then went on to tell her about my pony, Snowball, and the puppies that had just been born who were currently living in the stables and did she want one to keep her company? I finished by promising to research our family tree and looked forward to her next letter.

That evening, after the ritual kiss, I tentatively reminded my father about our little project. "Do we have a family tree father? Or any papers that may help me draw one?" He closed his eyes and sighed, as if he were reluctant to admit that such things existed.

"I suppose it will do no harm. There is a family tree in a trunk in one of the rooms in the west wing. I do not recall which one, but the chest is wooden, about one yard long and has the family crest carved onto the lid. There are other very important papers in the chest also, be very careful with them - do not tear any of them, do not write on any of them, do not fold them if they are rolled and make sure they are all returned to the chest."

Such was his encouragement.

The Hall had many rooms but over the years I had explored them all. I would often just stand at a doorway and study the rather old-fashioned furniture and try to imagine the days when people slept in the bed, hung their clothes in the wardrobes, sat warming themselves by the fire, or sat at the dressing table preparing for a ball given by a long deceased Lord and Lady Russell. I remembered seeing a chest such as my father described and the next day I only had to open five doors before I found the right room. I then sat cross-legged on the floor and painstakingly took out each sheet of paper and each roll of parchment, studying each one intently to see if it was the family tree that my father spoke of, or whether it offered any information about my ancestors. There were copies of the wills of generations of Russells; covenants restricting the use of certain parts of the estate; invoices for everything from building materials to repair the folly by the lake to oats for the horses; letters from solicitors, bankers and other worthies and estate accounts going back decades. It was absolutely fascinating and I made copious notes and wrote names, dates and relationships whenever I could. By the end of the first day I was astounded to see that I had barely scrutinised the top layer and that it would probably take me weeks to finish going through the whole trunk. There was no rush though, as Mrs Russell admitted in her almost weekly letters that Mr Russell's family documents were not so well organised as ours and were stored in various places all over the house, and that she didn't seem to have any time anyway because she spent all her time visiting, being visited or dandling young Maurice on her knee and singing him nursery rhymes.

I learned an enormous amount from reading those old pieces of paper: of the meanness and generosity of people on their death-bed; of the pettiness of neighbouring tenants; of the increase over the years in the price of basic vittles, such as flour, ham, eggs and milk; of the pomposity and condescension of everyone who worked in the legal profession; of the amount of effort and money it took to maintain the estate; of the changes of style in letters written in the late 1700s to those written one century later. I had not realised the extent that the Russell estate affected other people's lives and it made me feel proud to be part of the family. I wondered whether my father would have preferred a son to pass it all on to; perhaps that was another reason why he didn't love me.

For the following weeks I forsook my painting and resented any time not spent on my research. My haphazard notes covered pages and pages and I suspect that it was a good thing that I eventually found the single document that provided the answers, so that I did not have to try and interpret my scribblings into anything meaningful. It was not the very last scroll of parchment but it was certainly one of the very few left at the bottom of the trunk. When I started to unroll it the first thing I saw painted at the top was the family crest: a golden shield with a black cross fillet, which my father had once explained represented dominion and authority. In each of the quarters there was a symbol: in the first a bunch of blue berries for peace, in the second a lion for strength and power, in the third a cock for perseverance and courage, and in the fourth a red heart for kindness and charity. I had always been very proud of our crest and often signed my painting with it rather than my name.

As I unrolled further I saw that it seemed to be a family tree, most of the names and dates penned in a tiny but neat hand. In case of any doubt the paper was headed "Russell of Kent Family Tree" in a beautiful script and in the bottom right-hand corner there were the letters "AFR" and the date June 1858. I knew these to be Mama's initials, Anne Florence Russell, and I concluded that she must have done her own research, maybe doing what I had done and gathering the details from the contents of the trunk. I wondered whether she had sat in this very spot; the thought made my throat dry and my eyes moist.

I carefully studied the page searching for my father's name. I then traced and re-traced the web of lines until I found the path from my father to Sheridan Russell. A Lord Walter Russell, my great-great-grandfather, was our common ancestor. He and his nameless wife had had seven children, the eldest son being my great-grandfather Richard Russell, who had sired many children, the eldest son being my grandfather Samuel Russell, who produced two sons, John (b. 1820, d. 1832) and my father Albert. The title "Lord" was inherited by each of the elder living sons, which was why my father was Lord Russell of Kent. The tree had my father's date of birth 1823 and the fact that he had married Anne Florence Hetherington (b. 1832, d. 1860) in 1855. It also had my own name and my year of birth, 1860. I realised with a pang that my own details and the date of my mother's death had been added in rather less tidy writing and I recognised it as being that of my father.

I put my finger back up to Walter and followed the line through his fourth and last son, Maurice, through his son and heir Andrew and saw that he had had five children, one of whom was Sheridan. There were no marriage details, of course, but I would ask my father if I could add the details of his marriage to Sarah MacAdam in 1868 and the birth of their son, Maurice, in June 1870.

When I next wrote to Mrs Russell I reproduced the family tree and admitted to her that the results were not from my own efforts, but rather those of my mother. It was in her response that she shared with me that I would have to add another box to the family tree for the name of her second child, due in August that year.

My correspondence with Mrs Russell continued on a regular basis and the receipt of one of her letters was always a high point. It was beyond either of our capabilities to determine our exact relationship, but I certainly felt a bond between us because of our shared surname. Even without this connection we would still have got on well, for we had the same sense of humour, a same disrespect for proprieties and the same belief in ourselves as individuals. I felt very grown-up and proud when she said I could call her Sarah rather than Mrs Russell in my letters, for she said that friends always called each other by their first name didn't they? We shared not only the minutiae of our daily lives, but also the peaks and the troughs. I was with Sarah in spirit, if not in body, at the birth of her daughter. My father allowed me to add her name to the family tree having proven to him one hundred times that I could write the name small and neatly enough. The ink had hardly dried having written "Catherine, b. Aug 1871," when I had to add "d. Aug 1871." At only eleven, I did not understand the grief that she wrote of and was unable to offer anything other than my childish condolences followed immediately by amusing tales of the antics of Max, my new puppy, and my inability to conjugate my Latin verbs. It was many months before Sarah's letters returned to be as rambling and entertaining as they used to be, and it was with great relief that I was able to add "Georgina May, b. 1872" to the family tree.

Both Sarah and I mourned the fact that we were not able to meet again but Mr Russell was something important at the Embassy and soon after the loss of their first daughter he took the family with him to Australia. Despite the huge distance between us Sarah wrote so vividly that I had no trouble imagining myself there, sharing her adventurous life. I loved her witty descriptions of the country and its diverse landscapes of sea, mountains and the "outback", along with its weird and wonderful animals. Once, she attempted to draw a kangaroo, which made me laugh out loud, for how could anything so ridiculous really exist? For my fourteenth birthday she sent me a wooden boomerang beautifully and delicately painted by a young Aborigine man who worked in her house. I practised and practised throwing it as she instructed in her letter, but it only ever came back to me in Max's gentle mouth.

***

One of my few pleasures was to write to Sarah, which I did as soon as I had settled myself in London.

Russell House
Bloomsbury
London
September 27th '80

My dear Sarah,

Thank you for your condolences and those of your family. That I was in your thoughts has been a great comfort to me. I too wish you could have been with me.

You will see from the letterhead that I have moved, temporarily at least, to our London home. I love the Hall but I just felt I needed to be somewhere a bit more lively for a short time. When we first arrived Bessy suggested, albeit rather tentatively, that I should continue to wear black for at least a year, and perhaps curtail my exploration of the city until at least another three months. I carefully explained that the wearing of an unbecoming and uncomfortable dress would make no impression on my father, God rest his soul, nor on God Himself; that staying indoors for months on end would most likely turn me into a mad woman with murderous tendencies; that one of the benefits of our having minimal involvement with "society" all the years we had stayed in London, meant that I cared nothing for the opinions of "society." You do agree with me, don't you?

You will never guess who I met yesterday in the park? Lady Fenshaw! Do you remember I wrote of her about four years ago. Her husband was a colleague of my father's and she heard of me and invited me to a party to celebrate her son's seventeenth birthday. It was an excruciatingly awful affair and I am convinced that this is when I made the discovery that all boys are idiots and should be avoided at all costs and that I will never marry! Lady Fenshaw was effusive with her commiseration at my loss, although not grief-stricken enough to make the journey to the funeral! She then took my hands in hers, looked up into my eyes - she is very short - and said quite seriously, "I feel honour bound to take you under my wing, you poor thing. How old are you now? Twenty? Well, that is no age to be motherless and fatherless. You need looking after, and I shall be the one to do it." Well! How I stopped myself from laughing I do not know. Even Bessy, who has far more decorum than I have ever possessed went quite red of cheek. She meant well, I suppose, but I had to tell her that I had managed quite well up to now without a mother and that Mr Wilkes was on hand to be as fatherly as necessary. I was very polite and thanked her profusely. She looked quite flustered and let go of my hands as if I had some dreadful disease. Then she smiled brightly, said how independent young people are these days, and then told me that the least I could do is to attend a soiree she is holding this very night. It is to be a very discreet affair, just a few close friends and I would go wouldn't I? Even I felt I could not refuse.

September 28th - the day after the soiree!!!

Another disastrous affair! I tried very hard, honestly I did. You know I am taller than most women - and most men too if it comes to that - and being as thin as the proverbial stick I tend to wear dark, simple gowns with few adornments. Last night, however, I did wear one of Mama's beautiful pearl necklaces and matching earrings, and I even put a diamond pin in my hair - purely as decoration.

Lady Fenshaw lied! It was not a small do at all - there must have been at least one hundred people there, all of whom looked like they were trying to be the most sparkly person there. Even the men looked more gorgeous than I did. I thought Lady Fenshaw was being very kind when she came over, made small talk with me for quite a few minutes and then took me over to her younger son, Matthew, who was standing alone by the punch. She introduced me as "Lady Russell of Kent, recently lost her father and the sole beneficiary of his estate, poor thing." She then went off to be sociable elsewhere and I of course explained that I was not in fact a Lady, but I confirmed, to his eager enquiries, that yes I would indeed inherit the estate when I am twenty five. You should have seen his eyes light up! I know that I can be quite an innocent, but even I knew exactly what was happening. I allowed him to serve me a cup of punch, to fetch me a plateful of food and even to waltz me around the dance floor, but when he tried to kiss me behind the palm tree, well! I explained that I am not the slightest bit interested in being courted as I have absolutely no intention of ever getting married and his time would be better spent making love to one of the glittering belles in the other room. He left me - still behind the palm tree - his shoulders slumped and head hanging, I felt quite sorry for him. When I went back into the room Lady Fenshaw glared at me, whispered something into her neighbour's ear, who turned to me and glared also. After that I helped myself to another punch then asked to be taken home.

I doubt I will be bothered any more by amorous young men!

All my very best to you and yours,

Hannah

Chapter 2 – The Story of Trevina

1880 - 1881

"So, girl," she cried, in a dreadful voice, "not content with rejecting my son's noble offers, you would try and put an end to his life. It is lucky, indeed, for him that, with a mother's care, I have been watching him and you, when he thought me far away. I was sure no good would come of it, when he honoured you, a common human being, with his love, instead of offering it, as I wished, to the snake-princess. But now you shall be punished. Bitterly may you regret your unfeeling conduct ... Yes! You shall be well punished, for you shall become a tigress; and, left by yourself in the enchanted land, you will wish you had been grateful to my son for his kindness in offering to make you his wife."

("The Story of Trevina," from "The Hair Tree," in *On a Pincushion* by Mary De Morgan)

Our routine did not vary very much over the following months. Christmas was a quiet affair. Bessy knitted me a scarf and matching gloves, and I painted her a picture of her favourite cat, Tiger, who unfortunately was run over by a carriage on Christmas Eve, thus making my gift more poignant than it was intended to be. Occasionally we made an effort and went to the theatre or a concert, but I was happy to stay in and read, sketch or write to Sarah.

One day in February, we went out for a drive to Stepney Green Park but it was not a particularly

32

interesting place and rather than drive straight back to Bloomsbury, I suggested that we stroll around the streets. The tea houses that were to proliferate a decade or so later were not yet in evidence; my intention was merely to stretch our legs. We were ambling along Stepney Way when we came across St. Philip's, a rather stunning example of gothic architecture. I had left my sketch pad in the capable hands of Fred the driver, whom we had left chatting to some of his colleagues at the park, but I was fascinated by its numerous spires that seemed to be too thin to support themselves, its arched doorways, and the gargoyles, whose faces were too far away to be seen clearly but whose hideous expressions I could well imagine. The main door was open and I could hear someone practising on the organ. I did not crave a haven for my spirit, but rather for my body; the temptation to sit for a while in the quiet and study the interior architecture was too great.

Bessy remained outside, saying that she preferred to sit on the low wall that surrounded the building and enjoy the weak but relatively warm sunshine. I stepped quietly inside, the suddenness of the drop in temperature making me shiver and button my coat right up to the top. I walked down the central aisle, my shoes clicking noisily on the tiled floor, despite my attempts to be as quiet as the proverbial church mouse. I worried that I was distracting the organist so I slipped into the nearest pew. My eyes were drawn upwards, not to the heavens, but to the sweeping wooden arches that held up the roof and the golden stars that adorned the otherwise pristine white ceiling. I was in this position, with my head right back, when a voice startled me to such an extent that I yelped out loud and jarred my neck as I brought it back to a more normal angle.

"Oh, I am so sorry. Did I frighten you?" The voice, with a very faint Scottish lilt, came from a middle-aged woman, who was clutching a pair of scissors and some leaves that she had obviously just cut from one of the flower arrangements that adorned the front of the church.

"I was enchanted by the stars. How simple, but how very beautiful." I felt that I ought to mention God. "I think that they make one consider the wonders of God's world far more than a painting, or a statue."

"I am so glad that you like them. I am Adelaide Ross, the vicar's wife, how do you do?"

She managed to transfer all her bits and pieces into one hand and then held the empty one out to me. I stood up awkwardly, banging the back of my knees on the wooden seats, and shook her hand.

"Good day. I am Hannah Russell. My real home is Russell Hall in Kent, do you know it? But I am living for now in our town house in Bedford Place in Bloomsbury and we, that is Bessy and I – Bessy used to be my nurse maid but of course I don't need a nurse maid now, she is now my lady's maid - anyway we just came here to visit the park really, but it was not particularly interesting, and so we decided to walk for a bit and I have just come in to look around. Bessy is outside"

I realised I was gabbling somewhat, but could not stop myself from adding, "I am not a regular church goer. I'm sorry."

Mrs. Ross smiled gently, put the scissors and greenery onto the pew and took my outstretched hand in both of hers, as if it were a delicate bloom whose petals she did not want to crush. "Please do not apologise to me. You are here now, that is all that matters. If you don't mind me saying, you look as if you could do with some refreshment."

I had not realised that I might look so in need, but I accepted her offer gratefully, despite my usual aversion to meeting new people, asking if Bessy could join us.

"Of course, the more the merrier. I am expecting another guest in about fifteen minutes and you are both very welcome to join us."

I surprised myself by not even attempting to rescind my acceptance. Mrs. Ross radiated a sense of serenity and compassion that wrapped itself around me like a comfortable blanket, and I was willing to share her company with a stranger if it meant I could remain with her for a while longer.

We went to find Bessy and then we all walked across the road to the Rectory, which was surrounded on all sides by a large garden that showed signs of Mrs. Ross's valiant attempts at control, but which I suspected would revert in a very short time to its natural state, as God surely intended it.

When we were inside the sitting room she took my hand again, squeezed it hard, and told me what was

35

missing from my life, having heard the pertinent details of my history in the short time it had taken to walk from the church to the sitting room. "What you need is a purpose in life. You have the money, the time and the energy to make a real difference. All you need now is the will."

With that she left us to tidy herself up and to tell Cook to cater for two more people. Bessy and I sat together quite at ease on the old but very comfortable settee, and before long I heard a knock at the front door and female voices in the hall and soon after Mrs Ross came in followed by a dark-haired woman, slightly older than myself and quite a bit shorter, and one whom I recognised but could not put a name to.

"Mary, this is Miss Hannah Russell and Miss Bessy Cartwright, her companion. Miss Russell, Miss Cartwright, this is Miss Mary De Morgan."

Mrs Ross had a gentle smile and looked pleased with herself, as if she already knew that she had brought together two people who would become the greatest of friends. Mary smiled broadly, her head tilted to one side as she looked up at me with wonderfully bright, blue eyes. She grasped my hand and shook it energetically. I knew the name and was intrigued to find out whether she was indeed the writer of the fairy tales that I so admired and also the daughter of the man whose funeral I had attended all those years ago.

The group broke up and Mrs Ross, sensing that Bessy was feeling uncomfortable, asked her if she would go into the kitchen and help prepare the tea, at which she left the room as quickly as politeness allowed her.

Mrs Ross, or Adelaide as I later called her, explained to Mary how we had just met, at which Mary threw her head back and gave the laugh I was to learn to love; one that was unrestrained and joyous.

"How absolutely marvellous. How do you do it, Adele? The poor girl just pops into the church for a few minutes' peace and solitude and she suddenly finds herself one of your army of helpers."

"I have done no such thing, Mary. Miss Russell is here to share our tea and cakes, that is all. Please do sit down and stop giving her the wrong impression of me. Honestly, you make me sound like an absolute bully."

Their banter made me smile and Mary was so friendly and approachable that I felt no unease in talking to her. "We have met before. Well, not met exactly. My father took me to a Mr De Morgan's funeral about nine years ago and I am sure it was you I saw there?"

"I'm afraid I don't recall seeing you. There were a lot of people at Papa's funeral. It was all a bit of a blur."

"Of course you won't have seen me. I was only eleven. I am so pleased to meet you. So you are then the writer of the wonderful fairy tales that I read so avidly." I stopped to take a breath.

She looked pleased. "I am surprised that you know of my little stories. Do you have lots of darling little nephews and nieces to whom you have to spend endless hours reading?"

"No, I have no siblings; it is I who am the admirer. I have always loved fairy tales and have a large collection of them in the library. I am always buying new copies and

I have *On a Pincushion*, well a very dear friend bought me a copy for my sixteenth birthday, and I am waiting anxiously for *The Necklace of Princess Fiorimonde*, which I believe will be available soon? They are truly wonderful tales and I am very, very pleased to meet their creator."

Mary tilted her head again and looked at me seriously. "Why do you like them so? They are not like the fairy tales of the brothers Grimm or of Hans Christian Andersen. What is it about them that appeals to you?"

I did not want to give her a trite or pompous answer and I considered my response carefully. "When I was a child I read the traditional tales of Perrault, the Grimm brothers and Andersen, and yes, I loved them. I was good at drawing and I would do my own pictures but as I got older I made up my own tales, but through illustrations rather than words. I thought that there were no rules in fairyland and I felt I was allowed to be whomsoever I wanted to be, so I always had myself as a heroine, rather than a victim, as in the traditional fairy tales. I had no comprehension then of social niceties or what girls and boys *should do*, so I merely drew what I thought; and I thought that there was no reason for a girl not to be the one to kill the dragon, or climb the bean stalk, or rescue someone from the wicked witch."

I paused and she reflected upon my response. "That is admirable! You are a girl after my own heart. What happened to the girls at the end of your stories, did they always marry the handsome Prince?"

"No! Well, only if they loved him and really wanted to. I'm afraid I always made the men weak and not very interesting, so usually the girls just had the castle or the gold and lived happily ever after by themselves. I was, am, not a typical girl, you see. I am quite independent and do not *need* to marry. I do hope you do not think me odd."

At that Mary threw her head back and roared with laughter. "I do like a girl that's a bit odd! Let's have no more heroes, just feisty heroines! One day I will write a fairy tale with you as the heroine, shall I?"

We all laughed and I blushed a little. I concluded my confession.

"As I grew older, I realised that fairy tales are not just entertaining stories, but that they can show us what is wrong with our lives, and how things *could* or *should* be. I like that about them. I like that about yours."

I don't know what it was about Mary that attracted me to her. She was short and had thick dark hair coiled on top of her head, just like Mama, but that was the only similarity. She wasn't pretty exactly, but she had an open, friendly expression that I found striking. She exuded such a warmth and obvious interest in me as a person that I felt I wanted to tell her everything about myself, even secrets I had only hitherto written to Sarah.

The entrance of the tea trolley interrupted our conversation and we concentrated for a few minutes on the sipping of tea, the nibbling of cake and the contemplation of the weather and the health of the Reverend Alexander Ross who, at sixty, was some ten years older than Adelaide. Mary then changed the subject completely.

"Adele, my dear, we need to get young Maisie Brown out of that house and into service. If she stays there much longer she will turn out like her sister, and we don't want that do we?" On seeing my puzzled expression Mary explained. "I do visiting to some families in the East End for my sins. Maisie is twelve and a little simple, but still an innocent and can be saved. The father does welding at the docks when there is work, which isn't very often, and he has a tendency to drink. Her mother also likes a tipple, gin being her preference. The eldest son has his own family to support although he is a chip off the old block and hands over more coin to the barman than to his young, pregnant wife. The Brown's eldest daughter, well, she is beyond help, shall we say. The two youngest boys are too young to do much with, but there is a chance to save Maisie. The Ross's run a charitable organisation that helps get young girls off the streets and into service, where they can make an honest penny and retain their honour."

Adelaide had listened quietly whilst Mary talked and now she sighed. "It is not much that we do, but I always think that if we can save just one wee girl from a life of ..."

She hesitated so I offered up the word she seemed loath to use, "Prostitution?" She nodded, "yes, if we can save but one, then that is a blessing and is worth all the hard work."

By the time I had finished my second cup of tea I had offered my services and so it was that I became one of Adelaide Ross's band of helpers, a more "useful" member

40

of society and had a purpose in life. It was also the start of my friendship with Mary De Morgan.

I agreed to meet Mary the following Wednesday to accompany her on her visits to some of the East End families. I felt curiously restless and excited all week, marking off the days until I could do something constructive. We had arranged that I should pick her up from her house in Hampstead. I duly arrived at ten o'clock and was ushered into a small sitting room to await Mary's arrival. As I stood warming myself by a fire that really did not warrant such a name, the door opened and a small, grey-haired lady marched in but stopped suddenly on seeing me, her expression one of crossness rather than welcome. I recognised her from Professor De Morgan's funeral, and I held out my hand. "Good morning, Mrs De Morgan. My name is Hannah Russell and I am awaiting your daughter, Mary." She continued to look crossly at me and I gabbled on. "We're going visiting. Poor people, that is. In the East End. This is my first time. I am quite excited."

At that Mrs De Morgan's brows furrowed even deeper. "There is nothing exciting about helping the poor, my dear. Poverty is a disease that needs to be cured once and for all. It is not there so that those of us who are more fortunate can feel better about ourselves." With that she turned around and left the room, as briskly as she had entered.

When Mary came into the room a few minutes later, tardiness, I learned, being one of her failings, I had

41

recovered my composure and I made no mention of my brief conversation with her mother. I put out my hand but she hugged me instead.

"We don't need to stand on ceremony with each other. We are going to be great friends, I know it. Can your man drive us part way to where we are going today? Perhaps at the end of Commercial Street? We don't want to turn up in a carriage, it would be like shouting 'Look at us! We are richer than you!' We can easily walk the rest of the way."

Fred duly dropped us off at the chosen spot and we continued on foot. This was not an area of London I had visited before and I looked around me with interest at the row of shops which seemed to sell predominantly utilitarian clothes and utensils, frequently interspersed with public houses and the occasional church. There seemed to be a large number of men loitering on the pavements, especially outside of the public taverns. Women too, with rouged cheeks and large bosoms, hanging onto the arm of a man, or propped up against the wall. The smell of gin that emanated from these people quite made my eyes water. It was the children, however, who shocked me the most. They were everywhere, running hither and thither, getting under the people's and horses' feet, darting in and out of shops with the shopkeepers running out seconds later shaking their fists and shouting pointlessly for them to stop. They all, the boys and the girls, looked the same to me: all dressed in dirty rags; bony legs and arms that looked like twigs stuck into a potato; grubby faces that had never seen soap and water; hair a tangled mop, doubtless the happy home of families of fleas. I heard a noise behind me and when I glanced over my shoulder there was a crowd of the little urchins following behind.

"Spare us a penny, missis."

"Ma 'as got a new baby and no milk."

"I'm so 'ungry, m'lady. I a'int etten in days."

They all looked at me with large, doleful eyes, and I felt tears spring to my own. I went for my purse but Mary suddenly waved her arms in the air and shouted,

"Be gone, you scallywags! You all know me and you know you will not get a penny from me, not this way. Now, go, be gone!" They all scampered off laughing and went about their nefarious business. Mary smiled at me and patted my arm. "They can smell an innocent a mile away. If you had given them money you would never have got rid of them, they would be like leeches. Money is never the answer. I know they all need good clothes and a proper meal, but anything you give them gets handed over to their parents and then just gets spent on beer or gin. No, never, ever give them money."

We carried on walking, Mary occasionally nodding to people she met, who all smiled back and greeted her affectionately. We had just turned into Mile End Road when I noticed a piteous group of people shuffling along the road, dressed in rags and laden with pathetic bundles. Their attire made the clothes of the East Enders I had seen hitherto seem positively resplendent. They were all going in the same direction and seemed to be led by a better dressed man, who kept turning round to speak encouragingly to them. Mary noticed my interest.

"They are Jews, Russian Jews probably. They come over here to escape persecution. They look as if they have just arrived and being taken to one of the Jews' shelters."

"My God, they look absolutely exhausted and so, well, so pathetic. How will they survive? They won't have anywhere to live and they won't be able to get jobs surely?"

"Ah, that is where you are wrong. The Jews are very clannish and always look after their own."

Before she could explain what she meant, a couple, who had been standing on the curb and were not much better dressed than the Jews, hissed and shouted at the motley group.

"'Ere are more of them bloody Jews again! Ain't there enough of us wivout work or food wivout these buggers coming 'ere an' stealing our jobs and the very bread outta our mouvs! Why don't you go back to yer own country, yer bloody Yids? Go on, go 'ome!"

With that, the man picked up a stone and threw it at the Jews, catching a young woman on the shoulder and causing her to yelp in pain and to hold her baby even closer to her breast. I was incensed and started forward to intervene, but Mary held me back.

"Don't get involved, Hannah, you won't be helping. Look, the couple have gone now. There will be no more trouble."

"But why were they so awful to those poor people? They were hardly a threat to them."

44

"Well, that is not strictly true. The people round here fear the Jews very much and they do in fact see them as a tremendous threat. That small group we have just seen will very soon be living in a Jewish community. In a few weeks' time you will not recognise them. They will be properly dressed and they will be working in one of their compatriot's shops or even running one and in a few months' they may even own one themselves. They work hard, make money, which they don't waste on drink, and they become successful by their own efforts. And the native workers are jealous of them for doing something they could just as well do if they had the will. And what is more, the Jewish men treat their women with respect, which is more that can be said for most English men!"

By this time we had reached Middlesex Street and there were stalls strewn across the road and the pavement, displaying an odd assortment of goods and manned by men and women in strange, outlandish clothes. There was a man selling theatrical costumes whose face was painted in many colours and was wearing a bright red velvet jacket and a blonde wig. There was an extremely large, ugly old woman selling meat that, according to the notice pinned to the front of the table, was *kosher*. The woman had a black wig on that was not quite straight and I began to giggle, until Mary glowered at me.

"Ssh, Hannah! It is the tradition for married Jewesses, especially the older ones, to wear a wig to cover their natural hair so as not to draw the attention of other men."

I could not believe that any man would be attracted to the old woman, with or without her wig, but I held my tongue. Mary continued with my education.

"Did you know that earlier this century this used to be called Petticoat Lane? But in a fit of Puritanism the name was changed to Middlesex Street, not that it stopped the sale of such garments, of course."

Mary strode quickly past all the stalls but I had time to see the goods that each was selling: pots and pans, all kinds of kitchen ware, flowers, dried fish, foods and spices I did not even know the names of, haberdashery and clothes, including, of course, petticoats. The stall keepers were shouting, either to advertise their wares or at the customers, who shouted as loudly back, haggling over the cost. The air was filled with a babble of German, Polish and Russian and the guttural Yiddish that is a mixture of Hebrew and any one of these other languages. As I walked on a high-pitched sing-song voice penetrated the cacophony of noise and caught my attention. I stopped and pinpointed the source to a young girl standing behind a chair, with a couple of pairs of stockings draped over the back. She was dwarfed on one side by a stall laden with shiny pots and pans, and on the other by rolls of colourful cloths but she sang out her pitch as if she had an abundance of wares to sell. She was really very beautiful with long black hair flowing freely, black arched eyebrows and shiny black eyes. She saw me looking at her and she smiled, revealing tiny white teeth with a rather charming gap between the top two. I could not just walk away so I approached her and felt the stockings although I had no need of another pair.

"These are very fine stockings. I will buy this pair, thank you."

"Thank you very much Ma'am. You are my very first customer. When I have sold these two pairs, I will have enough to buy four pairs. And when I have sold them, I will have enough to buy eight pairs. One day. Ma'am, I will have a shop. You come back and see how well I am doing, come and see Salome." She exuded such enthusiasm and confidence that I bought the second and last pair and promised I would come again to see how well she was doing.

Mary had noticed that I had stopped and was waiting for me by a stall selling vegetables. I told her about Salome and her enterprise.

"You see, Hannah? These people work hard and have ambition. I have no doubt that she will succeed. When we come again she will have a bigger chair, or perhaps a table by then!"

We walked on through the market. I found the scene fascinating and wished I could sit in a corner and paint the flamboyant colours, the bizarre costumes, the flashing black eyes, the sheer vitality that these people exuded; to capture somehow the sounds and smells that were so tangible that I felt I could gather them in my hands and put them in my pocket.

We soon turned off the main thoroughfare, however, and walked down a street of terraced houses. The difference in atmosphere was palpable. There were no colourful stalls here or garish costumes. Instead, a pall of grey despair and black despondency seemed to lie over everything like a fine dust. The people walking along seemed bowed down by an invisible heavy weight and their eyes were dull and apathetic. The only hint of colour was the occasional flake of paint that tenaciously hung onto a front door, or a faded piece of fabric covering a window.

"These houses are very small. I cannot imagine more than a couple of people live in them?"

Mary threw her head back and let out a loud laugh. "Oh, Hannah, you have led a very sheltered life, haven't you? An East End family can often consist of parents, grandparents and more children than you can count on all your fingers. It is quite common for everyone to sleep in the same bed. At least that way they manage to keep warm." She shook her head. "These people live a very hard life. We try and help by finding work for them, or providing essentials in an emergency, but it is a drop in the ocean. We do what we can and for now that has to be enough."

We stopped outside one house whilst Mary retied her shoe laces and I could not but help overhear an argument taking place within.

"You good for nuffink waster space," screeched a female voice. A man answered back but I could not hear what he said because his words were very slurred, although I gathered from his tone that he was saying something conciliatory. To no avail, however, for as a baby started wailing the woman continued to berate him.

"Now look what you've done, you great useless piecer lard, you've woken our Lizzie." I heard no more of this saga, so I never knew if the couple became reconciled or whether the babe was successfully lulled back to sleep.

About half way down the street we came to the house of the Jones family, who was first on the list for a visit. Mary knocked loudly on the door and it was immediately opened by a young boy who shot out and raced off down the street, with his mother's words chasing after him.

"And don't come back until you've got them pieces of 'addock!" The owner of the voice stood in the doorway, her round, shiny face beaming at Mary. "Why, Miss De Morgan, no less. How nice of yer to come a visiting. Come in, come in. Make yerself at 'ome."

I followed Mary into the room and looked around with mounting horror as Mrs Jones bustled round shooing a couple of scruffy girls off some wooden chairs so that I and Mary could sit down. A small, square table was pushed to the far wall. It was covered with an oilcloth and piled high with dirty plates, which had bits of unrecognisable dried food hanging resolutely onto their edges. There was a big double bed in one corner, its sheets rumbled and of a suspicious colour. There was a shelf on the wall, upon which sat some knick-knacks, which I couldn't quite identify, and a couple of candles, the only source of light that I could see. The final piece of furniture was a large mirror with a surprisingly ornate gilded frame that hung over the empty fireplace. The glass, however, was a network of cracks, which made the mirror totally ineffectual. The girls who had given up the chairs sat on the edge of the bed, both sniffing and wiping their noses on threadbare sleeves. Suddenly there was a cry from the floor. One of the girls leant over the end of the bed and gathered up a grubby bundle from a box and proceeded to gently rock it until the sobs subsided.

My inspection was interrupted by Mrs Jones putting her face about six inches from mine and shouting at me.

"Do yer want a cuppa, Missus?" I was about to shake my head when I felt Mary kick my ankle so I turned it into an eager nod. Mrs Jones then shouted to the girls, "Make yerself useful you two and go an' make some tea. In clean cups, mind!" The girls scurried out of a door in the back wall into what I presumed was the kitchen, as the smell of boiled pork and cabbage wafted in from the opening.

The mother placed her ample posterior onto a chair that creaked ominously under her weight. As she and Mary chatted together about people I didn't know and circumstances I had no knowledge of, I studied our hostess. She was a large and buxom woman and was wearing a faded floral dress, its only bit of bright colour a splash of egg down the front. Her dark brown hair was greasy and hung in tendrils around her fat, flushed face. She used her hands to emphasise her point and often jabbed her stubby fingers at poor Mary's arm, until I am sure she must have been black and blue under her sleeve.

The girls eventually came back, each one carrying a white cup and taking great care not to spill any. My cup was chipped and had a black crack running from top to base and the tea was a grey colour with globules of grease floating on the surface. Despite this, I smiled kindly at the girl who handed me mine. She blushed and gave me a hint of a smile back, before returning to sitting on the edge of the bed. For a moment she had looked almost pretty and my heart went out to her.

The least said about the taste of the tea the better.

I was trying hard to swallow the liquid when I heard Mrs Jones say the word "Kent" and without thinking I blurted out "I come from Kent. I was born and grew up there. I have only been in London for a few months."

Mrs Jones turned to me in great delight. "Oooh, we go 'oppin' there each summer. The old man, an' the kids, an' even Ma and Pa. We loves it there don't we?" This last she shouted out to the girls, who both nodded enthusiastically. "Did you ever go 'oppin' when you lived there, Missus?" I didn't like to say that I actually owned acres of hop fields and that she and her family could quite possibly have spent their summers helping me to increase my fortune. So I shook my head and tried to look as if it was my deepest regret that I had not experienced the joys of 'oppin.'

"Though I ain't sure we will be goin' this year, what with 'Arry being out of work 'an all." Mrs Jones was no longer smiling and her shoulders drooped. "For every job at the docks there are ten men awaiting. And 'Arry, he ain't what you call robust. So it is always the youngsters what get chosen. No wonder he likes a sip of beer to keep his pecker up, otherwise there ain't no knowing what he might do." She looked at me sadly. "A sip of beer ain't much to ask is it Missus?" I shook my head and supposed not. Mrs Jones continued her tale of woe. "Our Charlie

51

works at the market of course, but he can't give me much now he's betrothed to that Sally, and 'er due any day now. I manages to do some mending now and then and the girls 'elp me, but it never brings in enough, no, never enough." She sighed and shook her head, the two girls on the bed shaking their heads in unison.

Mary opened her mouth to say something but before she could I had taken out my purse and thrust a handful of silver sixpences into Mrs Jones's open palm. "Buy the girls some shoes and the baby a warm blanket."

Mrs Jones's face broke into a beaming smile. "Well, God bless you, missus. I never expected nothing of the sort. You are a real lady, that's what you are, a real lady, ain't she girls?" The two girls on the bed nodded their heads in unison. The only person in the room not smiling was Mary. Her mouth was a thin line and I could see her jaws clenched in anger. Not at me, surely?

Her voice was harsh as she said we must be going and that she would come again the following week. She didn't wait for me after we were back in the road but marched back the way we had come, head held high, back ramrod straight. Despite my longer legs I had to run to keep up with her. It was only when we turned off the street and out of sight of the Jones's house that she abruptly stopped and turned on me like a ferocious terrier.

"What were you thinking, you stupid, stupid girl? What did I say not an hour ago? Never, *never*, give them money! Do you honestly think she is going to go and buy those poor girls some shoes and the baby a lovely warm blanket? Are you really so stupid?" By this time she had taken me by the shoulders and was shaking me as she ranted on. "I can guarantee that she has left the girls looking after the babe and she is now buying everyone a glass at her local gin shop. You have ruined everything!" At which I burst into tears. She stopped shaking me and instead hugged me to her. "Oh, there, there, you silly girl. Don't cry. I'm sorry I am so cross. I know it breaks one's heart to see such poverty, but there are other ways of helping, really there is. I have a plan for her and the girls, but it can wait until next week. Come on, stop crying now. No real harm done." In truth I had stopped crying, but her arms holding me tight was so comforting and the smell of her perfume was so intoxicating that I could have just stood there for hours.

I slowly extricated myself, and gave my eyes a final wipe. "I am so sorry, Mary. I just didn't think. I promise I will never, ever give anyone any money ever again. Honestly, I won't. So, where next?"

Mary cocked her head and gave me a smile that made my whole body tingle before leading me on to the next family on the list.

Chapter 3 – The Story of the Cat

1881 – 1882

The days passed, and Christmas Day came, and again the snow fell, and the ground was white. The wind whistled and blew, and on Christmas morning the old gentleman stood and looked out of the window at the falling snow and rain, and the grey cat stood beside him, and rubbed itself against his hand. He rather liked stroking it, it was so soft and comfortable, and when he touched the long hair he always thought of how much money he should get for it.

This morning he saw no old beggar-man outside the window, and he said to himself: "I really think they manage better with the beggars than they used to, and are clearing them from the town."

("The Story of the Cat," in *The Windfairies*, by Mary De Morgan)

I never became hardened to the visits to the poor East End families.

After only a couple of weeks, having witnessed the abject poverty and degradation they had to suffer day after day, and listened to the endless tales of hopelessness and despair, the guilt of my own wealth and comfort overwhelmed me. I didn't need two houses so I could sell Russell House and I didn't live an expensive life-style, so I could exist quite well on a reduced annual income. I shared my thoughts with my friend.

"Just think what could be done with that money, Mary. I could buy all the children shoes and warm clothes.

I could buy food and coal. I could really make a difference."

We were having tea at Twining's and Mary considered me for a long few seconds over the top of her cup, before putting it down carefully. She nibbled at a biscuit and then proceeded to quash my idealistic dreams.

"And what about when all the money is spent, what then? You will have made a difference for a very short time to a very small number of the poor. But how will those few feel when there is no more money to buy shoes, clothes, food and coal when next time they are needed? Do you think they will still be grateful and say 'well, it was nice whilst it lasted, now let's just go back to being poor'?"

Mary gave me time to digest her words. I quickly realised that she was right but did not see how things could ever improve permanently. "But what can be done? Even an army of women such as we two will not change things for ever, will it? I am rich, not because I have worked hard but because I was born to a rich family, whilst others remain poverty stricken despite working all the hours God sends, and more. It is all so unfair." Mary took my hand in hers, causing a tingle to travel from my finger tips to my toes.

"You are perfectly correct. Hannah. Life is not fair and our small efforts will not make it so. There needs to be a transformation, perhaps even a revolution."

"A revolution? Like in France? Surely not! That would lead to terrible bloodshed, wouldn't it? Our own Queen would be executed!"

Mary smiled at the expression on my face. "Oh, Hannah, you do not need to look so horrified! I am *not* advocating that the working classes overthrow and massacre the aristocracy. I *am* advocating more equality between men and women and between the rich and the poor. If workers are paid a decent wage, if workers only have to work eight hours a day, if landowners and industrialists are not so greedy, if men and women have an equal say in how the country is run, if girls are given the same education as boys, if women are given the same work opportunities as men, then, and only then, might we see a fairer society." She watched my face intently to gauge my reaction.

"It sounds like one of your fairy tales! That is an awful lot of changes. Who is going to make them? Gladstone?"

"Maybe Gladstone, maybe others. My brother William is in with a set of people who do a lot of talking about reform. You have probably heard of some of them - Edward Burne-Jones and William Morris?"

I nodded. I knew them both for their art, rather than their politics.

Mary continued. "I find their ideas interesting, but I don't know whether they will ever do more than just talk about it."

My curiosity in Mary's family took immediate precedence over the state of the nation. "I didn't know you had a brother! Is he the only one?"

"Goodness, no. Let me see." She put her head to one side, closed her eyes and recited her family tree. "The first child my parents had was Alice but she died at the age of fifteen, when I was three years old. Then came William, who is eleven years older than me; he makes tiles. Then there was George but he died in his mid-twenties; he was going to be a mathematician like my father. Then there was Edward, he unfortunately died a few years ago when he fell from a horse, leaving a wife and four children. Then there is Anne who is married to Reginald, and Chrissy, who died ten years ago. Lastly there is me. Alice, George and Chrissy all died of the De Morgan Curse."

Mary said this last with a straight face but I could not help myself from laughing.

"What do you mean, the De Morgan Curse? You make it sound like something from a penny dreadful!"

"It is William's phrase for consumption, or tuberculosis."

I was immediately chastened. "To have lost so many brothers and sisters, how absolutely awful for you. I am so sorry."

"It is hard, yes. But I would rather have had siblings and lost them, than have had none at all, like you. But it was Chrissy's death that finished poor Papa off. She had been on a long sea voyage to Madeira, as we all thought that the warm air would be better for her chest. I still have the letters she wrote to me from the ship; they are full of humour and fun and she had great plans for the future. We all thought she was so much improved but as soon as she returned to England she relapsed and died within a few days. Poor Papa. It was just too much for him."

"And your Mama, surely?"

Mary hesitated for a second. "Mama firmly believes that after death we all become spirits. She mourned the passing of Chrissy so early in her life, of course she did, but she considers death to be a blessing for the deceased and she looks forward to meeting with them again when she dies. Papa was not such a strong believer."

"And you, what do you believe?"

Mary smiled ruefully and drained her cup of tea. "That conversation is for another day. Remind me to show you a notebook of my mother's sometime soon. Now, it is time to go home but talking about William makes me think I should arrange for us to visit him. He is very artistic, just as you are. He works very hard and makes very beautiful tiles; they are much sought after, but he doesn't have much of a business head and he never seems to have a farthing to spend. You will like each other, I am sure. You two can talk about colours and different types of paint brushes!"

A few weeks later Mary was good on her promise and took me to visit her brother William at his workshop at Merton Abbey. He lived in Stone Cottage, a small one story stone building, and he had constructed a simple workshop and kiln in the garden. Mary told me that sometimes there were young women who painted the tiles, but this day William was alone. When I saw him my first thought was that someone had opened every single paint pot and flung them at him, for there was no inch of his smock that was not covered in paint, and it was spattered on his hands, beard and even the end of his nose. Mary and I laughed out loud when we saw him and Mary asked whether he was having a good or a bad day.

"Oh! Excellent, Mary, very good indeed. Look what I have made."

It was a tile about nine inches square decorated with an absolutely stunning peacock; the colours of blue, emerald, turquoise, crimson and daffodil yellow glowed and rippled and it seemed as if the bird might walk off the tile onto the table and fly out though the open window.

"All I need to do now is to make a few hundred and sell them at a vast profit." He threw back his head and let out a loud laugh, curiously high pitched for a man. Unlike Mary, William was tall and thin. His lankiness was accentuated by a long, straggly beard, the colour difficult to tell due to the splashes of paint and clay that adhered to it. The hair on top of his head was grey and thinning, revealing a high domed forehead, signifying, so the phrenologists say, a man of intelligence. He was not a handsome man, but he was an attractive man because of his wit, his cheerfulness and his consideration for others. William had illustrated Mary's first collection of fairy tales, *On a Pincushion*, and when I praised him for them he laughed in his inimitable way.

"Oh, they were mere trifles, I am no Burne-Jones or Rossetti. No, my forte is ceramics. I like to use my hands, bury them in the clay and feel it as it transforms from a cold lifeless lump into a living, breathing work of art. Now, enough chat, how about a cup of tea?"

Mary chaffed her brother, "As long as we don't have to use any cups you have made, as they will doubtless leak!"

My friendship with Mary blossomed, watered by tea.

Not only were we invariably offered the refreshment at the families we visited each week, which I learned to endure, if not to enjoy, but we also started to meet at other times and we usually revived ourselves with a pot. Mary was such good fun and seemed to take a great interest in me. She was the first real friend I had ever had. Hitherto I had always been perfectly content with my own company, that of Bessie and my correspondence with Sarah. Now, however, I found that I counted the days and hours until we were together; she made me feel loved, a very new experience for me.

She had an enthusiasm for life that rubbed off onto me.

"Hannah, I have had a marvellous idea! Let's pretend to be tourists and visit all the sites in this fair city. As a Londoner born and bred I have never visited anywhere just for the sheer pleasure of it. What do you think? Are you willing?"

I was so thrilled that she wanted me to share in her scheme. "Oh Mary, what a wonderful idea. We could go to the British Museum and I have been meaning to go back to the National Portrait Gallery for years. Where else is there?"

"Well there is the Natural History Museum, it has just opened and is apparently free, which is very unusual these days. And do you know where I would really love to go to?" She didn't wait for me to answer. "Madame Tussaud's!"

"Who is she? She sounds like someone who runs a brothel!"

"Hannah! What do you know about brothels? You are a dark horse."

I blushed with embarrassment and she laughed at my discomfort.

"Silly goose! Madame Tussaud's is a museum in Baker Street which contains copies of famous people made out of wax. They are apparently so good they cannot be told apart from the real thing. I am particularly looking forward to the Chamber of Horrors!"

We visited Madame Tussaud's the very next day. I had walked down Baker Street many times before but I had never noticed the museum. Fred dropped us off at the door. It had started to rain and in my haste to get inside I bumped into a lady standing in the hallway. I excused myself profusely; she was an elderly bespectacled lady, dressed severely in a black dress and a bonnet tied under her chin. She did not respond to my apology and I wondered if she were ill, as her face was pale and had a feverish sheen to it. I put my hand on hers but quickly pulled it away again at the cold, waxy touch. Mary was watching me with a wry smile.

"I believe you have just met Madame Tussaud herself." She came closer and studied the face intently. "She is indeed very life-like. Look at those lines around her eyes and mouth, and the individual eye-lashes. What patience it must take."

I gave an embarrassed laugh and felt a little discomfited at my mistake, but also disturbed. I myself copied people's faces onto paper, but no-one would ever consider them to be anything other than an artistic depiction. This life-like figure, though, was uncanny. It was as if someone had managed to preserve the real Madame Tussaud so that she would live on for ever. My feelings of unease were not appeased as we went around the different rooms, inhabited as they were by a strange medley of house guests: the Duke of Wellington, Napoleon, Voltaire and Jean-Jacques Rousseau all rubbing shoulders with Benjamin Franklin. It was, however, the so-called Chamber of Horrors that had me running out in search of light and fresh air.

The room was dark and cavernous, with gas lamps positioned so as to light up only the macabre death masks and bloody scenes. The first to greet us was a row of heads on pikes, all dripping very realistic blood and gore. These, so our guide gleefully told us, were the heads of King Louis XVI, Marie Antoinette, Robespierre and others who had fallen foul of the guillotine, a model of which was the next stop on our tour. The blade was at the apex, but with a flick of his hand the guide released it and it fell with a metallic swoosh, slicing effortlessly through a melon, one half of which landed with a sickening thud into a basket placed underneath. The guide smirked at my horror stricken expression.

"They say, they do, that the eyes still blink for minutes after. And some, they grins at yer. Not that they 'ave much to smile about, mind you. Are you alright, m'dear?"

62

"Yes, yes, of course. It is just rather warm in here. Please carry on. Fancy, still blinking. How very interesting." I didn't find it interesting, though, I found it sickening. I imagined what it must have felt like to lie under such a blade, knowing that the sound as it hurtled towards my neck would be the last I ever heard. What if, God forbid, I was still conscious for minutes afterwards? What if I was still aware, aware of the noise of the crowd as they cheered my demise, aware of the intricacies of the inside of the wicker basket, now spattered red with the blood pumping out of my veins?

I had lagged behind in my reverie so I hurried to catch up with Mary and the guide who had stopped at a recess in the wall. I peered in and wished I hadn't. It was a scene from hell. There was a heap of bodies, all naked, some decapitated, with the heads strewn haphazardly on the floor, their glass eyes staring into the abyss.

I knew they weren't real. Even so, I could smell the blood and sweat, I could feel the warmth their bodies were still radiating, I could see the horrendous heap shifting. My forehead was damp with sweat but my whole body shivered. I felt the bile rise in my throat and, turning on my heels, I ran back the way we had come. I did not stop until I was outside again, the raindrops cooling my brow, and the familiar smell and taste of the London air settling my stomach.

I couldn't go back into the museum, I just couldn't, so I decided to sit in the carriage and wait for Mary. By the time she sat down beside me, some fifteen minutes later, I had recovered myself and could return her smile. She stroked my cheek gently and brushed something off my sleeve, keeping her hand resting on my arm.

"I didn't come straight after you; I thought you might like some time to yourself. I am so sorry, Hannah. I should have known that such ghastly scenes would affect someone with such an imagination as yours. Me, I just see the paint and the wax, whereas you, well, to you it is real blood and flesh."

I shuddered involuntarily. "I am sorry too. I have ruined the afternoon. Would you mind awfully if we went home now?"

***

The weeks passed into months and we continued to visit "our" families. Mary and I became familiar faces in the Jewish markets where the stall holders would shout to us, trying to entice us to buy their wares. Whenever we walked down Middlesex Street I kept my eye open for Salome. She was there come rain or shine and it was no surprise to us when she swapped her wooden chair for a trestle table, and then soon after she moved to a bigger pitch so that she could put up her very own stall. Over time she expanded her wares from just stockings to everything a lady needed to adorn herself: a pretty selection of lace; gloves for day and evening wear; plain and patterned shawls; jars of bone, shell, pewter and glass buttons; ribbons and even parasols.

We always stopped at Salome's stall and purchased an item, needed or not. One afternoon, on a cold damp December afternoon, just a few weeks before Christmas, I could not but help notice that the young Jewess wore a self-satisfied smile and had an air of suppressed excitement about her.

"You are looking particularly pleased with yourself today, Salome."

Her cheeks flushed as she packed some buttons into a paper bag for me. She looked up at me shyly and then broke into a wide grin.

"I am the 'appiest girl alive!" She paused until she was sure she had our undivided attention. "I am betrothed. To Daniel Cohen." We both congratulated her enthusiastically. "We will be married once we have saved enough money. Two years it'll take - no more. I will invite you, Miss Hannah, and you Miss Mary." She sighed contentedly and then turned to the next customer who was waiting to contribute to Salome's wedding fund.

Mary and I carried on our way through the market.

"Do you think you will ever marry, Hannah?"

"Me? Goodness, no!" Surely she knew me better by now, perhaps she needed my reassurance? "I cannot imagine that any man would want to marry me and anyway, I have absolutely no inclination to partake in the sacrament of holy matrimony."

Mary linked arms with me. "You really should stop putting yourself down. You are a lovely person and anyone who marries you will be very lucky. Now me, I am far too old to contemplate marriage but you are still young and very eligible."

"There is nothing about being married that appeals to me, nothing at all. I have no desire to share my home or my life with any man."

"How about with a woman?"

"Maybe with a woman. We would have to be very good friends though and she would have to tolerate my peculiarities, of which there are many."

Mary laughed and repeated, "Don't put yourself down all the time."

She had sown the seed.

Christmas that year was very different to any I had experienced before. My father's only concession to the festivities had been to attend church in the morning and to allow the staff a day off. Once back in Russell Hall he would lock himself away in his study as normal and leave me to my own devises; I had always accepted Cook's invitation to join the staff in the kitchen for their Christmas dinner. It was always a merry occasion with much laughter and singing, especially after the sherry and brown ale had been quaffed. Everyone always seemed to be very appreciative of the little gifts I had made each of them. I never felt like an intruder but on the other hand, I never felt completely at home either.

The previous year, of course, had been my first having moved to London and I had spent Christmas with just Bessie for company.

This year, Mary invited me to share in an informal family celebration, which I was gratified to accept. I arrived at the De Morgan household on a very frosty Christmas morning. As I unwrapped the many layers necessary to keep out the biting cold, a young boy of about six years old came out of the living room and stood to attention, with his right arm stuck out straight in front of him. He stayed patiently in that position until Mary came into the hall and quietly told me that the boy was waiting to greet me. I put out my hand and he grabbed it with his two little warm ones, and pumped it enthusiastically up and down.

"How do you do, Miss Russell, and a very merry Christmas. My name is Pet. Uncle William gave me the nickname, it is short for petit Reginald, to dis ... to dist ..." His confidence disappeared instantly and he looked beseechingly at Mary, who knelt down beside him and whispered in his ear. He listened intently, nodded then continued, "To dis-tin-guish me from my father, who is also called Reginald."

"Well, I am very pleased indeed to make your acquaintance, Master Pet. You are very kind to welcome me in such a manly manner and thank you so much for allowing me to share your Christmas."

Pet blushed and keeping his hands encircling mine, he led me into the room where a group of chattering people was standing next to a roaring fire. The mantle-piece was decked with holly and there were sprigs of ivy placed over pictures and mirrors; in the far corner I saw a Christmas tree.

First of all, Pet pulled me over to Mary's mother, who was sitting on a sofa upholstered in a fabric I recognised as being a design by William Morris. Since my first embarrassing meeting with her, when she had rebuked me for feeling excited at the thought of visiting the poor East End families, I had only seen her a few times and she had continued to look on me, so I believed, with disdain. She looked so regal sitting bolt upright in her plain, unrelieved black dress, that as I took her cold, dry hand in mine I curtsied to her, feeling awkward and self-conscious.

Rather than the expected cold look, she smiled softly and gently squeezed my hand.

"You are very welcome, Miss Russell. Mary has nothing but good to say about you. Please make yourself at home and consider yourself as one of our family."

I felt my cheeks burn with pleasure. Pet took my hand again and continued solemnly to acquaint me with the others. First there was an elderly couple whom Pet introduced as great uncle George and great aunt Josephine. The man seemed frail and his hand trembled as he took mine and put it chivalrously to his lips, but his voice was strong and clear.

"Well, my dear, I very much hope that you are a good influence on Mary. By the time she was born her parents had given up trying to discipline their children, so she was left to grow up wild. She has always been incorrigible and has never done anything anyone has ever told her to do, especially her Uncle George."

I was shocked and felt my face redden in anger, but then I saw the twinkle in his rheumy blue eyes and realised he was making fun. Before I could make any further conversation Pet took my hand and pulled me to the next couple, being Mary's sister Anne and her husband Reginald. Anne was nothing like Mary, being a buxom, motherly type whose conversation revolved around her home and her family. Within the first few minutes I learned that Augustus was studying medicine and that Reginald was the youngest and had been something of a "surprise". With hardly a break to breathe, she explained that her husband was a doctor at Brompton Hospital, he specialised in, and was indeed at this very time, writing a definitive book on pulmonary haemorrhaging. I did not know what this was nor did I ask; looking at her husband's grim expression, I decided it was not a conversation to be had on Christmas Day.

Last of the group was Mary's brother William, whom I had met quite a few times by then and whose company I enjoyed immensely. He shook my hand and bowed with great decorum, then winked at Pet and tousled his hair affectionately.

"Uncle William, *please* don't do that. I am not a child anymore."

William looked suitable chastened.

Having done his duty I expected Pet to leave, but he looked up at me and shyly asked if I would like to see the Christmas tree. It really was a magnificent specimen. It was only slightly higher than me but its base was almost as wide as its height so it completely filled the corner of the room. The needles were a green, so dark they were almost black. The strands of tinsel, ribbons and coloured beads that were draped over the body of the tree glistened in the light of the candles that were fixed, somewhat precariously I thought, to the tips of the branches. It was the hand-made decorations, however, that Pet wanted to show me. He pointed out the paperchains that he and his Aunt Mary had cut out and coloured; the little muslin bags of peppermints and toffees; the sugar mice with pieces of liquorice for eyes, nose and tail, the prints from small awkward fingers clearly visible; the crackers he said would be distributed during dinner that contained jokes written by uncle William and a paper hat we all must wear; and finally the silver star in pride of place, slightly askew on top of the tree.

Pet's cheeks were as red as the holly berries with the heat of the candles, with pride at his endeavours and with shyness as he plucked a bag of sweets from the tree and handed them to me. There was a label, larger than the bag itself, upon which a childish hand had written, "Happy Christmas to Miss Russell, from Master Reginald De Morgan." I blinked furiously to stop my tears from embarrassing both myself and Pet.

There were many more Christmases over the years, of course, but it is always this one that I remember the best. We had a wonderful dinner of goose with a sage and onion dressing, potatoes both mashed and roasted, and a choice of gravy or dark port wine sauce. Afterwards there were mince pies and a flaming plum pudding, which Pet proudly announced he had helped stir. William made a great pretence of choking on the silver penny and had us all shrieking, first with horror and then with hilarity. In fact, he kept us entertained throughout the meal with his anecdotes, and although I rarely knew the people he referred to, I laughed along with the rest of them.

By the time we finished our meal it was early evening and we all gathered round the piano and sang carols until we were hoarse. Mary played the piano, not well, but with much gusto.

When I reluctantly left to go home I said my farewells to everyone in the warmth of the living room, but Mary came out into the hall to see me out. I shivered in the cold air and she put her arms around me and hugged me to keep me warm until my outer clothes were fetched. When she released me I impetuously kissed her on the lips. She looked a little taken aback but she then stroked my cheek, kissed me on my forehead and then helped me on with my layers.

That night I dreamed that Mary and I lived together in a huge house in the middle of nowhere. I awoke the next morning feeling happier than I could ever remember being.

Mary and I did not see each other every day, of course. Mary wrote to maintain her financial independence and would often be closeted in her room for days on end, working on articles or short stories. I was disappointed if she sent me a note in the morning cancelling an outing, but I tried to be understanding, recognising that her writing was as important to her as my painting was to me.

It was in the February of the next year that I painted Mary an imaginary garden for her birthday, which she claimed to be an exact copy of the jewel garden that she had dreamed of when she was but six years old. Her mother had recorded her daughter's dreams and her own visions in a little leather-bound notebook which Mary had shown me.

Mary's mother had been convinced that Mary was a true seer and I hated the thought of a mother interrogating the child about her dreams, and putting thoughts of death and spirits into her young, susceptible mind. I restrained my inclination to throw the notebook into the fire where it belonged and instead handed it back to Mary.

"So, tell me about being a seer."

Mary settled back in the armchair, more relaxed now.

"It was a number of years ago now. I was at a dinner party, I can't recall whose, but the conversation turned, as it often did, to palmistry and clairvoyance. I don't know what made me do it, but I admitted that I had had some success at reading people's palms. A gentleman immediately stepped up, offered me his hand and asked me to read it. He was obviously a non-believer, but I decided to play the game. I traced the lines on his palm and then, honestly, I just made up some random events. I told him that he would soon travel to another country, that there would be some sort of accident involving a carriage that he would be unhurt but would rescue a woman from the wreckage, whom he would later marry. It was all very ridiculous and we all laughed heartily.

"A year or so later, I was at a different dinner party, how I loathe them! when this same gentleman approached me and shyly introduced me to his new wife. After I congratulated him he proudly declared that after our last meeting he had indeed travelled to France and that on the road from Paris to Nice the carriage had overturned. He was unscathed but another passenger was trapped under one of the wheels and he managed to pull her out. They married soon after, and here they both were!"

"Oh, Mary, you are making this up, aren't you?"

"No, it is the honest truth. I was terrified he would ask me to read his palm again and tell him what lay in their future, but instead he moved on to tell other people about my prowess as a clairvoyant. It is all too ridiculous, but not as ridiculous as séances!"

"I have never been to one. They are just hoaxes, surely?"

Ever the story teller, Mary settled even further into the chair and proceeded to relate a tale of when her mother had arranged a séance whilst the whole family was holidaying in Betws-y-coed, when Mary had been about twelve years old.

"Imagine, if you will, a darkened room, the curtains drawn tight to block out the early evening light, the only illumination coming from the flickering flames of the fire. There are six stout, middle-aged men and women sitting soberly around a rectangular table that is positioned in the very centre of the room. Their faces are grimly serious and they are all sitting erect and motionless; the only movement is that of their shadows dancing crazily in the firelight."

I had had to stop her at this point for I knew that her mother was far from stout and had she not been present also?

"Oh, alright then. There are five stout, middle-aged men and women, one quite skinny lady, and one young girl, who is neither stout nor skinny. They are all sitting with their backs ramrod straight, their arms resting on the table holding each other's hands. One of the stout ladies, an American, is the medium and she closes her eyes, starts to rock backwards and forwards slightly and asks, nay demands, that any spirit who wants to make contact should knock once."

Mary paused here, her head tilted slightly to one side, as if listening for that elusive rapping sound. "Nothing, not a knock to be heard. The medium tells everyone to close their eyes, to concentrate as hard as they can and calls out even louder, just in case the spirits are hard of hearing. I have to close my eyes, not because I am concentrating, but because otherwise I know I will just burst out laughing. So I do not see who knocked, but knock they do."

Mary knocked loudly on the wooden arm of the chair she was sitting in, making me jump slightly. "What a hoo-hah! Hands are gripped tighter, eyes open wide and backs straightened even more. And so begins a very long, and I must say rather tedious, evening of dialogue by rapping. In this day and age there must be a quicker and more efficient means of communication between the real and the spirit world!"

By this time I was having to hold my sides because they hurt so much with laughter. From that day on I never looked at Mrs De Morgan without thinking of her trying to read more into young Mary's dreams than there ever was.

When I went home that night I looked at the lines on my own palms and wondered what Mary would see there.

Chapter 4 – The Pedlar's Pack

1882 – 1884

A pedlar was toiling along a dusty road carrying his pack on his back, when he saw a donkey grazing by the wayside.

"Good-day, friend," said he. "If you have nothing to do, perhaps you would not mind carrying my load for me for a little."

"If I do so, what will you give me?" said the donkey.

"I will give you two pieces of gold," said the pedlar, but he did not speak the truth, for he knew he had no gold to give.

"Agreed," said the donkey. So they journeyed on together in a very friendly manner, the donkey carrying the pedlar's pack, and the pedlar walking by his side. "

("The Pedlar's Pack," in *The Necklace of Princess Fiorimonde*, by Mary De Morgan)

One day in June Mary came to visit. Without even wishing me 'good day' she thrust a magazine into my hands.

"Page one hundred and fifty three," was all she said, but she had a satisfied smirk on her face.

It was a copy of the illustrious *Westminster Review* and when I turned to the specified page I looked in amazement at an article entitled 'Co-operatives in England in the 1880s' by Miss M A De Morgan.

"What on earth do you know about co-operatives?" was all I could think of saying.

Mary looked rather cross at my apparent lack of enthusiasm. "As you know, I am helping my mother write her reminiscences and she is, as I now am, a great supporter of the concept of co-operation. I submitted the article about six months ago and the editor thought it interesting enough to publish in this quarter's edition. Read it, tell me what you think."

I sat at the table and read through her treatise on the benefits of co-operative societies for all parties, from producer to distributor to consumer. The article was dry and factual, as I suppose it had to be.

"It is indeed interesting and, well, yes, very interesting, Mary." What else could I say?

"Well, the editor thought it was interesting enough to pay me. He has asked if I could write some more articles for future editions. So, you may find it dull but at least it earns me money."

"Oh, Mary, of course I'm pleased for you, you must be very proud. But do you really need money? Why don't you let me help you?"

"Hannah! Take your *money*? How could you even think of such a thing? Mother and I are not poverty stricken; I think it would be very boring to be as rich as you are. I enjoy earning my own money, especially when I can do so by writing."

Tea was then served and we settled down to refresh ourselves.

"Do you really need to earn more money? You got well paid for your two collections of fairy tales, didn't you?"

"I got paid, yes, but not well paid. Once the publishers have taken their third and the illustrators their third, well, one third of even a reasonable sum does not amount to much and does not last very long. But if I can sell a few articles throughout the year and maybe some short stories, then that will suit me very well."

I busied myself pouring the tea and passing the cakes.

"I know you want to be independent, but promise me that you will ask me if ever you are in need of something. I can't bear the thought of you going without anything whilst I sit here with so much, too much really for just one person."

She squeezed my hand and then brought it to her lips and kissed my palm gently; I held my breath as she did so and delighted in her light caress.

"You are a very generous woman, Hannah. If ever I am in dire need I will be sure to come a-knocking on your door. Now then, what do you suggest I write my next article about?"

"Well, what do you know sufficiently well to write about?"

"I don't need to know anything - I can find out everything there is to know about everything and anything at the library of the British Museum."

My puzzlement must have shown on my face, for Mary smiled enigmatically and proposed that our next visit should be to this bastion of learning.

"Not only can you marvel at the architecture and be amazed at the mass of knowledge that is bound within the book covers, but I can also do some research for my next article, when I have decided what it will be about."

I had always thought that the library at Russell Hall was large, but when I walked through the doors into the cavernous domed reading room of the British Museum a number of weeks later, my mouth actually dropped open. The curved walls were lined with bookshelf after bookshelf that went up so high I wondered how anyone could possibly reach them, until I saw that there were two balconies running around the walls, allowing people access to the higher books. The dome itself was sky blue with huge arched windows all around its base as well as its crown being made of glass. The afternoon sunshine shone through onto the bowed backs of the people sitting at the tables.

"There must be millions of books here," I whispered. "Millions and millions. How on earth do you know where to look for something?"

Mary smiled at my obvious awe, pulled me inside and took me over to a cabinet that contained multiple drawers; each was tightly packed with neatly written cards.

"All the books are categorised and numbered. There are different indexes so that you can look for books on a particular subject or by a specific author. If you want to read books on witchcraft, for example, then you go to the subject index drawers, look under W for witchcraft, and see, there are about ten cards here for books on your chosen subject. You then write down the numbers of the books you want to read and hand it to the librarian. Each number indicates the level and section they need to go to in order to find the book you are looking for. Very simple, but very effective."

I continued to stare around me; the air itself seemed thick with the world's knowledge and I imagined that all the men and women bent low over piles of books must surely be great philosophers and scholars. Mary smiled when I whispered this to her and she whispered back that most of them were there because it was warm and dry. I looked again and indeed I saw that many were in fact fast asleep, that some wore the clothes of the poverty-stricken rather than the academic, and those that were writing seemed to be merely copying from the numerous open books that were spread out before them.

"Is that what you do? Just copy what someone else has written?"

"Certainly not! I read many accounts and then create another in my own words. Now, I have decided to write something for an American magazine. Apparently they are always interested in anything relating to the old country, so I am going to write about boys' public schools in England. I need some books on Eton, Harrow, Winchester and Rugby to start with. Will you help me look?"

It was not long before we were sitting at a table with a stack of books in front of us and we spent the rest of the afternoon with Mary taking copious notes from texts that I found for her. When the article was published some months later I felt immense pride in seeing my name in print after Mary's, albeit very small: "by M A De Morgan (research assistant H A Russell)."

We continued to visit the East-End families and different tourist attractions, as well as going shopping together and taking tea at each other's homes. Time passed quickly and before we knew it, it was Mary's birthday again; she was thirty-three. A few weeks previously I had asked her if she would stay with me for a few days, including her actual birthday. I was thrilled when she agreed and I spent the following weeks happily having the bedroom next to mine re-decorated. The wallpaper was a Morris design, as were the curtains and chair covers and I even had the fireplace decorated with some of her brother's tiles. I replaced all the furniture and the overall effect was very colourful and modern.

Mary arrived in the early evening of the day before her birthday and I took her up to her room myself. I was quite nervous as I opened the door; I so much wanted her to like it. She was chattering away as she entered the room but as she took in her surroundings she became silent, a slight frown furrowing her forehead.

"You've redecorated the room. Why? It was perfectly alright before, wasn't it?"

"I did it as a surprise for you. I thought you would like it. Don't you?"

Mary slowly walked around the room, inspecting every aspect, stroking the fabrics, caressing the woodwork and finally came to me and put her arms tightly around me.

"You did all this for me? Oh, Hannah, there was no need. I am only going to sleep here for a few days."

"I enjoyed doing it, it gave me a lot of pleasure. It needed doing anyway," I lied.

That night, as I lay in my bed, I listened contentedly to Mary pottering around, humming to herself. When she finally settled I fell into an unquiet sleep.

My dream woke me in the early hours of the morning but evaporated into the blackness, leaving nothing but a thumping heart and a feeling of foreboding. I lay listening but heard nothing. Surely it had been Mary's rhythmic breathing that had lulled me to sleep the previous night?

The silence was absolute.

Had she stopped breathing?

Was she at this very moment on the threshold between life and death?

Without a further thought I leapt out of bed and went to the interior door that joined both bedrooms. I opened it as quietly as I could, but it squeaked nonetheless, and I stood in the doorway, listening.

Nothing, nothing but the blood pounding in my ears.

I held my breath, too frightened to move.

The blackness was palpable; the fear rose in my gorge and leaked out of my mouth as a whimper.

"Hannah, I hope to God that is you. What are you doing? Are you ill?"

The relief flooded through me, forcing the air out of my lungs and tears out of my eyes. I opened my mouth but could only produce inarticulate sobs. I heard Mary strike a match and then the candle flame pushed back the darkness and revealed her sitting upright in bed, her hair in slight disarray, a concerned expression on her face. I suddenly found my voice.

"Oh, Mary. I thought you were dead!"

"Dead? Why on earth did you think that? You are such a goose, sometimes." She put out her arms to me. "Come over here."

The warmth of her arms around me and her breath on the back of my neck was proof enough that she was very much alive.

"I had a bad dream that woke me up and then I couldn't hear you breathing. I convinced myself that you were dead. I am so sorry to have woken you."

She stroked my hair and continued to hold me against her breast. She hummed quietly and I felt my eyes droop. I wasn't asleep but I pretended to be, and I let Mary lower me onto the bed and cover me. She blew out the candle and lay down beside me, still humming.

The next morning I woke curled on my side, with Mary wrapped around me like a coat. I lay for minutes just savouring the sound of her breathing, the warmth of her skin against mine, the very smell of her. My toes curled with pleasure and I felt a longing in the pit of my stomach that I could not explain.

There was a tap on the door and Mary shouted out, "Hang on a second." She then whispered to me to go quickly and waited for me to close the connecting door before then calling to the maid to enter. Her haste in sending me back to my own room puzzled me.

It was as if she was embarrassed, or guilty even.

I bought Mary a beautiful Paisley shawl for her birthday; the primary colour was a peacock blue that matched her eyes perfectly. It was a cold, frosty morning and we decided to parade her gift by going out, so we went for a brisk walk around Richmond Park. We laughed at the ducks slipping and slithering on the frozen lake and at the children sliding on every conceivable piece if ice. We marvelled at their stamina, at their resilience to the cold, to their imperviousness to the hardness of the ground and to their tenacity, regardless of the numerous tumbles and scrapes.

By the time we returned home, her cheeks were flushed and her eyes sparkled as if the cold had turned them to crystals of ice. As we were removing our outer clothes in the vestibule there was a knock on the door and as I was close by I opened it, to be faced with an enormous bouquet of red roses on legs. Then a small head popped out round the side, "Flaars for a Miss Mary De Morgan."

Mary looked puzzled and took them off the young boy who waited patiently whilst I found a coin in my bag; he thanked me with a cheeky wink and then scurried off on his next errand.

"Who are they from, Mary? Who knows you are here?"

"There's no label, it must have fallen off. I suppose they must be from William."

I opened the door to try and call back the boy, to see if he knew who had sent them, but he had already scurried off and was nowhere to be seen.

84

Mary buried her nose in the fragrant blooms, her cheeks almost as red as the roses; she was crying and the tears fell like drops of dew.

She looked so beautiful.

She placed the bouquet carefully on the table, broke off a head and came over to me and put the stalk through a button hole on my blouse. The touch of her hand on my breast sent a shiver right down to my toes and I kissed her on the lips and wished her a very, very happy birthday.

Mrs De Morgan and her brother William came round for a birthday tea and I had never felt happier than when I stood in the doorway waving them both goodnight, my arm around Mary's shoulders.

It was only later that I remembered she had not thanked her brother for the flowers.

That night I remained in my own bed, the connecting door was locked.

The weeks passed uneventfully. Mary seemed in a particularly happy mood and we continued to follow our usual routine, apart from one day, when she sent a note saying she felt a little unwell and could I visit the Murphy family by myself? I had grown to love this family over the previous months, although I still could not remember the names of all the children, so many of them were there. I dressed in very plain, dark clothes, despite it being a summer's day, all the better to hide the sticky finger prints that would doubtless decorate my skirt once the smallest of the Murphy brood had finished playing peeka-boo among the folds, and the older tots had clambered onto my knee to hug me and tell about their day.

After I arrived I waited for the initial chaos to calm down, then I told the mother and fifteen year old daughter to sit down and listen to me.

"Rosaleen, I have some very exciting news. We have found you a position as a nursemaid with a good catholic family in Brighton. You can start on Monday, the week after next."

Mrs Murphy's cheeks went even redder and she clapped her hands. Rosaleen, though, bit her bottom lip and looked uncertainly at me, and then at her mother. "Brighton, isn't that ever so far away Ma? I won't never see you again! Can't you find me somewhere 'ere abouts Miss Russell?" She lowered her head dejectedly.

"Brighton is not so far away, Rosaleen, really it isn't. The family are called the O'Connors and they have twin nine-month old babes. Mrs O'Connor needs help looking after them, now that they are crawling."

Rosaleen smiled; she was the eldest daughter and had helped her mother look after the Murphy brood ever since she could walk and knew the mischief mobile babies could get into.

"The house is really beautiful and you will have your own room. I have seen it Rosaleen, and it is so pretty. It is newly decorated, bright and airy and it overlooks the sea. You will love it there, I know you will."

Rosaleen lifted her head and I could see that she was more interested.

"There is an enormous garden that you can walk and sit in with the babes. There is even a pond, though you will have to be careful your charges don't go swimming in it, of course!"

Rosaleen chuckled and I knew I was starting to persuade her.

"You will get four shillings a week, be provided with a uniform, have a full week's summer holiday and, of course, you will live in a lovely house and eat decent meals every day. And, the best of it is that you will have a Sunday off every month so that you can come and see your family. You won't get a better job than this, Rosaleen."

I watched her face brighten and her eyes sparkle as she realised that this was indeed a wonderful opportunity for her and I smiled in satisfaction as she too clapped her hands with excitement.

I felt particularly pleased with myself as I walked back down Middlesex Road, shadowed as always by the indomitable Fred. I decided to treat myself to something from Salome but when I got to her spot I was surprised, then worried when I saw a gap where her stall had been only a few weeks previously. I stopped at a nearby stand and waited for the stall keeper to take a breath in his flow of cheerful banter.

"Excuse me." I had to shout above the din of voices that filled the air like humming birds, hovering and swooping around my head. "Excuse me! Do you know where Salome is? She had a stall right next to yours. She sold haberdashery."

"Salome? She's too good for 'ere these days." He gave a toothless grin that belied his criticism. "She's got 'er own shop now, you know, over there."

He gave me instructions and I went directly there. I opened the door, whose little bell announced my entrance, and when Salome saw me she greeted me with a beaming smile. She proudly showed me around her little empire and I willingly complimented her on her achievement. I bought some stockings and some sewing thread to add to my collection of largely unused sewing materials and congratulated her once again. When she handed me my change she looked at me shyly.

"Do you remember last year, Miss Russell, I said I was betrothed and that we would be married within two years?"

I nodded.

"Well, we 'ave saved and saved, and even with leasing this shop, we 'ave enough to get married. I, that is we, would be so 'onoured if you an' Miss De Morgan could join us."

She explained that as Gentiles, Mary and I would not be able to attend the wedding at the synagogue, but she handed me a tiny card on which I read that Mrs Shelski would be happy to receive congratulatory visits on Sunday, August 19th between 9 and 12, in honour of the marriage of Mr D. Cohen and Miss Salome Shelski. Reception at 4 Cobb Street. I of course accepted with the greatest pleasure.

I visited Mary the next day. She looked surprisingly well and I asked her if she was feeling better now.

"Better? Oh! Of course. Yes, thank you. It was just a very slight headache, but I thought it might get worse if I spent the morning with the rumbustious Murphy family. Did it go well? Will Rosaleen take the position? She would be a fool not to."

I told her how the visit had gone and then showed her the invite.

"Goodness, a Jewish wedding, I have never been to one of those before. I wonder what one wears on such an occasion?"

We discussed possible outfits and then Mrs De Morgan came in and Mary showed her the card.

"Cobb Street is it? That is in a very poor area. You will not want to swan around in your refinery. Dress down rather than up, I suggest."

Eight weeks later Mary and I, both dressed smartly but not too splendidly, arrived at the terraced house to find a crowd of people peering in through the windows. We knocked on the newly painted front door with a certain amount of trepidation. When it was opened we entered into the front parlour, where there were about a dozen chairs placed around the room, all occupied by chattering women of different ages and sizes. As we stood shyly on the threshold, a short, overweight woman stopped mid raucous laugh and waddled over to us, her round face split into a toothless smile. She had blacker than black hair pulled tightly into a bun on the back of her head, out of which stuck a peacock feather that swayed dangerously at each step. Her eyes were like shiny jet buttons that twinkled merrily at us. She introduced herself as being Salome's mother and before we could explain who we were she let out a peal of laughter and shouted to everyone that here were her daughter's very good gentile friends, at which everyone swarmed round us trying to shake our hands.

The room was decked all in white: there were clean white sheets covering the walls, the tables and an assortment of chairs, so that it looked like we were inside a great slab of icing. The table was laden with scented candles, flowers, a variety of cakes and sweets and even wine and spirits with which to toast the *kall*, the bride. The whiteness was further broken by the women's finery; they sported brightly coloured shawls, a vast amount of quite gaudy jewellery and the hair feathers that seemed to be the de rigueur adornment. We eventually sat politely on our chairs and nibbled at the food that some young girls passed around, whilst other visitors streamed in and out, congratulating the bride's mother, sampling the fare, drinking the health of the *kall* and then being ushered out to make room for the next influx.

After some time Salome entered the room, looking absolutely radiant in a pearl grey satin dress, with orange blossom in her dark hair. It was hard to believe that just a few years ago she had arrived in England wearing rags, carrying all her possessions in a small case and with not one penny to her name. She was surrounded by her relatives who all wanted to kiss and congratulate her. Even so, she still noticed Mary and I sitting rather uncertainly at the side of the room and she came over, hugged and thanked us for finding the time to join in their celebrations.

After a couple of hours the mother suddenly stood up and clapped loudly. She took her daughter's arm and together they walked slowly around the room, stopping at each person for a smile and a word. When they came to us we kissed Salome on each cheek and wished her the best for the future. After they had completed the circuit they walked out of the door and down the street towards the synagogue, followed by her kith and kin, many of whom by this stage in the proceedings were very much the worse the wear for drink.

***

A gloriously warm and dry summer turned into a cold damp autumn and an even colder and damper winter. Everyone seemed to have a cough but whereas mine lasted only a few weeks, Mary's dragged on for weeks including the Christmas period, so that I celebrated the festive season alone, but for Bessy. We communicated daily and her letters were usually full of banter, despite her being unwell. Her first letter in January, however, held no humour.

6 Merton Road,
Hampstead
2nd January 1884

My dear Hannah,
1884 has not started at all well, I am afraid. I am not talking about my own silly cough, for that is much better and will be gone in days, I am sure. I am referring instead

to the health of my dear sister Anne. I am afraid she has succumbed to the De Morgan curse and she now lies prone in bed. I cannot risk going to see her yet until my own cough is completely gone, but if you are free from it, would you mind visiting her? I am sure she would benefit from the very sight of you.

I miss you terribly but you must still avoid me at all costs, for mine is the sort of cough that you can catch, whereas Anne's is not. If you manage to see her please tell her how much I love her and hope that she recovers very soon. Tell her that I am in fine fettle, that my cough is merely a tickle and that mother and I will visit her as soon as we can.

There is very little else to say. I am feeling more energetic day by day and have even put pen to paper today. I am thinking of trying my hand at a novel!

Please keep well and tell me all about your day.

I hope to see you very soon.

Always your very dear friend,

MDEM

I visited Anne the very next day and was shocked at how pale and how very small she looked. She was propped upright in bed, this being the best position for her breathing, as she managed to explain in between coughs that shook her whole frame. She held a kerchief to her lips but I saw the tell-tale spots of blood that stained it. I smoothed her pillows, washed her face, brushed her hair and helped her change into a fresh nightgown. When I left there was slightly more colour in her cheeks from the exertions of her ablutions, but the effort had exhausted her and she lay with her eyes closed; she could not even muster the energy to say goodbye.

Anne never recovered and died on the 18th January, just a few days before her thirty-ninth birthday. She was just five years older than Mary.

Thereafter I watched Mary like a hawk and at the slightest cough I plied her with *Gee's Linctus.* Mary tolerated my nursing but was resigned to her fate.

"There is nothing I, or you, can do about it, my dear. The De Morgan curse will get me in the end. You cannot fight a curse. William is as convinced as I am of this fact and he is certain that his lungs will be the death of him in the not too distant future."

"Oh, for goodness sake, Mary, of course you're not cursed. You just need to look after yourself properly, keep wrapped up and eat well. What you need, what we both need, is a holiday."

I waited for her to refute my opinion, but she put her head on one side and sucked the end of her pencil.

"A holiday? Now that would be fun. Where could we go?"

I had already pondered on this and visited Cooks to ask their opinion of possible holiday locations which would be of benefit to someone with a tendency towards ill-health.

"Egypt."

"Egypt! Don't be ridiculous, Hannah. It would take months to get there, it would cost a fortune and there is nothing there but sand. What on earth made you think of Egypt?"

"The man at Cooks said it is just the place for someone with a cough. The air is dry, the sun warm and it is apparently *the* place to be."

"Well, it is not the place where *I* want to be. There must be somewhere in England that will do just as well." She continued to suck on the end of her pencil, her eyes closed. I let her muse whilst I admired the shape of her head, the clearness of her complexion, the sheen of her dark hair, the upwards turn of her lips, the slight laughter lines around her eyes. I was just about to suggest we went to Russell Hall for a week or so when Mary suddenly opened her eyes wide.

"I know! William went to a place a few years ago. He wrote to me and it sounded delightful. In fact there are two places, one on a hill directly above the other, which is by the sea. They both begin with the letter L, but I can't recall their names. They are in Devon, so it is bound to be warm. I'll go and get his letter."

Mary returned, muttering the names "Lynton" and "Lynmouth" repeatedly. Mary bought a county map with her and we eventually found the two names nestled closely together, right on the north Devon coast and the border with Somerset. Mary continued to read the letter to herself, speaking aloud at the pieces of interest.

"Lynton is on a hill vertically above Lynmouth, which is a small fishing village and they are linked by steps. Both villages are very pleasant ... there is a hotel in Lynton and the rates are very reasonable. That sounds ideal, doesn't

94

it? We can walk along the cliff tops, drink lots of tea, eat too many cakes and ice-cream, read, write, paint, even go fishing, should we so desire. It will be marvellous. We can decide each day whether to stay in Lynton or walk down to Lynmouth."

"And walk back up again," I reminded her.

"Oh, goodness, Hannah, going up and down a few steps will do us both good."

"It will not be dry, though Mary. That is what you need for your cough, dry air."

Mary's head went up and she stuck her chin out like a recalcitrant child. "I am not going to Egypt. North Devon or nowhere."

I hadn't really expected Mary to agree to go to Egypt, it was indeed too far away and doubtless dangerous, so although it was not an ideal location I was pleased that she had agreed to go away with me. I had to make quite a few more visits to Cooks before the holiday arrangements were finalised but eventually it was organised and all we had to do was to count the months, then weeks, then days until July 10th.

Neither of us had a wardrobe suitable for a summer by the sea and I managed to persuade Mary to let me take her shopping to buy us both some light cotton dresses, short-sleeved blouses, loose-fitting skirts and a sun hat. Despite a very tenacious sales girl we did not purchase a bathing costume.

Fred took us and our trunks to Paddington railway station and got us settled into our carriage. It was very plush with red velvet upholstery, shiny brass fittings and walnut wooden table and wall panels. We had the compartment to ourselves and we sat facing each other, both grinning like young housemaids on an annual excursion. Before the train had even pulled away from the station we had been brought tea and a plate of dainty biscuits. We ate with relish and then settled down to enjoy the journey across England. We arrived in Exeter at three o'clock and had a short wait before catching a smaller train to Minehead.

This one had no first class carriages and we had to sit on hard wooden seats, along with other families going to the seaside for their holidays. It is difficult to sit primly and properly when there are toddlers pulling at your skirt, babies exercising their lungs to the full, little girls stroking your lace gloves and little boys offering you a lump of sticky toffee in none too clean hands. It did not take long before Mary and I were rocking with laughter at the children's antics and the parents' anecdotes.

We arrived at Minehead quicker than we wished and we said goodbye to our new found friends, none of whom were staying at the Beach Hotel. We had an excellent dinner, a good night's sleep and a hearty breakfast and were back at the railway station in plenty of time to take the horse-drawn carriage to Lynton. We sat outside whilst we were waiting, the sun already warm on our uplifted faces. Mary sighed contentedly and when I took her hand in mine she did not remove it.

The relative silence of the morning was broken by the clip-clopping of four gleaming black horses that trotted towards us. They pulled a large, dark brown carriage, beads of water from its' morning wash glistening in the sunshine. Each of the doors was emblazoned by a prancing red deer. The conveyance was large enough to carry eight passengers inside, and then there was room for another couple sitting at the front next to the driver, and then another four or so on the back seat who could only see where they had been. The trunks and cases were tied onto the roof of the carriage; they looked very precarious but the driver assured us that they were quite safe. I had purchased first-class tickets and for six shillings and sixpence each, Mary and I were entitled to sit inside. We were joined by a middle-aged couple who neither spoke to us nor to each other during the whole of the journey. By silent mutual consent Mary and I would have much preferred to sit outside in the cheap seats, so that we could have participated in the entertainment offered by one of the families whom we had met the previous day. The woman was large and her very ample figure took all the available seats at the front next to the driver, but she also carried a babe-in arms, and two of the toddlers crouched on the floor as they clung to her knees. Her much thinner husband sat at the back with the remaining children, all boys, who wriggled, chattered, punched and pulled hair and generally had a good time.

We had eighteen miles to go and the driver told us we would arrive at Lynton at around one o'clock. After an hour we stopped just the other side of the village of Porlock to allow the horses to drink from a stone trough at the side of the road, and for us to stretch our legs. The boys scampered around, shouting at the tops of their voices, their skinny white arms flailing around like pieces of string in a strong wind, and their even skinnier legs pumping up and down like the great brass pistons in the railway engine that had carried us from London. The dour couple's frowns got deeper and their lips thinner.

We were about to get back into the carriage, when the driver stopped us, his brown, wrinkly face creased even more with a big grin.

"Nah, missus. You 'ave to walk some ways now. That there is Porlock 'ill. 'osses can't pulls you up thar. Jes' take it easy and we'll meets you at top."

With that he led the horses and empty carriage slowly up what transpired to be one of the steepest hills in England, whilst we followed behind. The boys let out hoots of delight and immediately started to race to the top. The adults followed at a more sedate pace. The middle-aged couple were well prepared and both had sticks to aid their ascent. The mother carried the babe and took each step slowly but remorselessly, stopping frequently to catch her breath and mop her brow. At first the father tried to carry both toddlers but after a short time he had to put them down and holding their hands almost drag them up the incline. Mary and I soon left them behind but even though we were unencumbered we almost immediately had to encourage each other onwards, for our leg muscles ached, our breath came out in short gasps and our clothing stuck to our bodies with sweat. We convinced ourselves that the top of the hill was around each corner. We had almost given up ever reaching the end when we finally came upon the horses, who were contentedly grazing, and the four boys, who were still running around dementedly, as if they had done no more than just cross a street.

Mary and I sat on a fallen tree trunk and gratefully accepted a long, remarkably cool, glass of lemonade proffered by the driver. Mary suggested he went and helped carry the little ones to speed things up. He did so and before much longer we were all ensconced once again in the rumbling carriage; the mother fanning herself with a piece of card; the babe still asleep in her arms; the toddlers still clutching their mother's knees as if their life depended on it; the husband trying to doze at the back; the four boys as boisterous as they had been at the very start of the journey.

We duly arrived at the Royal Castle Hotel in Lynton in time for a late lunch.

When we were shown to our bedroom and Mary saw both trunks were at the bottom of the bed, she looked askance at me, but said nothing until the porter had left.

"Hannah, surely you can afford a room each? I have never slept with anyone before, only that time when you were frightened. I don't sleep well and sometimes I get up very early or stay up late to write. I really think it would be better if we had separate rooms."

I was disappointed; I had been looking forward to sharing those intimate little practices that only occur in a bedroom but she looked so worried at the thought that she might disturb me that I went down to reception.

I was even more disappointed to find that there was a room available.

Royal Castle Hotel
Lynton
Monday 16th July '84

My dear Sarah,

I hope this letter finds you and the family well, or is poor Sheridan still suffering from his bad chest? I am in rude health and Mary seems to have finally got rid of the nasty cough that has plagued her since winter time. We are now happily installed in a very pleasant hotel in Lynton. Henry James stayed here ten years ago; if it was good enough for him it is certainly good enough for us! Although it is July and the height of summer we have not had a day without rain, albeit warm rain! It usually clears up by late afternoon and the sun gets quite hot, though to someone who is used to the Australian heat it would probably seem positively wintry.

Our hotel is right next to the cliff railway, for which Lynton is rightly famous, and which links it to Lynmouth, a fishing village at the bottom of said hill. We are both quite used to mechanical transport, of course, but to slide up and down an almost perpendicular incline by means of machinery powered entirely by just water, is a totally new experience that both thrills and terrifies us! Each time we decide to go to Lynmouth we debate whether we should put our trust in a wooden box and cables that must surely snap, plunging us to our certain gruesome death! Nonetheless, we always take the risk and continue to use the contraption rather than exert the energy that is required to climb down and up the steep path between the two villages. We are, after all, on holiday!

Lynton is a bit like the sophisticated, upper-class cousin to Lynmouth, which comes from the working-class branch of the family. Lynmouth's income used to be from herrings, of all things, but has recently become a bit of an artists' haven. Consequently there are a large number of tea shops, guest houses and hotels, but there are still the quaint fishermen's cottages, which are doubtless damp, dark and cold when the sun is not shining! Fishing still goes on and sometimes, when we walk along the harbour front and the wind is in a certain direction, the smell of fish is so overwhelming that we have to run in the opposite direction!

I had hoped that Mary and I would spend all our time together, but she says she needs to write and locks herself in her room for hours on end scribbling away. Luckily, I brought my painting paraphernalia with me so I set myself up in the garden, if it is dry, otherwise at my bedroom window, and try to capture the ever changing colours of the sea. No sooner have I got just the right silver grey colour than it changes to cobalt blue, and then in a twinkling of an eye, it is a glorious turquoise. It is very frustrating!

I must admit to being a bit disappointed that I have so much time to myself, but I have to accept that Mary earns her money by the pen, and writing is not a shared activity. I do worry about her, though, for I don't think she is getting enough rest. She is always up before me at the crack of dawn, even before the post has arrived, as over breakfast she always shares the news received from her mother or brother - they seem to write almost daily. When

I settle down to sleep at night, I can hear her in the next room still working. I had such expectations that this holiday would bring us closer together but sometimes I feel that Mary is not quite here with me; she has a distant look and I often have to repeat myself.

Goodness, how things change in a heartbeat!! No sooner had I written the last sentence, than the rain stopped, the sun came out, a magnificent rainbow arched across the sky and Mary popped in and told me to get my coat on, as she is going to take me out for tea and cake at our favourite tea shop in Lynmouth to apologise for being such a bore these last few days!

I am already feeling much happier. I will write again at the end of the holiday.

Give my love and regards to all the family. Tell Georgie she is very naughty as I have not received a letter from her for a couple of months.

Your ever loving,
Hannah

It started to rain heavily almost as soon as we stepped outside. Although we were wearing coats and had borrowed the hotel umbrella, we decided to go to a tea shop just along the road, rather than get soaked walking to and from the cliff railway. Although the distance was short, the rain was quite torrential and by the time the bell over the door announced our entrance our hair was damp, our hands cold and our feet wet. We were the only customers so we took possession of the two much used, but nonetheless very comfortable armchairs that stood on either side of the fireplace. The owner had had the foresight to light a small fire and Mary and I gratefully put our feet as close as physically possible without setting fire to our toes and were soon laughing as steam rose from our stockings. We raised our cups to each other and sampled the excellent scones, clotted cream and jam.

"I am sorry, Hannah, if I have not been as sociable as you would like. I am afraid I get like that when I am writing."

"That's quite alright," I lied.

"I am going to write another collection of fairy tales. I have a few ideas and I really need to get them down on paper whilst they are still fresh in my mind." She sipped at her tea and then smiled mischievously at me. "I am going to write one about you. I promised when we first met, do you remember?"

Of course I remembered.

"Me? A fairy tale about me? Will I be the princess or the wicked witch?"

"Hannah, you know I don't write those sorts of stories. No, it will be about a feisty girl - that's you, of course - who has to go on a quest whilst her lover has to wait at home. You will have all sorts of adventures - isn't that what you said to me when we first met, that girls can slay dragons too?"

I nodded my agreement and felt pleased that she had remembered the details.

"In the end you naturally succeed in your search, marry and live happily ever after."

"Do I have to? Get married I mean."

Mary tilted her head to the side, and considered.

"Yes, you do. I know you would far prefer to remain single and be independent but although I don't always follow the rules when I write my fairy tales, my readers do expect a happy ending and for now, that means marriage. I think I will make her just a normal girl, not terribly clever or frightfully beautiful. Perhaps I will make her taller than average, like you. I won't call her Hannah, of course, but I will have you in mind when I write it. What do you think?"

"I like the idea of being the heroine and I know I am not terribly clever or frightfully beautiful, but that doesn't mean you will make me stupid and ugly, does it?"

Mary laughed and shook her head. "No, she will just be Miss Normal. I want young girls to read the story and think 'she is like me and if she can be active and assertive, then so can I.' Women have got to start to think for themselves and to take control of their lives, not just wait to be told what to do by the men. Why shouldn't women make some of the rules, even help run the country?"

"Now that really is a fairy tale!"

Mary looked seriously at me but then smiled almost sadly and just said, "Small steps, Hannah, small steps."

The rain continued to beat down outside so we ordered another pot of tea and a plate of biscuits.

"You know, Hannah, many of the princesses in the traditional fairy tales don't have a mother, so you are a very suitable candidate."

"I would rather have had a mother and not been a 'suitable candidate' for a fairy tale, thank you very much."

"You have never spoken much of her, do you remember her at all?"

"No, she died just a few days after I was born, so all I know of her I learned from Cook."

Mary snuggled further down in the arm chair and commanded, "Tell me."

I gathered my thoughts and cast my mind back twenty years or so. The warmth of the tea room fire reminded me of the heat from the range in the kitchen that had always seemed to be on, roasting meats, boiling water, baking bread or simmering soups.

"I remember I used to have my own little stool that I stood on because I was too small to reach the top of the table, it was called 'Missy's lift up.' It is still in the kitchen; I think the girls use it to stand on to reach the higher shelves. Cook used to give me some flour, water, a bit of butter, some sugar and even a few raisins to make biscuits." I smiled at the memory of the misshapen offerings Cook and Bessy had had to eat after each of my cooking sessions.

"Cook was a lovely lady, short and round, a bit like bread dough that has nicely risen, just before you put it in the oven. She had a broad Cockney accent and always called my 'poor Miss 'annah'."

"Why 'poor'?"

"Oh, she called me poor because I was not as beautiful as my mother, who looked like a princess, but instead looked like my father; because my mother died giving birth to me; because my father didn't love me."

Mary's smile slipped from her face, and she looked at me intently, the concept of an unloving father obviously incomprehensible to her.

"Is that true, really? Why?"

"He blamed me for Mama's death. He would have preferred me to die and for his wife to live. I can't say I blame him, but it is hard for a child to understand such things."

Mary bit her lip and a frown creased her brow.

"He loved your Mama, then? He was capable of love?"

"Oh, yes! Cook often told me the story of how Father turned from being a solemn young man into a lovelorn swain. She said it was just like in a fairy tale. Father had lost his parents at the age of twenty five and so became Lord Russell at quite an early age. According to Cook he took the role very seriously and "'e were just plain gloomy, not an ounce of fun in 'is bones!'"

Mary's mouth twitched at my poor attempt at a Cockney accent.

"Then, one day, whilst walking the estate, he came across a young lady, Cook always referred to her as 'Miss Hetherington, as she was then.' She had fallen from her horse and sprained her ankle and Father carried 'Miss Hetherington, as she was then' to the Hall and arranged for a doctor to come. Father, according to Cook, became a changed man. Cook said it was just like in *Beauty and the Beast* and not only was father transformed, but so was the Hall. It's hard to imagine, but there were guests in all the bedrooms, there were balls and soirees and everyone was always laughing. Well, so Cook said."

"So they got married and expected to live happily ever after."

"Yes, until I was born and Mama died."

A log shifted on the fire sending a shower of sparks up the chimney startling both of us.

"Cook says my father was never the same after Mama's death. I will never forget once, when I was small I was outside the open kitchen door, playing with some kittens. I overheard one of the maids tell Cook that in her humble opinion Lord Russell was a 'cold fish.' The kitchen was always full of dead things and I had often seen dead trout lying on a slab having just been gutted. You know how their eyes go, all milky and their mouths are open and if you touch them they are cold and clammy? I imagined such a fish with my father's face and I scared myself so much I began to cry. Cook heard me and came outside and when I tried to explain to her about dead fish with my father's face, she just hugged me and said 'he just misses her, he won't be sad for ever.' But he was; he was sad and cold, just like a dead fish, until the day he died." I sighed deeply. "I do so wish I had known Mama. *She* would have loved me."

Mary took my hands in hers. "You are not 'poor Miss 'annah' now, though are you? You are strong and brave and independent. You are not to blame for your mother's death, nor for your father's attitude to you, you know that, don't you?"

107

I nodded silently, relishing the closeness of her. She began to stroke the back of my hand. Our heads were almost touching and I could feel the warmth of her breath on my cheek.

I wanted so desperately for Mary to hold me, to stroke my arm, my face, my back, my whole body. I moaned with longing. I actually started to lean forward to kiss her but the clank of the bell heralded more customers and we pulled apart and sat back demurely in our chairs.

I wondered what I would have done if Mary had spurned my kiss.

I wondered what I would have done if she had not.

Although nothing had actually happened between us, something nonetheless changed. We went back to the hotel and met again over dinner. I thought Mary looked pale and commented on the fact, but she said she was just tired and would have an early night. When I later walked past her bedroom on the way to the bathroom I stopped to listen, just to see if she was still awake, just to say "goodnight." What I heard was muffled sobs. I knocked on the door.

"Mary. Mary, it's me Hannah. Are you alright?"

No answer. The crying had stopped but I could still hear her shallow breathing.

"Mary, please let me in. What's the matter? Can I help?"

More silence, then, "I'm fine, Hannah. Please, just leave me alone. I'm tired and want to go to sleep."

I could hear the tears in her voice but there was nothing I could do except to call out "good night" and hope Mary would explain the next morning.

She didn't.

She came down to breakfast looking pale and as if she had not slept at all. She responded to my "Good morning" but said little else throughout the meal, after which she said she needed to write and spent the rest of the morning in her room.

She came down again for lunch and we had a stilted conversation about what she had been writing but when she talked to me she didn't look me in the eye but at a spot just over my right shoulder. I couldn't bring myself to ask her what was wrong in case it was something to do with me, so I spent the afternoon writing a long letter to Sarah whilst Mary continued with her work.

The rest of the holiday followed this same pattern, apart from a few occasions when Mary deigned to walk with me, if the weather was fine, or sit in the drawing room if it was wet.

Mary was so tense and withdrawn; it was as if we were separated by a thick pane of glass that meant we could see each other, but it was difficult to hear and impossible to touch. I felt too dejected to paint so I whiled away the time by searching the little shops for gifts for the staff, by reading novels that other guests had left behind and by replaying that afternoon in the tea room to see if I had said or done anything to warrant this change in Mary. I could think of nothing.

The morning of our final day finally came and it was glorious - the sort of weather we had hoped for but never experienced for the duration of our holiday. Mary seemed brighter; there was colour in her cheeks and she even chatted to me over breakfast. I didn't want to ruin her good mood, but I had to know.

"Mary, have you enjoyed the holiday?"

She put her head to the side and paused as if choosing her words carefully.

"On the whole, yes. I have managed to do an awful lot of writing which I probably wouldn't have done if I had been in London. This is a lovely part of England and I am glad I have visited it. The weather could have been better, but on the whole, yes, I have enjoyed myself."

She nibbled some toast and took a sip of tea.

Nothing about how she had enjoyed my company; no "we", only "I". She didn't ask if I had had a pleasant time myself.

The journey back was a mirror of the one we had made two weeks earlier. This time, however, we asked if we could sit outside, so we swapped our tickets with a young couple on their honeymoon who didn't care where they sat, just so long as they could look at each other and hold hands.

We sat at the front with the driver and as we trundled along the warm breeze seemed to blow away my ill humour and my spirits rose with every clip clop of the hooves. When we came to Porlock Hill the driver asked us all to walk down, in case the horses found the slope too steep and careered out of control. We happily obliged, not wishing to end up smashed into pieces against the wall at the bottom of the hill. It was, of course, easier going down than it had been walking up, but even so after a while the backs of our legs hurt and we had to keep stopping to rest and to get our breath. The slope was so steep in one place that we had to link arms to hold each other back. Even when the need was not there, Mary kept her arm in mine until we were back in the carriage, which was thankfully still in one piece. My heart soared and joined the eagle that I saw circling high above.

The nearer we got to London, the brighter Mary became; she seemed as excited as a child about to go on holiday, rather than an adult returning from one. When we arrived at Paddington Fred was waiting for us, and we took Mary back to her home first. Before she alighted she gave me a quick peck on the cheek; she seemed almost embarrassed.

My happiness disappeared instantly and my mood matched the drizzle that greeted out return to the capital, turning everything to a uniform slate grey.

Chapter 5 - The Bread of Discontent

1884 - 1886

Once there was a baker who had a very bad, violent temper, and whenever a batch of bread was spoiled he flew into such a rage, that his wife and daughters dared not go near him. One day it happened that all his bread was burnt, and on this he stamped and raved with anger. He threw the loaves all about the floor, when one, burnt blacker than the rest, broke in half, and out crept a tiny black man, no thicker than an eel, with long arms and legs.

"What are you making all the fuss about, Master Baker?" said he. "If you will give me a home in your oven I will see to the baking of your bread, and will answer for it that you shall never have so such as a loaf spoiled."

"And pray what sort of bread would it be, if you were in the oven, and helped to bake it?" said the baker; "I think my customers might not like to eat it."

"On the contrary," said the imp, "they would like it exceedingly. It is true that it would make them rather unhappy, but that will not hurt you, as you need not eat it yourself."

"Why should it make them unhappy?" said the baker. "If it is good bread it won't do anyone harm, and if it is bad, they won't buy it."

"It will taste very good," replied the imp, "but it will make all who eat it discontented, and they will think themselves very unfortunate whether they are so or no; but this will not do you any harm, and I promise that you shall sell as much as you wish."

("The Bread of Discontent," in *The Necklace of Princess Fiorimonde*, by Mary De Morgan)

Over the next few days I spent my time sorting out my sketches and paintings. Some I threw away, thinking them uninspired and uninspiring, some I placed in the racks I'd had specially made and others I kept out, meaning to finish later. Then, on a morning when I was wondering what to do with myself, I received a note from Mary in her characteristic scrawl:

Apropos marriage - talk tonight at Fabian Society by Annie Besant. Will be good. Do come. 7:30 at Essex Hall. Meet me there. MDeM

I was not the slightest bit interested in politics, nor indeed in marriage, and I knew nothing about the Fabian Society, but I had heard of Annie Besant. She was a campaigner for the rights of women and I had read that she was separated from her husband. I wondered why Mary thought I would be interested in a talk by such a woman but I was desperate to see Mary, so I sent a note by return saying I would be there.

Fred dropped me off outside the hall a few minutes early. Mary was not yet there and I was uncertain whether to stay outside or to follow the small groups of people who were walking inside, all with an air of confidence I envied. I stood to the side of the front door out of everyone's way, feeling certain that they all knew that I was a Fabian pretender. Everyone seemed to know each other and they chatted happily together, making me feel more and more awkward and conspicuous.

I had almost made up my mind to flag a hansom cab to take me back home, when I saw Mary running down the Strand towards me, hat askew and cheeks flushed with the exertion.

"So sorry I am late, Hannah. I decided to walk and then wished I hadn't! We are still in time, though, let's go in."

No hugs or kisses, just her hand at the base of my spine propelling me forward into the hall, which, from what I could see of it, had little to differentiate it from any other utilitarian space used for the purpose of worthy gatherings. There was row after row of wooden chairs facing a makeshift stage at the far end. I would have sat at the back but Mary continued to push onwards until we were near to the front. We then had to squeeze past the people already sitting, in order to reach the two empty seats in the middle of the row that Mary seemed determined to occupy. She apologised brightly to each person as they stood to let us past seemingly unaware of the disturbance we were causing.

We were still settling ourselves when a man came onto the stage and clapped hesitatingly in an attempt to gain everyone's attention. He was tall and thin, probably in his late twenties, clean shaven but with a mop of unruly dark brown hair. He wore a black suit that was obviously brand new, and one he did not feel comfortable wearing. He was breathing heavily and his face was flushed, as if he had just been running. A group behind us were still

114

shuffling and whispering and I was startled when Mary turned around, glared at them fiercely and told them to be quiet. The man smiled gratefully at Mary; I could see that he was nervous and I felt quite sorry for him. He started speaking but though I could hear that he had a pleasant, deep voice it did not travel well and a man shouted out, none too politely, "Speak up, mate, can't 'ear a bleedin' word!"

The nervous speaker blushed, closed his eyes, took a deep breath and started again, reading from notes that shook uncontrollably. "Good evening, ladies and gentlemen. Welcome to the meeting of the Fabian Society, and to tonight's talk by our very own Mrs Annie Besant."

He continued speaking, outlining some of the key Fabian principles, reminding members of forthcoming events and inviting everyone to tea and biscuits after the meeting. I soon stopped listening and instead took out my pad and did a quick sketch of him. I was rather pleased with it and turned to Mary to show it to her. She was on the edge of her seat leaning forward, her whole body tensed, her lips moving as if she was reciting a prayer. I tried to get her attention but failed to do so until the nervous speaker - I called him this as he forgot to introduce himself - had finished his introduction, after which they both visibly relaxed.

Our whispered conversation was very soon curtailed by the rapturous applause that greeted the arrival on stage of a short, compact middle-aged woman with greying hair pulled back into a tight bun at the back of her head. What she lacked in height she made up for in energy and she bounded onto the stage, her arms wide open as if gathering everyone's approbation to her bosom. She smiled widely and despite my previous prejudice against her, I liked her immediately. She stood patiently waiting for the clapping to cease and for everyone to settle back down. She scanned the audience, nodding and smiling at those she obviously knew, and when she started speaking it was in a strong, passionate voice that easily filled the hall.

"How many of you women are unmarried?"

I was rather shocked at the abruptness of the question but Mary obviously felt no such qualms and she put her hand straight up in the air. I looked around the room to see other hands held confidently aloft and so I followed suit, but rather more tentatively.

"You, ladies, are the lucky ones. You, ladies, can own property. You, ladies, have absolute control of your own body. You, ladies, even if you have a child out of wedlock," a shocked murmur rippled through the audience at such a thought, "yes, even if you have a child out of wedlock you, ladies, have the right to the custody of that child. But once a woman marries ..." Mrs Besant paused for effect. "... then she has no rights. It is the institution of marriage that imposes injustice and degradation onto a woman, and it is all done perfectly legally."

She took a sip of water from a glass handed to her by the nervous speaker. "Let me describe some of the injustices that are inflicted onto the woman once she has said 'I do.'"

She then proceeded to explain the losses that a woman endured once she entered the so-called blissful state of marriage. She was a forceful speaker but perhaps because I had no intention of ever getting married, I soon became bored. I concentrated instead on doing a sketch of her as she strode about the stage, her whole body expressing her anger and protestation at the unfairness and inequality of marriage. Mary too seemed to lose interest; each time I glanced at her she was not following Mrs Besant but was instead staring at the back of the stage where the members of the Fabian Society were sitting in a row. I noticed the nervous speaker sitting at the end of the line, more at ease now that his ordeal was over.

The audience participated throughout Mrs Besant's speech with shouts of "Unfair!" and "Disgraceful!" and such was their disdain at one point they even stamped their feet. After an hour Mrs Besant stopped pacing and faced the audience for her conclusion.

"So, ladies and gentlemen, I think you will agree that the law must change. The rights I have told you about are fair and reasonable but should apply to both men and women, married or otherwise. They are *human* rights. Marriage should not be about ownership. Marriage should not be a crime for which women are punished and given a life sentence. No! Marriage should be about love. Marriage should be about equality. Marriage should be about happiness, for both the husband *and* the wife. What say you?"

A loud "Aye!" erupted from the audience and they rose to their feet, clapping and shouting enthusiastically. Mary and I stood pretending to be as fervent as everyone else. After many minutes the applause died down and we both sat back down again whilst the rest of the audience made their way to the back of the hall, where the refreshments were. I began to screw up the sketches I had done, one of the nervous speaker and the other of Mrs Besant, meaning to throw them away, but Mary took them from me, smoothing out the creases.

"May I keep them? They are very good, Hannah. You have really captured Mrs Besant's energy and almost manic fervour extremely well. Now, let us go and have a cup of stewed tea and a stale biscuit."

As we queued waiting to be served, the nervous speaker came and stood behind us. I turned and smiled at him but Mary ignored him, quite rudely I thought. When we had the cups in our hands we moved away and went to stand in the corner. I felt sorry for the nervous speaker and wanted to ask him to join us, but Mary's expression was so fierce I decided she would make him even more anxious. Mary seemed agitated; her face was flushed and I noticed a sheen of sweat on her forehead.

"Are you feeling alright, Mary?"

"Yes, of course! Why wouldn't I be? Wasn't Mrs Besant marvellous? She is so right. I think I will do an article on her. What an inspiration to us all! Who would think that such a small woman could exert such energy?

Everyone loved her, didn't they?" Mary spoke so fast she almost gabbled and her tea slopped into the saucer in her excitement.

"Hush, Mary, dear. Calm down. What on earth is the matter? Are you feeling ill? I am sure she was very good but I wasn't really listening to be honest and I didn't think you were either. Come, Fred will be here soon. Let's get out of this hot hall and wait outside for him."

"No! No, I am perfectly well. I will make my own way home. Really, you go."

Try as I might I could not persuade her to come with me.

"There are some people here I would like to speak to. In fact, Mrs Hogarth over there, the rather large lady all in purple, lives just down the road and I am sure she will take me home. Please, Hannah, you go."

She actually gave me a small push towards the door. As I finally turned to go, feeling disappointed and a little hurt, Mary suddenly took my arm. "I'll come tomorrow, shall I? We'll plan what we are going to do over the next few weeks." She smiled beguilingly and then put her arms around me and hugged me tightly before turning and walking towards the lady in purple. I left, feeling much happier.

When Mary arrived the following morning I was surprised at the change in her. She radiated an aura of contentment that painted her cheeks with a pink blush and sowed a sparkle in her eyes. I did not know what caused this change but I revelled in it and our relationship seemed to be as good as it was before the holiday, if not better.

We soon settled back into our routine of visiting the East End families, exploring London attractions and paying social calls on those whom we both could tolerate. Mary still insisted on having her own time to write but we always saw each other at least once a week, even if it was just to sit together, read and talk. It was on such an occasion one spring morning that Mary put her book down and asked me if I would like to do some work for Miss May Morris, one of William Morris's daughters, who had just been given the responsibility of the embroidery department.

"Embroidery? You know full well, Mary, that I have no skill in that quarter. What on earth makes you think that I would be of any use to Miss Morris?"

Mary laughed at my discomposure.

"I bumped into May yesterday and she said that although she has a paid work-force of girls, she thought it would be fun for a few friends to gather each week to form a sort of embroidery circle. She has asked Lily Yeats, Maude Deacon, Florence Emery and a few others I don't know. You remember we bumped into Lily and Florence last year at Brown's?"

I remembered the occasion and the rather riotous time we had spent over a pot of tea.

"I do see that it might be rather fun. But it doesn't change the fact that I can't sew."

Mary looked disappointed.

"I just thought it would be pleasant to sit and gossip and perhaps help May out at the same time. But if you don't want to go then of course you needn't, but I shall go."

I felt a sense of panic as I realised I had potentially lost the opportunity of being with Mary. I forced myself to sound casual. "Of course I would love to come, Mary, I just don't want to be a hindrance. Maybe I could embroider something that will go underneath or behind something and so will never be seen!"

Mary accepted my volte-face and we agreed to join the embroidery circle the very next day. Miss Morris had set up her studio in a converted stable adjoining the family home in Hammersmith. When we arrived the workshop was a hive of activity. The paid working girls were all sitting around the edge of the large space at long tables, with the cloth spread out in front of them, and the coloured threads scattered like a shattered rainbow. Miss Morris walked briskly from girl to girl, explaining and correcting. She was about my age but seemed very capable and rather bossy. When she saw Mary and I standing at the threshold, she strode over to us, shook our hands then led us to a table in the corner. There were other ladies there, some of whom I knew, heads bowed over their pieces of embroidery. They greeted us cheerfully, although Miss Morris's expression remained somewhat dour and daunting. I nervously explained that sewing was not my forte and I was surprised when, rather than dismissing me out of hand, she suggested I sat next to Miss Yeats, who was a very skilled embroiderer and would teach me the intricacies of the craft. She then gave a smile that lit up her face and I realised she really was rather pretty.

"Don't worry, she will soon turn you into an expert seamstress."

I continued to attend the embroidery circle even if Mary was not free to accompany me. Her periods of silent withdrawal occurred more and more frequently. If she turned up at my house bright-eyed, cheerful and brimming over with happiness, then I knew she had had a productive time writing articles or the fairy tales she had started at Lynton. If, however, she arrived with a face pale and drawn, and eyes red and swollen, then I knew she had been suffering from a bout of dejection that would often take days of gentle cajoling and loving to alleviate.

"Why don't you come and live here with me? You know there is plenty of space and we get on so well together, don't we? I could take care of you and all you would have to worry about is your writing."

Mary sighed and shook her head.

"Hannah, I know this is what you want, and I want it too, really I do, but it isn't the time. That is all, it's just not the right time."

We had been going to the embroidery circle for almost a year when May Morris came over and sat at our table whilst we were having a refreshment break. She tapped on the table with a thimble to get our attention.

"On March 24th it is my father's birthday and we are holding a small dinner party for him. I am going to give him the set of cushions most of you have all been working on for the last month, so it would be lovely if you could all attend."

All the members of the embroidery circle accepted with pleasure. Mary was a great friend of William Morris but I had never had the chance to meet him, and I looked forward to the opportunity.

Three weeks later Mary and I arrived at Kelmscott House, which was an imposing almost square building, five rooms wide and three storeys high, with a central front door flanked by two white fluted columns. The stark symmetry was somehow emphasised by the twisted trunk and stems of a still bare wisteria that climbed up the side and over the top of the entrance.

Mary had been there many times before, of course, but as a first time visitor I found it very difficult not to exclaim out loud as I saw Morris's distinctive designs in the curtains, chair covers, carpets and wallpaper that decorated the rooms that we passed by. I was especially thrilled when I also recognised some of Mary's brother's tiles surrounding one of the fireplaces and I asked Mary if she was not proud, to which she merely shrugged.

Mary and I were led up to a small garret bedroom where we could finish our toilette. It was a charming room, probably originally a servant's room, but now used for guests. This room too was papered with one of Morris's intricate designs, with slender entwining stalks, pale green leaves and blooms of dusky pink.

It did not take long to remove our outer clothing, change our shoes and straighten our skirts and hair. Mary wore an emerald green velvet gown, quite unadorned with lace or frills and I thought she looked beautiful. She radiated such vitality and energy and I was so happy and proud to be there with her. Before we went downstairs I brushed a piece of fluff off her sleeve. I could feel the warmth of her skin through the smooth nap as my hand slid down her arm. My stomach inexplicably knotted and I had the urge to cry. Mary did not notice my agitation but took my hand and eagerly led me downstairs.

When we entered the drawing room I was overwhelmed by the number of people that were there, all standing in little groups, holding a glass and chattering away. Even though I was nearer thirty than twenty, I was still not accustomed to large social gatherings and I clung to Mary's arm. We stood in the doorway for only a short while before a large hirsute gentleman came over to us, kissed Mary on each cheek and pumped my hand up and down in his bear-like paws. "You must be Miss Russell. Mary has spoken very highly of you. Welcome, welcome to my little celebration."

This, then, was the great William Morris, larger and louder than I had expected, but a handsome man, who exuded bonhomie with no sense of superiority, although he was surely quite justified in doing so. Morris had a head of grey shaggy hair and a matching beard. He wore a resplendent waistcoat which, I could not help but notice, was not correctly buttoned. I liked him immediately.

Morris took me by the elbow and steered me around the room, introducing me to everyone as "Miss Hannah Russell, Mary De Morgan's friend." We went at such a pace that I barely had time to take in people's names before we moved on. The Burne-Jones's were there, and the ladies from the embroidery circle, and I recognised some people from different events that Mary had taken me to over the last few years. I was pleased to see Mary's brother, William, along with his fiancée Evelyn Pickering, but our meeting was fleeting as Morris dragged me to the next group of people. The vast majority of guests were from Morris's artistic or political circles, some falling into both camps.

At the end of my tour Morris left me with May, who was standing quietly watching over the proceedings. I looked around for Mary and I was surprised to see her in heated conversation with a young man. I recognised him as being the nervous speaker from the Fabian Society evening we had attended a year or so previously.

I stood chatting to May for a few minutes; she was relaxed, telling me about her sister Jenny, who couldn't be there that night, when her eyes suddenly lit up, she straightened her posture and her cheeks took on a pink bloom. A dark haired gentleman, only a couple of years older than ourselves, approached us.

"May, my dear, you look ravishing."

He bowed deeply, then took both her hands in his and kissed each of her fingers, far too slowly and sensuously. I felt very embarrassed and turned to move elsewhere, but he stopped me by saying, "And who is this charming lady? I don't believe we have met, I would surely have remembered."

I disliked him immensely, even though May was obviously quite infatuated by him. "My name is Miss Hannah Russell."

"And I, my very dear lady, am Bernard Shaw. I cannot understand how our paths have never crossed."

Before I could think of a worthy retort May told him not to be such a flirt and that I was a friend of Mary De Morgan. At that his expression changed from one of benevolence to one of malice.

"Ah, the Demogorgon. I was not aware that she had any friends."

I felt my face redden in defiance.

"What on earth do you mean? What is a Demogorgon? It does not sound like a suitable name for the most caring and beautiful woman I have ever met!"

He looked slightly abashed and tried to take my hands, no doubt to kiss away my anger, but I put them behind my back, leaving him bowed and nothing to do but to straighten again.

"I apologise, dear lady. I did not mean to offend you. It is a play on her surname, do you see? I cannot claim the credit for so naming her - I believe it was Sir Claude Phillips, who found her demeanour somewhat alarming. You have, however, convinced me that those who consider that she should be endured rather than endeared are misguided in their opinion and that your perception of the dear lady is the right one. Please accept my sincere apologies. Ah! Speak of the very devil!"

I watched with misgivings as Mary made her way over to our little group. Shaw was polite enough but I could see a glint of malice in his eyes. Thankfully May chose this time to present her gifts to her father. There was much laughter as he pretended to try and guess what was beneath the wrappings and then polite clapping when he tore off the paper to reveal the embroidered cushions that had taken the embroidery circle so much effort. I knew there was a slight mistake - my mistake - in the corner of one of the cushions, and I was sure everyone would be able to see it. Luckily, a bell was then rung and we were all invited to partake of supper.

The room in which we dined had a number of large, oval tables, which necessitated the guests splitting into groups. I pulled Mary away from the one Shaw was seated at, explaining that he was flirting outrageously with May Morris and that I found him to be an odious man. We ended up on the table with Morris himself, and his wife Jane, still a beautiful woman, whose dark wavy hair cascaded down her back. Mary told me that she had been Rossetti's lover and it was rumoured she now had another. I could not understand why she needed a lover when she had such a charming, talented and humorous husband. I nodded to the nervous speaker, who was also at our table. I quietly asked Mary what his name was and what they had been arguing about.

"I can't recall his name, Green or Greenaway or something. We weren't arguing, just discussing socialism."

We were interrupted by the soup and we both engaged in conversation with our immediate neighbour. Mine was Henry Holiday, a painter and designer of stained glass windows. Holiday was much older than me and well-known but he was easy to talk to and we chatted together quite comfortably. He was a good friend of the De Morgans and he took great pleasure in relating an incident when both families were holidaying together.

"We were all staying at Betws-y-coed, many years ago now. I can't remember when exactly but Mary must have been about twelve or thirteen. She was, how can I put it, an outspoken child, who never believed in being polite for politeness' sake. We were all walking up quite a steep path, I recall, when she suddenly whipped round, pointed a finger most rudely at me and declared at the top of her voice: 'All artists are fools! Just look at you!' She didn't say what had prompted the accusation she just turned back to the path and continued walking."

We both laughed out loud and Mary wanted to know what was so funny. She was equally amused and turned away from her own neighbour, some old woman whom she obviously did not find so entertaining.

Soup was followed by a dish of braised beef and vegetables. I became aware of Morris's voice raised in anger and I, along with the others at the table, stopped to listen.

"That, young sir, is not a flaw!"

Morris was holding up a glass, which even I could see from the other side of the table, had an imperfection in the bowl.

"That, young sir, is the mark that makes it unique. There is no other glass in the world exactly like this one."

Morris glared at the poor young man - I saw it was Mr Green or Greenaway, the nervous speaker - who was red of face.

"Are you saying that you would be happier if all glasses were *exactly* the same? That you could have twenty glasses in front of you and you could tell none of them apart? Is that what you are saying?"

The nervous speaker opened his mouth but made no sound.

"Are you saying that you would prefer to drink out of a glass that has been made by a soulless *machine* rather than by a man, who has poured his heart into the making of each glass and has made each one unique? Is that what you are saying? You want everything the same and the workers can go hang?"

The nervous speaker shook his head fearfully, wiped the sweat off his brow and took a large swig of wine from his imperfect glass.

"Quite right, young man. We need to stamp out mass-production and go back to hand-made goods, each of which contains the soul of its maker."

I thought what he said made a lot of sense and no longer felt worried about the mistake I had made in the embroidery. Others were nodding their heads in agreement and I was surprised when Mary put up her hand and spoke in a tone I had never heard before, strident and somewhat arrogant.

"That is all very well William, but these so called mass-produced goods are so much cheaper than those made by craftsmen, so that the poorer people can afford them.

What are the poor meant to drink out of? It is surely not your belief that only the rich should have beautiful things in their home?"

The room went absolutely silent, and Morris's face went so red I was worried he might have a heart attack. The buttons on his waistcoat strained as he tried to control his anger and I had a terrible desire to giggle.

"Mary, you are talking absolute rubbish, I am surprised at you. These machines that are churning out these cheap goods are taking the place of men, so that they have to fight for the fewer jobs. That means that the employers can reduce the wages as there is so much competition for them. The men that are lucky enough to have jobs may as well be machines themselves, they have no individual identity. They have no pride in their work, and the goods that are produced are shoddy and of no intrinsic value. The only people that are benefitting are the manufacturers, who get richer and richer as the workers get poorer and poorer."

He paused for breath and took a long draught of his wine. One person clapped, and then another, until the room was filled with thunderous applause. I didn't know what to do for best, I didn't want to go against Mary but neither did I want to stand out by not clapping. But then I saw that Mary was clapping as enthusiastically as everyone else, so I joined in. When it was quiet she spoke again.

"You know, William, you really ought to think about going into politics!"

We all waited to see what William's reaction would be, and when he gave his enormous belly laugh we all joined in. I could not help but notice that Shaw was whispering something in May's ear whilst looking directly at Mary with a spiteful look, and that the nervous speaker, Mr Green or Greenaway, was nodding and smiling at Mary.

Mary leaned over and whispered in my ear, "I do so love rubbing William up the wrong way. He knows I only do it to tease."

The rest of the meal passed without incident. When it was time to go back to the little garret room to get our things I could not find Mary anywhere, so I made my way up thinking she was there already. She wasn't so I got my things together and sat and waited. She did not come up for another thirty minutes, by which time I had fallen into a light doze. The cross words died on my lips as I saw her distraught face.

"What on earth is the matter?" I thought of Bernard Shaw. "Has someone said something horrid to you?"

"In a way, in a way. It is nothing. Really, Hannah, it is nothing. Just words. Come let us go home. Poor Fred will be waiting for us."

Try as I might on the way home I could not get Mary to tell me what had caused her distress. As we dropped her off she took my hands and looked at me intently.

"You are my one true friend, Hannah. My rock. You will never leave me, will you? You will always love me?"

She flitted away before I could answer with a resounding "yes!"

131

After that evening Mary seemed dejected and listless and she sometimes did not contact me for days on end and when she did, it was just a short message saying she would be in touch very soon. One day in August I had not heard anything from her for over a week, despite my sending little notes to her each day. I was worried so I asked Fred to take me round to the house she still shared with her mother. When I arrived I was shown into the library, where Mary's mother was sitting in her late husband's leather armchair. Being much slighter than her husband she had to prop herself up with cushions in order to be comfortable and not get lost in the corner of the seat. She was white haired and bespectacled and looked her age of nearly eighty years old, but nonetheless she was still heavily involved in her social reformation projects. She greeted me warmly and indicated that I should sit down. We exchanged pleasantries and she held up the hand-written papers she had been perusing.

"I am writing an article on vivisection. I am a member of the Victoria Street Society, you know, which lobbies against all experimentation on animals. It is not a pleasant article to have to write and I am pleased of an interruption."

"I really came to see Mary, but it is of course always a pleasure to talk with you. I have not heard from Mary for a while and I just thought I would call to see if everything is alright?"

"Oh, my dear, she is not here."

I felt my shoulders sag in disappointment. "Do you know when she will be back?"

"No, Hannah, I mean she does not live here anymore."

Chapter 6 - The Ploughman and the Gnome

1886 - 1888

Next morning, at breakfast the wife came down with the new comb in her hair, and said to her husband, "See, husband, I bought this of the pedlar yesterday, and he tells me they are quite the newest fashion, and all the great ladies in town are wearing them."

"Well," quoth the ploughman, "such a fashion may be all very well for the great ladies who have scarce any hair of their own, but, for my own part, I had rather see your beautiful hair just as it is without any adornment."

...

When her husband was gone, the wife went to her glass and looked at herself, and took out the comb and put it in, and tried it every way. "'Tis true, for sure," said she, "my hair is very beautiful, and maybe it looks best done up as I used to wear it, still it seems a pity not to use the comb when I have bought it."

("The Ploughman and the Gnome," in *The Windfairies*, by Mary De Morgan)

If I had not already been sitting I would have fallen.

Mrs De Morgan saw my distress and rang her bell vigorously to order tea. "Oh, Hannah, Mary would have told you, of course she would. Her note must have got mislaid, that's all, dear. Yes, I am positive she told me she had written you a note with her new address."

"But why? Why has she moved out?" I didn't pose the question I really wanted the answer to, "Why did she not come and live with me?"

"She has been working very hard recently and she said she just needed to be on her own for a while. She isn't far away and to be perfectly frank, Hannah, it will do her good to live on her own. I won't be here for ever. Now, let us have a cup of tea and then I will write down her address for you."

As much as I liked Mrs De Morgan, the next half an hour was excruciating; I just wanted to leave and drive round to Mary's lodgings and demand to know what on earth she was doing. I refused a second cup of tea and Mrs De Morgan, perhaps sensing my impatience, wrote down the address and when she handed it to me squeezed my hand and tried to reassure me. "The note just got mislaid, dear, that is all."

Between taking my leave of Mrs De Morgan and taking my seat in the carriage I decided to go home and write a carefully worded letter to Mary, but when I opened my mouth to give my instructions to Fred I heard myself repeating the address written on the paper I clutched in my hand. It was a journey of about fifteen minutes, after which we arrived at a wide street flanked on both sides by three-storey houses. There was an air of dejection about the place and a sense of pervading decay that the occasional window box of dusty summer flowers did nothing to dispel.

Telling Fred to wait, I climbed the stone steps up to a front door that bore a badly written card stating this was the lodgings of a Mrs Clitheroe and all visitors were invited to knock loudly, which I duly did. I heard the shuffle of slippered feet upon a tiled floor and then the door opened slightly; just wide enough for a very short woman to peer out. I introduced myself and asked if a Miss De Morgan lived there. I showed her the paper with the address written on as justification for my enquiry.

"Mister Morgan? Nah, no-one of that name lives 'ere."

Her eyes were level with my waist, so I had to nearly crouch down in order to talk to her face to face.

"No, I said Miss De Morgan. She is a lady."

She squinted up at me, evidently puzzled that Mister Morgan was a lady. I raised my voice and spoke my words slowly.

"Miss De Morgan!"

"Alright, m'dear. I ain't deaf, no, nor stupid neither. Upstairs. Nummer free."

She opened the front door wide enough to let me squeeze past and as I went up the uncarpeted wooden stairs I heard her shuffling back down the corridor towards the source of the cabbage smell that permeated the air. At the top of the flight was a mirror corridor leading God knows where, with closed doors leading off on either side. Each door was painted rather badly in a different colour, "for those residents who do not know their numbers" I thought maliciously. A bright red door on my right proclaimed itself to be number three. I felt inexplicably nervous and I knocked rather timidly with my knuckles, there being no knocker. I waited for a few

136

seconds and having decided the sound had not been loud enough for anyone other than myself to hear, I raised my fist in readiness to make my presence known more forcibly. Before I struck wood, however, the door was jerked open and Mary looked out angrily.

"What is it *now*!"

She was glaring at my middle section and seemed surprised at what she saw. It was quite comical to see her eyes rise slowly up my body to my face, and to see her expression turn from irritation to recognition.

"Oh Hannah! I thought it was Mrs Clitheroe, yet again, asking me all sorts of stupid questions. I have only been here a week and she already knows my life story and that of the entire De Morgan family back to great grandfather John. What are you doing here?"

I was nonplussed at her abruptness and took a step back as if she had slapped me.

"I went to your house. Or what used to be your house."

I paused, but Mary said nothing.

"Your mother told me you had moved out. She said your letter to me must have got lost. Did it?"

"My letter? Yes, of course! Did you not get it? I wondered why you had not at least written to me. Yes, it must have got lost. Oh, what a pity. I hope you didn't think I had moved away without telling you?"

I bit my lip, for indeed that is what I had thought.

"Oh, Hannah, how could you think that I would do such a thing?"

We both stood awkwardly, me clutching my handbag and Mary holding the door so close to her that I could see nothing beyond her. I suddenly wished I had just gone home and written to her after all, rather than impose myself on her uninvited.

"Do you want me to go?"

Mary tilted her head characteristically and gave me a smile that wiped out all the ill feeling that had lain like a stone in the pit of my stomach.

"You are a goose! No, of course you must come in. Just don't look too much at the decor; it is hardly to Morris's standards. I haven't really got everything sorted yet, but come into the sitting room and I'll make you a cup of tea."

The room was large and bright; the sunshine streamed through the bay window revealing the shabbiness of the room: the dull wallpaper, the unfashionable furniture and the faded, frayed carpet. In the bay was a table upon which Mary had placed different piles of paper, each prevented from fluttering away in the breeze from the open window by a glass paper weight. Mary's tools of her trade lay near at hand: a jar of pencils, an eraser and a pencil sharpener.

Mary bustled around removing her coat and bag from the sofa to make room for me to sit. She then went behind a curtained-off corner of the room and by the clattering sounds she made I gathered this was the kitchenette. I could think of nothing to say. I was not going to lie and say what a charming room it was. Instead, I voiced the question I desperately wanted the answer to.

"Why, Mary? Why here and not with me?"

I heard her pour the water into the teapot, and take the lid of a tin and empty the contents onto a plate. And I heard her give a long sigh. She came back into the room carrying a tray which she carefully placed on a low table and then sat in the arm chair opposite me. She did not speak nor look at me until she had dispensed the tea and proffered a plate of biscuits.

"I don't expect you to understand, Hannah. I am thirty six years old. I have always lived in the parental home; I have always been a dependant. If I lived with you it would be no different."

I opened my mouth to contradict her, but she put up a hand to ward off my words.

"No, Hannah, I would be a guest at yours and I want, in fact I need my own place. I need my independence. You have always had it and I don't think you realise how very precious it is."

"But you would have your own bedroom; I would convert one of the other rooms into a study for you. You could be as independent as you like. You can even pay me some rent if you insist."

Mary just shook her head and as she did so there was a noise from the bedroom that sounded like a creaking floorboard. I turned my head involuntarily towards the room and Mary gave a small gasp then chuckled. "I have not yet got used to the noises this house makes. I sometimes lie awake at night convinced there is someone in the room with me! But it is just the draught under the wainscoting or a window that is not closed properly, banging in the breeze."

We spent the next half an hour chatting about trivial things and drinking more tea, so much so that I had to ask where the bathroom was, thinking it was off the bedroom.

"It's further along the corridor on the left; you can't miss it, it has a large hand-written sign announcing the fact."

The bathroom was indeed impossible to miss; the door this time was painted white with a piece of roughly cut wood hanging by some string from a hook not quite centrally fixed. No planning had gone into the writing of the word "BATHROOM" and the last characters had been written so small they were almost illegible.

The bathroom seemed clean enough but I found the thought of other people carrying out their ablutions there, people I didn't know, somewhat repulsive. The mirror over the sink was spotted and cracked, distorting my reflection into something ghoulish and unrecognisable. I ran the hot water into the sink to wash my hands and noticed a dark hair, too short to be Mary's, floating on the surface. I pulled my hands out as if I had been washing in acid, pulled the plug and held my hands under the running hot water and scrubbed and scrubbed until they were red, but at least I felt they were clean again.

How could Mary prefer this squalor to living with me?

When I got back to Mary's room she thrust my coat and bag at me before I could even cross the threshold.

140

"I'm sorry, Hannah, but I need to get on with my work. You don't mind do you? I'll come and see you next Tuesday. Yes, next Tuesday. We'll go and have tea somewhere and catch up. You don't mind do you?"

I did mind, of course, but I said nothing and hugged her tightly. As I did so I caught a hint of a scent that seemed familiar, but not one I associated with Mary. "Have you changed your scent, Mary? Has the bottle I gave you last Christmas finished already?"

Mary looked confused but then nodded. "Salome has started selling perfume and I felt obliged to buy some when I popped into her shop a week or so ago. I thought I would try it today. It is not as pleasant as the one you gave me, I don't think I will wear it again."

We hugged again and I left bemused that Mary had gone to Salome's without me; the smell of the new scent still in my nostrils. When I was in the carriage a memory suddenly flashed into my head of me as a young child giving my father the ritual goodnight peck. I laughed to myself when I realised that Mary's perfume reminded me of my father's cologne, and determined to tell her when we next met.

***

All through that summer and autumn we would spend the day together every week or so, but I never felt that she was truly with me; she often had a faraway look in her eye and her mind seemed elsewhere - I assumed it to be in fairyland. I still visited the East End families and continued to attend the embroidery circle, but there were still long periods of time I needed to fill between seeing Mary, so I started painting again.

I never got bored with sitting in the park capturing an instant in time that would never be repeated, no matter how long or how often I sat in the same spot. I loved to sketch the people as they walked past and I often wondered about their lives. Was that couple who walked so demurely at some distance apart, courting? Were they desperate to hold hands, to kiss, to be together always? Was the old man who marched briskly along in a military manner hiding from the world his grief at the loss of his beloved wife? Was that young girl a nanny because she loved babies or was it just a job and she might as well have been pushing a pram full of laundry? What great unhappiness had befallen that dark-haired woman that she should look so desperately sad?

It took me quite a few seconds to realise that it was Mary walking dejectedly towards me, her eyes lowered, her shoulders slumped.

"Mary, Mary! It's me, Hannah. What's wrong? Has something happened? Is it Mrs De Morgan? Mary!"

She continued walking, oblivious to my cries until I reached her and grabbed her arm. She looked up, startled, and I was horrified to see her red, swollen eyes, the dark smudges that told of lack of sleep and her pale, almost translucent skin. I took her cold, clammy hands in mine and made her stand still. "Mary, what on earth is wrong?"

She looked at me, seeming only then to recognise me. She opened her mouth but instead of giving me an explanation she started to cough in the most dreadful manner. She bent almost double as her whole body convulsed. She made an awful sound as her lungs tried to both expel the ill humours and inhale the life-giving air. Eventually her seizure eased and she was able to stand upright. I gently took a kerchief and dabbed the blood that had gathered at the corner of her mouth. My heart almost broke at the sight of her and I felt guilty at not noticing how her cough had got worse over the last few months.

"Right, Mary. You are not staying in the lodging one day more. It is killing you. I am taking you home and I am going to look after you until you are well again."

I expected her to argue but it was as if all her spirit had been sucked out of her, leaving just a passive shell. "Yes please, Hannah. I need you now, the time has come." And she burst into tears that did nothing to dampen the feelings of elation that her words elicited in me.

Despite Mary being quite unwell I cannot remember being so happy. She never asked to be left alone and her desire for independence seemed to have been forgotten. My greatest pleasure was to sit in my studio and paint or read, whilst Mary wrote her articles or stories. She would sometimes read me what she had written. I never told her that I thought her fairy tales were lack-lustre and her short stories depressing. Instead I suggested small changes and I felt so proud when she took notice and scribbled out or added bits accordingly.

Mary's cough improved but never quite went away and before we knew it she had been living with me for a year. One of the habits we got into was for me to go to her bedroom each morning and evening. She would sit at the dressing table in her nightgown and let me drag the brush through her tangled locks. As the months passed I noticed her hair becoming greyer and greyer, which somehow made me love her more. The different coloured glass bottles and the silver vanity set all glittered in the firelight or the sunlight, making me think I was in Aladdin's cave. When I had finished we would swap places, although my short hair needed the minimum of care. Mary always brushed thirty-two times, counting quietly under her breath. How I relished the touch of her fingers on my neck, the heat of her body on my back, her face reflected in the mirror, returning my smile.

In the evening we would kiss each other and I would go to my own room. I ached to just lie with her but I could not bear the thought of rejection, so I never suggested it.

The months came and went. Mary seemed happy most of the time but some days she sank into despair I didn't know how to get her out of. I don't know what triggered it but I knew the signs: she would not get out of bed in the morning but say she was tired or not well; she refused food; her face would be pale and the lines around her eyes and mouth more defined than normal; she would cry unceasingly for hours. I learned quickly that there was nothing I could do other than leave her alone, or if she could tolerate my presence, then to sit quietly and just stroke her hair and tell her how everything would be alright.

Then almost as suddenly as it appeared her despondency would lift and she would greet me with a bright smile and ask me to brush her hair. She never apologised for her bouts of depression and we never discussed it; it was just part of our life together that we coped with. I liked to think we were like any normal, happily married couple - comfortable with each other's company and each other's weaknesses.

Mary would go to see her mother each week to ensure that she was alright and to collect any letters from people who did not know that she now lived with me. We always read our letters to each other over breakfast. Mary's were from publishers or admirers of her fairy tales or occasionally from members of the De Morgan family; mine were from Mr Brown the estate manager at Russell Hall or silly notes from female acquaintances.

Our greatest pleasure though, was a letter from Sarah, who was still in Australia. One day, in the spring of '88 an envelope with the familiar hand-writing and post mark was presented to me and after we had finished breakfast we went to the living room to sit in comfort and prepare ourselves to be entertained. This letter was no exception and we both laughed at Sarah's description of the antics of her Aborigine house boy, the kangaroos that came into her garden and nibbled at anything that had the temerity to pop its head out of the soil, the saga of the successes and failures in education and society of her son and daughter, eighteen and fifteen respectively. We both expected the letter to finish with the usual terms of endearment but in fact Sarah's final sentences took us completely by surprise.

My dear Hannah, could you do me the greatest favour? Could we come and stay for a while whilst we look for somewhere to live? Yes, we are coming back to England! Mr Russell yearns to see green fields once more and he wants the children to see their home country. We intend to arrive by September, is that convenient? I know you have enough space but please, please, please, my dear, do not go to any bother - promise me you won't! We will only be with you for a very short time, I am sure we will find a place in London quickly.

I am so looking forward to seeing you again - do you think we will recognise each other? I am sure we will. Georgie looks the spitting image of you and your father - long face, brown hair - a true Russell! I am very excited about meeting with Mary. I feel I know her already and I am sure we will be great friends. Now remember, I don't want you to do anything other than allow us to sleep in a bed and sit at a table, nothing more!

Not go to any trouble? Mary and I spent that summer totally redecorating three bedrooms, converting another into a study for Mr Russell, another into a room for Sarah and yet another into somewhere the youngsters could go to do whatever youngsters do.

Mary still suffered periods of depression but when she was well she threw herself into the project, helping me chose modern furniture, fabrics and wallpaper. I was thrilled with the effect and I was so excited at the thought of having the Russell family stay, and was determined that their visit would be longer than Sarah had indicated. How lovely it would be to hear young people's laughter in the house, the first time in living memory.

Sarah continued to write, entertaining us with her tales of the preparation for the journey and their plans to stay in Cairo for a few weeks as they knew some people there. Mary and I had started to count the weeks to their arrival when I received my first ever cable; I knew it could not be the bearer of good news.

Cairo, Egypt
27th August '88

Hannah Russell

Mr Russell died 25th cannot travel to England sorry Sarah Russell.

Chapter 7 - Leila's Gold

1888

One thing all the people thought very strange, and that was that every day the new queen grew paler and paler, and weaker and weaker, and none of the doctors or physicians could do her any good, though she summoned them from all parts of the world, and no one knew that she was bleeding herself to death. Every day she grew worse and worse, and in spite of her great wealth and her being queen she never appeared to be happy, but always looked discontented and anxious.

At last she grew so ill that she could not walk at all, and she lay down on her bed and ordered that no one should come and disturb her, but that she should be left quite alone to rest. "I shall not want any more gold just yet," she said to herself, "so I will rest here and grow strong," but before the day was passed her ladies came and told her that the officers were asking for money with which to pay the soldiers.

"I have no money yet. They must wait," said Leila. And she dared not press any more blood from the wound on her hand, for she was so weak that she feared it might kill her.

("*Leila's Gold*," by Mary De Morgan)

157 Dar Al-Shifa
Cairo
Egypt
1st September '88

My very dear Hannah,

I very much hope you received the telegraphic cable I sent last week but in case you didn't I am very sorry to have to tell you that my dear husband passed away on 25th August. As you know, he has not been well for a number of years and I think the journey was just too much for him. I am so sorry that he didn't get to see his beloved England once more.

We were staying with some good friends, Robert and Amelia MacDonald, and they have been marvellous; they have two boys who are of a similar age to Maurice and Georgie. I didn't want to be a burden on them and so they have helped me find a very pleasant house to live in.

Hannah dear, I cannot bear the thought of continuing the journey so I have rented the house for at least six months.

The children seem happy here, although they are, of course, devastated at the loss of their father. There are quite a few families here that we knew in Sydney as the men folk all worked at the embassy. I am surrounded by some very dear people who are helping me cope with all the administration that seems to accompany death, but are also helping me to come to terms with the huge gap in my life that used to be filled with Mr Russell. I know you and Mary would have been a tremendous support, but I feel at home here - and the weather is what we are used to.

Why don't you and Mary come over here? There is plenty of room in the house and the dry air will do Mary the world of good.

Forgive me, I tire very easily at the moment and I can't write any more.

Please be assured of my love for you,
  Sarah Russell

Both Mary and I sat silently, alone with our own thoughts. Mary had never known the Russells, of course, so I did not expect her to feel anything other than the natural sympathy for another who has suffered such a loss. I, on the other hand, had been in touch with Sarah for the last seventeen years or so and considered her to be one of my dearest friends; I should have felt real sorrow at her obvious grief, but my main emotion was disappointment that she wouldn't be coming to England. I felt too guilty to articulate my regret and we separated without saying anything about poor Mr Russell's untimely passing.

Mary kept to her room all morning and I spent some hours completing a sketch of a late flowering rose that I had come across in the back garden. When she joined me for a cup of tea, she seemed tense and I was worried that she was on the edge of another one of her black moods. Mary perched on the seat, biting her lip and creasing her brow. She took a breath to say something then seemed to decide against it.

"What on earth is the matter, Mary? Are you feeling unwell?"

She continued to bite her lip, continued to look at me, her cheeks becoming flushed. Then the words burst out like champagne out of a shaken bottle. "I feel very sorry for Sarah and I was thinking that maybe, well, maybe we should go out there. Go to Egypt. She did suggest it in her letter, didn't she? It was almost an invitation, wasn't it?"

I was so taken aback that I didn't know what to say. Mary took the letter she must have put in her pocket earlier and read through it quickly.

"Yes, look, Hannah, she says 'why don't you and Mary come over here?' She even says it would do me the world of good."

"Go to Egypt? Go to *Egypt*? Do you know how far away it is? It would take weeks, maybe even months! It could be dangerous; Sarah said it was the journey that killed Mr Russell. And what would we do when we got there? By then Sarah would have quite got over her husband's death. We would just be a burden to her. Mary, you are not thinking straight, we cannot possibly go to Egypt."

Mary took a deep breath and then held up a finger. "First of all, the journey actually takes about twelve days - that is not even two weeks." She held up another finger. "Secondly, Mr Russell has been ill for years and he may well have died even if he had stayed in Australia. The Blunts have been there many times and William tells me they have bought a huge estate just outside of Egypt. It is *the* place to go because the climate is so conducive; even

William is talking about going out there." She held up a third finger. "I am not sure how long Sarah was married for, but I am sure she will not have got over her husband's death after just a couple of weeks." She tilted her head as she tried to recall my other objections.

I aided her memory. "I said we would be a burden."

She held up her fourth finger triumphantly and waved the letter in front of me with her other hand. "Ah yes. She says here that there is plenty of room in the house, so why would we be a burden? Friends are all well and good, but at times like this you need your family, and you, Hannah, are family."

She held up her thumb. "And was it not you who suggested we go to Egypt, when we actually went to Lynton? *You* suggested it, not me."

Mary's eyes were bright with an excitement that I did not share.

I, in turn help up a finger. "One, twelve days is still a very long time; it will not be like travelling in a train to Minehead. Do they even have trains in Egypt? Two, Sarah said quite categorically that she thought it was the journey that killed him. You are not strong, Mary, and I am certain that you would not be able to cope with such an arduous journey. Three, we are not the Blunts - they are adventurers. They think nothing of riding across the desert, which, by the way, nearly killed them so Lady Anne told me. And four, I may be family, but I have only seen her once when I was about eleven years old. She has been with her friends for much longer, some of them for years if they were also in Australia with them. Maybe we wouldn't be a burden exactly, but what help could we give her?" I held up all my fingers and thumb, mirroring her gesture. "And, yes, I did suggest going to Egypt, but I didn't mean it. I just said it so that you would agree to go somewhere in England. Anyway, neither of us has ever been married, and have no idea what it is like to lose a loved one."

Mary's head snapped up and she glared fiercely at me. "I *know* what it is to lose someone I love. I *know!* Do you not think I feel the loss of my darling Papa, my brother Edward, my sister Chrissy, my ...?" She stood up, her eyes now bright with tears. "If you loved me at all you would go just so I could get better." With that she left, leaving her tea untouched and my senses reeling.

I wanted desperately to go to her and tell her that of course I loved her, but when I tapped on her closed bedroom door she told me to go away, her voice thick with tears. I spent the afternoon pacing up and down my studio arguing with myself. My rational side argued that the trip would be exhausting for Mary and could quite likely kill her, if indeed the whole ship did not flounder in the perilous seas with all hands lost. And anyway, had anyone ever actually been *cured* of consumption by staying in Egypt? My emotional side, on the other hand, could only repeat that Mary would think I didn't love her and she might even leave me. My emotional side won in the end, of course, for the very thought of a life without Mary was unbearable.

Having made my decision I tapped on her door again, slipped a note underneath and made my way back downstairs. I had not been sitting at the dining table for more than a minute before Mary came flying through the door, pulled me up from my seat, hugged me until I could hardly breathe and soaked my bodice with copious tears.

Cooks did all the planning and a few visits to Harrods ensured that we were both suitably attired for a climate neither of us could even imagine. England was suffering from a particularly damp autumn, which exacerbated Mary's condition. We duly said farewell to friends and, in Mary's case, family and publishers, and on Tuesday November 20th we travelled to Southampton, the first leg of our journey to Egypt, quite certain we would be returning the following year in time to enjoy the start of the English spring.

We spent the night at the Royal Victoria Hotel and boarded the ship during the afternoon. I had seen pictures of liners, of course, but they were always at sea and gave no indication of their immense size. My first sight of the *S.S. Pegu* stopped me in my tracks. I had never seen anything so vast in my life.

"How on earth will that take us to Egypt? It will surely never float."

Mary stared at it, her head tilted to one side. "I don't understand how it floats, but it obviously does. Come on, I can't wait to see what it is like inside."

I had managed to book two of the best cabins, each of which consisted of a sturdy iron bed, an armchair and a chest of drawers. The steward was very proud to tell us that we were privileged to have two of only four cabins that had the luxury of a sink and water closet. We also had a porthole apiece, through which the afternoon light painted the walls with a pale yellow wash that made the rather Spartan decor seem quite cheerful. We unpacked quickly as we only had one small trunk each, the main ones having been put somewhere in the belly of the beast.

There still being a few hours until the evening meal, we decided to explore, using a printed map that the steward had given us.

"This reminds me of the maze at Hampton Court. Do you remember, Hannah? It's a good job we have a map otherwise we may be wandering around these corridors until the end of time! Mind you, we don't seem to be getting any nearer to the upper deck."

We were trying to get to the open air but each staircase we came across only went down, and therefore so did we. Many of the doors were open and we quickly saw that our first-class cabins were well worth the cost. These others had no portholes to lighten the tiny rooms that had nothing in them other than bunk-beds as furniture. I sometimes counted as many as six people trying to fit themselves and their trunks into the confined space. As we went lower and lower, the air got hotter and hotter and the noise of the machinery that kept the lights burning and the ship afloat got louder and louder. I began to feel quite claustrophobic. Luckily, we bumped into a man in uniform, who gladly accompanied us along more corridors and up more stairs until we reached our destination. We gratefully felt the cool breeze on our flushed cheeks and inhaled the fresh air into our lungs.

We were not the only ones who preferred to be outside and the deck was crowded with passengers either strolling arm in arm, or leaning over the railings waving and shouting to those standing on the dockside. We had no-one to bid us farewell, but even so we waved and laughed enthusiastically, so infectious was the jovial atmosphere.

The steward had marked on our map the most useful routes that we would need during the journey, and so it was that we managed to find our way back to the cabin in order to get changed, and then to the dining room in time for the evening meal. There was one large room with a long table that accommodated all but the first-class passengers. We, to our chagrin, had to sit at a table just big enough for the eight privileged guests, in a small room adjoining the larger one. We benefitted from oak panelling and silver cutlery but Mary and I would have preferred to sit with the other passengers, who sounded as if they were having a very jolly evening, compared to the polite, dull conversation we had to endure.

The meal, however, was excellent, cooked, so the maitre d' proudly told us, by one of the best chefs in England.

"He is here on the insistence of Lord Macintyre, who is gracing us with his presence on this trip." The man bowed his head reverently as he spoke the name and Lord Macintyre himself, who was sitting opposite me, inclined his head in acknowledgement. "His Lordship" another bow - he reminded me of a picture of an Emperor penguin I had recently seen - "travels nowhere without his chef and so all the passengers benefit."

"Not all," retorted Mary. "I wager the second and third class passengers out there are not eating as well as we are."

The maitre d' smiled coldly. "Of course not, madam. That would not be appropriate."

It had been a tiring day and I fell straight into a deep sleep and did not awake until eight o'clock the next morning. It was only when I got out of bed and staggered a little as the floor moved slightly under my feet that I realised we were finally at sea. Now that we were here I felt excited by the prospect of our journey and I ran to the porthole but was disappointed to see nothing but a dark grey sea topped by an even darker grey sky. I wondered if Mary was awake yet, so knocked and was greeted by groaning. When I stuck my head round the door I saw immediately that Mary may have been of a sea-faring race but was not blessed with an ocean-going constitution. Her face was unhealthily pale; her hair was dishevelled and dark with sweat; the bedclothes had been flung to the four corners of the room but she was now curled up on her side shivering with cold. I quickly collected the bedding and made her warm and comfortable, washed her face and hands and a damp cloth and then rang the bell to summon help.

The doctor arrived thirty minutes later, hardly looked at Mary and asked no questions but advised me to ensure that she drank only water with a little ginger and ate only dry crackers and green apples, all of which the cabin attendant would be happy to provide. He also suggested that she sit outside as much as possible when it was warm enough to do so, so that she could see the horizon. When the doctor left I tentatively asked Mary if she would like something to eat or even to get up but all she seemed capable of doing was groaning. I completed my ablutions then sat with her for the rest of the day, eating my meals on a tray and managing to read a complete novel, whilst Mary alternately dozed and vomited. The cabin attendant, Denis, provided fresh sheets and in the evening I sponged her whole body and changed her nightdress. I tried unsuccessfully to persuade her to eat a few crackers and an apple, which Denis confirmed were of great benefit to those who suffered from the "mal de mer." I was loath to leave her but Denis said he would ensure a female attendant came in every hour to make sure Mary was alright, so I went to bed and had another dreamless, undisturbed sleep.

The next day followed the same pattern, but I was happy in my role as nurse. When Mary was sleeping peacefully later that morning I took a stroll on the upper deck to get some fresh air. It was another grey, cold day but all the deck chairs were taken and there was quite a crowd of people ambling along. I guessed that they all preferred to brave the damp winter elements rather than to breathe in the stale, thick air of their cabin. I had a warm coat, scarf and gloves and walked briskly along the deck, but even so it was not many minutes before I was so chilled that I had to return to the cabin. I found Mary awake and struggling to sit up. She was still pale but there was a tinge of pink on her cheeks and she managed to give me a ghost of a smile.

"Oh, good, are you feeling a bit better? You have had a horrible time of it."

I plumped up the pillows and wrapped a bed jacket around her shoulders. I stroked her cheek and kissed her brow.

"I can at least now look at a cracker without wanting to be sick and the room is no longer spinning around. I'll try eating something and then see if I can get out of bed."

It was, however, another couple of days before Mary felt well enough to leave the cabin and join me for a walk along the upper deck, and yet another few days before she felt confident enough to eat in the dining room. As each day passed I was aware of the weather improving, the temperature getting warmer and the sky and sea bluer. By the time we stopped at Malta Mary felt completely well and we spent a pleasant day walking around Valletta with a group of other passengers. It was warm enough to sit outside for afternoon tea and it pleased me to see Mary lift her face to the sun and sigh contentedly.

The next morning I awoke early. The sun was only just rising and had not yet warmed the air, but I decided to wrap myself up well and to sit on the upper deck and to savour the birth of the day. There were already a few passengers already on deck, but I managed to find a deck chair that offered protection from the cool breeze, but provided a wonderful view out to sea. When I first looked out I thought that there was nothing to see but the vast flat expanse of blue that stretched to infinity. But the longer I looked the more I saw: the smudge of smoke from another ship on the horizon; a flock of black cormorants skimming the surface of the ocean, coming from goodness knows where, going to goodness knows where; a single small white cloud marring the otherwise clear azure dome. And the sea itself, not flat after all, but just like blue icing on a Christmas cake that the cook had patted with a spatula and then brushed with sugar. I imagined rather than saw the brightly coloured shoals of fish that darted hither and thither in the dark depths. The surface was suddenly, joyfully, broken by five shiny porpoises, arching in synchrony through the air. I saw them for but a few seconds, then no more and I wondered if I had imagined them.

I was entranced and it was only when she sat next to me that I realised that Mary had joined me. We sat, unspeaking, just relishing the serenity and the watery sound of the ship forging its way through the waves. A warm wave of love flowed through me and I took Mary's hand and squeezed it tight.

"Isn't this absolutely wonderful?"

Mary laughed and took her hand away to loosen her coat as the sun got hotter.

"And to think you didn't want to come. Just imagine, we could be in London coughing and sneezing in the cold and damp. Come, let's have breakfast. I feel inspired to do some writing today. It was my turn to sit next to Lord Macintyre last night, and he bored me rigid about the amount of money he has. I had a sudden desire to stick my fork in him to see if he has blood or gold coins in his veins, and then I thought that would make a rather good story. I'll work on it today and read it to you tonight."

I had packed all my painting paraphernalia in a trunk that was stowed in the hold so I only had a sketch pad and a small assortment of pencils. Although the seascape was fascinating there was nothing I was inclined to draw, so instead I asked Mary what the basis of her story was so that I could do some sketches to accompany it. She thought for a few moments and then began her story in a sing-song voice.

"Once upon a time there lived a girl named Leila, who dwelt with her father, who was a woodman, of course. She was a pretty girl, but she had one great fault - she loved money. She hoarded every penny she could find, and never gave any away because she wanted to become a rich woman. One night she sat in front of the cottage counting her silver pennies when a poor woman came across the hill-side and stopped in front of her. She was dressed in rags, and carried a baby in her arms. The old woman asked Leila for a silver penny so she could buy her starving baby some food, but Leila refused. The old woman begged and begged but Leila just carried on counting her money." Mary paused and chuckled, "Do you think it would be too obvious if I called her Leila Macintyre?

"Anyway, the old woman finally gave up but before walking away she suddenly took a small knife from her pocket." Mary changed her voice to be that of an old crone. 'You love money more than anything else in the

161

world. You shall have as much of it as you like, and see what good it will do you.' Before Leila could stop her the old woman had scratched her hand with the sharp point and drops of red blood fell to the ground, and as they fell each drop turned into a bright gold coin. Rather than being horrified Leila was thrilled, for now she could become as rich as her heart desired, merely by pricking herself."

Mary paused again and looked out to sea for a few moments. "There will have to be a boy in the story, one who loves Leila but whom Leila spurns, for he is but a poor shepherd." The cabin attendant came in at that moment to clear away some cups. After he had gone Mary continued. "I'll call him Denis and as his love was not reciprocated he departs and we don't hear of him until the end. So, Leila grows richer and richer, and as she gets richer she becomes more and more powerful. She lives in a glittering palace and has servants galore. She wears silks and satins and has trunks full of gold and precious stones. She becomes the greatest lady in the country and when the old King dies she pays an army of soldiers to take his son prisoner. She shuts him up in a strong tower and then she has herself crowned queen."

Mary stopped again and nibbled on the end of her pencil. I was mesmerised and my head teemed with images of palaces and jewels and of this coldly calculating girl. "One thing that everyone notices about their new queen is that each day she becomes paler and paler and weaker and weaker. None of the doctors can help, of course, because they don't know that she is effectively

162

bleeding herself to death. At last she grows so ill that she cannot risk bleeding herself anymore in case she kills herself, and so she cannot pay the soldiers' wages. When they hear this they break into her palace, seize her from her bed and drag her back to her humble cottage. Leila lies there all night, weeping and wailing and when she sees smoke rising from her burning palace she weeps and wails even more. Then a shepherd comes by and asks her if she is alright. It is Denis, of course, but Leila looks so awful he doesn't recognise her. She repents, he forgives her and they live poorly, but happily, ever after."

I clapped my hands in admiration. "Oh, Mary, that is excellent, well done! You must include that in your next collection of fairy tales. Do you mind if I try doing some sketches? It will amuse me and I don't mind if you don't use them in the end."

The next few days were spent on deck, each absorbed in Leila's world and before we knew it we had arrived at Alexandria. We docked just after midday, having spent the morning re-packing. Once we had walked down the gang plank we stood to one side, savouring the feel of solid ground beneath our feet. The heat was intense but it was the noise that was so overpowering that it was like a physical barrier that prevented us from moving forwards: there were the smaller vessels hooting their welcome to the giant liner from England; there were the bangs and scrapes as enormous wooden crates were lifted, shifted and deposited by contraptions of metal, rope and manpower; there were the cries of the vendors vying for the attention of anyone and everyone; there were the screams of the Arab children running around for no apparent reason other than getting under everyone's feet; there was the banging of doors of a nearby train and then a long, piercing whistle as it slowly left the station, chugging with the effort.

"My God, Hannah, this surely is what Hell is like - an incessant cacophony of noise and a seething sea of impenetrable humanity. How on earth are we going to find Sarah?"

One of the benefits of being tall was that I could scan over the heads of the hundreds, if not thousands of people milling about the dock, seeking out the woman I had only met once when I was eleven. There was constant movement over every inch of the ground as people bustled here and there, but my eyes were drawn to a couple who were standing perfectly still near to the entrance, like the calm eye of a storm. There was a middle aged woman who was staring fixedly at the gang plank, just to the left of me, and a young man who, even at this distance, I could tell was closely related to the woman. I raised my hand tentatively and her gaze shifted to me and then she waved, first uncertainly, and then with great enthusiasm. She grabbed the man by the arm and then pushed him in our direction. He may have been young, but he strode towards us with great authority, elbowing his way through the throng.

When he was still some five yards away he shouted, "Miss Hannah Russell? Miss Mary De Morgan?" We smiled and waved in agreement and when he reached us he shook our hands warmly. "Welcome to Egypt! I'm

Maurice Russell and I am very pleased to meet you. Come, I'll take you to Mama, she is beside herself with impatience to meet you. Then I'll make sure your baggage gets sent to the right hotel." He turned around and retraced his steps, pushing people aside like a modern-day Moses parting the Red Sea, creating a people-free passage for Mary and I to traverse.

When we reached Sarah there was much laughing, hugging and inconsequential chatter. After the initial excitement Sarah hooked an arm in each of ours and led us away from the dock to a horse and carriage that was waiting patiently on the road.

"We'll go straight to the hotel and you can have a short rest, by which time Maurice will have got the luggage delivered. You can then change for dinner. Oh, it is so good to see you both! How long have we been writing to each other, Hannah? It must be, what, at least fifteen years? In each letter we always said how we wished we could see each other again, and here we finally are!"

I took her hands in mine and kissed her gently on the cheek. "I am so sorry that it is under such circumstances. I can't imagine what you have gone through. But Mary and I are here now and will help as much as we can, won't we?"

Mary nodded and although her expression was suitably serious I recognised the excited sparkle in her eyes.

"Thank you Hannah, dear. Mr Russell was ill for so many years that it was not totally unexpected. Of course it was still awful when it finally happened. One can never be totally prepared." She paused, looking straight ahead, her face muscles taut as she tried to control her emotions. She sighed deeply. "People in Cairo have been so friendly and supportive; there is quite an English community here, you know. Maurice has started to work at the Embassy and is already doing very well. Georgie goes a few days a week to an English school; she has lessons herself but also helps teach the little ones. She so wanted to come today but I thought it better if she stayed at home; you will meet her tomorrow. We all feel very at home, as I hope you will whilst you are here." She had talked without taking a breath and now stopped, her chest heaving.

A few minutes later we arrived at the hotel but so deep had we been in conversation that I had taken little notice of our surroundings. The inside of the hotel was dark and deliciously cool; I wondered how the potted palm trees thrived so well without the sunlight - maybe they didn't and had to be regularly replaced for the indulgence of the guests. We were led to our rooms by an Arab boy who looked no more than ten years old. I was pleased that I was sharing with Mary. As our luggage had not yet arrived there was little we could do except lie on the beds and rest, which we duly did; I felt unexpectedly tired.

A knock on the door startled me awake and I was surprised to see Mary now sitting at the dressing table avidly writing. She opened the door for the porter, who carried in our trunks and cases; when he had finished she gave him some coins, as instructed by Sarah, and also an envelope for him to give to the concierge to post.

"Couldn't you sleep? Who were you writing to so urgently?"

Her brow creased into a frown. "I wasn't writing urgently, I just wanted to finish it. It was to my mother of course, who do you think it was to?"

I didn't have an answer so instead I went into the bathroom to refresh myself and get changed for dinner, at which Maurice regaled us with outrageous tales of their life in Australia - so much so that my side hurt with laughing. Sarah smiled at him fondly throughout the meal and occasionally made a contribution to the story, but it was her son who held court.

The next day we had a late breakfast and then caught the train to Cairo. We had a private carriage and yet another young Arab boy served us with tea and biscuits and tiny triangles of sandwiches. He spoke no English but bowed and smiled all the time, his grin widening even more when Maurice gave him some *baksheesh*.

The landscape that we passed through was so totally different to what Mary and I were used to that we both spent most of the journey just staring out of the window. The railway went alongside the river Nile, whose banks were verdant and lush. The green belt, though, was narrow and beyond we could see the sands of the desert stretching out, seemingly to eternity. We passed an occasional settlement, just a few rough mud dwellings built haphazardly on the bank. We saw women washing in the river water - they stopped their labours, waved and grinned, their teeth startlingly white in their nut brown faces - it took a while but we eventually sloughed our English-bred inhibitions and waved back. We saw donkeys trudging along paths, laden with huge melons or crops just harvested; we saw naked children, as brown and skinny as twigs of an oak tree, running and playing as all children do.

"I bet these scenes have not changed for hundreds, if not thousands of years. I wonder what they thought when they saw a train for the first time? That it was a new Egyptian god perhaps!" Mary's eyes were bright and her cheeks were flushed.

When we arrived at Cairo some four hours later there was another horse and carriage waiting for us and within a very short period of time we arrived at the house that Sarah had rented and which would be Mary's and my home for the next two months or so. It was a large, square three-storied building, the outside of which was the colour of the desert. Inside the walls were whitewashed and the floors were black and white squares of marble, so that I wondered whether we could play a game of human chess on it. It was a relief to get out of the heat and into the relative coolness.

Our baggage had already arrived and someone had unpacked for us into adjoining rooms. I didn't want to cause a fuss so I accepted this separation, although I would dearly have loved to share Mary's bed again. We had a wash and changed our clothes and then joined Sarah in the garden for afternoon tea.

It was a large garden whose centre-piece was a flamboyant marble fountain, with horses and cherubs frolicking and forever cool in the cascading waters. Tall palm trees afforded ample shade to those who wandered along paths that meandered around beds of the most gorgeous roses, narcissus, lilies, oleander, geranium, dahlia, chrysanthemums and violets. The colours of the flowers were dazzling; their perfume hung heavily in the warm air, which was filled with the buzzing of insects who fed on the abundant nectar.

We sat under the canopy of an enormous sycamore tree, next to the fountain that tinkled and sparkled in the sunshine.

"If the dock at Alexandria was hell, Mary, then this is surely heaven."

Mary merely nodded and sighed happily. I too was contented for I was sitting with the two women I loved most in the world.

"I am surprised, Sarah, at the abundance of flora. I expected there to be nothing but a few cacti."

"That is a common belief but the Nile soil is some of the most fertile on God's earth. When you go into Cairo you will see that the flower shop is one of the most common that there is."

Whilst we were sipping and nibbling, Georgie arrived from school. She was sixteen but still young enough to clap her hands excitedly at the sight of us, to race eagerly down the path and to trip on a raised stone and fall inelegantly into my lap. Undeterred, she righted herself. "Oh, you are here at last! Mama would not let me come and meet you and I did so want to be there. But she said it was too long a journey and I would be better here making sure everything was ready, and it was, wasn't it? Your rooms are alright aren't they? I personally supervised each one to make sure it was absolutely perfect. Oh! Did they remember to put fresh flowers in your rooms? I do hope so. I reminded them this morning. Flowers make a room so welcoming don't they? Oh! I have not introduced myself, and I don't know which is Miss Hannah and which is Miss Mary. Oh dear."

Georgie finally stopped speaking, like a wind-up toy that had run down. She looked so dejected that we had to smile. Mary and I stood up and formally introduced ourselves to her but rather than shake our outstretched hands she hugged both of us tightly, and kissed us quite passionately.

"I am so glad you are here! I have been longing to meet you for ages."

Sarah looked on with a wry smile. "Do sit down Georgie and act like the young lady I would like you to be. Poor Miss Russell and Miss De Morgan, they must feel quite battered and bruised by your torrent of words and over-zealous embraces." So Georgie sat down and started eating cake with great gusto, and I was able to take a good, uninterrupted look at her. I saw immediately that she was a Russell; she had the same long face, light brown hair and deep-set eyes as my father and me. I had already seen that she was quite tall for a girl but perhaps not as tall as I was at her age.

Mid bite Georgie suddenly sat bolt upright, gave a gasp and took an envelope out of her pocket. "Oh, Miss De Morgan, I quite forgot! This letter came for you this morning. I am not prying, honestly, but I could not help but notice that it has an Egyptian postmark. Do you know someone here?"

Sarah looked horrified at her daughter's frank curiosity. "Georgie! Don't be so rude. Just give Miss De Morgan the letter and keep your inquisitive nature to yourself."

Mary almost snatched the letter from Georgie then held it tightly to her breast as if she was frightened it would blow away, but she did not open it. I too was intrigued; I caught her eye and looked at her quizzically.

"It's just from my nephew Gus. You have not met him, Hannah." She turned to Sarah to explain the genealogy. "Gus is one of my brother Edward's boys. Edward was seven years older than me and died eight years or so ago, leaving behind a wife and four children. Gus is the oldest and is a doctor at a goldmine in Egypt - it has a strange name and I can't remember it. I told him I was coming here and gave him this address - that was alright wasn't it?" She didn't wait for an answer. "I think I will go to my room now, if you don't mind, I have a slight headache probably due to the heat."

I didn't see Mary until the next morning at breakfast and she seemed fully recovered. The next few days were spent being paraded before Sarah's friends. Any new face was apparently of much interest to the tight-knit community. We both had to relate our life stories at each

171

visit to such an extent that Mary suggested we save our breath, write them down and merely hand them out for everyone to read.

They were all very pleasant people, still hanging onto their English traditions for dear life. They all had English cooks; they attended English churches; they sent their children to English schools; they associated only with other English people; they spoke English with no attempt at learning the language of the country they lived in.

After a week we begged Sarah to give us a respite as we wished to explore the real Cairo, rather than the pockets of England we had hitherto visited. She agreed on the condition that Abdul, one of the house boys, accompanied us at all times. He was not a boy but rather a man of middle years, with a rather melancholy air; he reminded me of a bloodhound with his downward drooping eyes and his wrinkled brow. Abdul spoke enough English to understand Sarah's instructions to take us to the *souk*, to stay with us at all times and not to leave our sides under any circumstances. He bowed and then beckoned to us imperiously, as if he was a school teacher and Mary and I were two very naughty pupils.

We followed him obediently into the carriage, trying hard not to laugh. We drove down the main thoroughfare and then along side streets until I lost all sense of direction. On turning yet another corner we found ourselves on the edge of a large square so filled with stalls and people that the carriage could go no further. We alighted and with Abdul leading the way we became part of the throng of milling humanity. There was so much to

172

see it was hard to take everything in: pots and pans piled into towers that teetered on tables; bales of colourful cloth rolled out for people to admire visually and tactually; bowls of herbs and spices, the names of which I did not know; dried meats hanging from hooks; displays of leather goods, the warm smell more enticing than the sugary sweets that were covered with swarms of flies. It reminded me of the Jewish market in the East End, with the stall holders shouting out their wares, trying to persuade the passers-by to taste, smell or feel.

Abdul led us further into the market. He had a stick which he swished side to side to clear a path, unconcerned about any injury he might cause to shin or ankle. I could see no other white person, which explained why we seemed to be the centre of attention. Not only the stall-holders were trying to entice us into their shops, but a gaggle of children were hanging onto our skirts and holding out their hands in the universal plea for alms. They all wore the minimum of clothes, had brown skinny arms and legs, black unkempt hair and huge dark eyes that looked at us beseechingly. They were all pushing each other out of the way, prattling in their high-pitched voices. I didn't understand a word, of course, but I knew from the expressions on their faces what they were asking for. Without thinking I went to open my purse.

"Hannah!" Mary grabbed my wrist and slapped the back of my hand. "For goodness sake, what are you thinking? Did you learn nothing in London?" She looked at me crossly. "You know you must never, ever give money to the poor. Even you, Hannah, don't have enough money to cure the poverty here." She faced the crowd of children that had gathered around us and flailed her arms and shouted at them. "Begone, you horrors! We have nothing for you, go on, shoo!"

Some of them stepped back surprised at the strange foreign lady with the swinging arms and loud voice, but they soon settled back into a unit that continued to follow us around. They hoped, no doubt, that their doggedness would melt our cold English hearts.

Although November is one of the coolest months in the year, it was still a glorious 75°F and we wore summer dresses and protected our heads from the sun with white lacy parasols. We enjoyed the thought of the people back in London, wrapped in their heavy overcoats, gloves and scarves, protecting *their* heads from the driving sleet and snow with dull black umbrellas. Even though I was wearing the coolest dress I owned, after a time even that felt too cumbersome with its belt like a metal band round my waist, its collar rubbing the back of my neck sore, and the material sticking to my skin with sweat.

"What we need, Mary, is to wear garments like the Arab women - look, they all seem to wear pantaloons and long loose tunics, nothing fitting tight to the body, nothing to prevent the air flowing around their bodies to keep them cool. If I don't get this dress off soon I fear I will melt into a puddle and disappear into the sand." I looked around the nearby stalls. I espied one selling materials and grabbed Abdul's arm to change his direction.

There were some beautiful materials on display but in the end I decided just plain, pastel would be more appropriate. I stretched out my arms and held up my fingers to indicate how many yards of each bolt I wanted and then stood back as Abdul and the stall holder shouted at each other until both seemed satisfied with the deal they had made.

On completion of the transaction, rather than walking away the stall holder beckoned me inside the shop and Abdul indicated that I should follow. The contrast between the light outside and the dark interior was so great that at first I could see nothing - it was if I had gone completely blind. But after a few seconds I began to distinguish the shelves laden with more materials, a counter, chairs, the stall keeper and what appeared to be a dwarf. The latter turned out to be a very small, elderly woman, made shorter by a hunched back that meant that the top of her head was actually level with her shoulders. But this impediment did not seem to prevent her from carrying out her job as a seamstress. She reminded me of a clothed hedgehog as she scurried around me measuring every part of me, the stall keeper lifting her up to reach my upper body.

When she had finished she circled round me, muttering under her breath. Then she stopped, started to chatter, nodding her head energetically. Abdul translated for me. "Three days, Missus and they will be ready. I come, pick up."

So it was that three days later Abdul handed me some brown paper packages that contained the most beautifully made pantaloons and tunics. I took them upstairs immediately and tried them on then went downstairs and into the garden, where Mary and Sarah were sitting, sipping lemonade and reading. I twirled in front of them, delighting in the feel of the cool cotton on my skin, the sense of freedom at the lack of belts, buckles and buttons.

"Hannah, my God! What on earth are you wearing? For goodness sake, take it off, what will the servants think?"

I stopped mid-twirl, surprised at Sarah's reaction.

"I am wearing what all the women wear here, clothes that are practical and comfortable. I don't see what anyone could possibly object to."

Sarah looked worried. "Hannah, dear. You just look so, how shall I say, so very odd. No-one will respect you if they think you have gone native."

I felt a surge of anger. "I am not looking for people to respect me. I don't care if people think I am odd. I *am* odd!"

Mary stood and took my arm, preventing me from flouncing off, as I was inclined to do.

"You are not odd, Hannah, stop being so melodramatic. I am sure you have no intention of going out in public like that, but Sarah, they are perfectly suitable for indoor wear, surely?"

Sarah nodded. "I'm sorry Hannah, I did not mean to shout. You just took me by surprise." She looked at me for a few seconds. "They do actually look quite cool and comfortable. Of course you may wear your outfits indoors, but please, please, do not go outside."

I joined them at the table and Mary poured me a lemonade and then suddenly blurted out, "I'm going away for a few days. You don't mind do you? It's Gus. He is going to Alexandria for stores and we have agreed to meet up. We will both stay at the same hotel as we all stayed at when we arrived. That is alright, isn't it?"

Both Sarah and I talked at the same time.

"But Mary we can all go can't we? I would love to meet your nephew. You surely don't mean to go alone."

"Of course it is alright you going, my dear. It is important to take every opportunity to be with family."

Mary held her hand up and looked at me sheepishly.

"Hannah dear, of course you must meet him one day. But not this time. I want it to be just him and me so we can catch up. I don't want him to feel he has to be on his best behaviour. You do understand don't you?"

I didn't but of course there was nothing I could say that didn't sound churlish and selfish.

"When do you go?"

I expected her to say next month or next week.

"Tomorrow. I catch the early morning train, so I will probably be gone by the time you get up."

And so she was.

Chapter 8 - Siegfrid and Handa

1888 - 1889

As Siegfrid walked along he kicked something with his foot, and found it was a trap in which a poor little Hare had been caught, and was held by one leg.

"Poor Hare," said Siegfrid, "perhaps you used to play about us when I walked here with Handa. I will let you go, and then another time you will be careful not to be caught"; so he undid the trap, and the Hare sprang from it, but instead of running away, as Siegfrid had expected, it sat quite still in front of him, looking into his face..

"I saw Handa last night," it said at last, in a wheezy voice.

Siegfrid started, but he was so overjoyed at hearing again of Handa, that he quite got over his surprise at hearing a Hare speak.

"Saw Handa!" he cried. "Oh, where? Is she alive? Oh, tell me."

"She is in a cavern underground," said the Hare. "She and all the other little girls are sitting there in a row, and they cannot move or speak, because on their feet are magic shoes that the old shoemaker made for them, which hold them as still as marble. He waited for them one by one near the village, and gave to each a pair of pretty yellow shoes, and when she had put them on, they ran away with her, and she could not stop try what she might; and the shoes took her right into the middle of the forest. Then the ground opened, and the shoes ran right down into the cavern underground, and the earth closed up again; and

there sit Poor Handa and the other five little girls, who were all brought there in the same way; and they will never move till someone pulls the shoes from their feet."

("Siegfrid and Handa," in *On a Pincushion*, by Mary De Morgan)

I didn't want Sarah to think that I couldn't function without Mary being around, so rather then just sit and wait for her return, which I was inclined to do, I sat in the garden and attempted the impossible task of capturing the vibrant colours of the flora by means of water colours on paper. I was not satisfied with the results but continued nonetheless whilst listening to Georgie's tales of the ups and downs of her daily existence at the school, partly as student and partly as teacher. I liked this young girl, she made me laugh and I found her sheer enthusiasm for life exhilarating.

It was Georgie who suggested that we visit the *souk* after luncheon, as she wanted to buy some trinkets for a friend's birthday present. Abdul was again our guide. This time we walked as it was really not that far, and Georgie proudly taught me the few words of Arabic she had already learned: "*sabah alkhyr*" for "good morning"; "*tab masayik*" for "good afternoon"; "*shukraan*" for "thank you"; "*min fadlik*" for "please" and "*wadaeaan*" for "goodbye". By the time I could recite these to her liking, and to Abdul's obvious amusement, we had arrived at the *souk*.

Before we had gone three steps we were surrounded by young Arab children. Abdul shouted at them and waved his stick. They did move away, but only a few feet and they then reformed and re-gathered around us. They reminded me of a flock of swallows back in England, the individual birds swooping as one entity from one invisible point to another, always on the move.

Georgie and I browsed the shops and admired the wonderful array of goods both inside and out. The bowls of spices scented the air and made my mouth water; the colourful cottons, satins and silks decked the tables like giant bunting; the burnished copper pots and pans that were piled in gloriously shiny heaps reflected the bright sunshine and dazzled us; the plates of sticky sweets attracted hoards of black flies but not us, the baskets of glittering, gaudy bracelets and necklaces, however, did. We spent some pleasurable minutes holding up the trinkets for each other to admire. Georgie finally made her purchase and we continued on. I was particularly drawn to a table on which rows and rows of leather footwear were laid. I wanted to purchase some sandals that were more comfortable than the constricting heeled shoes I had brought from England-only to be worn inside the house, of course. Having made my purchase, we could not resist going into the dark shop, drawn by the enticing smell of the leather, which hung in the air and wrapped itself around us like a shawl. We both stood for a while, just breathing in deeply, as if smelling a beautiful bouquet. I glanced around and saw that the shelves were overflowing with belts, boots, shoes, briefcases, saddlebags, pouches, wallets, even saddles and harnesses, but very little to interest two females.

We both turned to leave, smiling politely at the shopkeeper whose own face looked like an old piece of dark leather, so creased that I was quite tempted to stroke it to try and smooth it a little. He had moved from the back of the shop into the doorway and blocked our exit. I am sure he knew that speaking to us was of no use, but he chattered away nonetheless, grinning toothlessly and holding out various articles that were of no interest or use to us. I shook my head at each offering and I was about to walk purposefully forward, believing that he would not physically prevent us from leaving, when something glinting in the shadowy recess of a deep shelf caught my eye. When I pulled it out I found that it was a most beautiful carpet bag. It had a thick leather base and a frame of a dark, polished wood, with an intricate silver filigree clasp. The body of the bag was made from a dull brown hard-wearing material, akin to thick tweed, but the sides were decorated with patches of the most exquisitely coloured satin. The turquoises, blues, greens, reds, yellows and oranges shimmered and blended like oil on the surface of a puddle, and the gold thread that had been used to sew on the pieces glinted and gleamed, even in the darkness of the shop. I knew that I had to buy it.

"This will make a perfect gift for Mary."

"Is it her birthday?"

"No, not yet anyway. I just like buying her gifts and I am sure that this will give her immense pleasure."

I was about to hand the bag to the shopkeeper, who stood expectantly on one leg, when Abdul firmly took it off me and put it back from whence it came. He winked at me, put a finger to his mouth and then turned to the shopkeeper, shook his head dismissively and marched towards the door, beckoning for us to follow him. Georgie, not having seen the charade, opened her mouth to object, but, knowing the shopkeeper would not understand, I said, "We apparently have to play the game. I don't think we should show too much interest too soon. Just leave it to Abdul, he knows what he is doing."

We had all just got into the street and were making our way along the street, when the old man ran after us, bag in one hand, holding up one finger of the other. Abdul shook his head vehemently and gave a contemptuous laugh.

"I think he wants one Egyptian pound. That is almost one English pound. That is quite extortionate. Absolutely not!" I shouted the last words and mirrored Abdul's firm shake of the head.

We continued our stroll, although Georgie looked tense and uncertain how she should behave.

"Don't fret, Georgie. I am sure Abdul has the situation under control. Just pretend the bag is the last thing on earth that we want to buy."

Although old, the shopkeeper was very sprightly and overtook us quite easily, held the bag up to me and asked what sounded like "*Nehua semmena.*" I guessed he was asking how much I was willing to pay. I shrugged, shook my head again as if I was not really interested at all and continued walking. He ran around to the front again and held the bag up, showing us how the patches shimmered

182

in the sunlight. I opened my purse and handed a handful of *piastres* over to Abdul. He took five and held them out to the shopkeeper, who looked horrified and it was his turn to shake his head fervently. I could see that Georgie was getting agitated, not yet understanding the art of bartering, and I decided to cut the ritual short. I took another five coins from Abdul's hand, put them into the old man's open palm, retrieved the bag which he had let drop to the floor, and walked briskly away, leaving him standing with his mouth open. Georgie ran after me, giggling like the young girl that she still was, and Abdul nodded his head in approval.

I left the carpet bag on Mary's bed with a little note, saying that it was an early Christmas present. At dinner that evening Georgie made us all laugh recounting our attempts at haggling with the natives. In a lull in the conversation, Sarah asked me when Mary would be returning.

"I don't know, she didn't actually say, did she?"

"It is just that I want to invite some people round for a soiree and I would like Mary to be here. Do you think she will be back in a week's time?"

"Yes, surely she will only be a few days? Her nephew was up to get stores so he would soon need to be back to the camp, wouldn't he?"

We agreed that she should be back within the week and for the next few days Sarah and I spent pleasant hours planning the supper and sending out invitations. Even though I was cross with Mary for leaving so suddenly and not saying when she would return, I ached for her. I missed her smile and somewhat raucous laugh; I missed her slight frown when she was concentrating on finding just the right word; I missed the sound of her distinctive light tread; I missed her smell and the taste of the air that she had recently walked through.

Six days after Mary's departure I was sitting reading during the quiet period after lunch. Sarah was resting in her room, Maurice was at work and Georgie was at school. When I heard a slight commotion at the front door and then the sound of Mary's voice, I resisted the temptation to rush out Georgie-like and hug her tightly. Instead I went calmly into the hall and waited for her to hand-over her small valise to one of the house boys and then to straighten her hair and gather herself.

"You're back then," I pointed out somewhat unnecessarily.

"I'm back. I had a lovely time with him. What have you been doing?" She tentatively opened her arms to me and as soon as we embraced any residual crossness evaporated into the hot, dry air. I gave her a potted history of my week; she told me she and Gus had merely sat in the hotel garden, sipping lemonade and reminiscing.

"I am weary, Hannah. I'll go and rest before dinner, if you don't mind."

I had forgotten the carpet bag and was pleased when she came back down and thanked me for it before retiring. That evening Georgie eagerly told Mary about the supper that her mother was holding the next evening and especially that she was now considered old enough to

184

attend as a junior hostess. Mary smiled gently at Georgie's excitement but I sensed a sadness that she could not quite hide, as did Sarah.

"You must have been sorry to see your nephew go again. Will you be seeing him again before you return to England?"

"Yes, it was hard to say goodbye. I don't know when I will see him again. We couldn't make any plans; it depends on the timetable of the mine and when they next need stores. I hope we can meet again soon." She bit her lip and looked sideways at me. "I was going to discuss this with you later on, but I might as well ask now. I wondered," she hesitated, "well, I wondered, whether it would be possible to stay a bit longer than the two months? I would so like to see him again and the weather is really doing me good, I have hardly coughed at all since I have been here. Would it be alright?" She looked at me then at Sarah then back to me again.

Georgie clapped her hands. "Of course it will be alright, won't it Mama, Miss Russell? You can stay as long as you like, oh, how wonderful it will be!"

Sarah and I laughed at Georgie's enthusiastic invitation but nodded our agreement nonetheless.

I was going to ask if I could join her and her nephew next time they met, but the sight of her unshed tears dried the words in my mouth and instead I suggested that she go to bed.

The next day Mary was still subdued, so I proposed that we go on a trip to see the Sphinx of Giza and the nearby pyramids. Khadir was our guide this day and we rode by open carriage up to the edge of the city, and then mounted sturdy donkeys who ambled their way slowly to the great stone statue that lay half buried in the sand. Khadir spoke no English or French but my copy of Baedeker's explained that the Sphinx had probably been carved out of limestone nearly three thousand years BC. The statue was enormous and I had to crane my head to look at its enigmatic face. We walked all the way round it, admiring its size, its realistic form and its antiquity.

"I wonder how many slaves it took to carve it and how long it took? And who is the face meant to represent? Does Baedeker say?"

"It says the face is probably that of the Pharaoh Khafre and that it is the largest sculpture in the world; I can't even begin to imagine where one would start to create something of this size. It also says that the nose was knocked off by a cannon ball fired by one of Napoleon's troops using it as target practise. It's a shame isn't it? He would otherwise have a very kind expression."

We walked around the recumbent lion one more time, then remounted our donkeys and rode out to the pyramids that incongruously stuck out of the undulating sands. I read out the incredible dimensions to Mary, who looked suitably impressed.

"They were built as tombs for the pharaohs and it took the slaves decades to complete. Instead of a 'thank you' at the end they were buried along with their master so that they could help him in the afterlife - it doesn't say whether they were killed first or just left to die. Either way, how horrible! The biggest pyramid is apparently one of the Seven Wonders of the World and is the biggest man-made edifice anywhere."

I looked at the structure with more respect. We sat on one of the huge stones at the base of the Great Pyramid and, shaded by our parasols, we ate our lunch and drank some iced tea that was now lukewarm. We needed to get back to prepare ourselves for Sarah's little gathering that evening so we made our way back through Cairo. On the way Khadir had to pull the horses up sharply as a young girl darted out of a shop and ran right in front of us, closely followed by a couple of policemen. It was almost farcical the way the girl avoided their attempts at catching her, but in the end she tripped and they managed to grab hold of her. I couldn't see what she had taken, but the shop she had run out of was a bread shop. I felt rather sorry for her, especially when the two policemen dragged her wailing along the street. We watched until they turned the corner and were no longer in sight, but the experience left us both feeling unsettled.

Sarah's soiree was a great success. She had invited all the people who she wanted to thank for helping her during her recent difficulties. Most of them were middle-aged couples from the Embassy, charming enough but dull. There was also Coles Pasha, an Inspector General of Prisons, who sat in between me and Mary. He was a short, rotund, dark skinned man with jet black, shiny hair and a small, square moustache that bobbed up and down when he spoke. He wore a tight-fitting black uniform; his jacket was only just held together by bright, brass buttons, and all evening I expected them to pop off and fly across the table like tiny cannon balls. He wore his bright red fez throughout the meal, its black tassel bouncing up and down in harmony with his moustache.

When I called him Mr Pasha he threw his head back and laughed. "It is a common mistake with visitors from Europe, my dear. Pasha is a title conferred on officials of the higher rank. My given name is Charles Edward Coles. Please just call me Coles Pasha until such a time that you feel comfortable calling me just plain Charles, yes?"

Coles Pasha was a funny and interesting man and he entertained Mary and I throughout the dinner with a humorous prison tale that I suspected accentuated the comic and expunged the tragic. When he had finished, Mary put her hand on his arm to stop him starting another anecdote.

"Hannah and I saw something today that disturbed us. We saw a young girl being dragged away by two policemen just because she had taken a small loaf of bread. She looked half starved. What will happen to her?"

Coles Pasha's mouth turned down and he looked downcast.

"Ah, that is a very common occurrence I am afraid. She will be taken to court and if found guilty, and it sounds as if she was, then she will spend at least a year in a juvenile reformatory. You have these in England, yes?"

We both nodded and Mary explained her own interest. "My mother was, and still is, an ardent campaigner for social reform. She is a prison visitor and is on a committee to improve the conditions of prisons and reformatories. I have accompanied my mother on many occasions to visit juvenile reformatories. I know the children there have broken the law, but their punishment seems so harsh and so out of proportion to the crime. But, I suppose you think that I am just a silly female who is too soft?"

"On the contrary, my dear. The children need to be punished, yes indeed, but I do not agree that they should be shut away from the sunlight, and just left for months on end with nothing done to guide them towards a better life. I hope I am not blowing my own trumpet - that is the English phrase, yes? But I have just had built new reformatories, one for girls and one for boys in Helouan, which is not that far from Cairo. The old ones were terrible places, dark, unsanitary, and they had no workshops or places where the children could run around and fill their lungs with fresh air. My reformatories are altogether better places, yes indeed, and if you are interested I would be most happy to show you around."

I was not interested but Mary obviously was, and she seemed quite intoxicated, despite having partaken of little wine. The two of them spent the rest of the evening head to head, discussing juvenile criminality, whilst I was left to listen to my other neighbour's woeful tales of the incompetence of her Arab staff.

189

The next morning two letters were handed to Mary. One was a thick one which I assumed was from her nephew, as she put it straight into her pocket to read later. I was surprised that he had so much to say having seen her only a few days previously but before I could comment Mary began to read aloud the other letter, which was from Coles Pasha inviting her, and me if I wanted, to join him in an inspection of the girls' reformatory the following day. We duly sent an acceptance and were ready and waiting, as instructed, having had our breakfast. A carriage arrived to take us to the railway station. We were escorted by a young policeman who was the complete opposite to Coles Pasha, being very tall and very thin. His cuffs did not quite cover his wrists, nor his trousers his ankles, but nevertheless he looked very officious and we both followed him meekly as he purchased our train tickets and led us into a first-class carriage. It was a short train journey, just twenty minutes, with the track running parallel with the Nile. As with the journey from Alexandria, we were flanked on one side by luxuriant greenery and on the other by sandy aridness. I found the contrast fascinating and promised myself that I would soon try and capture it. When we arrived in Helouan we had to take another carriage to the girls' reformatory, which was situated on the very edge of the town. We plodded slowly down the wide, tree-lined avenues, past the large, white villas that housed the elite; past hotels; past churches of all denominations and past the sanatoriums, for which Helouan was becoming more and more famous.

We arrived at the perimeter wall, which kept the young offenders in and the shifting sands out. We had to wait quite a few minutes as someone unseen opened the numerous locks and bolts, before the large wooden gates swung open, revealing a single storey building made of large blocks of stone and surrounded on all sides by sand trampled hard by hundreds of feet. Once inside the wall an ancient, hunched Arab laboriously re-locked and re-bolted and then hid the huge bunch of keys back inside the folds of his voluminous robe. We dismounted and the policeman led us into the reformatory and along a long corridor until we reached a door with the word *Directrice* neatly engraved on a wooden plaque. He knocked and opened it when a female voice barked "*Entrez!*"

Inside the office was Coles Pasha, sitting relaxed in a chair on the near side of an oak table that was covered with all the paraphernalia necessary for the administration of a large institution. On the business side sat a middle-aged woman, whom I assumed to be the owner of the bark. She stood as we entered and her hitherto grim features were transformed by a wide smile that created a multitude of laughter lines around her eyes and dimples in her cheeks. Coles Pasha made the introductions.

"Miss Hannah Russell, Miss Mary De Morgan, may I introduce Madame Genevieve Dupont, Directress of this reformatory but whom I am also honoured to call my colleague and friend."

She was dressed in a utilitarian white high-necked blouse and a full black skirt that swished as she walked round the desk, holding out her hand to grasp ours. She greeted us warmly with a slight French accent.

"I am very pleased to meet with you. I am always 'appy to show people around the reformatory. I am very proud of it and what we 'ave achieved; Charles and I 'ave worked very 'ard to make it a success."

We had a cup of tea and some biscuits, served by a young Arab girl dressed in a dark blue tunic. Her black hair was covered by a white, lace mop cap and she curtsied at every opportunity. Madame Dupont smiled encouragingly at her and thanked her when she left.

"That is Aisha. She has served her sentence but is staying on as one of the teachers. She is a good girl and deserves some 'elp in life."

"What did she do to be sent here? She looks so young and innocent."

` "She is sixteen, so not so young. She came from a good, industrious family but both her parents died in an accident when she was thirteen and she, along with her younger siblings, were looked after by relatives who were not quite so respectable or hard-working. Very quickly they had her stealing, something that she was not very good at and she was soon caught. She was sent here for a year and she was a model student."

She smiled as both Mary and I raised our eyebrows at this nomenclature. "I do not call my girls prisoners or inmates. They are all here because life has been cruel to them, not because they are evil and must be punished.

192

Non, they are here so we can teach them the skills to lead a better life. So they learn to read and write, in French, *naturellement*, they learn to cook and sew, they learn to be, 'ow you say, an upright citizen."

Coles Pasha nodded in agreement, his moustache and tassel bouncing up and down in concord. Madame Dupont continued "So, when she asked if she could stay here rather than go back I gladly agreed. I know she sends money to the family for her brothers' and sisters' upkeep - I doubt they see any of it. *Bon*, if you are ready, I will show you around."

As we walked down the corridor she explained that the reformatory was built in the shape of a cross. The arm of the cross that we were currently in was the administration block. Here were the offices, a communal lounge for the staff and their bedrooms. At the end of the corridor was a door that opened onto an open courtyard that was in fact the centre of the cross, off which the other arms radiated. It was a pleasant area with palm trees and trellises covered with bougainvillea providing shade. There were some forty girls lined up in one such area touching their toes and reaching for the sky as they went through a routine prompted by an instructress who shouted out the commands like a sergeant major at a military parade.

"As you see, this is where the girls take their exercise each day and they are allowed to sit here in the evening for an hour before they go to bed. We will go to the dormitories *maintenant*."

This corridor was empty now, of course. There were ten dormitories in total with twenty girls in each. Each girl had just a metal framed bed and a small locker to call her own. The bedding was folded neatly at the bottom of each mattress. The walls were plain white but I was intrigued to see that many beds had paintings pinned above them. I went over to look at one, which was of a childish representation of a camel. Madame Dupont saw my interest.

"Ah, Madamoiselle Russell, you like our art? The girls 'ave painting lessons once a week. It does them good, I believe, to let them be creative, you agree?"

"Oh, absolutely. I myself am a painter. It is a wonderful form of stimulation and inspiration, and often an emotional release. I think it is marvellous that you give them the opportunity."

The dormitories were all the same, of course, apart from the children's works of art. The next arm we walked down contained the kitchens, bathrooms, more store rooms and a small sick room.

"Unfortunately we do not have a full-time matron yet but Mrs Elliott and I do the best we can and so far there has been nothing we could not 'andle."

The final arm contained the classrooms. Here we walked past rooms where girls sat in a circle on the floor chanting out from their reading books; where girls had their heads down as they embroidered kerchiefs or darned stockings; where girls sat, many with tips of their tongues stuck out, as they concentrated on forming their letters with chalk and slate.

194

Madame Dupont led us into the final room where a small group of children were sitting on the floor in a semi-circle around the teacher, who I recognised as being Aisha. We stood quietly in the corner so as not to disturb them, listening as she read one of Madame D'Aulnoy's fairy tales. The children, none of whom could have been more than ten years old, were engrossed and it was strange to think that they were all considered by the courts to be criminals.

As we walked back I congratulated Madame Dupont on the reformatory but Mary was silent and it was only when we were again seated in the office that she spoke.

"Madame Dupont, I am truly impressed with what you are doing here. I ..." She looked at me, chewing her lip as she was wont to do when she was nervous. "I would very much like to help."

I was surprised, as seemed Madame Dupont.

"Help, Miss De Morgan? In what way?"

"Well, I am sure I can help with the nursing of any sick child and I can certainly help teach reading and writing. My French is very good."

This was not something I was aware of.

"Aisha's story and the girl we saw the other day being dragged away by the police because she stole some bread, probably because she was starving ... " Her eyes were brimming with tears. She looked beseechingly at me and before I knew it I heard myself saying,

"And I could teach them painting. My French is not very good, but you don't need words to teach art."

195

Madame Dupont and Coles Porter shared a quick glance; both had a knowing smile and I suspected that our volunteering to help was not totally unexpected. Madame Dupont turned to us with her wide, open smile.

"Well, that is *magnifique*, I know that you are only here for a few months but we are always very grateful for any help we can get." She gave a little frown and a Gallic shrug. "We cannot pay you, I am afraid. Your *rémunération* will have to wait until you are in 'eaven."

We agreed to come every Wednesday in the first instance, starting a week from that day. We all shook hands and then the young policeman escorted us to the carriage. I felt elated and excited.

"My goodness, Mary. What have we let ourselves in for?"

Chapter 9 - Dumb Othmar

1889 - 1892

"Othmar," she said, "I have thought and thought, and I know that the little man with the fiddles was a wicked fairy." Othmar nodded. "So I am going into the big world to find him, for if he has done this ill he will know how to cure you, and I have saved all my money for a year."

Then Othmar took her hand, and kissed it, but still wept, as he shook his head and made signs to her that she must not go, as it would be all in vain. But Hulda did not heed him,

"And now," she said, "I am going, Othmar, and it may be long years before I return, so you must do three things. First, you must give me a long curl of your brown hair, that I may lay it next my heart and wear it day and night, not to forget you. Then you must kiss me on my lips to say goodbye; and then you must promise that my name shall be the first words your lips say when they again can speak." Then Othmar took his knife and cut from his head the longest, brightest curl of his hair, and drew her to him and kissed her thrice upon the lips. And then took her hand and with wrote upon his lips her name, "Hulda," as a promise that her name should be the first thing they said.

"Goodbye, Othmar," she said; "you will wait for me." Then she turned away and started alone to go down the mountain-side, and she looked back as she went and called back, "Goodbye, Othmar," as long as he could see or hear her.

("Dumb Othmar," in *The Windfairies* by Mary De Morgan)

It quickly became very clear that what we had let ourselves in for was a commitment that we both took very seriously but also enjoyed immensely, such that it soon almost became our *raison d'être*. The one day a week very quickly became two and then three, and just four weeks after agreeing to help at the reformatory we were going every Tuesday, Wednesday and Thursday. We made the same journey as our original one and arrived in time for breakfast. The girls had all been up since six o'clock and had already had an exercise session and done their laundry and cleaning duties. At nine they had a light meal, which we shared with them. We asked if we could sit with the girls but Madame Dupont was adamant that we sit with the other staff at a separate table in order to maintain our distance and emphasise our authority.

"We are 'ere to guide them to a better life and *certainement*, we are not their *ennemis, qu'est-ce que c'est en anglais?*"

"It's the same, it's enemy."

"*D'accord*, we are not their enemy, *non*, but we are not their *amis*. Do not forget, *mademoiselles*, we are not their *amis*."

After the meal Mary and I separated to give our different lessons; Mary tended towards the more academic and I the creative. As well as painting and sketching, I taught cookery and sewing, both of which I had just sufficient skill to pass onto girls who had none.

Everyone had to speak French at all times, although I know the girls reverted to their native tongue if no adult was within hearing distance. I had had a French tutor at Russell Hall but had forgotten much that he had tried so valiantly to teach me. Madame Dupont allowed me to sit in on lessons and I managed to purchase an English to French dictionary, so I was soon able to hold a simple conversation.

The last lesson on the days when we were there was story-time, which very soon became Mary's domain. Aisha was happy to hand over the role of story-teller to Mary and she would sit, along with the other girls, and listen with great pleasure as Mary read from Perrault and Madame D'Aulnoy, or gave her translation of the Grimm Brothers, Hans Christian Andersen and her own wonderful tales. Story-time was meant to be just for the youngsters but prompted, I suspect by Aisha, the group soon grew as the older girls joined in, still themselves just children after all. I too always sat in. I loved to see Mary's bright eyes and flushed cheeks as she invited the youngsters into her world of the fey and magical. I loved to hear her voice as she took on the persona of each character, from ancient wicked crone to beautiful young princess. More than anything I loved to see the girls, wide-eyed in wonder, as they heard tales of underdogs who were cast off by society and considered unworthy, but finally winning through and marrying into royalty or becoming rich beyond their wildest imagination. I did wonder whether we were offering the girls false hope as it was unlikely that there would a "happy ever after" for them, but I was not going to be the one to crush their dreams.

I only saw Aisha at story-time; at all other times she was Mary's *petite aide*. Mary said she was like a little puppy, following her everywhere, fetching and carrying, waiting for a pat on the head and a tickle under the chin. But Mary spoke fondly of her and I reminded her of what Madame Dupont had said. "Never forget, Mees De Morgan, we are not their *amis*."

We helped at the reformatory with Sarah's blessing. It had become clear very early on that we could do little to help her as she coped with her grief and learned to adjust to a new way of life. We had never known Mr Russell and so we could not share reminiscences; instead she frequently visited her many friends in Cairo who had known them both and who offered her the support she needed. Sarah was, however, happy that we were there and living with her and the children. She said she enjoyed our company, as did Maurice and Georgie.

One of the things I liked to do, in the fond hope that I was being of some use to Sarah, was to accompany Abdul when he went shopping at the *souk*. I was doubtless more of a hindrance than a help to him but I enjoyed the outing and I took the opportunity to learn more Arabic phrases. The stall-holders soon became used to me and we would exchange simple greetings; they gave toothless grins and clapped when I hailed them with a new phrase. With Abdul's help I was soon able to comment on the fact that it was another lovely day: "*akhar yawm jami*" or to their query as to whether I was well, "*Marhaban! Kaifa haloki*," to thank them for their concern and say that I was indeed well, "*Ana bekhair, shokran*."

Mary spent much of her time in her bedroom writing; she was still working on her new collection of fairy tales. I enjoyed nothing more than when she sat in the evening and read her work out to me, or asked for my opinion. I reminded her that she had once said she would base one of the characters on me.

"It is very odd that you should say that, Hannah, for I want to read you that very fairy tale. Perhaps it is you who is the seer, rather than me? I am going to call it 'Dumb Othmar.'"

"That is a strange name for a girl."

"No, it is the boy's name. He has his voice stolen by a wicked gnome, which is why he is dumb. It is the girl who is the hero and goes on adventures to recover his voice. Her name is Hulda, that is you."

"Well, that is a strange name too. Where on earth do you get them from?"

Mary tapped her head with her pencil.

"They are all in there, in my imagination. Do you want me to read you this story or not?"

It was a wonderful, magical tale that I enjoyed all the better knowing that she had based the feisty, brave hero on me. As she had promised she would, Mary described Hulda as being a normal girl who was not frightfully clever or terribly beautiful, but she was caring and always helped others when she could. She loved Othmar, needless to say, and when she found that his beautiful voice had been stolen she decided to go out into the big world to search for it. So instead of the girl waiting patiently to be saved by the boy, as in most fairy tales, in Mary's it was the boy who had to wait patiently for the girl to come back with the prize - his voice. I listened spellbound from start to finish.

"And Othmar married Hulda, and his voice never left him again; but when long years after folk would tell him his voice was sweet and far more beautiful than the birds, he would say, 'But it is not really my voice, it is my wife's, Hulda's, for I should have been dumb for ever if she had not sought it and brought it back to me.'"

Georgie had come into the sitting room without either of us noticing her, but before I could say how good it was Georgie took the words out of my mouth.

"Oh! Miss De Morgan, that is truly, truly, wonderful! How good it is to hear a story where it is the girl that has all the adventures. It made it far more exciting for me to imagine myself doing all those daring deeds, rather than sleeping for one hundred years, or waiting at the top of a tower as we girls usually have to do!"

"Thank you kindly, Georgie. I am very pleased that you like it. I wrote it with Hannah in mind, but really it is for all girls everywhere who would rather be vigorous and active than submissive and meek."

"I'm glad they married at the end. After all the trouble she went through it would have been a shame if he had just said "thank you very much" and then married the local farmer's daughter!" Then Georgie asked something she had obviously wanted to ask for a while. "Why have you two never married? I know you are both rather old now, but you were young once and must have been quite pretty then? Perhaps I should make it my aim in life to get you both married to some rich Englishman, would you like that?"

Mary and I were quite used to Georgie's abruptness but even so we both howled with laughter at her candidness. I was the first who was able to speak. "Well, thank you for saying we must have been *quite* pretty once! And it is a very kind offer, but no thanks you, we do not need you to be a match-maker. It may surprise you to know, Georgie, that many women are quite content to remain unmarried. We don't all need a man to make our lives meaningful. Do we, Mary?"

Mary hesitated for longer than I liked, and then grinned at the expression on my face. "Of course we don't, Hannah. Men are bores. And anyway, who would marry us now that we are *rather* old? I'm going to write some letters now, so I'll say 'goodnight' to you both."

The sending and receiving of letters was an important part of our daily lives. I kept in touch with my estate manager, Mr Black, and my solicitor, Mr Wilkes. Mary, of course, wrote to her mother and brother and we all waited eagerly for their responses, which she shared with us all. Mrs De Morgan wrote of the campaigns and committees she was still heavily involved in, despite her advancing years, and William wrote wonderfully humorous letters of his life as a potter and of married life with his new wife Evelyn, who was an accomplished painter - a better one than I ever would be. Mary also received a constant flow of letters from her nephew, Gus, which she never read to us, but secreted in her pocket and read in the privacy of her room. I was intrigued as to what he had to say.

"I hope Gus is well, Mary?"

"Yes, very, thank you for asking."

"He always writes lovely long letters. You are very lucky to have such a thoughtful nephew; most would find it a burden to have to write to an aunt on a regular basis."

"He doesn't *have* to write to me, Hannah, he does so because he wants to. We are very close and we share family matters that only mean something to the two of us. They are of no interest to anyone else, I assure you."

"Of course, Mary, I am not prying, really."

About six weeks after her first meeting with her nephew, Mary told us during dinner that she would be going again the following week and would stay for five days.

"Five days, Mary? That is a long time. I would so like to meet him; there is no reason why I shouldn't join you, even if it is just for one day? I would be quite happy to spend the rest of the time exploring Alexandria if you two want to be alone."

Mary was silent for quite a while.

"Hannah, I know you would like to meet him, and of course you are very welcome, but I really think it would be too bad of us if we were both absent from the reformatory at the same time. Aisha can take over my lessons but she will need your help, you see that don't you? We don't spend *all* the time together; he has things to do in Alexandria so I just see him when he has some spare time. I will try and get Gus to come here one time, I really will; he is very keen to meet all of you - it is just not that easy to arrange. Are you happy with that?"

I had to agree and when I thought about it more rationally later that night, I did see that it would be very inconvenient for Madame Dupont if we were both away all week. So I good-naturedly kissed her good bye the evening before she left the following day, coped quite well with Aisha at the reformatory in her absence, and then welcomed her back with open arms.

She returned looking both exhilarated by her visit, but also exhausted, despite the fact that she assured me all they had done was sit and talk, or stroll leisurely around the parks of Alexandria. She was quite down afterwards, but she didn't succumb to one of her black moods as I feared and she soon reverted to her normal demeanour.

Our lives fell into a predictable pattern: Mary and I teaching at the reformatory each week, me assisting Abdul on his shopping excursions; all the female members of the household visiting and receiving visitors; Mary and I, often accompanied by Georgie, exploring Cairo and its environs; Maurice advancing at the Embassy and getting a well-deserved promotion; Mary disappearing to Alexandria every six weeks or so. She asked Gus if he could come to Cairo one time, but apparently his business was in Alexandria and he could not make the time for a trip to visit some friends of his aunt.

Before we knew it Georgie was seventeen and only went to the school to teach, no longer to be a pupil; Christmas came and went and it was 1890. Mary was forty that year and I was thirty. Mary and I no longer discussed going back to England. We were both content together in Egypt and Mary's health was so much better than it had been in England that it no longer occurred to me to even suggest going home - this was now our home. I paid a good rent to Sarah so that we would not be a financial burden on her and all in all I felt life was good.

Another year passed and Georgie transformed from a gangly, ungainly child into a tall, elegant woman, after reluctantly attending deportment and etiquette classes. Maurice was obviously destined to be "someone important at the Embassy," like his father, but he nonetheless had time to get engaged to a girl called Antonia. They had known each other since they had both been children in Australia and their close friendship had turned slowly into love.

The adults merely aged another year, and then another.

We celebrated the start of 1892 and then Mary went on her regular visit to Alexandria to spend some time with her nephew. It was Friday morning, so I was breakfasting at home. Abdul came in carrying an envelope on a silver platter. He handed it to Sarah who groaned when she read it.

"Oh dear, it is a telegram for Mary. It is from her brother. Here, Hannah, you read it."

London, England
6th January '92
Mary De Morgan

Regret to say Mama passed peacefully to her spirit world 5th Jan. No point in coming back. Will write soon. Chin up. Your brother, William

"Oh dear. She was a lovely, lovely woman. I got to know her quite well. Mary will be devastated. She needs to know. Should I go to Alexandria and find her?"

"No, Hannah. There is nothing that Mary can do now. Let her enjoy her time with the living. She will be home on Sunday. The news will keep until then."

I always looked forwards to Mary coming back but this time I almost dreaded it. How was I going to tell her that her mother was dead? How would she take it? Would it cause her to go into a decline?

I need not have worried. It was Sunday and I was in the garden with Georgie picking some flowers when Mary and Sarah came out to join us. I could see that Sarah had told her the news for Mary's cheeks were wet with tears and she was biting her bottom lip as if to stop herself from wailing. I hugged her gently and whispered how sorry I was into her ear. I felt her body shudder as she began to sob and I tightened my arms around her, letting her grief dampen my blouse. I was almost glad her mother had died as it meant I could hold Mary in my arms.

Eventually she stopped crying, wiped her eyes, blew her nose and straightened her shoulders.

"Well, Mama truly believed in the spirit world so I hope she is right and she is now with Papa, Alice, George, Edward and Chrissie." She sighed. "It is William who will miss her the most; they were very close. When he writes next I expect he will tell me about the funeral. A lot of people will have attended; she was a very well-respected lady. She wanted so much to make things better for people who couldn't help themselves. She took life very seriously but she had a good heart, yes, a good heart."

This thought brought on another paroxysm of weeping; it was the last time she ever spoke of her mother.

Our routine remained the same throughout the spring and summer. I was contented and I believe Mary was too.

One Saturday in September we were sitting in the garden. Even if I had not known by the date that Mary was due to go to Alexandria in a few days, I would have known from the excitement that she failed to completely suppress. I was idly flipping through the *Egyptian Gazette*. It is indeed strange how a familiar name leaps out unbidden from a list of names on a printed page: G. Eustace, W. R. Owen, A. De Morgan, E. G. Grenville, N. M Whyte.

"A. De Morgan, that's your nephew's name isn't it?"

Mary was darning a stocking that was in truth beyond repair, and she seemed glad to pause for a little conversation. "Yes. Why, is there an article about him? He is a doctor, has he discovered something to save mankind from itself? Or perhaps a cure for the De Morgan curse, now that would be something marvellous indeed!"

I wished I had not spoken so casually and I could find no words to soften the blow, so I merely handed the newspaper to her, pointing out the black-bordered article in which her nephew's name was listed as being one of five who had recently died of fever at Um Garaiart, a gold mine about one hundred miles from Assouan in the south of the country. The colour drained from her face and I saw the paper shake in her palsied hands. It was, however, quite a number of seconds later that she cried out loud and threw the paper from her, as if by doing so she could undo the deed. She began to wail and rock backwards and forwards on her seat, backwards and forwards, backwards and forwards, her keening like a sharp needle being thrust into my ear drums. "Mary, it is too awful, I know, but please do not take on so."

I was aware that my words were meaningless, so I went over to her, put my arms around her body and once again held her tightly to comfort her at the death of another of her family. She eventually stopped rocking, her wails turning into sobs. I murmured softly to her, in the hope that she would find succour in the tone, if not the words. "There, there. He is too young to be taken but it is all over for him now. He is not in pain and there will be no more suffering for him." I remembered Mary's words at hearing of her mother's death. "He will be with Edward, his dear father, and his grandparents, your own mother and father."

Mary slowly raised her head and looked at me with eyes already red-rimmed and streaming with tears. "This is not how it should have been." Her voice was low and strained, as if the very effort of speech was too great for her. "Oh, this is not how it should have been."

I continued to hold her, stroking her hair and repeating "there, there" until I felt the tenseness ebb away and she relaxed into my arms, lamenting as if it had been her own child, not that of her brother, who had died in so untimely a manner.

It was a terrible time. Mary would not, could not, settle and for the next few days she paced up and down her bedroom, muttering to herself, wringing her hands, pulling at her hair, ignoring her bed and the plates of food left for her. Neither of us went to the reformatory; instead I sat with her for an hour or so each day, but it was as if I were not there, and after a while I left her, distraught myself at the sight of such grief and my inability to soften it in any way. On the third day she came down at about midday looking gaunt, her hair and clothes in total disarray. Her face was as white as parchment, the only colour her too bright cheeks and her too bright eyes. Without any preamble she blurted out, "I must go to Um Garaiart. I must go there to see him. I must. I must."

And with that, she crumpled to the floor in a dead faint.

Chapter 10 - The Story of the Opal

1892

But when the Moon rose, after the Sun had set, the clouds cleared away, and the air was again full of tiny silver ladders, down which the Moonbeams came, but the Nightingale looked in vain for his own particular Moonbeam. He knew she could not shine on him again, therefore he mourned, and sang a sorrowful song. Then he flew down to the Stone, and sang a song at the mouth of the hole, but there came no answer. So he looked down the hole, into the Stone, but there was no trace of the Sunbeam or the Moonbeam - only one shining spot of light, where they had rested. Then the Nightingale knew that they had faded away and died. ... But through the Stone wherein the beams had sheltered, shot up bright beautiful rays of light, silver and gold. They coloured it all over with every colour of the rainbow, and when the Sun or Moon warmed it with their light it became quite brilliant. So that the Stone, from being the ugliest thing in the whole forest, became the most beautiful.

Men found it and called it the Opal.

("The Story of the Opal," in *On a Pincushion*, by Mary De Morgan)

It took another three days for Mary to recover; three days of mopping her fevered brow, of feeding her sips of cooling water and reviving broth, of whispering soothing words into her ear and stroking her face and hands so that her nightmares might become more pleasant dreams. On the third morning, when I had taken heed of Sarah's advice and was sleeping in my own bed rather than in the chair in Mary's room, Sarah came into my bedroom, shook me gently by the shoulder and told me that Mary was awake and was asking for me.

She was still pale but she looked rested and her hair had been brushed, so that she no longer looked like an inmate of Bedlam. She smiled at me and my heart almost broke. "I am so sorry to have been such a trouble. It was, it was just..." She closed her eyes and pursed her lips before forcing herself to continue. "It was just one death too many."

Tears followed a familiar track down her cheeks and she clenched her fists tight in an attempt to stop herself sobbing. She took some deep breaths and wiped her eyes with an ineffectual, sodden kerchief. "I need to go to see him. Will you help me?"

I had discussed this with Sarah and Maurice. There was a sleeper train from Cairo to Assouan and then it would take two days, or nights rather, in a horse-drawn carriage to reach the gold mine at Um Garaiart, and then back again, of course. We had all agreed that we could see no point in making the trip, which I tried to explain to Mary.

"It would be a very tiring journey and you are still weak. Why do you want to go? There will be nothing to see, probably at most just a wooden cross in the sand. You can go to church and pray for him, you surely do not need to go all that way."

212

"You don't understand, Hannah. I have to go there, I just have to."

She started to get out of bed, as if she meant to start the journey there and then. I held her down quite easily, so weak was she still, and I told her that she must first get strong and we would discuss it again.

When I told Maurice later that day that Mary was still adamant that she wanted to go, he said that he would go and speak with her immediately and convince her of the folly of making such a journey.

When Maurice came back down some thirty minutes later he looked uncharacteristically flustered and sheepish at the same time. "I could not persuade her, Hannah, she started to cry. No, it was worse than that, she was making this awful wailing sound and her whole body was shuddering. I couldn't stop her; she just got worse and worse until I said I would arrange for her to go. Then she calmed down. I'm sorry."

He looked at me, his face flushed from embarrassment. I knew that Mary was stubborn and had a bit of a temper sometimes, but I had never known her act in such a manipulative manner to get her own way. I was rather cross and went up to her room to have it out with her, but when I saw her curled up and sleeping more peacefully than she had done in a long while, I did not want to disturb her so withdrew quietly.

By the next morning my anger had dissipated into the hot, dry air and when I sat with Mary we talked as if it was all arranged and that it was a foregone conclusion that I would go with her. Now that the decision had been made

I was quite excited about the trip and more than pleased that I would be of use to her in her hour of need.

Maurice was wonderful and made all the arrangements for us, so that all we had to do was to wait the two long days before we could start our journey. Mary, usually more than capable, had lost the inclination to do anything but sit and stare out of the window, so I took it upon myself to pack her case. When I told Mary what I had packed she showed not one iota of interest. I think she would have gone in her nightgown if I had suggested it, or even naked, so preoccupied was she with her own painful thoughts.

I was extremely relieved that Maurice, with Sarah's and Antonia's blessing, said he would accompany us. We were to travel on the over-night sleeper from Cairo to Assouan and Maurice had received a telegram from the mine manager confirming that there would be a horse-drawn carriage waiting for us at Assouan. The train did not leave until six in the evening, so I had the whole day to feel at first excited, then impatient, then bored, whilst Mary sat in a chair looking out of the window, the whiteness of her knuckles the only indication of her state of mind.

When the time came to leave I took her elbow gently and steered her towards the waiting carriage. She walked as if in a trance and gave no response to any questions; it was as if only her physical body was there and her spirit had gone to a totally different place. The journey to the railway station was short and Maurice chatted away to me, politely ignoring Mary's vacuous air.

When we arrived at the station it was teeming with people, both Arabs and Europeans, and the noise of their chattering voices, the blowing of guards' whistles, the trundling of trolley wheels, the cries of the vendors and the disgorgement of steam echoed around the cavernous building and I imagined that this was what Pandemonium must have been like. The sounds seemed to arouse Mary, however, and for the first time in days she became aware of her surroundings and of the presence of Maurice and of myself. Although she must have been used to it, having gone by train to Alexandria every six weeks for the last two years or so, she seemed overwhelmed by the mass of humanity that swarmed around us and so I took her hand in mine and we threaded our way down the hall to our platform, where our train stood waiting for us like a dozing dragon breathing out its billows of smoke and steam.

The railway carriages were brilliant white and they gleamed in the sunlight, some still with the water that they had just been cleaned with trickling down the windows and glittering like strings of diamonds. Maurice led the way to our carriage and then one of the attendants led us down the corridor to our compartments. Mary and I were to share and Maurice was next to us. The compartment was already transformed into its night-time guise, with the seats magically converted into two beds, one on top of the other, and a tiny white ceramic sink with gleaming silvery taps released from its hiding place behind the wooden panel. Our cases were opened on the rack, our night

215

gowns placed on the beds, and our washing paraphernalia lain out neatly on the shelf above the sink. We had a quick wash and tidy up and were ready when Maurice knocked on our door.

The dining car was nothing if not luxurious, even a little ostentatious. The button-back seats were of a deep red plush velvet, each table was covered with a starched white tablecloth and decked with an array of cut glass and silver cutlery, which reflected the ornate gas lights hanging from the ceiling so that it seemed as if we were entering a crystal cave. The walls of the carriage were of dark wood panelling and the large windows were topped with ruched silken blinds, not yet pulled. The sound of our steps was muted by a deep-piled carpet, its colours not only harmonizing with the rest of the decor but also camouflaging any morsels of food that might be dropped by careless diners. A waiter with a brilliant white apron and bright red fez led us to our table and seemingly out of the air plucked a basket of bread rolls for us to nibble as we read through the many-paged menu, which any top-class London restaurant would have been proud to proffer.

The air was uncomfortably warm and Mary and I ordered a glass of ice-cold water as an aperitif, whilst Maurice chose a beer. As we pondered on whether our appetites could do justice to the chef's culinary offerings, the train pulled slowly away from the station, its departure accompanied by a long, mournful whistle and a loud, satisfying belch. The tableware clattered at the sudden movement and we all involuntarily held onto our glasses, but there were no spillages of course, the waiters knew full well how much liquid to safely pour.

As I dithered over the choices I was surprised to feel a sudden waft of cool air ostensibly coming from the roof. I saw other people lift their heads from the menus and look around in equal puzzlement. I noticed the head waiter standing at the end of the dining car, nodding and smiling at our bemusement, and after a few minutes he clapped his hands officiously to get our attention and then proceeded to explain the phenomenon by imparting a short lecture - his English vocabulary very much of his own making. "I am so very happy that you have all noticed our wonderful air-cooling that we have made for your pleasitude and comfortitude. Above you is not one, oh no, not one but two roofs therewith and henceforth, and inside we have hidden, oh yes indeed, hidden for your blessitude great blocks of very nice ice. As we move at this very great speed the air moves over the ice, gets itself very, very cool, yes indeed, and herewith and thenceforth it blows through these tiny holes in the ceiling, see, here and here and there and there, and violà, you, the lovely peoples in this carriage, are no longer hot and unhappy. We indeed are ourselves very happy that you can now eat in very great comfortitude and we very much hope that you are full of praise and are pleased to tell your family and friends of this wonderful invention, thank you very much, yes indeed."

He gave a bow and waited expectantly. One by one we all clapped politely and smiled and nodded in agreement that, yes indeed, this was a truly wonderful feat of modern engineering.

The cool air had heightened my appetite and I ordered pâté and Melba toast, followed by a lemon sorbet to cleanse the palate, then for the main course roast quail, potatoes and a mixture of vegetables. I ate my roll to keep at bay the hunger that had suddenly made itself felt, and then another, which magically appeared as soon as I had eaten the last crumb on my plate. Mary seemed to be reading the menu but when the waiter asked her what she wanted she just asked for the same as I was having, without at that point even knowing what I was going to order. Maurice and I kept up a desultory conversation that ceased when the first course arrived.

I have always enjoyed my food, I am lucky in that whatever I eat my frame remains slim, if not thin, and I ate my pâté with relish. My appetite, however, was soon ruined by Mary's total lack of it. She broke the toast into tiny pieces and piled them into a small pyramid, she squashed the pâte into such a thin layer that it almost covered the plate, and then she arranged the bits of salad around the edge, but not one piece did she actually put into her mouth.

"Mary, are you not going to eat that?"

She was startled by my voice and looked around her as if she did not know where she was. She saw what she had done to her food and was suitably embarrassed. She undid her work and mixed it all together but still did not eat anything.

"I am sorry, I am not really all that hungry."

She also apologised to the waiter when he took her plate, which now looked like something farmers gave to their pigs. Mary managed to eat a few spoonfuls of the sorbet, but when the main course was placed in front of her, she let out a sob and stood up suddenly.

"I am sorry but I cannot eat this. I need to go to my room."

With that she hurried out of the dining car, excusing herself as she bumped into concerned waiters and unwary passengers alike. I made to go after her, but Maurice put his hand on my arm. "Sit down, Hannah, let her be. She is better left alone for now. Eat and enjoy your meal."

But I could not enjoy my meal, and although I ate some of it I too pushed my food from one side of the plate to another, waiting for Maurice to finish before putting my knife and fork down. Maurice looked at me crossly.

"There is no point in you not eating either, that will not help anyone, least of all Mary. She needs to pull herself together and you need to help her do it, for which you will need strength and fortitude, not a rumbling stomach!"

How I loved Maurice, he was so honest and down-to-earth. "I know, but her misery just appals me. I can't even imagine what she is going through."

"All of us have lost someone close, but we get over it. Georgie lost her father at a young age, as you did. Neither of you went into a decline."

"Mary has lost so many of her family. She told me that her nephew's was just one too many. She was very fond of him. I imagine they got very close over the last few years; they must have done, they saw so much of each other. But she does seem to be taking it harder than one would expect, and she is not getting any better."

I did not want any dessert, so I left Maurice to his port and made my way to our compartment. Seeing that Mary was asleep, or pretending to be, I undressed and got ready for bed as quietly as I could. Mary had chosen the top bed, so I got into the bottom one, whispered a "good night" just in case she was awake, dampened the light and settled down to a sleep that refused to come. I lay on my back, then on one side, then on the other, and rather than the gentle rocking and the sound of the wheels over the rails lulling me to sleep, I found myself counting the seconds between each clickety-clack, the modern-day equivalent, I suppose, of counting sheep. I lay on my back again and let out a sigh.

The wonderful air-cooling did not extend to the sleeping compartments, and although I had kicked off the top sheet I was still hot, and my restlessness was making me even hotter. I desperately wanted a drink of water but I was loath to get up in case Mary was asleep and I disturbed her. And I was hungry. The longer I lay there, the hungrier I felt. I had noticed some biscuits that had been left for our refreshment and my mouth watered as I imagined myself eating them.

"Are you awake, Hannah?"

"Yes. Can't you sleep either?"

Her voice was thick with suppressed emotion. "I try and think of happier times, but they are always ruined by images of death and corruption. I am so tired, but I am afraid to sleep, I am afraid to dream."

I put on the light, put some water in two glasses, gathered the biscuits, climbed the wooden steps to her bed and sat on the side with my legs dangling over the edge. She sat up and as we shared the feast I reminded her of some of our times in the East End of London, exaggerating the funny little scenes we had witnessed, turning the dirty, slovenly women we had tried to help into comics and philosophers. I spoke quietly and in a purposefully monotonous tone, trying to lull her into sleep.

Mary didn't respond; she was looking into the distance, tears streaming down her cheeks. I took her in my arms and held her, all the while stroking her hair and rocking her gently. After just a few minutes her weeping subsided then ceased, and I felt her body become heavy in my arms as she fell asleep. I lay her down carefully on her side then, with my arms still around her, I lay behind her, our two bodies fitting like pieces of a jigsaw. Despite Mary's deep unhappiness, this was perhaps one of the most contented moments in my life, being wrapped around the woman I loved. I listened to her steady breathing and the next thing I knew Maurice was knocking on the door asking if we were ready to go into breakfast.

Mary managed a few slices of toast and conserve, and I broke my fast with scrambled eggs, bacon and

221

mushrooms. The scenery that we were travelling through was rougher than I had seen before, and the banks of the Nile nurtured groves of palms, mimosas and the strange castor-oil shrubs rather than the fields of maize and wheat that grew further north. The terrain was rocky, and we passed a number of ruins standing on the tops of precipices that bordered the river.

Maurice talked all through breakfast, saying that the previous evening he had got talking to some men who were returning to the mine at Um Garaiart, having been on a week's leave. One of the men had explained that the mine workers were taken back and forth by a number of horse-drawn carriages, and it would be in one of these that we would travel. This form of conveyance was now possible due to a road that had been laid between Um Garaiart and Assouan, in order to transport the gold and the men, meaning that the journey was easier, more comfortable and quicker than the four-day camel ride that had hitherto been the only means of transport.

We arrived at the modern town of Assouan late morning and Maurice had had the forethought to book us into a hotel for the afternoon so that we were able to freshen up and rest before we gathered in the market square at dusk, along with the returning miners. I counted six carriages, each pulled by two horses, and each large enough to carry six men. There was some bantering amongst the men, all of whom were European, about who should travel with whom, but they soon formed themselves into small groups and went and occupied a carriage. One man came over to us and introduced himself.

"Good evening, ladies, sir. I am Alistair McGregor, the site manager at Um Garaiart. Do you mind if I join you?"

We told him our names and were pleased to have someone else in our party, if only to have some different conversation. The carriages were no more than rough wooden boxes topped with a metal frame, over which was fixed a tarpaulin. Inside there were crudely cushioned seats and little else for comfort; they were made for working men, not for the ease of ladies. Our luggage was placed under our feet and within a short time we set off, our carriage sandwiched in the middle of the convoy. Maurice had warned us that we would be travelling during the night so that we avoided the heat of the sun and I had made sure that both Mary and I were prepared with warmer tops for the cold night air.

Nothing, however, had prepared us for the discomfort of the journey. The road was very rough and the carriage seemed to bounce over every stone that had blown off the desert; I was grateful that we could hold tightly to the leather hoops that hung from the frame that lay like a metal skeleton over the top of the cart. We travelled in this manner for mile after mile, the road meandering around the dunes. It got dark very suddenly and we could see nothing but each other and the soft glow of the gas lamps that hung from each carriage. We all managed to doze despite the bumping and bouncing and it was only when we stopped that I became fully awake. The sun was just rising and the air had not yet become over-heated, and I saw that we had reached our first shelter, a small settlement which boasted of a few rough buildings for the use of travellers. There were no oases in this region and so a large portion of the floor of each carriage was occupied by a large vat of water, along with a box containing cans of meat, vegetables and fruit, as well as biscuits and bottles of beer, hopefully sufficient for our needs until we arrived at the mine.

The Arab drivers doubled as cooks, and they were soon preparing a feast for us, which I found I enjoyed tremendously, seated on some large stones and balancing the plate on my lap, just like the miners did. The men did not really include us women in their conversations, but neither did they ignore us; they acknowledged our presence by keeping their language relatively oath-free, by passing to us a bottle of water with which we were allowed to refill our metal mugs and by averting their eyes when one of us had to walk away with a little spade that Mr McGregor had had to explain the use of, in a typically direct Highland manner. Mary listened to their conversations intently, as if trying to find out as much as possible about their lives at the mine, maybe she found that it passed the time. As the sun rose higher in the sky I understood why the shelter had been built here, for it lay in a deep shadow cast by an overhang of stone. It was by no means cool, but we would not burn and the drivers cum cooks brought us mugs of water every now and then, with which to moisten our dried lips and quench our thirst.

Some of the men played cards, others slept and some poked about in the sand to see if they could find any ancient relics, in which pursuit Maurice joined in. Mary and I sat on cushions on the floor of a small building, our backs against the surprisingly cool stone wall. I had brought some books with us but neither of us had the energy to concentrate so I tried to converse with Mary.

"I know there is a very sad reason for this journey, but it is quite an adventure, isn't it? Not many English women have made such a journey."

Mary merely shrugged.

"I am interested in seeing how a gold mine works - I cannot begin to imagine how one goes about finding it and then getting it out of the rock."

Mary gave no response.

"I didn't agree at first, but it is right that you should see where your nephew is buried; it will help you come to terms with his death."

Despite the heat, Mary shivered and closed her eyes, forestalling any further attempts at conversation. We dozed and had another meal, washed down with water or beer as gender dictated, and as the sun had settled down for the night, we set off for the last leg of the journey, a little refreshed but no more enthusiastic about the discomfort to come.

I don't know what time it was when I was awoken by the silence and lack of movement. I could vaguely see Maurice and Mary stretching and looking around to see why we had stopped. Mr McGregor was not with us but I could hear his Scottish accent along with the voices of the drivers. I then heard the site manager's voice moving around as he went from carriage to carriage, before finally coming back to ours.

"We have to hunker down, there is a sand storm coming our way. We need to form a protective circle and secure the carts as best we can. Ladies, please find something to wrap your faces with to keep the sand out. Don't be frightened, it is just a matter of sitting it out."

Maurice went to help tighten the purpose-made clips which held the tarpaulin to the sides of the cart. We sat in silence, waiting. The gas light started to sway and the driver, who had joined us in the back, turned it off after receiving a curt nod from Mr McGregor. He could not, however, stop the cart from being buffeted by the malevolent wind that tore around our circle of carriages, screaming in frustration and trying to find a gap into which it could force its pernicious tentacles. The tarpaulin was so taut that it thrummed like a drum, and my head beat in sympathy. I could see nothing but I felt Mary sitting stiff with fear beside me. I took her hand and pulled her down onto the floor, where we sat huddled together for what seemed an eternity. Despite our precautions sand found its way inside; very soon I was crunching on the hard grains and my eyes were dry and sore when I rubbed them. Even above the shrieking of the wind I could hear the braying of the horses, all of which had been unharnessed from the carriages and tethered together inside the circle.

I was wondering how long it would be before anyone found our desiccated bodies when the wind suddenly went totally silent and the tarpaulin seemed to relax and give a sigh of relief. I heard the men in the other carts moving about and our own driver lit the gas lamp again and went outside to brush away a miniature desert off the roof and to see to the horses. I looked at the others, unable to stop myself laughing out loud at their appearance. Each one of them was covered from head to toe in a layer of sand, their faces ghastly pale in the gas light, and their hair sticking out like stalks of straw. Maurice grinned, cracking his sand-mask. We all stood up gingerly and went outside to shake ourselves down. We had some water and biscuits, as did the poor horses, whilst the drivers swept out the carriages, and then we were on our way again.

We had perhaps lost about four hours and a mile or so out of Um Garaiart we were met by a group of men on camels who had been sent from the mine to find us and make sure we were alright. When they saw we were quite safe they turned around and raced off quicker than I expected, the camels' awkward gait making the men bob comically from side to side, each man's *keffiyeh* streaming out behind him like a sheet on a washing line.

When we finally arrived at the gold mine, the sun had warmed the air and the horses were sweating in the heat. There was a crowd of people waiting for us, miners waiting to greet their old friends or new work-mates, the Arabs, both male and female, who worked in the kitchens or cleaned, and a Mr Carmichael, who the men merely referred to as the Boss. Mr Carmichael himself handed us down from the carriage, and I stumbled when my feet touched the ground, being unsteady after sitting for so long.

"Welcome ladies and Mr Russell, to our very humble abode. I'm afraid it is not really fit for visitors yet, but I hope you will be comfortable for your short stay. Please, let me show you to your quarters and then we will have some refreshments."

Maurice and I responded politely but Mary blurted out, "Can I not go straight to the cemetery? That is all I have come for."

Mr Carmichael looked at her queerly. "It is too hot for anyone to go anywhere. The refreshments have been made and to be honest, you all look as if a wash and a rest will be of more benefit." With that he turned briskly around and strode off down the path. I grabbed Mary by the arm and hurried after him. Mr Carmichael eventually slowed so that we could keep up and pointed out the various buildings to us.

"That is the main sleeping quarters for the men, but there is a smaller one round the corner where you ladies will be housed; it has all the facilities. We are in the process of building some married quarters and a school, so that the men's families can live here also. It will make all the difference, but I'm afraid that they won't be ready for quite a few months. It is a shame that you did not wait to come then."

I was afraid that Mary would apologise for Augustus dying at such an inconvenient time, but I saw her purse her lips and bite on her retort. When we arrived at our room, Mr Carmichael explained how to find his office and then he left us to get washed and changed. The room was whitewashed and clean, containing just two simple wooden beds, a bedside table each, a couple of relatively comfortable chairs and a large tin bath with about twelve inches of tepid water.

"For goodness sake, Mary. That was very rude of you. The poor man has obviously gone to a lot of trouble to accommodate us, the least you can do is to have a cup of tea and eat a piece of cake with him. And he is right, it is not fair to ask someone to go out in this heat to take you to the cemetery. It will not hurt you to wait for a few hours more."

Mary looked sheepish and apologised. There was not enough room for both of us in the bath so I told Mary to get in first and I would wash her with the soap and flannel that had been provided. Even though I was cross with her I still took great pleasure in producing a rich lather which I spread all over her exposed body, and then sluiced it off again to reveal her pale skin, untouched by the sun. I washed her hair and she lay down in the bath to rinse off the soap. She was over forty but she had a body of a much younger woman. When she was done she stood up and wiped the excess water off herself before letting me wrap a bath towel tightly around her. I was not surprised to see that the water was now a sandy brown with a layer of scum floating on the top. I nonetheless stepped gratefully into the now cold water and immersed myself as best as I could, being far longer than Mary. I could feel a layer of sand under my buttocks and as Mary was busy drying herself and showed no inclination to repay my act

229

of kindness, I washed myself in the grimy water as quickly as possible and was dressed and ready before her.

We made our way to Mr Carmichael's office, where we found Maurice and Mr McGregor already ensconced. Mr McGregor acted as mother and I gratefully sat in an armchair that did not rock or bounce up and down. The men had obviously been talking about the building plans and Mr Carmichael continued. "A lot of the drive to build the married quarters and school came from the old site manager, Mr Grenville. I don't know for sure, but I think he may have had a sweetheart back in England, whom he wanted to marry and bring over here. His death is a great blow to the company. As all their deaths are, of course."

This last was directed at Mary, who sat bolt upright, her face as white as our bedroom walls, and a biscuit crushed into crumbs in her clenched fist.

"My very deep condolences to you, Miss De Morgan. Augustus was a good doctor and was well-liked by the men. He will be missed. They all will be. It is always the family and friends left behind who suffer the most, is it not? Ah, well."

The men continued talking about the mine, Maurice asking questions about the workings, which I neither understood nor wanted to. I kept my eye on Mary, who I saw was struggling not to cry, and when it looked as if she would not be able hold back the tears I stood and asked if we may be excused for a few hours as we were both rather tired from our journey.

When we got to our quarters Mary fell onto her bed and started sobbing, as if she had only just heard of her nephew's death. I was getting a little bit exasperated at her grief and spoke to her quite sternly.

"Mary, you must pull yourself together. Your grief is becoming quite unseemly. Dry your tears now, my darling. The pain will pass, I promise you."

Her sobs subsided and she rolled over and looked at me through puffy, damp eyes. "You are too cruel. You cannot possibly know what I am going through."

I was surprised and a bit hurt at her vehemence. She muttered that she was tired, rolled over and curled up into her habitual sleeping position. I followed suit.

We were woken by a knock on the door and Maurice asking if we were ready to visit the cemetery. We smoothed our clothes, in which we had slept, and brushed our hair. I collected two shawls in case we were still out when the air cooled, then followed Maurice back to the entrance of the site, where four camels were waiting, one for each of us and one for our guide. I hate camels; they are large, they smell, they are uncomfortable and they spit. I had had the misfortune, on one of our outings the previous year, to be persuaded by our guide to go for a short trek on the back of one of these misshapen and vicious beasts. I had not enjoyed the experience and I was not looking forward to repeating it. I am sure that the camel allocated to me this time gave me a sour look when I walked at a good distance from his teeth, but he obediently fell to his knees when the guide tapped him with a stick. It was easy enough to climb onto the seat, but I had to hold on tightly to the sides of the saddle when the camel lurched to his feet, with the sole intention, I was convinced, of throwing me off. I laughed at Maurice's attempt to remain in control, and scoffed at him as his hat fell over his eyes and he sat askew on his seat. Mary managed to mount perfectly.

The journey was short, but long enough for me to be thankful that we had not had to ride a camel the whole way from Assouan. The guide led us up and down a rocky path and then up an escarpment which led to a plateau, on which I saw crude wooden crosses, some twenty of them in rows of five; hardly a cemetery. Mary seemed loath to dismount now that we were here, but I held out my hand to her once her camel had knelt, and she let me help her off. Her breathing quickened and her cheeks, already pale, drained of all colour. I waited for her to compose herself and then led her to the first cross. I could not read the letters, so bleached were they by the sun, so I surmised that this was an old grave. I led her along the each row until we came to one whose lettering we could discern: "G. Eustace. Miner (36). 11th September 1892." Then "W. R. Owen. Miner (26). 9th September 1892," followed by "N. M Whyte. Miner. (28). 8th Sept 1892." Next was "E. G. Grenville. Site Mgr. (35). 12th September 1892," and lastly "A. De Morgan. MD (32). 9th September 1892."

I stopped in front of this last one and waited for Mary, who had stopped dead in her tracks just behind me. "This is the one, Mary. Here lies your dear Augustus."

Mary did not move but stood staring sightlessly at the crosses. "Too young. All too young to die. He, they, had so much to live for. How can God be so cruel?"

"God did not choose to kill them, Mary. You know you do not believe that. It was just their time. They are perhaps in a far happier place." I felt uncomfortable saying such trite words, but I could think of no others.

"Happy? How can he be happy, under this hot sand, without ..."

She did not continue, but bit her lip and took deep breaths. She joined me at Augustus's grave and looked sadly at the simple commemoration of a life. "Poor Augustus, poor, poor boy. Hannah, would you mind leaving me alone for a while?"

I hugged her and went over to Maurice and suggested we go for a walk for a few minutes and leave Mary to her mourning. We wandered along the path which continued along the plateau for a bit before ending in a sheer drop to the desert floor below. I admitted my interest in understanding a bit more about the workings of the gold mine and Maurice explained that there had been a mine here since the time of the ancient Egyptians and that this was probably the source of much of the gold jewellery that I had admired at the Cairo museum. This modern mine had only been here quite recently but in that time they had built eight shafts that led down to the gold-filled quartz veins that were embedded in the rocks under the sand beneath us. We stood watching a large group of tiny men scurrying towards the refractory, whilst another group moved less quickly towards the workings to start their shift.

We had left Mary for a good quarter of an hour, and as we walked back to her I was prepared to have to wipe her tears and lead her back to her camel. I was not prepared, however, to find her regressed to a whimpering child, sitting on the floor, arms tightly wrapped around her knees, rocking backwards and forwards. She had her eyes screwed shut, but the tears were falling nonetheless. I whispered to Maurice to go and wait by the camels and I knelt down beside Mary.

"Mary, dearest, we need to get back now. Come, I'll help you up."

I may as well not have spoken for all the notice she took of me. I touched her arm and she jumped as if stung by a scorpion and looked at me with her eyes wide and confused. "Come, Mary. We need to go. Say your last farewells."

She wiped her eyes with the hem of her skirt and fearing that she would use it to blow her nose also I thrust a kerchief into her hand.

"You are such a dear, dear friend, Hannah. I don't know what I would do without you."

And she kissed me quite hard on the lips, then rose, brushed the sand off her skirt and walked unsteadily without a backward glance, back to where Maurice was waiting.

I sat for a few seconds longer and said my own goodbye to a man I had never met. As I stood up I saw something glinting in the rays of the sunshine. It was by the cross next to her nephew, one marking the resting place of an E. G. Grenville. When I brushed the sand away I saw it was a beautiful opal brooch. With a shock I recognised it as the one I had bought for Mary one

234

Christmas in celebration of her fairy tale "The Story of the Opal." She had told me that she loved it and would wear it always. At first I was hurt that she was now leaving it here, but on reflection I understood that she was in fact leaving one of her most treasured possessions as a sign of her love for her nephew, to show that they would eventually be re-united, just like the Sunbeam and the Moonbeam.

I re-buried the brooch under the sand next to Augustus's cross, deeper this time so that no-one would see it and steal it, and made my way to where the others were waiting.

Chapter 11 - The Wise Princess

1892 - 1895

The King's servants found her lying on the shore, with her face white and her lips cold, but smiling as they had never smiled before, and her face was very calm. They carried her home, and she was laid out in great state, covered with gold and silver.

"She was so wise," sobbed her little maid, as she placed flowers in the cold hand, "she knew everything."

"Not everything," said the skylark from the window; "for she asked me, ignorant though I am, to teach her how to be happy."

"That was the one thing I could not teach her," said the old Wizard, looking at the dead Princess's face. "Yet I think now she must be wiser than I, and have learned that too. For see how she smiles."

("The Wise Princess," in *The Necklace of Princess Fiorimonde* by Mary De Morgan)

We had been back from Um Garaiart for a week. Mary had regained none of her vitality or colour and I was no less worried about her than when she had first collapsed on hearing of her nephew's death. I wanted so much to return to the life we had shared in London; I wanted us to be as close as we had been then.

"Mary, perhaps now is the time to go home, back to England? We could go to Russell Hall, see if you prefer it there rather than London? It is a beautiful place and so peaceful; I'm sure you would find it easy to write there. Let's go home."

Her shoulders drooped; she sighed and closed her eyes as if she couldn't both look at and talk to me at the same time.

"I don't ever want to go back to England, Hannah; there is nothing for me there now. My only living relative is William and he spends most of his time in Florence. Maybe we could go and visit him soon, but I want to make my life here. But ... I don't always want to be a guest and living off your generosity. I want to earn my own living and live independently. So I have spoken with Madame Dupont and she has agreed that I can become a paid member of staff and that I can live at the reformatory."

I could hardly take in everything she had just said. She had already spoken to Madame Dupont about this momentous decision without even discussing it with me? She felt she was living off my generosity? She wanted to live independently?

"But .... " I didn't know where to start. "But, Mary, we live together, as we did in London. You were happy then weren't you? I pay rent to Sarah so we are not guests. We can live in our own house if you prefer? I thought we would always live together, like ..."

"Like what?" She opened her eyes and glared at me. "Like what, Hannah?"

I wanted to say "like a married couple" but instead said "like sisters."

She gave a humourless smile. "Like two spinster sisters, getting older together, more bitter and twisted day by day? Is that what you mean?"

I felt a sudden surge of anger. "No! That is not what I mean. Why are you being so cruel? Where has all this come from, Mary? You've never said you were not happy living with me until now. What has changed?"

She bowed her head and took a few shuddering breaths before she whispered.

"I'm sorry, Hannah. You are right. I *am* a cruel and horrid person and I don't deserve you. Please just be patient with me. I need to throw myself into something and working at the reformatory is ideal." She lifted her head and looked beseechingly at me, the unshed tears trembling on her bottom lid, ready to fall. "Please, Hannah, don't be angry with me. I just need to do this. It may not be for long and we will of course still see each other when you come - you will still come won't you? And I will visit here every week. I promise. It won't be so very different, it's just ..."

I didn't know what to say; in truth what could I say? I didn't want her to live at the reformatory, to separate herself from me even more and yet I couldn't force her to live with me. If I argued with her I was frightened that she would sink into another bout of depression and God knows she was already so weak. Really, the only thing I could do was to agree with her and to support her, although inside I wailed and gnashed my teeth in frustration. I was hurt that she hadn't turned to me in her need and I didn't see how living at the reformatory and distancing herself from me would help. But I spoke to Sarah and on her advice I kept my thoughts to myself and pretended to be supportive and a few weeks later I helped Mary move into her room, her "nun's cell" as I called it because of its plain white-washed walls, uncarpeted floors and sparse furniture.

She took very few clothes and the only personal belongings were her books, writing implements and photographs of her family: one of her mother and father, one of her mother and her dead sister Alice, and one of her brother William as a young man in a formal pose, unsmiling and revealing nothing of his irreverent sense of humour. I was pleased that she also took the carpet bag I had bought for her.

When we had finished unpacking I went to take my leave. I stood uncertainly, not knowing whether I could hug her or whether it would be better just to walk away.

"I'll go now then, shall I? You'll be alright, Mary?"

"Of course I will, Hannah. I know everyone here and although the room is very basic, it has everything I need."

"Is this really what you want? You can still come back with me now, no-one will think any less of you."

Mary gave a twisted smile. "I would think less of myself. I realise you don't understand why I am doing this, Hannah; I'm not sure I really understand it myself. I just know this is the right thing to do at this moment. It has nothing to do with my feelings for you, please don't think that. And please don't stop loving me; in fact I need your love even more. Come and give me a hug."

I don't know if it was the dying rays of sun that found their way through the shutters, but she for an instant she looked as if she was wrapped in a shimmering cocoon, which shattered into a million tiny shards when she opened her arms to me.

"Oh, Mary, of course I won't stop loving you. Please, please let me help you so that you can come back to me soon."

I hugged her gently at first, and then tighter and tighter until she gasped and laughingly told me she couldn't breathe.

I still went to the reformatory for the three days each week and I tried to see Mary as much as possible, although we still had to give our separate lessons. But we shared meal times, I always sat in at story-time and we would spend a few hours in the evening before I returned to Cairo sitting in the central courtyard chatting about old times and making plans for the future. I went on a Saturday or Sunday also and we spent the day together amusing ourselves in Helouan, or she sometimes made the journey to Cairo and seemed to enjoy the company of the Russell family. Although I hated that we were not living together I did feel that we were re-establishing our relationship and that when she did come back to me, which hopefully would be very soon, it would be on a much stronger footing.

Sarah was very understanding and on the days when I was not at the reformatory she would try and entice me to go visiting with her, which I did sometimes, but often I would just sit in the garden and read or paint, biding my time until I would see Mary again.

Mary had promised it would be a short interlude, but it did not turn out to be so. She seemed quite content with the new routine but although I was deeply frustrated I did not dare challenge her again, for I feared for her physical and mental health. Almost a year after her nephew's death, Mary still had not returned to her old self. She rarely laughed out loud as she used to do; her eyes had lost their mischievous sparkle and there was no bounce in her step. Over the months I noticed that there were more and more white streaks in her hair and that the lines around her eyes and mouth became more and more deeply etched. Worst of all she started to cough; it was only slight to begin with but it was a sound I had hoped never to hear again.

One Sunday when I was visiting Mary we were walking along the street when she had a coughing fit that left her fighting for breath, and her kerchief spotted with blood.

"Oh, Mary, we have to get you looked at. We are surrounded by sanitoriums all with the sole aim of getting people like you well. Let me book you in. They'll treat you and make you better."

"You don't honestly believe all that propaganda do you? Do you actually know of anyone who has been cured?"

"Well, I don't know their names, obviously. But all these people wouldn't come here if no-one ever got well now would they?"

241

"All these people come here because they are offered false hope at a very high price. I have indeed felt a lot better here than I did in England but there is no cure for consumption, Hannah. Most of the De Morgan family have died from it - as you know, we call it the De Morgan curse. I am not wasting my time and your money on something that is a blatant confidence trick. If you want to spend money on me let's go the Hotel des Bains and you can buy me a mint tea and one of their splendid cakes."

That night I told Sarah about Mary's coughing fit and how she refused to visit a doctor.

"Mary is possibly the most stubborn woman I know, Hannah, but she is probably right about the effectiveness, or lack of it, of the so called 'cures' offered by the sanitoriums. All you can do, all any of us can do, is to be there for her, to make sure she doesn't over exert herself and that she rests as much as possible."

"It is just all so difficult for me to just sit back and watch her get ill again. I was wondering ..."

"Yes, dear?"

"Well, I was wondering whether you would mind very much if I moved to Helouan? If Mary won't come back here, then I need to be there. I want to rent somewhere and I hope Mary will come and live with me but even if she doesn't I will be nearer to her and able to help her more. But I don't want to leave you, if you need me here."

"Oh, Hannah, of course you must go! We will miss you, naturally, but we can still see each other often. In fact it will be a great relief to me to know that you are near to Mary. You are right, perhaps she will agree to live with you there if you rent a little place just big enough for the two of you. And she can pay you some rent if that makes her feel better."

When I told Mary my plans she tilted her head in the manner I found so charming.

"That is an excellent idea Hannah. Then we can be even closer together."

"Will you come and live with me Mary?"

"I might well do so, indeed I might."

I was overjoyed but my delight was not sufficient to make the wheels of property rental run smoothly or quickly. I joked with Mary that the cogs must be clogged with sand. So, instead of moving into my own little house, I initially moved to the Hotel les Bains for a few weeks and then, because so much time was passing with nothing progressing, I asked Madame Dupont if I also could move into the reformatory.

"Ah, Mees Russell, *êtes-vous sûr*? You are used to a place far more *élégant*. Here it *ees très humble*."

"Oh, Madame Dupont, I do not mind that it is not *élégant*! I am worried about Mary and I need to be near her. I cannot find a place to rent in Helouan, so living here would be ideal. I will, of course pay you rent, I will still take the same lessons but I do not expect any salary. Things will be the same as they are now except for me living here. May I?"

She agreed, of course; there was no reason for her not to.

Mary was horrified when she heard I was moving into the reformatory.

"Hannah, you can't be serious! You living in a place like this? You'll hate it!"

"Why will I? You don't think I can live with just a few possessions? All I need is a bed and somewhere to put my easel. What else do I need? Oh, and somewhere for a few of my clothes and books. This way we can be near each other; it will only be for a while, anyway, until we find somewhere to rent. I hate to say this, but I almost wish that someone's cure is not successful and they die, so that their rented villa comes free!"

"Hannah, that is a terrible thing to say!" but she laughed as she said it.

I moved in a week later; Khalid returned to Cairo with my trunk still half full with clothes as there was less space than I had envisaged.

But I was happy, oh so happy.

At last, I was living with Mary again, albeit with a few hundred other females.

I now saw Mary every day and we would spend every evening together, quietly reading, painting, writing, talking. We sometimes went to the communal lounge and played cards with some of the other staff, but usually we preferred to keep our own company. We even started to brush each other's hair at night, before kissing each other and going to our separate cells. Each day I felt more and more content, more and more hopeful about our future together.

Time marched relentlessly on.

We continued to look for a place to rent with no success.

In May 1894 Maurice and Antonia married. Sarah was both happy and sad; happy that Maurice was doing so well and had such a lovely wife but sad that Mr Russell was not alive to see it and that Maurice would no longer be living with her. It was a typical Church of England wedding; there were even peals of bells to celebrate the occasion, which sounded quite incongruous competing with the cries of the Mullahs calling the faithful to worship their God. Mary and I spent a few days with Sarah so that we could attend the wedding and enjoy the subsequent celebrations. The house was certainly quieter once Maurice had moved out.

Georgie was now twenty one and had turned into a beautiful swan. She was tall, though not as tall as me, and was slim but shapely. She had naturally wavy hair, which she kept long but coiled elegantly on the back of her head. She taught at the school full-time now and was walking out with a policeman called James, some five years her elder. It seemed no time at all before there was a diamond on her finger and Sarah told me that she was avidly reading wedding magazines ordered from London.

We continued to look for a place to rent with no success.

On July sixteenth 1895 it was my thirty fifth birthday. It was a Tuesday but Madame Dupont had agreed that both Mary and I could have the day off, so Mary and I went to Sarah's so that we could all celebrate my special day together. Sarah took us to Shepheard's for lunch and then we went back to the house where we sat companionably in the garden, talking and sipping lemonade, interrupted only by the singing of the cicadas and Mary's persistent coughing.

We stayed the night at Sarah's; Mary and I were going to travel to Helouan together the next morning, like we used to do. Mary excused herself immediately after dinner, saying she had a slight headache; she did indeed look particularly pale and drawn. Sarah and I sat drinking another cup of coffee. We waited until we heard Mary's bedroom door close before we started talking about her.

"She is getting worse and worse, Hannah. She really ought to stop working at the reformatory and you both should come back here so that we can look after her."

"Oh, Sarah, I know! I've suggested it but she just won't listen. She says the girls need her and that she needs something to do, that it would the sitting around all day that would kill her not the consumption. She always makes a joke of her illness. It's as if she doesn't want to get well. It's as if ... well, as if she wants to die and get it all over with. We have been much happier these last few years, but it could be so much better if we could find somewhere together and she let me take proper care of her."

Sarah took my hand and squeezed it gently.

"We can't force her to leave the reformatory. Maybe you could have a word with Madame Dupont? She may have some ideas."

Later that night, I sat at the dressing table and studied my face in the mirror. I was thirty five years old; half-way through my three score years and ten. My stomach ached when I remembered our life in London. Despite Mary's bouts of depression those days on London had been the happiest of times and I wanted them back. I determined to speak to Madame Dupont the very next day, to see if she had any ideas how we could ease Mary away from the reformatory, for the sake of her health.

But, so Aisha told us when Mary and I arrived at the reformatory the following morning, Madame Dupont had gone to Alexandria for a few days, leaving the reins in the very capable hands of Miss Elliott, the matron.

Aisha was now a competent young woman, much loved by both the girls and the staff. She took some of the classes all by herself but she still adored Mary and continued to sit at the back of the class at the end of each day, listening to the stories with great enjoyment.

During lunch that day I noticed a worried frown on Aisha's face. She was looking straight at Mary and when I too looked I was shocked by what I saw. She was trying to cough quietly into her kerchief, and she was hunched over, her bony shoulder blades protruding like angel's wings. When she lifted her head I could see that her skin was pale and waxy. One of the staff members handed her a glass of water, but she shook her head and quickly left the table. I followed her to her room, where I found her lying exhausted on the bed, a bloodstained kerchief clenched in her fist. I wiped her face gently and held her hand as she fell into a doze. I left her then to find Mrs Elliott.

"I have been giving her small doses of laudanum ever since she came to live here, Miss Russell. It eases her coughing but it is not a cure. I suggested once that she tried one of the clinics in Helouan but she nearly bit my head off, so I never mentioned it again."

She gave me some water with a dose of laudanum and I returned to Mary and sat with her until she woke. I gave her the drink then helped her settle for the night. The next morning I knocked on Mary's door and tried to open it, but it was locked.

"Mary, are you feeling alright? I was going to go to Sarah's but I can stay here if you need me?"

"No, I am feeling much better, thank you, I am just a little tired. Please go and see Sarah, she is expecting you. Tell her we will both go over at the weekend. I will get up shortly."

So I left.

Sarah and I had a lovely day together, walking round the *souk* choosing materials for new curtains and having a picnic in the beautiful Ezbekiyya Gardens. I had planned to stay overnight and return to Helouan the next morning, but at about three o'clock in the afternoon I was overcome with a feeling of such dread that I stopped dead in the street and my whole body shuddered uncontrollably. I didn't know why, but I knew I had to get back to the reformatory.

Sarah was wonderful; she told Khalid to get a carriage and they both accompanied me to the station.

"I'm sure everything is fine, but Khalid will come with you to see if he can be of assistance. He will return to

248

Cairo and let me know if you have need of me." She squeezed my hand and whispered something I could not quite catch but thought was "be brave, my dear."

When I arrived at the reformatory I went straight to her room. As I walked, then ran, down the corridor I heard sounds of groans and sobbing coming from behind her shut door. I opened it and was faced with a scene from hell.

Mary was laying on the bed, flailing wildly on the narrow mattress, the thin sheet thrown onto the floor, where it lay like a screwed up piece of tissue paper. Her body was writhing as if she was in unbearable pain and her skin was shiny with feverish sweat. She must have been coughing vigorously for there was blood splattered over the pillow and down the front of her nightdress, which was stuck to her. Her breathing was laboured and her eyes were those of a mad woman, wide open and darting from one unseen horror to another.

She suddenly looked at me, standing transfixed as I was in the doorway, and whether she saw me or some other being I know not, but she tried to rise and held out her arms in a heart-rending appeal for relief from her torture. She was too weak, however, and fell back onto the pillow, making a slow keening sound that jolted me into action.

Mrs Elliott was there along with Aisha; both were standing helplessly by the side of the bed, having obviously tried unsuccessfully to soothe Mary, for their aprons were spotted with blood, their hair was in disarray and their cheeks were flushed with the exertion. Tears of

249

frustration were streaming down Aisha's face and it was her sobbing that I had heard. She looked at me in anguish, the words that poured from her lips incomprehensible to me as she reverted to her native Arab tongue in her distress.

I was horrified at how quickly Mary had deteriorated.

Mrs Elliott and Aisha were exhausted so I took control, although I am not a particularly practical or well-organised woman. The next hour or so was a blur of activity, during which we managed to calm Mary down by laying her in a bath of cool water to reduce her temperature. I then dressed her in a clean nightgown, fed her some spoonfuls of broth and packed her carpet bag with everything that was on the top of her bedside cabinet, along with clean clothes and her wash things. When the sun had lost its debilitating heat one of the Arab men carried Mary to a carriage and I accompanied her to Helouan railway station, onto the train and finally back to Cairo, to the German Hospital.

Khalid left to give the news to his mistress and I asked for a trestle bed to be placed in the room so that I could sleep with Mary. Mary was heavily sedated and I managed to doze, lulled by her shallow breathing, but I was plagued by nightmares of gargoyles that spouted blood and fountains whose spray glistened like rubies in the sunlight. The next morning I woke feeling exhausted with every bone in my body aching.

Mary continued to sleep.

Sarah arrived shortly after a nurse had kindly brought me some tea and toast. She carried a bag of day and night clothes and my wash things, as well as a few books to read and a new sketch pad and set of pencils. Sarah sponged Mary's face and brushed her hair whilst I had a quick wash and changed my clothes, which I was glad to do having slept in the ones from the previous day.

"Hannah, you must prepare yourself."

"Prepare myself, for what? Oh! You mean for Mary to .... No! Look how peacefully she sleeps. All she needs is some rest and some care."

"Oh, Hannah. Of course we all pray she will get well, but I fear this is her last illness and that she will not recover. You must prepare yourself for the worst."

"No! It cannot be! I will not let her die! Please Sarah, just leave me with her. I will make her well, just see if I don't!"

Sarah sighed and shook her head sadly.

"Alright, Hannah. I will leave you with her. I will come back this evening."

She kissed Mary on the cheek and then me.

Mary continued to sleep.

Her hair and face was as white as the pillow on which her head rested; she looked like a marble effigy, the only colour the deceptive blush of health on each cheek. Her sleep suddenly became troubled for she started to make small whimpering sounds, her eyes moved rapidly under her closed lids and her breathing was too fast.

Mary stirred and then opened her bright iris-blue eyes. "Hannah, my dear faithful friend." Her voice was weak, and she had to take breaths between each sentence but her words perfectly clear. "I was with my

251

sister ... In the jewel garden ..." Her voice quivered with suppressed pleasure, "It was as it was before ... When I was small ... Alice was there then."

I remembered Mary telling me about her dream of the jewel garden when she was six years old that her mother had recorded in her little spiritual notebook. I also knew that Alice had died over half a century ago. I leaned forward and gently asked, "are you sure it was Alice?" She did not seem to have heard me and I leaned even nearer to repeat my query, just catching her whispered "very sure. She is going to take me to him."

Her breathing was now less hectic, and her eyes unfocussed, seeing into a world beyond the one that I inhabited. She drifted into sleep again and I took the opportunity to refresh the water in the vase of flowers and to tidy the items I had taken from her room and placed on top of the little cabinet by the side of her bed. There were not many things: a bottle of lavender water, a drinking glass, which I also refreshed, and a neatly folded kerchief, embroidered with her initials, MADeM.

Mary became agitated again, so I poured some of the lavender water onto the kerchief and wiped her brow but could not remove the slight sheen of her fever. Her breathing became shallow and fast and each inhalation seemed to give her great pain. Despite what I had said to Sarah, I knew I was losing her but I didn't want to believe it; I took her hand in mine and held it tight, whispering, "Don't go, Mary, oh please don't go."

I didn't think I had spoken loud enough for her to hear me, but she turned to face me and gave a gentle smile.

"Hannah, dear ... it is my time ... you know it is ... Please don't make ... me stay any longer." She paused whilst she struggled to get her breath and then she said, in a voice that faded into nothingness, "They are all ... waiting for me ... I must go to him."

She closed her eyes and with each breath the life seemed to seep out of her. As her breathing slowed mine quickened as I realised with mounting panic that there was not going to be a miraculous recovery; that this woman whom I had loved for the last quarter of a century was going to leave me alone; that my love was not going to be enough to save her.

Mary suddenly opened her eyes wide and looked straight at me, saying in a surprisingly strong voice, "Oh my love, my love, is that really you?"

"Mary, I am here," I said, "I am here."

My heart raced, as hers slowed. Tears streamed down my face and I wiped them away but in those few seconds she had gone.

She had called me her love, her love.

It was still early afternoon and, although the shades at the window blocked out the direct sunlight, the room remained warm, and the sky that I could glimpse through chinks in the material was, as always, a clear, coral blue. I was reluctant to lose physical contact, so I gently stroked the back of her hand with my fingertips, feeling a warmth flow throughout my whole body, even down to my toes.

I continued to stroke her hand, her cheeks, her hair.

I continued to stroke even as her flesh cooled.

I had been sitting for some minutes, my head bowed, when a movement over the hospital bed caught my attention. I was indeed exhausted after the events of the last few days, but I was not dozing. It was if the spirits from Mrs De Morgan's notebook had left the page and inhabited my weary brain, for what I saw was not of this world. I watched spellbound, trying to rationalize the form that hovered just a few inches above Mary's body. It looked as it was made of thousands of interweaving gossamer threads, each of which radiated incredibly fine beams of light that bounced off the walls, so that the whole room was suffused with a most beautiful, pulsating, pale pink glow. It was constantly changing but I thought I could make out a vaguely female human shape. It hovered over the bed for quite a few seconds and then floated towards the window. The blind vibrated slightly in the still air as the ethereal being slipped through out into the open air and up to the heavens. I felt immensely comforted and at peace for a while, despite the fact that my beloved was dead.

I continued to sit next to the bed, stroking, stroking, stroking, until Sarah arrived that evening holding a vase of flowers cut from her garden. I turned my tear-streaked face towards her. She understood. She laid her hand on my shoulder.

"My poor Hannah. She is now at peace. See how she smiles."

I was certain that this had not been the case at the time of her death, but her lips were now indeed curved into a contented smile.

"Just like the Wise Princess" I murmured.

Sarah smiled in agreement, for she knew Mary's fairy tales well enough to understand the reference.

Sarah stood for a while, massaging my shoulders, trying to ease the tension that permeated my whole body, but she could not melt the block of ice in my breast. She then gently kissed the top of my head and said that she would go and sort a few things out with the Matron, leaving me to say my last farewell.

How could I say farewell to this woman? Already her face was changing, and with a rising sense of panic I suddenly could not remember what she had looked like when we were in London, when we had first come to Egypt, even the last time I had seen her out of bed.

I was terrified that I would forget what she looked like. Then I recalled that Sarah had brought a sketch book that morning and without further ado I spent the next fifteen minutes sketching the face of the woman whom I had loved for so long and who, as she had just confessed, had loved me.

It is often said that the dead look at peace, but Mary looked more than that, with her small mouth curved into a smile, she seemed pleased with herself, even smug, as if she had just received a great accolade or won a prize. Her face was now relaxed and smoother than when she had been alive; death had ironed out the deep lines around her eyes and mouth.

When I had finished I saw that what I had drawn was Mary's death mask. I had only managed to copy the form; I had not managed to instil the vitality and passion that had made her the person that I had loved. I didn't want a constant reminder of how she looked in death, so I screwed the sketch up and put it into my bag, to throw away at a later time.

I knew that Sarah would be returning soon so I collected Mary's things and put them into the carpet bag. She had claimed that it was big enough to hold all her worldly goods and indeed, the few possessions it now contained hardly covered the bottom.

I heard the sound of Sarah's footsteps coming down the corridor and I closed the carpet bag and sat back down. She came briskly into the room. "It is time to go. The body must be prepared."

The body.

This was the body I had been going to spend the rest of my life with.

This was the body I had yearned to be near, to touch, to care for each and every day.

This was the body of the woman I had loved and now lost.

This was the body of my Mary, my dear, dear Mary, my beloved.

Oh God! How could I leave her, and yet how could I stay?

I knew that the body was already starting to decay in the heat.

I stood up so violently that I knocked the chair over. "Let's go. Now. Please."

Chapter 12 - The Seeds of Love

1895

"My tree is dead," sobbed Queen Blanchelys, "and the King loves me no more. Ah, tell me who has killed my tree?"

"Your cousin Zaire has killed it," said Love. "She asked Envy to help her, and Envy has given her a viper, which she laid at the tree's roots, and it has spat its deadly venom on to the red heart which is in the centre of the trunk and killed it."

"Tell me, then, how to make it live again," gasped the Queen.

"There is only one thing in the world that can do that!" said Love.

"And what is that?" asked the Queen?

"The blood from your own heart," said Love. "You must pierce your heart with a thorn from the tree, and let it flow to the tree's roots. Then, when it touches the snake it will shrivel and die, and the tree will bloom out afresh."

("The Seeds of Love" in *On a Pincushion* by Mary De Morgan)

There was a carriage waiting outside, with the old driver sitting contentedly in the late afternoon sun, flicking flies away from himself and the horses with a long swat. When Sarah and I were seated she told the driver, "*Yalla!*" We turned into the main road and immediately became one of the throng of horse-drawn carriages, over-laden donkeys, supercilious camels and what must surely

257

have been every Arab in the area congregated in that one street and all, seemingly, shouting at the tops of their voices. I was tired, both physically and emotionally, and I sat back and stared out at the chaos of everyday Egyptian life. It was like looking through a kaleidoscope as the bright, gaudy colours of the shop awnings and of the fabrics displayed in piles on tables, hanging on walls, suspended over extended arms, and wrapped around bodies, all swirled in and out of my view.

Our steady pace suddenly jolted to a halt as a donkey stood obstinately motionless in our path, having decided, apparently, that it could or would go no further with its load of copper pans and kettles that hung from it like Christmas-tree baubles. Our carriage was near the centre of the road and I could see right into the deep central gully, into which the people threw their rubbish. It took me several seconds to realise that I was staring straight at a dead cow, which lay on its back with its legs pointing straight up to the sky. It had probably only been there for a few hours, but already its body was bloated and it was covered in a writhing mass of flies. I had seen such sights before and they usually no longer sickened me, but as I looked my vision blurred and it was no longer the body of a cow but that of Mary. The buzzing of the flies filled my ears and the bile rose in my throat as I could see them working their way into her ears, nose and mouth, any place of darkness to lay their loathsome eggs. I shouted out loud and swung my parasol to try and disperse them, but only a few were disturbed and they soon settled back to the task in hand. The noise startled not only Sarah and

258

the driver but also the donkey, which slowly resumed his journey and allowed us to continue ours.

We soon arrived home. I could hear Georgie's footsteps on the tiled floor as she came to greet us but I could not face her grief when she was told of Mary's death.

Sarah nodded understandingly when I asked to be excused from dinner, saying truthfully that I was not hungry and just needed some time to myself. I went up to my bedroom, which was at the back of the house and overlooked the garden.

Although I was exhausted it was too early to go to bed, so I changed out of my dress into a loose, cotton robe. I sat in a rocking chair by the window, my favourite place in the whole house. I didn't want to think any more about the events of the day, of death and loss, so I closed my eyes and focussed on the different scents that danced in the air around me like butterflies fluttering around my head. I easily identified the sweet smell of the jasmine that grew right outside my window; this I imagined as four or five small white butterflies, happy to sit on top of my head, but ready for flight if threatened. I could also discern the deeper, richer fragrance of the roses in the beds directly underneath my window; I saw these as large, bright red, purple and orange butterflies, confident enough to settle on my hand and one even on the end of my nose. There was one fragrance I could not identify and I only discerned a hint of it occasionally; it had a slightly sickly perfume and in my mind's eye I envisaged a single butterfly that kept out of sight, daring to dart nearer for a split second only, then retreating back into the security of the gloom.

I felt a calmness settle over me like a thin gauze; the sun sank, the air cooled and the natural world settled down for the night. I even dozed, but eventually the drop in temperature roused me and I went back into the room. I suddenly remembered the sketch of Mary that I had drawn earlier that day and I retrieved it, flattened out the creases and studied it once more. I found no comfort in it, but I decided that I could not destroy it; I had very few sketches of Mary as she had always shied away from the idea of having her image recorded, by either portrait or photograph.

One thing that *did* always comfort me was to read Mary's fairy tales. I knew the stories all by heart, but still discovered something new at each reading. I took the first volume from the bookcase; it was my favourite book, not only because I loved these tales the best, but also because Mary had given it to me on my twenty-second birthday. I had already had a copy but this one was leather-bound and Mary had written inside: "To my very dear friend, Hannah, on the occasion of her birthday 16th July 1882." She had completed the entry with her flamboyant signature.

I didn't open the book immediately, but instead I stroked the dark green cover lovingly. I closed my eyes and started to trace the raised letters of the title, saying each one under my breath. "O.N. A. P.I.N.C.U.S.H.I.O.N."

Eyes still closed, I slid my fingertips down, over the embossed cherubs that decorated the cover - the relevance of which I have never been able to comprehend - and onto the letters of her name. "M. D.E. M.O.R.G.A.N."

As I went from letter to letter my heartbeat and breathing quickened. By the time I reached the final letter I was almost panting. A surge of emotion rose from the pit of my stomach and erupted as a dry sob, but I did not, could not cry.

My short nap had revived me and I was no longer tired but I did not want to light the lamps, so I crept into my bed and lay curled up on my side, clutching the book to my bosom. The blackness was now complete and I felt it almost as a physical presence, cocooning me from reality. I wanted to absorb that same blackness into my brain, to smother the memories that lay there, crouching in the corners of my mind, waiting to come to life and torment me. I clasped the book even harder and instead of images of a dead Mary, I forced myself to visualise the black and white etchings that Mary's brother William had done. In my imagination I gave the characters both life and colour and by a series of moving images, rather than words, I told myself the different tales. One of a vain girl being taught the lesson of loving others more than herself; one the story of a utopian village almost destroyed by greed; another story of two sisters and how the jealousy of one destroys not only her sister but also herself; another of how a fairy godmother replaces a young princess with a toy so that the real one can live a normal life; yet another of a little crippled boy who is cured through his own kindness to others.

261

I awoke the next morning feeling physically refreshed. For a few seconds I actually looked forward to a new day, and it was only when I stepped onto the book, which had fallen to the floor, that the events of the previous day came flooding back, threatening to overwhelm me. I had no further means of holding back the reality of Mary's death, and I went down to breakfast feeling emotionally crushed, as if my grief and despair were tied onto my back like a sack full of stones; inside, where my heart should have been, there was still the block of ice that only got bigger.

Sarah and Georgie were already at the breakfast table, discussing the funeral arrangements, although they stopped when I entered. Sarah asked if I had slept alright, and supposed I must be hungry as I had forgone dinner. I murmured an affirmative to both, although I did not think I would be able to swallow a thing, and they resumed their conversation as I helped myself to fresh fruit, bread and honey, and a cup of mint tea.

"I know you don't want to think about it, Hannah, dear, but we must hold the funeral as soon as possible. We are wondering about the music. Is there anything particular you want played? Did Mary have any favourites?"

I am not musical, as Sarah well knew, but one of Mary's short stories popped into my head. I knew the story almost by heart and spoke out loud.

"For whatever else she played, before the piano was silent for the night, there might always be heard the last of his "Nacht-Stücke," generally preceded by the "Romance in F."

Sarah gave me a bemused look.

"Mary wrote a short story called 'An old time tune' that tells of a piano teacher who plays these two pieces of music every night. Are they suitable?"

Georgie went over to the piano in the corner of the room and started playing Schumann's "Nacht-Stücke" from memory. We all agreed that the piece was appropriately sombre and funereal.

The rest of the day passed in a blur of activity, although it was Sarah's not mine; I merely followed her around as she met with the vicar to agree the funeral details, visited the cemetery to choose the plot, booked the carriages, and informed everyone who she thought may wish to attend. It all had to be done as quickly as possible due to the hot weather and by dusk everything was all planned to start at ten o'clock the next day. I was glad that I did not have time to think and that night, after a light dinner, I went straight to bed and straight to sleep, aided by two white tablets that Sarah gave me to take with my evening drink.

The next day was as beautiful a July day as ever it is in Egypt; a day for a wedding not a funeral. I didn't have any black gowns, and knowing that Sarah, if not the whole of the congregation, would be appalled if I donned my Arab robe, I compromised by wearing a light summer dress of a pale blue colour and wrapping a black Chantilly lace shawl around my shoulders. What did it really matter what I wore? I doubted that Mary would care one jot.

The block of ice meant I could hardly swallow the sliced peaches that I put on my plate.

"You must eat, Hannah. We can't have you fainting during the service." Georgie smiled at me kindly, which made me want to cry, but although I longed for the release that it would bring, I feared even more that if I started I would never be able to stop and I would drown in a sea of tears, rather like Alice in Wonderland.

Too soon I found myself sitting in one of the front pews of the church. I don't remember how I got there or who had given me the hymn book and order of service that I was clutching tightly. The church should have been cool, built as it was with walls of thick stone and just slits for windows, but the air was heated by the multitude of lighted candles, which very soon made me feel quite nauseous.

The service was a typical Anglican one, so much so that despite the heat and the faint smells of sewage that were ever-present, I could almost have been in one of the parish churches back in England; the vicar looked as if he had just strolled over from his Rectory across the village green and, as far as I could see, the congregation was made up purely of those of the English community that could be notified at such short notice. There were a surprisingly large number of people there; I did not think Mary had been particularly popular - being too outspoken and not sufficiently "female" for most of these imperialists – but I knew that the English liked to present a united front to the natives, who needed to be shown how to behave. In this instance the correct behaviour was to sit stiffly in over-tight clothes, sing some dirge-like hymns and hold in all emotions. The only other funerals I had ever attended were that of Mary and my own father; then too I had felt nothing but cynicism and denial. How much better I would have felt if I could have shown my grief in loud wailing, in the renting of my clothes and in the tearing of my hair.

It seemed to me that we, the mourners, were more dead than the dead.

I was glad to be out of the church into the relatively fresh air although by now it was nearly mid-day and the heat pressed down like a physical weight. I sat with Sarah, Georgie, Maurice and Antonia in the carriage, joined also by an elderly couple who had nothing better to do than to continue their mourning of a woman they hardly knew, and certainly never liked. The journey to the British cemetery in Old Cairo was long and although I had my parasol to protect myself from the direct sunlight, I felt the sweat trickle between my breasts and down my spine, and I longed to de-robe and don something cooler. The conversation was desultory and I didn't contribute other than an occasional nod or smile and to ask if we could stop at a flower shop so that I could buy some red roses to lie on the grave.

We arrived at our destination along with quite a few other carriages and we all filed through a wooden gate that was held open by an old Arab, who bowed his head courteously as each of us passed. The cemetery was surrounded on all sides by a high brick wall, which screened the sights, sounds and smells of the living. As well as the congregation, there was a entourage from the reformatory that had presumably not felt comfortable attending an Anglican church, but nonetheless wanted to pay their respects. Madame Dupont was there, along with Aisha and ten of the older girls. I was pleased that the girls wanted to show their respect. Or perhaps they just relished a day out.

Although all the girls were standing quietly, each neatly dressed in a khaki coloured tunic and with their hair constrained within a mop cap, I could see some of the English women looking at them suspiciously, as if they expected the girls to rush at them and steal their purses or, even worse, to act indecorously.

Even from a distance I could see that Aisha's eyes were still red and swollen from crying. I caught her eye and gave her a small wave and an even smaller smile, but she didn't return it, unused perhaps to the formality and restraint of the occasion.

Whilst we waited for the ritual to start, I stood with the Russells under the tree known locally as the Beard of the Pasha because of its long beard-like pods that hang down, which were rattling in the slight breeze that had sprung up. Appropriately Coles Pasha was also standing with us, although he did not have a beard, this being an absolute anathema for a man of his position. I knew he was a busy man and thanked him for making time to come to Mary's funeral.

"She was a splendid woman! Firm but fair, firm but fair. Saw goodness in everyone. That's why the girls respected her and worked hard for her. Everyone at the reformatory is devastated. Yes, a splendid woman. Such a shame. Such a shame. "

The cemetery was not very big, nor did it yet have a large number of inhabitants; I could see from the regular line of headstones near to me that those beneath were English and had died within the last ten years or so. I whispered to Sarah, "We must ask Mary's brother about a headstone. He will surely want to provide one." She was just about to answer when we heard the marching of feet outside of the cemetery walls, coming nearer and nearer.

The Arab held open the wooden door again and ushered in the coffin, carried on the shoulders of eight policemen, courtesy of Coles Pasha, resplendent in their dress uniform, all with fezzes perched on their heads, the tassels swaying in unison, and all with magnificent moustaches bristling with importance. Everyone fell silent and only the sound of the bearers' boots on the sandy path could be heard.

The Reverend said his piece, we all murmured our responses, the coffin was lowered into the hole and suddenly I was staring down at the wooden lid and a single spray of jasmine that Aisha had thrown in. I imagined Mary lying there, wrapped in a pure white shroud, her hair restored to the dark chestnut brown of her youth and her beautiful blue eyes open and full of fun. She smiled at me and I smiled back. But as I watched her eyes dimmed and her smile faded as her hair turned to white again and her face dissolved into dust. I let out a sob and sank to my knees as the reality of Mary's death hit me and my loss overwhelmed me. I was still holding the roses I had bought and one of the thorns pierced my chest quite deeply. The dark red droplets of blood, like those of Queen Blanchelys, fell to the ground and were instantly sucked in by the thirsty sand; how I wished that Mary would bloom afresh, as did the Queen's dead rose tree. As my blood flowed so did my tears, tears I could no longer hold back, tears that I thought would never, ever cease.

Chapter 13 – The Wanderings of Arasmon

1895

Then he began to play on his harp, and as he played the sheep stopped browsing and drew near to listen.

The stars grew brighter and the evening darker, and he saw a woman carrying a child coming up the hill.

She looked pale and tired, but her face was very happy as she sat down not far from Arasmon and listened to his playing, whilst she looked eagerly across the hill as if she watched for someone who was coming. Presently she turned and said, "How beautifully you play; I never heard music like it before, but what makes you look so sad? Are you unhappy?"

"Yes," said Arasmon, "I am very miserable. I lost my wife Chrysea many years ago, and now I don't know where she can be."

"It is a year since I have seen my husband," said the woman, "He went to the war a year ago, but now there is peace and he is coming back, and to-night he will come over this hill. It was just here we parted, and now I am come to meet him."

"How happy you must be," said Arasmon. "I shall never see Chrysea again," and as he spoke he struck a chord on the harp, which cried, "O Arasmon, my husband! Why do you not know me? It is I, Chrysea."

"Do not say that," continued the woman; "you will find her someday. Why do you sit here? Was it here you parted from her?"

Then Arasmon told her how they had gone to a strange desolate village and rested there for the night, and in the morning Chrysea was gone, and that he had wandered all over the world looking for her ever since.

"I think you are foolish," said the woman; "perhaps your wife has been waiting for you at that village all this time. I would go back to the place where I parted from her if I were you, and wait there till she returns. How could I meet my husband if I did not come to the spot where we last were together?"

("The Wanderings of Arasmon," in *The Necklace of Princess Fiorimonde*, by Mary De Morgan)

My robe billowed out and slowed my fall, so that I spiralled down the shaft like a maple tree seed on a blustery day. There was a small patch of light above me, which illuminated an object that lay far below me; from the shape I knew it to be a coffin. My robe suddenly slipped off and lazily drifted after my plummeting naked body, which hit the bottom so hard that I was sure every bone must be broken. I struggled to get the air back into my lungs and in the now absolute darkness I felt desperately around me, needing to touch the walls, to know the limit of my underground prison, but my fingers came into contact with nothing.

A high-pitched wail suddenly rent the silence and I knew beyond any doubt that it was Mary crying out in horror and panic, buried alive in the coffin upon which I now lay. I started scrabbling at the wood, feeling splinters tear at my finger nails as I tried to rip open the lid with my bare hands.

"Mary, Mary! I am here. I will get you out!" The wailing got louder and more hysterical as I could find no purchase on the wooden lid, now slippery with blood and tears.

"Hannah! Hannah!"

Mary was calling to me. Oh God! She must be so afraid. I had to open the lid, just had to. God, help me! "Mary, I am here, I am here. I will get you out."

"Hannah, dear, it is Sarah. Mary is ... It is Sarah, you have had a bad dream. It is just a bad dream."

And I found myself being held hard against Sarah's bosom as she rocked me gently, stroking my hair and cooing gently. I realised that indeed it had been a dream and I had fallen out of bed onto the wooden floor. I was naked, my nightdress having come off during my tossing and turning, but I felt no embarrassment and allowed myself to be calmed. I lay curled in Sarah's embrace like a frightened child and found such comfort from the warmth of her body and the very smell of her. I did not remember ever being so held.

I managed to sleep for a few dreamless hours, having taken some more of Sarah's pills. The next morning I was woken by the sound of a knock on the door, it opening and then the soft patter of bare feet; it was Khalid with my morning pot of mint tea and some biscuits lain out on a silver filigree tray. He put it carefully on the bedside cabinet, waited for me to sit myself up, and then placed a small white napkin over my chest. I felt so lack-lustre that

271

I wished he would feed me but he bowed slightly and walked backwards towards the door, giving me a shy smile when I thanked him, *"Shokran."*

I was surprised to find that I was hungry and I ate the biscuits with relish and decided to get up, put on a light cotton dressing gown and go down to the breakfast room. Sarah and Georgie were already there. Sarah didn't refer to the previous night's events, but merely asked if I had managed to sleep and what I intended to do that day.

"Yes, I slept well, thank you."

What did I want to do? I didn't want to *do* anything. What was there to do, now? What was the point in doing anything at all?

"I suppose I should go to the reformatory. Someone should clear out Mary's room. It needs to be done and I might as well do it today. I don't think it will take long, she didn't have very many things."

"If you are sure it won't be too exhausting? Do you want me to come with you?"

"No, there is no need for you to go as well. Perhaps Khalid can accompany me?"

Sarah and Georgie finished their breakfasts, kissed me on the cheek and then left the room, leaving me with their voices still echoing in my ears, the air settling after their retreat, and a plate of cold toast - my appetite having dissipated as soon as I had sat down.

The thought of just going back upstairs to dress seemed too much of an exertion, so I poured myself another cup of tea and peeled a peach as an excuse to remain seated and inactive for a while longer.

The day, and every day thereafter, stretched interminably ahead.

I knew that I had to clear Mary's room but I really did not want to go, to pace the same floor, breathe the same air, knowing that I would never see her again.

I sighed; I needed to go to the reformatory. I did not relish the task, but it was something that had to be done and it would not get any easier the longer I left it.

I decided to walk to the railway station, hoping that the exercise would invigorate my lethargic body and soul, shadowed by Khalid. The quiet, tree-lined residential avenue in which the house was located soon gave way to a bustling commercial street, teeming with people, camels, donkeys and horses-drawn carriages. Shoppers and merchants alike milled in and out of the shops, exchanging money and wares in a never-ending cycle; small street urchins wove in and out of adult legs, hands out for baksheesh or clutching stolen fruit.

I had walked along these streets many times over the last year or so, and the shop keepers knew me by sight and had come to accept me, although I think they considered me something of an oddity. I would sometimes repay their cordiality by going into their shop and purchasing a small item, or sharing a cup of their thick, black coffee and sampling some of their sugary sweets.

I had very soon realised that the *souk* was in fact not so very different from the Jewish quarter in Whitechapel that Mary and I used to walk through to get to some of "our" families in Bethnal Green. As I walked I reminisced about those first years with Mary, they were many years ago but I could remember some of the incidents as if they had occurred only yesterday.

These memories filled my mind as I walked towards the railway station in Bab-el-Luk Square, and it was only when I heard the sound of the train's whistle that the London streets faded and the Cairo streets came to the fore, rather like a chalk picture washed away by the rain, revealing another painted picture beneath. I hurried into the station, knowing that the whistle indicated that the train would soon be leaving. There was luckily no-one queuing for tickets and I quickly bought two returns for Helouan, thrust one at Khalid, who was hovering a few feet away, and then we both ran onto the train through the last open door, just before the guard slammed it shut. It was an open third-class carriage, with wooden bench seats, and I sat in the first vacant place as the train lurched forward. I gestured to Khalid to take a seat; the journey was only thirty minutes or so, and I did not mind sitting with the Arabs, rather than the Europeans, for such a short period of time.

In the first-class carriage I knew that the occupants would be sitting primly in their allotted seats, speaking only to those with whom they were acquainted, the men reading their newspapers, the women perhaps reading a book or conversing quietly to a companion, the children bursting with suppressed excitement but not allowed to show it. Here in the third-class carriage the only people who remained in their seats were the Arab women with their large baskets full of produce, dead and alive,

274

perched on their ample laps. Everyone else moved effortlessly around, stopping to talk to one person, exchanging cigarettes with another, chucking the chin of a random child, crying out greetings to some - usually at the other end of the carriage - and kissing others.

Outside we were passing through the outskirts of Cairo, a sight I was familiar with by now, but one which never ceased to upset me. The buildings, none of which seemed to be finished, lay in a haphazard manner, squashed together and all on top of each other like towers of wooden blocks that had been kicked over by a fractious child. The only bits of colour amidst the stone and sand and the blackness of the windows were the pieces of bright clothing hanging to dry on lines and over balcony railings. Everything shimmered in the heat and I saw only old men sitting smoking or dozing, and a few mangy cats and dogs sprawled out under whatever shade they could find. Compared to this hellish abode the slums of the East End that I had been recalling seemed almost luxurious.

I closed my eyes in an attempt to protect myself from the assault on all my senses. In my mind's eye I drew a map. I coloured a large black dot at the top of the page to represent Cairo, with the blue, wavy line of the Nile meandering down and off the page, like a cat's tail hanging over a wall. With quick strokes I painted a green ribbon on either side of the river to show the narrow band of lush arable land that bordered it, and I put another, smaller dot about halfway down the page, just on the eastern edge of the river to show where Helouan was sited. I mentally painted the rest of the page with a suitably sand coloured wash and then drew the black railway line along the right hand edge of the green swathe, joining the two dots.

I forsook my simple map and instead envisioned what I would see if I opened my eyes, had I been so inclined. By now we would have left the city and we would be flanked on one side by the fertile banks of the Nile. I imagined the date palms swaying slightly in the hot breeze, the men tilling their fields with ploughs pulled by bullocks, herds of goats at the waters' edge, a disturbed ibis swooping up into the air, a gaggle of chattering women washing clothes in the sparkling river, the laden feluccas sailing serenely by. On the other flank would be the barren expanse of nothingness that stretched out further than the eye could ever see.

The train rolled on, the carriages swayed slightly and the regular clickety-click of the wheels blocked out the chatter of the other passengers. My head dropped onto my chest and I could not have opened my eyes even if I had wanted to. The vagaries of a dozing imagination are such that although I actually sat in a railway carriage on my way to Helouan, my fancy took me to the carriage Mary and I had taken from Lynton back to Minehead a decade or so earlier.

I remembered we had actually walked down the steep Porlock Hill but dreams have a will of their own, and rather than being safely outside, I was suddenly alone inside the now inexplicably horseless conveyance that was careering down the hill, lurching from side to side.

276

The doors of the cab abruptly flew off and to prevent myself from being thrown right out I had to dig my fingernails deep into the edge of the red padded velvet seat. The carriage plummeted down, down, down, getting faster and faster until it ploughed into a wall at the bottom of the hill, sending me flying, up, up into the air. I was suddenly transformed into a giant bird of prey and my wings beat strongly, forcing me up higher and higher until I was able to soar on the thermals; I glided over the green English countryside and I knew I was over Kent when I recognised Russell Hall far below. I so desperately wanted to go down and rest in the shade of the huge oak that dominated the rear garden, but it seemed as if someone else was controlling me and I had no choice but to continue on my journey over the grey Channel, over the white mountains of France and Italy, across the blue Adriatic and Mediterranean seas and then over the golden deserts of northern Africa, back to Egypt. I took the opportunity to swoop over the Pyramids at Giza, did a loop-de-loop above the great head of the Sphinx and within but a few seconds was hovering over my railway carriage just entering into Helouan station. This was the end of the line and the train slowed right down, inching along until it hit the buffers with a jolt that woke me. I opened my eyes quickly, wondering whether I had embarrassed myself in any way but all the passengers were grabbing bags and each other's hands in their rush to alight and no-one took any notice of me at all.

I first of all went to Madame Dupont's office to tell her I was there. She hugged me tightly and we both cried on each other's shoulders.

"Oh, *pauvre chose*. It ees always those that remain that suffer the most, *non*? Come, 'ave a cup of tea first. That ees what the English do when they are sad, yes?"

I willingly accepted; anything to delay the task in hand. But I could not stay there for ever and after a second cup we both hugged, I promised to start coming to teach again and then I left and walked down the corridor to Mary's room. It was less than a week since I had last been there, but already the air was stale and musty although the window was slightly open, and a thin layer of sand lay on all the surfaces. A column of large, black ants marched unremittingly back and forth along the base of the outer wall, obeying their own natural instincts and caring not one jot for the concerns of mankind.

The bed had been stripped and the mattress turned, thank goodness, and nothing now remained as a reminder of Mary's final trauma. I put the carpet bag on the bed and sat beside it for a few minutes, gathering myself for the ordeal of going through Mary's things.

I had helped her unpack her few things when she had first arrived, and here I was, only three years later, re-packing them. I looked at the photograph of Mrs De Morgan and Alice, wondering if Mary was now with them. I shivered and opened the wardrobe door. The familiar smell of Mary wafted out and I breathed it in deeply, wanting to immerse myself in the fragrance and absorb it into my very pores. I shut the door again, suddenly distressed by the sight of her clothes; I would tell Madame Dupont to distribute them as she thought fit. On the top of the wardrobe was a hat box; I didn't remember seeing it before and I had never seen Mary in a hat. I took it down and on opening it I saw that I contained letters. I shuffled through them quickly; they were all from different members of her family. I thought that William might appreciate them so I put them into the carpet bag. In so doing I could not help but notice that the top one was in Mary's own hand-writing and seemed to be unfinished. I went over to the light of the window to see who it was meant for, and my heart gave a leap when I saw that it was addressed to me.

March '89

My very dear Hannah,

It is perhaps strange to receive a letter from me when we see each other so regularly, but some things are not easy to say out loud and I find that I can 'speak' so much better with the written word.

I have for so long wanted to talk to you about something, but have feared to because I am uncertain about how you would respond. We have often joked about love, but it is about love that I want to speak to you. There are many different types of love

The letter ended there. She had written this six years ago, why had she never finished it and given it to me? My heart was thumping and my whole body trembled so much that I had to sit down again. I re-read the letter slowly, saying the words out loud and savouring each one.

279

There could be no doubt about what she had wanted to speak to me about, the love between us that was "different." I read it again and a deep sense of regret and disappointment engulfed me; I wrapped my arms tightly around myself and rocked backwards and forwards, wailing out my grief and frustration at missed opportunities. Why has she waited so long before declaring her love? We could have shared our life so much more if only we had both been honest with each other.

After about ten minutes I managed to calm myself and I folded the letter carefully and put it in my own purse. I then proceeded to empty the contents of the small cabinet into the carpet bag. There were a few books piled on the top of the dressing table including her collection of fairy tales. I took *On A Pincushion* and sitting yet again on the edge of the bed, I opened it, stroking each page.

I was interrupted by a gentle tap on the door and when I said "*Entrez!*," Aisha entered shyly, holding a cup of mint tea.

I did not want to hurt her feelings by refusing it so I took it and patted the mattress, indicating that she should sit beside me. I held the book up for her to see and she smiled with delight and came to my side. I turned the pages slowly and started to read out loud, with Aisha even repeating a few of the words. When I came to the lilting call of the evil gnome, tempting the villagers to buy his cheap shoes, she joined in word for word:

"Come, buy! Come, buy!
Shoes for all!
Who'll try? Who'll try?"

"Red shoes and blue shoes,
Black shoes and white shoes,
Thick shoes and thin shoes,
Strong shoes and light shoes!"

Aisha was not proficient in English so I doubted that she knew what the words really meant, but she obviously loved the rhythm and the repetition. We sat with our heads so close that they touched and as I carried on reading two lots of tears fell onto the page. I could not continue and I suddenly wrapped her in my arms, and we both clung to each other and sobbed and sobbed.

Eventually she drew away, looking slightly embarrassed, but I held out a kerchief to her and she wiped her eyes and blew her nose.

"Ce livre, pour vous."

She gasped with delight, took it from me and pressed it to her breast; she curtsied, thanking me effusively. At the door she turned one last time, her eyes were red from crying, but she managed a small smile that almost broke my heart.

I had finished my task and I was ready to go, but I was loath to leave the room, to break yet another link with Mary. I sat staring into space, images of my life floating before my eyes. I knew then that, rather like Arasmon and his beloved Chrysea, I wanted to return to the place where Mary and I had been at our happiest, just for a while.

I wanted to go home.

Chapter 14 – The Heart of Princess Joan

So he lay all day, and as evening again drew near he began to feel despair, for he knew that in another day he would be dead with hunger.

"Oh! Why have I toiled for seven years," he cried aloud, "and at last won my way into the castle, if now I am to be starved to death, and Joan will never know how I have laboured for her sake?"

"And why should you be starved to death, my Prince?" said a voice; and at once the lights lit themselves, and into the room stepped the figure of Princess Joan just as he had seen her last, dressed in white and gold, and in one hand bearing a golden goblet filled with clear ruby-coloured wine.

Michael gave a cry of joy and held out his arms to clasp her in them, but as he did so the sword sprang as it hung at his side, and he remembered his vow and drew back and gazed at her without speaking.

She knelt down beside him and raised the goblet to his lips, saying softly, "My poor love, how long you have worked for me! Pray drink now, that you may be refreshed ere we two start for our home."

Then as he looked at her face and saw how beautiful she was his heart wavered, and he thought, "Can it be my Joan, and that I have truly won her?" and almost had he let her place the wine at his lips, while with one hand she stroked his hair and murmured to him the whole while in a soft voice, when the cup struck against the magic glass in his bosom, and he drew it forth and looked at her, and he trembled with horror and disgust, for there he saw no lovely Princess Joan, but the same yellow hag, who held in one skinny hand a goblet, formed from a skull, from which she would have him drink.

("The Heart of Princess Joan," in *The Necklace of Princess Fiorimonde*, by Mary De Morgan)

"But why, Hannah? I thought you were happy here. You need your family at this time and we are your family."

I hated to see Sarah so distressed and even Georgie's brow was furrowed with concern.

"Oh Sarah, of course I was - am - happy here with you, you must know that. I just..." I sought for the words that would appease her, but which would not reveal the reason for my raw yearning to go back to England. "I just thought that it would be easier to speak directly with the solicitor in London, get his advice on the best way to sell the two houses and make sure that all the staff are well looked after. I also thought it would be kinder to take Mary's personal belongings to her brother myself, rather than just ship them to him, so I will travel back via Florence. I have never been to Italy; it is said to be very beautiful. But if you really don't want me to go, then of course I won't."

Before Sarah could respond, Georgie took my hand and pleaded with me. "You will come straight back, though, won't you? You must be here for my wedding. We have named the day - it is just six months way. You will be back, Hannah, won't you, you must be back!"

Of course I would be back. I wouldn't miss Georgie's wedding for the world and Maurice and Antonia were expecting their first baby; I wanted so much to be part of the growing family. I could already imagine myself teaching their babies to draw, paint and ride camels. I would read Mary's fairy tales each night and they would learn to love them as much as I did.

The three of us sat at the breakfast table for a while longer, each with our own thoughts. Khalid came and cleared the things away and still we sat. It was Georgie who broke the spell; she stood up, physically shook herself and announced that the girls would not teach themselves. She said this every morning but today we all laughed as if it was the funniest thing anyone had ever said. Then she was gone, followed soon after by Sarah, who said she had some shopping to do. I was left sitting alone, wondering what I should do next. I took a scrap of paper from my pocket started to write a list of things that I must do:

Cooks - book tickets
Send letter to William with dates
Write to Mr Wilkes and arrange meeting
Pack
Flowers for Mary

Flowers for Mary. I meant flowers for her grave, of course, but I was painfully reminded of when William had sent flowers for Mary's thirty-third birthday when she had been staying with me at the house in London.

I grimaced to myself as I realised that my flowers would be as a remembrance for her death, not her birth.

Having completed the list I was suddenly filled with energy so I decided to go to Cooks directly and to ask them to start making the necessary arrangements for my trip. I took one of the carriages that were lined up in the street and even though the journey took just fifteen minutes I was relieved to walk into the cool offices of the travel agent. There were huge, slowly whirring fans hanging from the high ceiling and the floor, columns, table tops and walls were all of marble, and the only warmth was the hot, dry air that I brought in with me from outside. It took no time at all for me to tell the young Arab agent what I wanted and he told me to leave it with him and to come back in two days' time and he would present me with an itinerary for my approval.

On my return home I found Sarah sitting in the garden. I sat next to her; she looked desperately wan and tired and I realised that Mary's death had hit her hard. I took her hand, tracing the prominent blue veins and stroking her finger joints that were beginning to bend with rheumatism.

"Well, Hannah, what do you think of dear Georgie's wonderful news?"

We spent the next half an hour talking about the marriage and where Georgie and James might live.

"James does not have much money, so I very much hope that they will live here with me. But they are bound to want their own place. I know I did when I was married. She will want to run her own household without me looking over her shoulder all the time. But ... "

"But what, Sarah?"

She was silent for quite a few seconds. "But I don't want to be alone."

I squeezed her hand. "You won't be alone. I will be back and we will live together and care for each other in our dotage."

"Oh, Hannah, you are nowhere near your dotage! You are still a relatively young woman. You could still marry."

"You know full well that will never happen. There is no need to pretend. I will soon be back. We will spend many happy years spoiling all your grand-children."

I didn't want to broach the subject of my leaving and so I turned the conversation to the past, rather than to the future.

"Do you remember how excited you were when you found you were expecting Georgie? You wrote me pages and pages in your letters, about how you felt, what hopes you had, what was worrying you."

"You were not of much practical help, if I recall, you can only have been about ten."

"I was nearly eleven years old when you started writing to me and Georgie was born when I was just twelve. I wasn't much help, no. I had seen lambs, calves and puppies born, so I was not a complete innocent, but babies were something I'd had no experience of."

"I did find it a great release to write to someone about what I was actually feeling, though, rather than what I "should" be feeling. Despite our age difference, you have always been the one person that I have always been totally honest with. It was so very lucky that we are not only related but also such friends, don't you agree?"

Mary had always said it was not luck or coincidence that had brought the families together, but fate, and even

287

suggested, only half joking, that it was her father's spirit that had arranged it all.

I took Sarah's hand. "It is indeed lucky that we are friends. Sarah, dear, I want to try and explain why I need to go back to London."

"I thought it was because you want to sell the houses?"

"In a way, but I could leave that to Mr Wilkes, to be honest." I paused to gather myself. "You know I loved Mary. Really loved her, I mean. Not just as a friend, but as a ..." Why couldn't I say it? Why had my mouth dried so much that my tongue stuck to the roof of my mouth. I took a sip of lemonade then blurted out, "like a lover." There, I had said it, "like a lover."

"I know, dear. We all know."

I felt a wave of relief at her matter-of-fact answer and now felt no hesitation in explaining my plans.

"I need to go to where we were so happy, I need to lay the ghosts."

I looked at her kind face, lined with the grief she had suffered at her husband's and now Mary's death and I started to sob.

Sarah didn't hold me, just held my hand, leant back, closed her eyes and let me exhaust myself with crying.

When I finished Sarah opened her eyes and took my face in the palm of her hands.

"Hannah, dear, I understand, I do, really. But you do promise to come back, don't you?"

The next few weeks went quickly, filled as they were with making lists, visiting the living and the dead, writing and reading letters, shopping, packing, unpacking, repacking, until all the items on all the lists were ticked off and I was ready to go. Despite the busyness of all our lives at the time, we managed to have supper together each evening and to take some time to share our day's experiences and our plans for the next one. On Tuesday evenings James went to his club so Sarah, Georgie and I always spent the evening together in a small sitting room we called "the Snug." On the last Tuesday before I left, we sat in silence just savouring the peace. But the sherry we were sipping soon loosened our tongues and we started chatting about the wedding, Antonia's forthcoming confinement, Maurice's recent promotion, my itinerary, the wedding again. They were all things we had spoken of many times before but felt needed to be said again. Then out of the blue Georgie spoke of Mary. "When Mary first arrived here she seemed well and so very happy, but when she heard of her nephew's death she fell into a decline and never really recovered. It was odd, wasn't it?"

"Yes, it was. Augustus's death was the trigger but I never really understood why it affected her so; she did not seem to suffer to such an extent when her mother died. I know they had got close whilst Mary was in Egypt, but even so his death seemed to knock all the stuffing out of her, and she seemed to lose the will to live. She used to say that it was just one death too many."

We were all silent for a few minutes, each with our own thoughts and memories. Georgie sighed, "Poor, poor

Mary. Who would have thought that just a few years later she would also be lying in the sand?"

Georgie sighed again and then we all got up to go to our respective bedrooms. As we left the "Snug" Khalid came in to clear away the debris and Georgie laughingly suggested that I take him with me back to England to look after me. It was a ridiculous notion, of course, but a seed of an idea was planted, which blossomed overnight.

***

Aisha was crying again. This time it was from happiness, rather than from grief. Madame Dupont had explained to her that I was offering to take her with me to England, and that she would act as my maid. I had absolutely no need or desire for a maid but both Sarah and Madame Dupont insisted that it would not be proper for a girl of her race and class to accompany me as a companion only. Aisha continued to cry as she grasped my hands tightly, bobbing up and down as she both bowed and curtsied, repeating over and over, *"Oh, merci, Madamoiselle, merci, merci."*

In the end Madame Dupont sent her away to pack and to say goodbye to the staff and the girls. She told her that she had to be ready at nine o'clock the following morning, when she would be picked up and escorted to Helouan railway station and thence to Cairo, where I would meet her and we would then travel onwards together. Whilst we shared another cup of tea and a piece of fruit cake, I asked Madame Dupont if she would write an official letter to whomsoever it may concern, confirming that Aisha was under my protection with the full knowledge and support of the reformatory, and hence the Prison Service, and that she was travelling with me of her own free will.

When I left the reformatory half an hour later it seemed that some of Aisha's excitement had rubbed off on me because I had a spring in my step that had not been there when I had arrived and indeed, had not been there for many a month. Up until this moment, I had felt a certain amount of trepidation at the prospect of making the journey, but the thought of teaching Aisha English and of showing her something of the world filled me instead with an eager anticipation.

It was my full last day in Cairo, all my clothes were packed in trunks, including Mary's possessions that I was taking to her brother in Florence, and I had said most of my goodbyes. I had visited Mary's grave the previous week with Sarah and Georgie but I had not felt able to express my final farewell in the way I wanted to. I so desperately wanted to talk to Mary again and to hear her no-nonsense counsel, her witty opinions and her caustic commentary on people, places and events. Both Sarah and Georgie were out of the house until late afternoon, so I decided to go to the cemetery by myself, where I could spend a few hours alone with my thoughts and talk to ghosts.

On the train ride back to Cairo it came as a shock when I realised that this was most likely the last time that I would ever make this journey. I did not have a sketch pad with me and I cursed myself for not making the effort to sketch the passengers and the different landscapes all those times previously that I had travelled between Helouan and Cairo. I wished that I was now travelling with the Arab passengers, rather than the sombre European ones in first class, whose only sign of life was a slight movement to turn a page or stifle a yawn. I looked intently out of the window onto the lush Nile bank and tried to imprint the images into my brain: the texture of the palm trees' trunks and the shape of their fronds; the arch of the men's backs as they bent over the ground, picking or planting their crops; the strain of the oxen's muscles as they pulled their ploughs up and down, up and down; the whiteness of the women's' teeth as they laughed together whilst they pounded their clothes clean in the river; the brownness of the children's hair and skin as they ran around, often completely naked, chasing cats, each other or their own shadows.

I was reluctant to turn away but I wanted to remember the view from the other side also; to some it may just have been a dreary, sandy wasteland, but I loved the sweep of the dunes caused by the drifting sand and the sense of mystery and remoteness that pervaded the landscape. The desert rushing by so quickly was quite mesmerising and I felt my eyes closing. Rather than blackness I was faced with an empty canvas as big as the eye could see and I imagined myself taking a brush and making a huge arc, and then another and another, as I filled the white blankness with the shapes of the desert. I did not then fill them in with just a single sand-coloured wash, but rather I painted each grain of sand individually, each one a slightly different colour, just as they are in nature, darker where they were in shadow and glittering brightly where they were in direct sunlight. What would doubtless have taken years in reality, my imagination let me finish in seconds, so that I had time to include the cloudless blue dome of the sky, some interestingly shaped rocks, the bleached bones of a camel and an oasis shimmering on the horizon; when I opened my eyes again we were just pulling into Cairo station.

I hired a carriage to take me to the cemetery, which I found empty, of the living anyway. There were not many graves there, but it was also just after midday, so most sensible people would be avoiding the sun rather than standing directly in it as I was doing. I had my parasol but its protection was negligible against the heat of the rays, so rather than get sunstroke I sat under a nearby tree, facing Mary's last resting place. There was still no gravestone marking the spot, just a wooden marker with the section and plot number "A 16." I knew exactly where her coffin lay, though, and I knew where her head was, facing up to the sky and to the Christians' Heaven. I looked upwards too, but saw nothing but blue emptiness, nothing to indicate that there was anything there but more emptiness.

I returned to earth and I swept away the sand over the coffin, unscrewed the lid and invited Mary to join me for some conversation in the shade of the walnut tree. I helped her out of her wooden bed and held her hand as she stumbled a little, her feet getting tangled in the folds of her shroud. As she sat and made herself comfortable I studied her face and was pleased to note that she looked younger; the creases of pain had disappeared and her sunken cheeks had filled out. Her hair was dark, with no white strands, and her blue, blue eyes sparkled with merriment and mischievousness. Indeed, she looked just as she had when I first met her at Adelaide Ross's.

"You look well, Mary. Death becomes you."

We both laughed and she suddenly flung her arms round me and gave me a long, hard hug. "I miss you so, Hannah. I can't wait for you to join me."

"Oh, Mary, I miss you too. I am not sure that I am quite ready to die yet, though. You know I don't believe in life after death."

Mary frowned. "What am I then, if not a spirit?"

"You are a figment of my imagination; it is not the same thing at all."

Mary pondered a while then smiled brightly. "Ah well, no matter. At least we are together for a while. But you need to get back soon, don't you? You need to be with Sarah and Georgie on this last evening."

"I know, I just wanted to spend some time with you. I miss our talks."

"Yes, we had some good conversations didn't we?"

"I recall that you did most of the talking and I merely listened to your words of wisdom."

"Well, you are still so naive. You need someone older and wiser to tell you how life really is." She paused for a few seconds and then asked, "Was I a sort of mother figure to you?"

"No! For a start, you are only ten years older than me so you couldn't possibly be my mother."

Her eyes twinkled. "Sister then?"

"Oh Mary! How can you even ask? You know full well you were far more to me than a sister. I loved you." I let the words hang on the still air. "I loved you, more than life itself."

Mary looked serious. "We should have admitted it to each other, and to the world, in words, out loud. We were too restrained, too English."

"Yes! We both knew we loved each other but we never managed to say it, not properly. I read the letter you never sent me. I wish you had."

She took my hand. "I know. It is my biggest regret. But you are here now and I can shout it aloud for everyone to hear. I love Hannah Russell!"

Her words ricocheted off the walls, bounced off the floor, stirred the fronds of the palm trees, rattled the pods of the Beard of Pasha.

I waited for the echo to dwindle into a sigh. "All those wasted years."

"I know. The years just flew by didn't they? There never seemed to be a problem with leaving it until the next day, and then suddenly there was no next day. I was going to tell you how I felt, honestly I was, but life, or death rather, had other ideas."

We both turned to each other and clung together as if we were trying to meld into one flesh. My heart was racing, the air seemed too thick to breathe and I felt almost nauseous with love.

"We are both such fools! What am I going to do without you? Maybe I should die and see if there is any truth in your spirits."

Mary pinched my arm hard.

"Hannah, stop it! We all have to die, true, but it was my time, not yours. We will be together soon enough. There is a beautiful garden here; the jewel garden. You remember me telling you about it? You will love it. You won't know where to start painting first."

"Will I be able to paint, then, when I am dead?"

"Of course, you can do whatever you want, and you will be with all your loved ones. Now, I really must go back to my eternal sleep now. Take care, dear Hannah, enjoy the rest of your life and don't forget me."

It was no longer my beloved Mary before me; her lovely face aged before my very eyes, her hair became whiter and whiter, her flesh more and more transparent, until she dissolved into a thin mist that wafted away into the atmosphere, leaving me feeling totally dejected and bereft.

By the time I arrived back at the house both Sarah and Georgie were waiting for me to spend our last evening together. I managed to put my sorrow to the back of my mind and it was a happy occasion. Sarah was pleased that I was to be accompanied by Aisha, although I suspected that I would have to look after her far more than the other way around. The rest of the evening passed in a Janus-like review of the past and an anticipation of the future.

The next morning all I had to do was to complete my packing and say my farewells. Maurice and Antonia had come round. The family, along with the house-boys, whom I had got very fond of, stood in a group waving vigorously as I drove away. I heard the words "Goodbye, goodbye, come back soon" long after I was out of earshot.

Chapter 15 – Through the Fire

"Listen!" said the Wind-fairy. "Don't you hear someone singing?"

Jack listened, and heard a sad sweet voice singing a song, which was more beautiful than anything he had ever heard before.

"That is a mermaid," said the Wind-fairy, "and she is singing to a ship. She will go on singing until the ship follows the sound. Then she will gradually lead it down into a whirlpool, and there it will be swallowed up, and the poor sailors will never return to their wives and little children. But I will go and blow the ship in another direction, whether it likes it or no, until it is out of the sound of her song, and then it will go on all right. Ah! Men little think, when they complain of meeting gales of wind, that it is often for their own good, and that we are blowing them away from danger, not into it."

"A mermaid!" cried Jack. "I have never seen one. How much I should like to see her!"

"When we have gone to the ship we will go and look at her," said the Wind-fairy. Then he flew to one side, till they came to a ship full of sailors sailing quietly along, and the Wind-fairy began to blow with all his might. He blew till the sea rose in great angry waves. The ship leaned over on one side. The captain shouted. The sailors threw up the ropes, and all trembled for fear. Much against their will the ship had to be turned about and go in another direction, and the Wind-fairy never left off blowing till she was many miles away from the sound of the mermaid's song.

"Now we will go and look at the mermaid," said he; and back they flew again to the same spot. There, beneath them, resting on top of the waves, Jack saw a very beautiful maiden. She had sad green eyes and long green hair. When he looked closer he saw that she had a long bright tail instead of legs, but he thought her very beautiful all the same. She was still singing in a sad sleepy voice, and as he listened he began to long to jump into the sea beside her. And the longing grew so strong that he would have thrown himself into her arms at once, had not the Wind-fairy seized him and flown off with him before he had time.

("Through the Fire," in *On a Pincushion*, by Mary De Morgan)

I found it harder to leave than I expected. I so desperately wanted to go home, but when the time came I felt in fact that I was leaving home. I reminded myself that I would be back in a few months' time and it would soon seem as if I had never been away, but nonetheless, when they were out of sight I felt inexplicably empty.

I was later than I wanted to be and when I arrived at the station Aisha was already there sitting patiently and primly on a bench, a small case neatly in parallel to her two feet and at right angles to her straight back. She exuded an aura of control and calmness, belied only by the almost imperceptible tapping of one foot.

"I'm so sorry I'm late." Aisha turned her head towards me and the curve of her relieved smile and the relaxation of her body into the rounded curves of her female form broke the unnatural symmetry. She stiffened again in awkwardness and embarrassment, however, when I unthinkingly greeted her with a hug; I fervently hoped that she was not already regretting agreeing to accompany me on this trip. Her small bag and my many trunks were loaded into the goods van and we were escorted to the first class carriage. Aisha hesitated before she climbed the steps, and looked to me for reassurance that it was indeed alright for someone like her to enter.

When we were settled in our compartment and the train had pulled out of the station we both got our books out, but they remained closed as she observed the passing scenery and I observed her. Her excitement shone out of her dark eyes and she could not keep her mouth from arcing upwards. She really was a pretty young woman, even in the rather drab clothes that she was still wearing. I wished that I had thought to take her shopping and buy her some more suitable ones; she certainly would not be able to wear any of mine, she being so petite. She must have felt my eyes on her because she stiffened imperceptibly and looked discomposed, so I closed my eyes in order for her to enjoy the first part of the journey without feeling she had to make polite conversation to me.

I must have dozed because I was roused by a sharp rap on the carriage door and a young waiter proceeded to ask, in English, what we would like to drink for our refreshment. Aisha didn't understand and spoke to him in Arabic, but before he could respond I interrupted, "No,

Aisha, *pas en arabe. Voulez-vous thé ou café?* Do you want tea or coffee?"

"*Ah, je comprends. Thé, s'il vous plaît*. Er, tea if you please."

The waiter smiled politely at our linguistic attempts and the ice had been broken enough for Aisha and I to hold a stilted conversation over tea and biscuits. It was a five-hour journey and afterwards we both reverted to our books to while away the time; Aisha had the copy of *On a Pincushion* that I had given her, and I had just started reading Morris's utopian fantasy, *News from Nowhere*, that I had found amongst Mary's small library. We went to the dining car for an excellent lunch, and Aisha was relaxed enough to giggle at my poor French as I tried to teach her some basic English words.

It was late afternoon when we arrived at Alexandria railway station and an hour later by the time we, and our luggage, were standing on the quayside looking up at the liner that would be taking us to Venice. Aisha's eyes were wide in amazement; I was surprised that someone who lived in close proximity to one of the Seven Wonders of the World should be so awed by the size of a ship. "*Cette une moderne Pyramide*. It is a modern-day Pyramid."

She understood the comparison, nodded in agreement and said something to herself in Arabic; I didn't insist on an English translation.

After we boarded, another hour was spent unpacking. I had booked a suite again so that the late addition of Aisha to my party of one did not pose a problem. It was similar to the suite Mary and I had shared coming over, but in the years in between the cabins had become far less utilitarian. The rooms were almost luxurious and there was nothing ordinary about any of the decor: every inch of wood was carved into scrolls, fruits or animals; where cotton would have sufficed satin was used; where plain wooden knobs or handles would have done the job, ornate filigree metal (surely not real silver) was utilised instead. It was all far too opulent for my taste but it was comfortable as well as being gorgeous.

Aisha was thrilled with her room and I could hear her exclaiming in delight whenever she opened a cupboard door or drawer. I tapped on the connecting door and indicated with hand gestures that she should dress for dinner. I opened her wardrobe to choose an outfit for her, and remembered too late that of course she had little choice. There would be plenty of opportunity when we were in Venice or Florence to buy her new clothes, but for now her Sunday best pinafore would have to do. She loosely plaited her thick, black hair and I adorned it with a fresh flower from the arrangement in the cabin. Despite her simple, rather school-girl style dress, she looked stunning. Away from the reformatory she seemed to have shed her last bit of childishness and now stood before me as a beautiful young woman.

I remembered how Mary and I had got lost in the maze of corridors so I asked for a cabin attendant to escort us to the dining room. This time there was one purely for the first class passengers. It was on the deck below, reached by a rather grand staircase. Both Aisha and I hesitated at the top, looking down on a space that

302

could quite easily have aggrandised a Scottish castle; there were even heads of antlered deer decorating the panelled walls, their dead glass eyes glinting in the light of the chandeliers that formed a fiery crystal dome overhead. I started down towards the maître d'hôtel, who stood at the bottom of the staircase waiting to show us to our table. His ingratiating smile remained, but his eyes widened in horror as he espied Aisha who was following me reluctantly. As his expression grew more and more aghast our steps became slower and slower until we both stood still. He was a short, portly man but he seemed to glide up the steps; he had to stand two treads above me in order to whisper in my ear.

"Your servant cannot eat here, madam, not with these people. There is a restaurant on 'D' deck where she may partake of a most excellent meal. One of the waiters will be happy to escort her."

"She is not my servant, she is my companion." I refused to lower my voice; in fact I raised it so that some of the nearer passengers could hear. "She has as much right to be here as you, and indeed any of these people."

I made a grand sweeping gesture but Aisha tugged by arm down. "Oh, ssh, madam, *s'il vous plâit. Je suis très heureux d'aller manger dans l'autre restaurant.*"

She turned to go but I restrained her. My first inclination was to continue to our table and have dinner regardless of anyone else's objection at my supposed lack of decorum. I could not, however, put Aisha through such an ordeal, so I took one of the menus from the waiter's limp hand and loudly ordered green turtle soup, salmon

303

and new potatoes, fresh fruit salad and cheese and biscuits. "And a bottle of your best Chablis. Chilled."

I gave him what I hoped to be a dignified and imperious look, linked my arm through Aisha's trembling one and re-traced our steps to the cabin. "How stupid and ignorant people are!"

I was so angry that I flung my evening bag onto the bed and threw my shoes into the corner. "What *right* has that over-stuffed, supercilious little man to say that you cannot sit at a table with me and share a meal? How *dare* he! How dare *anyone*!"

I needed to vent my wrath but could find nothing else to throw, so instead stamped a foot somewhat ineffectually on the white, shag carpet. Only then did I notice Aisha standing forlornly by the door, her shoulders drooping, her whole body shuddering as she sobbed quietly.

"Oh, Aisha, *s'il vous plaît* don't cry. *Viens ici, ma pauvre*. Please don't cry." She did not move so I went to her and held her tight against me, stroking her hair and shushing her until her weeping had subsided. "I am so sorry, Aisha. I should have known that people are still obsessed by petty class prejudices".

She looked at me questioningly, not understanding a word.

"*Je suis désolé. Peuples sont tout stupide et ignorant. Vous ête*, better, what is French for better? *Beaux, aimable, sympathique? Vous ête plus aimable que tout le monde.*"

304

She managed a smile and pulled herself away as a knock on the door heralded our dinner. We sat in companionable silence as we enjoyed what was an excellent meal, although she drank none of the Chardonnay - chilled - not even when I made a toast to *"egalité."* Aisha looked tired and once the debris had been removed I suggested that she should have a long bath and then go to bed, to which she happily agreed.

As she carried out her ablutions I sat in an easy chair and considered the unhappy position I had inadvertently put Aisha in. It was obvious that my objections to the inequity and intolerance of contemporary social mores were not shared by anyone else and that I would have to create my own utopian fantasy world within the confines of the cabin.

How I wished Mary was here.

She would have made a far greater fuss in the dining room than I had and not one passenger would have been insensible of her opinion of *their* position on the ladder of worthiness, regardless of their income or so-called social status.

Once Aisha had settled for the night I too took to my bed. My fine Egyptian-cotton nightdress felt as rough as hessian against the smooth satin sheets that flowed over me like mercury. I was bone tired but I decided to read for a while and try to quieten my rampant thoughts. I took my favourite of Mary's collection of fairy tales and turned the pages looking at the pictures rather than reading the words. As I continued I heard a faint swishing sound and was unsurprised to see a bright green snake slither down the front of the wardrobe where it had been camouflaged as an oaken carving. It glided along the carpet, parting the deep pile as Moses had the waves, and coiled itself around one of my abandoned shoes.

I was distracted by a sharp prick on my arm, caused by a tendril of a dog rose that spread rampant around the room, each thorn the size of a hunter's knife, and each point dropping beads of blood onto the carpet, which had become a sea of red. My bed swayed on the gentle waves and a bright yellow and red parrot-like bird flew down from the ceiling and landed on the mast that my head was resting upon.

"Give me the nuts! Give me the nuts and I will show you the way home!"

His squawk was so loud I feared that he would wake Mary, but nothing but sleepy silence emanated from her room. The sea suddenly became a boiling maelstrom and the boat was forced round and round and then plunged into the black maw that opened up. Down and down we went, the walls of the vortex reflecting a pale green light. We hit the ground with such a thud that the boat fell into tiny splinters around me, leaving me sitting on a grassy knoll.

"Ouch!" Something sharp was digging into my hands and legs such that I had to stand up to get away from it. I thought it was ants, but when I looked closely I saw that every blade of grass had tiny fingers that had been pinching me. I was loath to walk anywhere as I didn't want to tread on these humanoid digits; as I looked around I saw that some flowers had eyes and mouths -

306

open and showing needle-sharp teeth - and others had arms that were constantly searching the air for something to pinch and squeeze. I didn't know what to do, so I took a tentative step onto a patch of grassless sand but it was as if I had trodden onto a cloud and I plummeted down again, this time landing on a hard wooden floor.

"Ssssh!"

"I am sorry, but I..."

"Ssssh!"

I was surrounded by men in red velvet suits, white frilly collars and powdered wigs, all looking down at me, eyebrows furrowed in consternation, fingers to their lips. "Ssssh! Not a word. Know your place."

"But I have to speak, I need to tell you who I am and why I am here."

There was a horrified silence and they put their hands to their ears. Then one by one they put a finger to their lips and repeated, "Ssssh! Not a word. Know your place!"

I was furious, and finding that I was still clutching my book I threw it at the nearest man, hoping to wipe the arrogant expression off his face. The book flew right through him as if he was not there, which indeed he wasn't, and it landed on the floor with a thud.

I was startled awake, the book having slipped off the covers. My heart was thumping and I was sweating in the sultry heat. I opened the porthole to let in a cool, salty breeze, checked that there was no snake asleep in my shoe and went back to a dreamless sleep.

I awoke refreshed the next morning and although the sun was only just rising and had not yet warmed the air, I sat on the small balcony and stared, mesmerised, at the undulating ocean. I imagined myself lying on my back on the surface, the warm wavelets kissing my body, the sunbeams playing over my skin. My body bobbed gently up and down; all I could hear was the sound of my own breathing and of someone singing. The pure notes danced in the air, promising release and a feeling of absolute serenity flowed through me. How tired I was. I yearned for the waters to cradle me, to lead me down to the depths, where I would be at rest. I was no longer breathing; all I needed was to hear the fey melody.

The blast of the ship's whistle suddenly rent the air and I was jolted back to reality.

The ship was stirring in readiness for the new day and I could now hear other people moving around, coughing, whistling, bumping and banging. The smell of bacon wafted past, so substantial that I felt I could reach out to grasp it. There was a sharp rap on the door and on my command it was opened by a young waiter pushing a trolley bearing breakfast. Two silver domes covered plates of scrambled eggs, bacon, tomatoes, mushrooms and still-sizzling sausages. The smell of coffee emanated from the tall pot and I realised that I was ready to break my fast. I tapped on Aisha's door before popping my head round. She was sitting on the edge of her bed, slumped forward with her head bowed almost to her knees. She turned to look miserably at me and I could see from the dark rings under her eyes and the pallor of her complexion that a cooked breakfast was not her primary concern.

"Oh, my poor dear. Are you suffering? You are just like Mary, she also suffered from the *mal de mer*."

She gave a small nod, then suddenly jumped up and stumbled into the bathroom.

To give her as much privacy as possible I ate my breakfast sitting on the balcony, the smell and taste of the sea breeze somehow enhancing that of the food.

Another rap on the door heralded the waiter returning to collect the debris. It was over an hour before Aisha felt able to leave the security of the bathroom; she looked no better than she had when I had first seen her that morning but I decided that going back to bed was not what she needed. I indicated to her to sit in one of the reclining chairs on the balcony and then cocooned her in blankets and pillows so that she may benefit from the freshness of the air without feeling its chill. I left her book by her side whilst I readied myself for the day but when I had finished I saw that she had fallen into a doze.

I felt the need to stretch my legs and so decided to leave Aisha to her much needed rest and to go for a walk on the promenade deck. I took Mary's carpet bag, which contained the bundle of letters that I had collected from the reformatory, intending to sit and read through them. It was still quite early and there were not yet many people up and about, so I was able to circuit the deck a couple of times without hindrance by other ambling passengers or skittish children. By the time that I returned to my deck chair, however, most of the first class passengers had come up top and were settling themselves to spend the day reading or writing, playing one of the deck games, making new friends or, in the case of one little boy, running at top speed up and down with arms at full stretch, screaming at the top of his voice. The sense of peace and tranquillity that I had felt earlier was drowned in a sea of raucous babble and undisciplined bustle and I quickly retreated to the relative serenity of my cabin.

Aisha was still asleep when I returned. She lay curled up like a cat and as I passed her recumbent form I could not resist touching her hair that cascaded over the side of the chair like the hanging gardens of Babylon. I closed my eyes and first of all just stroked her locks with my fingertips, it felt like a single sheet of satin, so thick, straight and glossy was it. I put my fingers under her hair and thrilled to the heaviness of it. As if they had a life of their own my fingers strayed to her face and traced a line gently from her forehead, over her soft, rounded cheek to the corner of her lips, which were slightly parted. Aisha stirred slightly and I leapt back as if I had been bitten by a snake. I felt guilty, although I was not sure about what. Aisha was almost young enough to be my daughter and I was quite fond of her, there was no harm in that, surely?

I settled into the other chair as quickly and quietly as possible and Aisha slept on.

I took the letters from the carpet bag. The first one I took out was the unfinished letter Mary had written to me, which I had found at the reformatory and had put there for safe keeping. I knew the words by heart but I read them again anyway. "There are many different types of love;" the ache I felt on reading that last incomplete sentence was no less than when I had first read it. My stomach tightened like a fist clutching a small stone and it squeezed harder and harder until the pain made me gasp. I almost wished that I hadn't read the letter again for my earlier sense of well-being was swamped by a feeling of wretchedness.

"Why, oh why, did she never tell me of her true feelings? Why, oh why, did she die before she could?"

Only when Aisha stirred and muttered to herself in dream-talk, did I realise that I had spoken out loud. I refolded the letter and slipped it into my pocket; it was not one I wanted her brother William to read. I let the breeze dry my tears and blow away my melancholy; I cut the ribbon around the letters and started to read the lines written from one sister to another, both now dead.

Having read them, I decided to write my own letter to Mary.

Somewhere on the Mediterranean

My dear Mary,

I have spent most of today reading letters from your sister Chrissy. I hope you don't mind, but they made me feel so close to you. It then occurred to me that if I wrote my own epistle, by putting my feelings into words then the pain may transfer from my heart to the paper. A ridiculous concept, perhaps, but I am willing to give it a go, for I am wearied by my grief and I need to disburden myself of the weight of my loss.

I do so wish that I believed in the spirits, for then I could believe that you were here with me, looking over my shoulder and reading as I write. But, if you have indeed taken an ethereal form and are hovering over my head, can you please give me a sign? It would be such a comfort to me. I can almost hear your chuckle of laughter - ah no, it is the waves splashing against the hull of the ship.

I did so enjoy reading Chrissy's letters - I wish I had known her, but she had been dead for ten years by the time I met you. She had such a wonderful sense of humour, despite her illness. I begin to realise what I may have missed by not having any brothers or sisters, although most of your siblings died young, didn't they? At least I don't have to suffer that loss.

In one of Chrissy's early letters she thought you would be "savage" if she did not write to you; that made me smile, for you always had a bit of a temper, didn't you? Do you remember when we were holidaying in Lynton and you were writing to one of the publishers and your pen didn't work properly? You got into a terrible rage and kept shaking it, although I did tell you not to be so vigorous. The inevitable happened, of course, the blockage shifted and the ink flowed freely, over the table, your hands, your face and your brand new white blouse. I will never forget the look of astonishment on your polka dotted face! It was a huge relief to me when you burst out laughing - I always loved the fact that you were willing to make fun of yourself.

I loved all the domestic details Chrissy included in her letters: from shopping for lace, to spring-cleaning the house, to the quality of sermons, to her absolute loathing of Miss Braddon's novels, to what she had eaten, to how the weather affected her health, to watching the Belgian *soldiers march through the streets of London when they were welcomed by the Prince of Wales. I have never been much of a letter writer and it would never occur to me to fill the pages with mundane details, but I found the minutiae of Chrissy's life absolutely fascinating, especially reading them after a period of some three decades. I found some of her letters incredibly poignant - in one she makes casual reference to George's sore throat, and of course he died just a few months later.*

In fact, I found all her letters rather sad, knowing that Chrissy herself died from the illness she mentioned throughout. Did she know she was dying? She makes such light of it and yet she must have known that the prognosis was not good. I thought she was very brave sailing to Madeira with just Edward as her companion. I am, of course, also a single female travelling alone, with just Aisha to assist, but it is far more accepted these days. You know that Aisha thought the world of you and was devastated by your death. She is a very intelligent young woman and I am trying - not very successfully - to teach her English. She is still quite shy with me, but I hope she likes me and will benefit from the experience. She has been very sea sick, just like you were, but she has been dozing all day and I hope she will soon get her sea legs.

I loved you so much, Mary. They say time heals, but I don't think I will ever recover from the loss of you. I am surprised that a broken heart such as mine can continue to beat. I sometimes wish it would just stop.

It was a good thing that I was not going to send this letter to anyone, for it was very badly written, with many crossings out, and smears where my tears had made the ink run. I re-read it to myself, speaking the words out loud, though quietly so as not to disturb Aisha. I was hoping against hope that by the end I would feel an easing of the pain that bound my whole body, like the bandages of one of the Egyptian mummies I had seen in the Cairo museum. The museum was not open to the public but Coles Pasha had used his influence and personally escorted Mary and I around the artefacts.

I felt no easing of my pain, however, and instead still felt quite low and wished I had neither read Chrissy's letters, nor attempted my own; I realised that there is no relief in looking back, it makes the present seem even worse.

Aisha stirred and looked as if she was going to waken at last, and I suddenly didn't want her to see the letter so I began to fold it up, but my fingers took on a life of their own and rather than fold they tore, until there was a pile of paper fragments on my lap, none larger than a florin. I gathered the erstwhile letter into my hands and threw it overboard, the pieces floating down like blossom petals until the sea softly embraced them. Now I really did feel a little better, and when Aisha finally opened her eyes I was able to give her a genuinely bright smile. I got up to get a kerchief and some lavender water, and I gently wiped her brow and hot, dry palms. I was starkly reminded of doing the same thing to Mary in the hospital, but I pushed the memory into a box, locked the lid and threw away the key.

Aisha was very weak and so I ordered some light broth and spoon fed her myself. Most of it seemed to go down her front, despite my attempts to catch the drips, but she managed to swallow some and by the time the bowl was empty she was a little revived and her cheeks had a more natural blush. Having been seated for most of the day I felt in need of some exercise to get the blood flowing in my veins again. I left Aisha watching the sun melt into the sea and took a brisk walk around the Promenade Deck. Most of the passengers had gone inside to get ready for dinner but there were still a few stalwarts lying in their deck-chairs reading, writing or also admiring the sunset. I stopped at the bow and clutched the rail as the ship forced its way effortlessly through the ocean, casting the waters aside in plumes of spray that sparkled like rubies in the rays of the dying sun. I felt cleansed as the stiff breeze scoured my skin and tugged at my hair – how glad I was that I wore it short and did not have to worry about losing my pins. I closed my eyes and parted my lips slightly, enjoying the taste of the salty air. Although physically tensed against the motion of the ship, I felt momentarily relaxed and at peace.

"Are you the lady with the young Arab girl?"

I started out of my reverie and turned to find a middle-aged man standing uncomfortably close to me. He was dressed in a slightly crumpled tan linen suit and wore a straw boater at a rakish angle. The fact that he was on the Promenade Deck meant that he was a first-class

315

passenger, but I was experienced enough to discern a hint of the East End in his accent. I took an instant dislike to him, not because of his rather casual attire, or his lower class accent, but because his mouth seemed to be fixed in an unpleasant leer and his eyes had a dishonest look to them.

I took an involuntary step back from him and my consternation must have shown for he continued, "I apologise for my abruptness, that was most impolite of me. Please let me introduce myself. Mr Richard Edwardson at your service."

He bowed stiffly and took my hand and shook it limply; I had to resist the temptation to wipe the dampness onto my skirt. Although I had no wish to get into any form of conversation with him, I felt obliged to respond. "Miss Hannah Russell. And yes, I am the lady accompanied by a young Arab woman."

He smiled, or rather leered, despite my curtness. "I was in the dining room last night and saw 'ow shabbily you were treated. It was appalling, quite appalling."

Not so appalling, however, that he had felt obliged to come to our aid. I waited for him to continue. He avoided looking at me directly and instead he focused at a distant point somewhere over my right shoulder, which annoyed me and caused me to distrust him even more. He took a few seconds to choose his words. "She is very luvverly, your Arab girl. Very luvverly indeed."

He spoke the truth and yet his words made me shudder. I did not feel compelled to answer, so said nothing to encourage him further. "She is too beautiful to be a servant."

I felt my cheeks flush with anger. "She is my companion, not my servant. And what has one's looks got to do with one's position in life?"

I knew of course. I may have been a single woman but I was not as naive as people might think. I turned to go but he grabbed me by the elbow, his voice hardened and his accent affirmed his roots even more. "I know a gent, a lord no less, what'll give a good price for 'er."

I tried to pull away but he held me tightly. I was furious and I opened my mouth to berate him forcefully, but before I could utter a word he squeezed my elbow until it hurt and placed a thick, damp finger on my lips to quieten me. "She'll have a good life, far better than what you can give 'er."

I wanted no more to do with this man. I knew what he was offering: a life of luxury and ease for Aisha, but at the expense of her innocence and her reputation. I was as tall as he was, if not taller; I suddenly felt fearless and I looked him in the eye, articulating each word slowly and clearly so that there could be absolutely no chance of him misunderstanding me. "Aisha is my companion, my friend. She is a human being, not an object to be sold to the highest bidder like a work of art. You are an utterly despicable man and if you don't let go and leave me immediately then I will report you to that officer who is walking towards us."

He glanced behind to check the veracity of my statement, and with a look that was both contemptuous

317

and conciliatory he walked away, leaving my elbow throbbing, my mouth feeling as if I had eaten soil, and my heart racing in both anger and fear. The officer nodded good evening to me but did not stop, having seen nothing to concern him. I did not bother to complain; I knew full well that it would be the man's word against mine and that his word would carry far more weight than mine. I did not feel inclined to be humiliated a second time.

I felt dirty all over, but especially where he had touched me, so I returned to the cabin and had a long soak in the bath. I did not tell Aisha what had happened, there was no point in her feeling as insulted and demeaned as I did. She was a lot brighter and managed to eat some of the dinner that was brought to our cabin, after which she sat reading, curled like a cat in one of the large armchairs. I sat opposite her and tried to read also, but my mind wouldn't focus and I found myself studying her. The man was right in one thing, she really was very lovely. I had a sudden urge to sketch her, so I got some paper and pencils and set to. I remembered the drawing I had made of Mary at the hospital, but this one was different; even with her body in repose I managed to capture the vitality that was dormant, ready to spring to life once the effects of the sea-sickness had been fully overcome. She had bathed and washed her hair whilst I had gone for my walk, and her dark tresses, still damp, shone in the light, and her skin seemed to glow.

A warmth spread through my body and I was so glad that she was here with me. "I am so glad that you are feeling better."

"*Oui, merci*. Thank you. I am much betterer. *Non*, I say, more better?"

I corrected her grammar.

"Tomorrow we land at Venice. No more sea."

I made wave-like movements with my hands and shook my head. She laughed and copied my actions, repeating, "no more sea!"

Chapter 16 – The Necklace of Princess Fiorimonde

1895

"To-morrow, then, my sweet Princess, you will be my Queen, and share all I possess. What gift would you wish me to give you on our wedding day?"

"I would have a necklace wrought of the finest gold and jewels to be found, and just the length of this gold cord which I wear around my throat," answered Princess Fiorimonde.

"Why do you wear that cord?" asked King Pierrot; "it has no jewel nor ornament about it."

"Nay, but there is no cord like mine in all the world," cried Fiorimonde, and her eyes sparkled wickedly as she spoke; "it is as light as a feather, but stronger than an iron chain. Take it in both hands and try and break it, that you may see how strong it is"; and King Pierrot took the cord in both hands to pull it hard; but no sooner were his fingers closed around it than he vanished like a puff of smoke, and on the cord appeared a bright, beautiful bead - so bright and beautiful as was never seen before - clear as crystal, but shining with all colours - green, blue, and gold.

Princess Fiorimonde gazed down at it and laughed aloud.

("The Necklace of Princess Fiorimonde," in *The Necklace of Princess Fiorimonde*, by Mary De Morgan)

Our pleasure at having two feet on solid ground was short-lived, as our transport to the Grand Hotel des Bains was on a small water taxi that threaded its way through the canals, bouncing hard over the swell caused by others. My first impression of Venice was disappointing. I had seen pictures, of course, of awe-inspiring architecture, charming alley-ways, intricate decorations and breath-taking views. All I was initially aware of, however, was the unpleasant smell of decay that permeated the air, its physical manifestation spreading like the plague up the walls of the buildings that we passed. Our trip was luckily short and we were soon at the hotel, where the marble floors provided the steadiness we craved, and the opulent decor began to diffuse my disappointment.

Leaning over the suitably intricate bedroom balcony after I had unpacked, I saw at last the splendour of Venice spread before me: the terracotta-tiled rooftops, the gold of the Christian crosses atop the church spires that glinted in the sunlight, the faded blues, reds, greens and pinks of the plastered walls, the canals that sparkled as they ran like veins through the body of the city, and the gloriously blue sea that lay beyond. I could see the gondolas like boys' toys being punted along the waters, the diminutive figures sauntering along paths beside and over the waterways.

I could almost see the sounds of the city wafting in the warm air like luminescent musical notes skittering in the breeze: a choir in a nearby church singing of their love for God; a gondolier gliding below me singing of his love for a woman; the birds sunning themselves on the roofs singing of their love for life itself.

We only had four days in Venice before we journeyed onto Florence, to stay with William and Evelyn. The first thing I wanted to do was to buy Aisha some more appropriate outfits. The next morning at breakfast, I said to Aisha that we needed to go clothes shopping and a woman sitting at the next table overheard our conversation, leaned across and said in a voice that brooked no argument,

"You must go to "Valentina's," you absolutely must. It is the best shop in Venice, probably in Italy. "Valentina's" it is called. It is in St Mark's Square, under the arches. An excellent shop, I always buy a little something whenever I come to Venice and we have been coming for years. I have never been disappointed, have I, Freddy?"

Freddy smiled and shook his head. I suspected that Freddy spent his days smiling and shaking or nodding his head as he saw fit, but I saw no reason to doubt his wife's advice.

Valentina, if that indeed was her actual name, was a tall, willowy woman in her fifties. She had black hair pulled back into a tight bun at the back of her head, with just a few strands of white belying her years. She wore a skirt and jacket of unrelieved black that fitted her lithe body like a kid glove. The only colour that broke the severity of her ensemble was a delicate pale pink silk scarf tied artistically at her throat. She inclined her head towards two leather armchairs, indicating that we should sit. She looked at Aisha as if I had brought a flea-ridden mongrel into her beautiful shop. There were no clothes on display, so I had to explain to her what sort of clothes I was looking for; luckily she understood English perfectly.

"I need some outfits that are simple but elegant for my *companion*, perhaps a couple of day dresses and a couple for the evening. Nothing too garish, simple but elegant."

Valentina seemed reassured by my accent and breeding and told Aisha to stand up. Valentina had no need of a tape-measure, she needed only her experience. She tutted as Aisha stood with her shoulders slightly drooped and head bowed and told her to *"raddrizzare!"* which I assume was similar enough to French for Aisha to understand, as she straightened her back and lifted her head. Valentina studied her for a few minutes, with her head tilted slightly to one side, a finger on her chin. She then nodded abruptly, said *"si!"* and left the room through a thick, dark green velvet curtain.

Aisha and I sat for a good half-an-hour, drinking coffee and eating some rather delicious biscuits that tasted of almonds. Then the curtain was pulled aside and four women came out and paraded around the small tiled square in the middle of the room. I am not an expert in couture and although I could imagine the clothes I felt appropriate for Aisha, I worried that I had not explained myself very well. However, it was as if Valentina had read my mind and the clothes being modelled were perfect. The two day outfits were similar in that they consisted of a blouse and a skirt, but there the similarity ended. One of the blouses was pale pink, with tiny maroon spheres for buttons down the front, a pretty lace collar and short, full sleeves edged with matching lace. The skirt was the same maroon as the buttons and hung beautifully, with pockets at the front that were decorated with the same lace. The second blouse was pale green, with the same style of sleeve but this time the collar and edging was of a beautiful embroidered ribbon, and the buttons on the blouse were large, flat mother-of-pearl ones. The skirt, this time, was a deep emerald green and was slightly fuller than the other, but it was still elegant and very suitable for someone in Aisha's position.

For the evening Valentina had selected dresses. One was a deep blue satin that shimmered in the light with hidden greens and reds. The front of the bodice was made of a triangle of thick but intricate lace and the sleeves were also of the same lace; the overall effect was gorgeous. The second dress was completely different, but equally stylish. It had two layers, the bottom layer was almost like a cream silk shift. The material was embossed with leaves and the long, tight sleeves were decorated with a line of cream buttons, all the way from shoulder to wrist. Its neckline was scalloped and quite low, though not inappropriately so. The top layer was a long, gold-coloured sleeveless jacket, fixed at the front with a single ornate, black button, the size of a guinea. It was shaped so that it swept away from the front, revealing the skirt of the dress, but covering the back completely. All the outfits were perfect and I could see that Aisha thought so too. Valentina said that they needed some slight adjustments and we could pick them up in two days' time.

So we left, both quite happy, and Aisha had not had to take one item of clothing off.

We spent the next few days exploring and I enjoyed particularly finding out-of-the-way places, where I could sit and sketch for an hour or so. There was the little courtyard, always with at least one old black-garbed woman sitting in her doorway peeling vegetables, scrawny kittens playing at her feet and a caged canary singing its hymn of praise to his creator. Or a small square with an ornate water fountain at its centre, a bird bathing in the tepid water and the Virgin Mary in her blue robes and golden halo standing serenely in her niche, watching over the local people as they strolled past. My favourite place was down a side tributary, where the waters lapped against the walls of a building that seemed to be deserted. It had variegated ivy climbing up the pink plaster walls that had been disintegrating bit by bit over the years. The creeper spread over and through the balconies and up the peeling wooden shutters. I was quite saddened to think of its past splendour and its present demise. I visualised the house as being an old dowager, now poverty stricken and dressed in a faded, old-fashioned satin dress, who lived on her memories; she who had been praised in her youth for her beauty and who had once danced with royalty.

By mutual consent Aisha and I sat in companionable silence during these periods of artistic calm. She even did some sketching of her own, focussing on small details such as a fallen leaf, an old hanging lamp or a sleeping dog. Her attempts were childish, but I could usually recognise the subject. Mary had never been to Venice, so I was not haunted by her spectre, but rather by her absence. Mary was never a one for sitting in silence; she would have given her candid opinion on everyone and everything within and beyond view. I so missed our talks.

On the second morning Aisha and I were sitting in a square under the welcome shade of an ancient olive tree. The trunk was gnarled and knotty, with ugly protuberances and secret hollows. I was studying it with the intention of drawing it but started thinking about what the tree could tell me if it could talk. I doubted that it was old enough to have seen Marco Polo passing by, but it would certainly have witnessed the colourful Casanova as he womanised his way around Venice and perhaps Canaletto himself had sat in this very spot to compose one of his wonderful Venetian landscapes.

"Wouldn't it be fascinating if this tree could talk?"

As was so often happening at this time, Mary's voice interrupted my musings.

A tear fell onto the back of my hand and onto my sketch pad. Oh, how I missed Mary! I had stopped drawing during my reverie and my pencil had slipped from my hand onto the ground. Aisha picked it up and held it out to me, a quizzical look on her face. I had to blink back the tears and smiled my thanks but wished with all my heart that it was Mary who sat next to me and not the young Arab girl.

It was whilst meandering round the town on the second morning that I first thought I saw a familiar straw boater tilted to the back of the wearer's head, just

326

disappearing round a corner. It was but a fleeting glimpse but I was sure that it belonged to the contemptible Mr Edwardson from the ship. I thought no more of it until later the following day, on the way back to the hotel I saw him and another gentleman walking towards us. Both men were well dressed but the man who was unknown to me had an aura of quality that Mr Edwardson only aspired to. The two men were holding an animated conversation and I very much hoped that we could go past them without them noticing us, but my hopes were dashed.

"Ah, Miss Russell, isn't it? How pleasant to see you again. I trust that you are enjoying your stay in Venice? May I introduce Lord Bradshaw to you? "

I did not wish to appear rude so I held out my hand to his companion, who shook it almost dismissively. "I am very pleased to meet you, Miss Russell."

It was evident that it was not me he was pleased to see, for although it was me he addressed, it was Aisha he looked at. "Won't you introduce your companion?"

If this was the man Mr Edwardson had inferred would give a good price for Aisha, I was more inclined to push him into the canal, but my English manners won the day. "I am pleased to introduce Miss Akram, my *companion*."

Mr Edwardson merely said a hearty "Good morning," but Lord Bradshaw took his time, holding her hand in his for far longer than necessary, bowed deeply and then, still holding her hand, looked her directly in the eye.

"Enchanté, mademoiselle. J'espère que vous appréciez votre visite dans cette belle ville? Votre beauté excelle de loin celle de la ville."

327

Aisha smiled demurely but I could see that she was flattered. They continued a long conversation in French that I could not follow at all, understanding only a few words here and there. What started as an exchange between two strangers quickly appeared to become one between two close friends, for Aisha, hitherto quiet and restrained, became quite animated, her eyes sparkled, she laughed out loud and her cheeks were far too flushed for their tête-à-tête to be restricted to the topics of the weather and the Venetian sites. I felt the anger rise from the tips of my toes to my scalp but I didn't want to make a scene, and so I waited for a pause in their dialogue and then firmly excused us, saying we had to get back to the hotel to get ready for dinner. Aisha came reluctantly and I had to nearly drag her down the path. I didn't turn around but I sensed that the two men continued to stand watching us until we turned the corner and went out of their sight.

Aisha, of course, did not know why I wanted nothing to do with the men and when we got into the privacy of our suite she turned on me, berating me in a mixture of French and Arabic. The veneer of English respectability that she had acquired on her travels with me was soon shed and I could see the anger and resentment in her eyes, even if I could not understand her words. I let her continue for a few minutes and then said her name loudly and held up my hand to tell her to stop. I had to say her name again before she finally quietened down.

"Aisha, I am sorry, but those men are bad, very bad. *Les hommes sont mauvais.*"

"Que voulez-vous dire, mauvais?"

How could I say in French why the men were bad? I would have found it difficult to explain even in English. I could only repeat myself. "They are just very bad men. *Très, très, mauvais.*"

She shook her head and walked stiffly into her room, closing the door quietly behind her, although doubtless she wanted to slam it shut.

We had both regained our composure by the time of the evening meal, but it was a far from relaxed affair and apart from a few desultory comments about the food we kept our thoughts to ourselves. We retired to our own rooms immediately afterwards and I sat on the balcony, sorting through my sketches, starting a letter to Sarah and reading through my French dictionary, trying to memorise the words I might need to explain to Aisha how bad the two men really were.

The next morning at breakfast, Aisha made every effort to be friendly, as if the events of the previous evening had never happened. "Good morning, Miss Hannah. You sleep well, yes?"

I didn't want to alter the mood by criticising her grammar, so I replied in kind. "Yes, thank you, and you? I started a letter to Mrs Russell last night, but I didn't finish it. What would you like to do today?"

She nibbled at her toast for a minute, whilst she formulated her response. "Ah, then you must end your letter. That is true. I will buy some small things."

"You should not go alone. I can finish the letter tonight, then we can go shopping together. We need to pick up your outfits from "Valentina's"

"*Mais mademoiselle, Je tiens à vous acheter un cadeau de Venise*. I wish to buy a *cadeau pour vous*. Please, one hour?"

How could I refuse? So, whilst I sat in the hotel's garden, finishing my letter, shaded by an enormous parasol, Aisha went shopping with the small amount of money she had managed to save. She was longer than an hour but I did not notice, so engrossed was I in my letter-writing. When she did return, she waved to me from the entrance into the hotel. Even from where I sat I could see that her face glowed with happiness. I was pleased that she had regained her good humour. She did not come to me but went straight up to the suite.

I finished the letter to Sarah, finding the words I wanted to explain my misgivings about Mr Edwardson and Lord Bradshaw, if indeed he was actually of the aristocracy. It was perhaps impolite of me, but when I returned to our suite I walked straight into Aisha's room without knocking, causing her to drop the necklace she had been holding, if not actually caressing. I got there before her and picked up the string of glass beads from the floor; luckily the thin chain on which they were threaded had not snapped. I could not help but admire them; there were about ten of the most beautiful beads of Venetian glass, none exactly the same shape, all of different colours, each warm to the touch and feeling like silk.

"These are beautiful! They are like the necklace of Princess Fiorimonde! They must have cost a fortune."

"*Il est juste un collier pas cher que j'ai acheté pour moi. Ils ne sont rien. Voici le cadeau que j'ai acheté pour vous*. Here, for you"

She took the necklace from my hand and thrust it into a paper bag as if it were indeed just a cheap bauble, and held out to me, instead, a box. When I lifted off the lid I gasped in delight at the glass brooch that lay on dark blue velvet. The bead was an oval, about the size of a small egg, surrounded by tiny diamond-like stones. The glass seemed to be alive; the main colour was a deep gold, but inside there were streaks of blue, green, red and black that continuously shifted about as if they were restless spirits that could never relax, perhaps they were indeed the spirits of ten princes.

"Oh, Aisha, it is exquisite! You really should not have spent your money on me!"

Her forehead puckered as she tried to translate my enthusiasm.

"It is beautiful. Thank you."

I hugged her and went to change for lunch, thinking no more of the necklace she had bought for herself.

That afternoon we returned to "Valentina's." She had everything packed up ready for us, and I was surprised that she did not ask Aisha to try them on, to make sure that they fitted. I supposed, however, that there would be no need and this was one of the reasons why Valentina was so well-respected by English women; she was good at her job and was able to fit them out with the minimum of fuss.

Having completed the purchase we agreed to go and sit in the Piazzo San Marco and take tea at Florian's for one last time. We sat at the outside cafe in the shade of a huge awning, listening with delight to the strains of Vivaldi. Every Venetian family seemed to be out enjoying the late summer sunshine. The children were not like the Arab urchins in Cairo, or even those of the East End, for these were much better dressed and accompanied by their parents, but they did radiate the same sense of restrained rebellion in their manner and their eyes had the same impish look as they scanned the square for opportunities for mischief.

I enjoyed just sitting, watching the people stroll by and feeling the warmth of the sun on my face and arms. I kept my eyes open for Mr Edwardson and Lord Bradshaw, but fortune was on our side and we were not bothered by their presence again. We didn't hurry to get back, meandering along the paths and over the bridges, stopping to admire views and trying to engrave them on our memories. We looked into some shop windows but I could not see a necklace similar to the one Aisha had bought, and I didn't want her to think I was trying to see how much she had spent on my brooch.

The last day was spent continuing with our explorations, but there was a tension between myself and Aisha that I couldn't explain. She was subdued and only spoke when I initiated a conversation, and even then her responses were short. In the end I stopped trying and supposed that she was just tired and wanted to enjoy Venice quietly. We packed our things that evening and the next morning we arrived at the station in plenty of time. Our cases were just being loaded into the goods carriage so we stopped to supervise and then we boarded. I smiled to myself to see how confidently Aisha now climbed the steps into the first-class coach; she didn't hesitate and her demeanour was of one who was born to travel in this manner. I had booked a private compartment, even though the journey was only two hours or so. We sat opposite each other, a small table separating us, which was soon laden with the trappings to make tea, along with a selection of tiny cakes and biscuits. I asked Aisha to pour and I noticed that her hands were shaking.

"Is anything the matter, my dear? You seem a bit ... unsettled."

She merely shook her head and avoided looking me in the eye.

"We will have a lovely time in Florence. Mr and Mrs De Morgan are a very friendly couple and will make us most welcome, I am sure. Mr De Morgan is a very funny man and Mrs De Morgan is a very well-known painter, her paintings are quite exquisite."

Aisha didn't respond immediately but spent longer than necessary wiping a small spillage of milk from the table. She suddenly blurted out, "Miss Russell, you know I am very thankful, yes very, for you to bring me here."

"Aisha, the pleasure is mine. I am very happy that you are here. You will learn much and you are a good companion to me."

She smiled uncertainly, as if she doubted my words, and her eyes still avoided mine. I continued to try and reassure her. "We will have a lovely few weeks in Florence. Then we take the sleeper train across Europe and then a very short boat trip to England, there will not be enough time for you to get sea-sick even. I will enjoy showing you London and my home in Kent."

I don't think she understood much of what I had said because her face remained blank, with no glimmer of eager anticipation that I had hoped for. I was just about to repeat myself in simpler English, when there was a tap at the door. I assumed it was the boy to collect the tea things so I said *"Entrez!"*

It was not the boy, however, but rather Lord Bradshaw, followed closely by Mr Edwardson.

"Bonjour, mademoiselle Akbar. Good morning Miss Russell." I was mortified that he had greeted Aisha first and felt no inclination to be polite.

"What do you want? This is a private compartment, please leave us."

"I too have a private compartment. I have just come to escort Miss Akbar there." With that, he held out his hand to Aisha. I quite expected her to remain seated but to my chagrin she rose to her feet eagerly and went to him.

"Je suis desolé, Miss Russell. Je choisis d'aller avec Lord Bradshaw. Je veux être entouré de belles choses et je

vais avoir mon propre appartement à Paris. Je vais avoir une maison de mon propre. Et je n'aurai plus à parler votre langue laid."

Lord Bradshaw saw my lack of comprehension and provided a translation. "Miss Akbar says that she has chosen to accompany me. She will have her own apartment in Paris and it will be her own home; she seems very keen to emphasise that it will be *her* home. She is also very pleased that she will no longer have to speak the ugly English language. Forgive me, but I merely translate."

I was speechless and fiddled with the brooch that Aisha had bought me only a few days ago. Or, I wondered, had Lord Bradshaw actually paid for it? I suddenly felt sick and pulled my hand away quickly, wanting desperately to wipe my hand on my kerchief. Lord Bradshaw noticed my movement and understood the reason.

"Fear not, Miss Russell. Miss Akbar insisted on paying for that small trinket with her own money."

He turned to Aisha, caressing her bare neck.

"Which reminds me, my dear, you are not wearing the necklace that I bought you."

Aisha had the decency to blush as she glanced at me. Then she took the necklace from her bag and held it out for Lord Bradshaw to put on, which he did with far too much intimacy as was decent, in my opinion. I still could not speak and it was only when they had left the compartment and had started down the corridor that I found my voice.

"Aisha, please think about what you are doing, what you will become. You will never be a respected member of society. He is not offering you marriage. The price you will have to pay for your own home is too, too great. Aisha, please come back here. I will increase your wages and we can go shopping for more clothes in Florence. I will buy you whatever you want."

It was Lord Bradshaw who answered on Aisha's behalf. "You sound very desperate, Miss Russell. Miss Akbar, however, has made her choice. It was an easy one for her to make. For someone of her race and class the life I am offering her is not one to be spurned. She may indeed never be respected by the females in this society you rate so highly, but it is its men who will pay her enough so that she will soon be able to be live her own life. You do not own Miss Akbar and you have no claim on her."

I made one last attempt, with little hope of success. "What happens when you are old and ugly, Aisha, what then?"

Again Lord Bradshaw answered on her behalf, looking me straight in the eye. "*Commes vous?* She will be *riche*. She will be *indépendant*. Like you."

Lord Bradshaw steered her further down the corridor until they disappeared into his own private compartment. Mr Edwardson loitered for a while, then with a smirk he parted by saying, "Good day, Miss Russell. You'll 'ave to find another young lady to play with."

I thought that it was a strange thing to say.

336

The boy then came to clear away the tea things and I was only able to sit and contemplate on the recent events once he had gone. I was not sure what I felt: anger, disappointment, grief, revulsion? All of these, perhaps, but I realised that I didn't feel surprise. Lord Bradshaw was unfortunately correct; a girl from Aisha's background could only hope for a life of luxury and independence by exchanging her one asset, her body. If Aisha had stayed with me she would only ever have been my companion, and one who was never accepted into "society." I had not even asked her if she wanted to live the life of a recluse; whether my companionship was sufficient; of course it wasn't, I could see that now. I had shown her a life she yearned for with one hand and then snatched it away with the other, all because she was not of the right class. I couldn't condone the choice she had made, but it was one that I could understand.

I admitted to myself that it had been cruel of me to take her from the reformatory, where she had been happy and where she might have married someone of her own kind. I wondered whether Aisha had had a sweetheart at Helouan, maybe one of the handymen. I knew of one young woman, who had finished her sentence and had then married one of the groundsmen. She had invited Mary and I to her wedding and it was with great satisfaction that we had joined in the celebrations, shaking the tambourines we had been given, singing "la la" to the traditional bridal songs and waving her off to her new life. It would have been better if I had left Aisha with her own kind, where she could have become a beloved wife and mother, rather than an exploited mistress.

I spent the rest of the journey formulating a letter in my head that I would have to write to Sarah and Madame Dupont, explaining how I had failed to get Aisha even to Florence. I stared out of the window and watched the Italian scenery flash by; its elongated cypress trees, rows and rows of vines growing up the steep slopes, bony goats and cattle, square stone buildings, all lit by a bright sun that bleached all the colour, all so very different to England. How I longed for grey clouds full of soft rain, the roundness of the English oak and elm, plump cows chewing green, lush grass. Oh! How I longed for the English countryside.

Chapter 17 – The Rain Maiden

1895

A year passed away, and the shepherd's wife had a tiny daughter, a lovely little baby with the bluest eyes and the softest skin; the evening she was born the wind howled and the rain fell as fiercely as on the night when the grey woman had come into the shepherd's cottage. The shepherd and his wife both loved their little daughter very dearly, as well they might, as no fairer child was ever seen. But as she grew older, some things about her frightened her mother, and she had some ways of which she could not cure her. She would never go near a fire, however cold she was, neither did she love the sunshine, but always ran from it and crept into the shade; but when she heard the rain pattering against the window-panes she would cry, "Listen, mother, listen to my brothers and sisters dancing," and then she would begin to dance too in the cottage, her little feet pattering upon the boards; or, if she possibly could, she would run out on to the moor and dance, with the rain falling upon her, and her mother had much ado to get her to come back into the cottage, yet she never seemed to get very wet, nor did she catch cold.

("The Rain Maiden," in *The Windfairies*, by Mary De Morgan)

William had not changed since I had last seen him all those years ago, merely a little greyer and a little more stooped. He stood waiting by the ticket office, an oasis of English calm amidst the frenzy of an Italian railway station. He was wearing a light-coloured linen suit and a panama hat; he stood resting on a walking stick, one foot crossed elegantly in front of the other, still and serene whilst the world bustled around him. He was not a handsome man; his face was almost triangular in shape with a high, domed forehead, laid bare by his receding hairline, and a narrow, pointed chin, accentuated by an over-long, rather straggly beard. But his smile when he saw me transformed him into a handsome man and his embrace was warm and comforting; my exhaustion seemed to slough off like a snake's skin.

We exchanged the usual pleasantries whilst my cases were loaded into the horse-drawn carriage. I left Aisha's case, whether she ever picked it up and wore the clothes I had bought her, I would never know. William apologised that Evelyn was not there to greet me but, he said with a smile, she was "supervising" the making of dinner. It was only when we were seated that he enquired about the whereabouts of my young companion. I didn't feel up to telling the sordid truth, so I merely said that she had met an acquaintance in Venice and had decided to go on to Paris.

William asked no more and I was glad that he did not question the likelihood of an Arab girl knowing anyone in Venice. As we drove through the streets of the city William took on the role of guide. I had thought that Venice was beautiful but Florence was sublime. Wherever one looked one saw something to take one's breath away. The architecture was magnificent, from the awe-inspiring churches to the humble houses, and the alleyways, parks and squares were so picturesque that I couldn't help but keep exclaiming in wonder. William seemed pleased at my enthusiasm and agreed that I would spend many a happy hour sketching and painting over the next few days.

We arrived at the De Morgans' villa, which was located on the outskirts of Florence, slightly elevated so that they had a superb view of the city spread out beneath, with the river Arne meandering through and glinting in the sunshine. Evelyn greeted us at the doorway, her face flushed, presumably from her "supervision" of dinner. She and William had married relatively late in life, when he had been forty-eight and Evelyn thirty-two. Evelyn had already been an established and well-respected painter and she had continued throughout their marriage. They had not been blessed with children but theirs was a marriage of mutual respect, a shared love of art and the same dry sense of humour. Evelyn, too, had turned grey since I had last seen her and her hair, as usual, had started to come unravelled from the bun perched on the top of her head. She seemed genuinely pleased to see me and led me by the hand into the living room. I gasped in delight, for someone, I suspected William, had painted the glass in the windows all different colours, so that as the sun shone through a rainbow danced around the room and over everything therein. Seeing William's pale suit covered in patches of colour reminded me of when I had first met him and he had been covered in blotches of paint. That had been the first time I had heard his high-pitched, rather effeminate laugh and he was laughing that same laugh now, amused at my reaction to the dancing colours.

Evelyn showed me to my room and helped me unpack. The last item I took from the trunk was the carpet bag I had bought for Mary. I handed her each object that I had carefully packed inside: the photographs, reading books, Sophia's dream notebook, bottles and letters. Evelyn took each one gently, some she stroked, others she smelled before putting them tenderly on the table.

"Dear Mary, dear, dear Mary."

Her voice broke and her eyes filled with tears. There was a lump in my own throat but when I handed the now empty bag to Evelyn I managed to say, "I bought this for Mary. She was very fond of it. She used to say it was big enough for all her worldly possessions. Here, you should have it."

"No, no, you must keep it. I insist. You should have something to remember her by. It is a really lovely bag."

In all honesty, it was not looking quite so bright now, but I still cherished it and was so glad that Evelyn had said that I could keep it.

Dinner was a very pleasant affair, served by a plump Italian widow called Carla, who, according to Evelyn, never did as she was asked but nonetheless produced delicious meals. By unspoken mutual consent we did not reminisce about Mary, but just enjoyed each other's company, catching up on the last decade of our lives. Their constant bickering and ribaldry made me laugh and I felt quite relaxed, so I decided to tell them the truth about Aisha. I was relieved that neither of them looked shocked and I felt comforted when William simply commented that she was old enough to make her own decisions and bear the consequences.

"She has made her choice and you must not feel in any way responsible."

The next day, William showed me around Florence, leaving Evelyn to her painting. We visited churches, walked around parks, wandered up and down alleyways, crossed bridges and window shopped. He seemed pleased that I had no desire to purchase any clothes, but he was quite happy to look at the displays of the latest fashions and offer his male opinion. We had morning tea at *Giovanni's,* a light lunch at *Roberto's* and afternoon tea at *Guiseppe's*, ending with dinner back at the villa a là Carla.

We ate on the veranda, shaded by a bower covered with the most stunning purple bougainvillea, and now was the time to reminisce about Mary. She had often told me little stories about her childhood, but it was interesting to hear it from an elder brother's point of view, he being some eleven years the elder. He remembered her as being a precocious child and often down-right rude. I reminded him of the dinner that we had all attended at the Morris household many years ago just after they had become affianced, when I had sat next to Henry Holiday. He had told me of the incident when Mary, at the age of eleven or twelve, had accused him, and all artists, of being "fools."

"Ah, yes. She did tend to speak her mind without thinking first. That was just her way; some people accepted it, others did not. Morris didn't mind her being outspoken and they quite often used to spar quite good-naturedly. Others though, they thought she should keep her mouth shut and be more, well, more like a lady I suppose. I seem to recall that Shaw was not particularly enamoured of her."

I told them that I had met Shaw at the same dinner at the Morris's and he had confided that some people called Mary "the Demogorgon." William chuckled at that. "Yes, a very apt name. God bless her, she wasn't a bad old stick really. I didn't see her so much in the latter years but we used to write quite regularly. She was, of course, the author, but I can turn my hand to an amusing missive."

I admitted that I enjoyed Mary's fairy tales and that I still read them often. "The more I read them, the more I read into them. I know children love them, but I think she really wrote them for grown-ups."

William agreed and closed his eyes as he reminisced, "I can see her now at Kelmscott Manor, sitting in the garden with the Morris and Burne-Jones children and young Rudyard and his sister at her feet; they were absolutely enthralled. But you are right, the parents were also listening and enjoying the tales. She even read some to Morris himself, who always had time for her. He is not well, you know. I don't see him nearly enough these days; we were good friends and spent our ill-spent youth together. How time scurries by, like a beetle running for cover under a stone."

Evelyn laughed at his metaphor then became more serious, her thoughts still on children. "Mary would have made a good mother. It is such a shame that she never

344

married. I think most men found her rather over-bearing and feisty. But William, weren't there rumours that she had an admirer quite some years ago?"

It was as if someone had slapped me. "Never! She never had an admirer, never!"

William looked at me with a concerned expression, then frowned, trying to remember. "Yes, my dear, I do believe you are right. It was indeed years ago now. I am sure he was something to do with eggs. Did he run a poultry farm? Or maybe his surname was Yolk, or White? Or Omelette? Goodness, my memory is getting very bad. Do you recall his name Evelyn, old thing?"

Before I knew it, I blurted out, "She never had an admirer. I would have known. I would have known." In my agitation I knocked over a glass of red wine. In the ensuing confusion I regained control of my emotions and having refused a refill I promptly made my excuses and retired for the night.

Lying in bed, a cool breeze wafting through the open window bringing with it the smell of jasmine, I looked back over the years and tried to remember the times I had ever seen Mary with a man. There was the nervous young man from the Fabian Society who she spoke to at Morris's, and whose name she could never remember. And there were the men from Morris's circle, but there was no-one who stuck out as being anyone special.

She had loved me.

She had said so.

The following morning we had a pleasant breakfast outside, none of us referring to the previous evening's conversation. I wanted to be alone so I asked if I could take myself around Florence to do some sketching. I had the loan of a carriage and the old Italian driver drove me from location to location, helping me set up my paraphernalia and then sitting happily in the sun, brushing the flies away from himself and his horse with a long swat. The sun was intense and I had to sit under the shade, either of a tree or a parasol. The stones themselves seemed to have had enough of the heat and threw it back into the faces of the passersby. I sketched the basics and then went back to the villa, trusting to memory to recreate the colours. Evelyn looked over my shoulder on one occasion and complimented me on my rooftops. Praise indeed from a professional artist.

At breakfast on the fourth day, Evelyn said that they were going to visit her Uncle at his Villa Nuti, just outside Florence, and I was very welcome to join them. I didn't know her relations and asked if I may be excused. I said I would stay in the cool of the villa and do some reading and write some letters. Having carried out these tasks, I wandered around the villa and peeped into Evelyn's studio. I realised that I was just an amateur, and always would be.

The post arrived at lunchtime. Carla brought me a letter from Sarah and even before I opened it I knew it contained bad news, for it had no bulk, being just a single sheet.

My Dear Hannah,

It is with great sadness that I have to tell you that Antonia's baby, Francesca, was stillborn. She is recovering but we are all devastated, as you can imagine. Come home soon, we need you.
With much affection, Sarah.

A tremor of sadness rippled through my body, but I did not seem to have any tears left to weep. Poor Antonia. Poor wee baby that had only ever been a dream and had never been given the chance to become reality. Although the villa was quiet I wanted to sit somewhere more peaceful, so I went to the nearest Catholic church and sat in a back pew, calmed by the faith of the thousands who had worshipped there over the centuries. There was a faint smell of incense from the last service and someone was practising quietly on the organ. Even as a non-believer I felt at peace and I sat for over an hour, just letting my memory recall images from the past in random sequence, images that bought me a sense of tranquillity. Then the church bell rang, calling the believers to mass, so I left.

Over dinner that evening I told William and Evelyn about the baby and they gave their condolences. Then Evelyn said something that surprised me. "She is at peace; her grandfather will look after her."

William noticed my bemusement. "Evelyn and I are both firm believers in the spirits."

I know I looked dubious. "Mary was very derogatory about séances. I will never forget her telling me of one that your mother held, William, whilst you were all holidaying in Betws-y-coed. She was only about thirteen, I think she said, but she remembered every detail. I laughed so much my sides hurt! She did make me laugh when she said that she thought that in this day and age there must be a quicker and more efficient means of communication between the real and the spirit world!"

Evelyn smiled but then said, "We also don't believe in the veracity of séances, but we really do communicate with the spirit world. We have been experimenting with automatic writing for some time and have had a modicum of success. We spend about an hour each evening and over time we have progressed from just squiggles to legible words and now to whole sentences. We both need to be present and one holds the top of the other's hand lightly. It is very strange that whichever of us is holding the pen the resultant hand-writing is the same. Not absolute proof that we are writing on behalf of a spirit, perhaps, but interesting, don't you think?"

"Sometimes," announced William, "what we write is something quite profound!"

Evelyn went to fetch some examples and I looked at a few sheets with feigned interest. I could not read all of it, but there were a few phrases that were very clear:

"I am growing into the light."

"Life is a struggle."

"It is glorious here."

Despite their obvious enthusiasm and trust in the spiritual source of the writing, I still thought it was their wishful thinking, although it would have given me so much comfort to know that the soul of my loved one lived on.

I told them about the dream notebook that I had brought with me, and William went to fetch it as he had never seen it. When he finished he said, "Mother always said that Mary had a gift, that she was a seer."

"She often had a far-away look, perhaps she was seeing into the future, although she never told me what she saw."

I told them my plans for the future, that I planned to return to Egypt once I had settled my affairs in England, to return to living with Sarah. Evelyn looked at me quizzically. "Is that what you really want, Hannah?"

"Of course! It is what we have planned."

That night I dreamed of rain. Big raindrops that fell in slow motion and clung trembling from the leaves of an oak tree before falling to the lush grass with a splash. There was a girl dancing, her arms outstretched, her white, drenched nightdress clinging to her body, her head thrown back; she was singing. The sound she made was fey, the undulating notes carried to earth on the raindrops. She whirled and twirled in harmony with the sound she made and she looked joyous. She stopped suddenly and turned towards me and I saw that it was a young me, prettier than I ever remember being. She smiled at me and beckoned to me to join her.

I awoke the next morning, my pillow damp with tears and a yearning to go home so strong that it hurt.

I remained in Florence for a further few days then both William and Evelyn accompanied me to the railway station. We hugged and kissed and promised to keep in touch and then I was away on a sleeper train to Paris. The journey took three days during which time I wrote a long letter to Sarah, finished reading my novel and admired the changing scenery as we sped through Italy and France. Although I relished the time to myself I wished Mary was there with me.

I stayed an afternoon and a night in Paris and as I strolled down the Champs Elysees I wondered whether I might see Aisha on the arm of Lord Bradshaw. Or perhaps some other man, for Lord Bradshaw had said that it was the money of the upper-class men that would pay for Aisha's eventual independence. I shivered at the thought of the life she had chosen.

I didn't see her, of course. I spent a pleasant time and caught the train the next day to Calais, and then a short boat trip to Southampton. As we docked I could not but help remember when Mary and I had arrived at Alexandria on the first day of our Egyptian adventure. How long ago that now seemed. When I stepped off the gangplank, ready to take a carriage to London, it started to rain. I stood and let the drops wash my face. How glad I was to be back in England.

Chapter 18 – The Gypsy's Cup

1895 - 1915

"And now one last thing," she cried, "and that is, that I will make you a cup that has a spell in it, and it shall be a present for you to remember me by. It will be very plain, and there will be no gay colours in it, but when you give it to your true love to drink from, if once you have drunk from it yourself, you will have all her heart, but beware that she doesn't take a second draught. For though the first draught that she drinks will be drunk to love, the second draught will be drunk to hate, and though she have loved you more than all else on earth, all her love will turn to hate when she drinks again."

(From "The Gypsy's Cup," in *The Windfairies*, by Mary De Morgan)

I had arranged to see Mr Wilkes the solicitor in two days' time, so I took advantage of this free time to revisit some of the places Mary and I used to frequent, hoping to recapture some of the happiness we had felt. I started by going to the church where our friendship had begun. St. Philip's had not changed, churches rarely do. There was a different lady arranging the flowers, of course; the Ross's had left the parish a few years previously. I sat in the same pew and remembered how Adelaide Ross had befriended me, invited me to tea, and I had had my very first meeting with Mary. It was nearly twenty years ago now, but I remembered everything so very clearly. I had known then that it would be a special friendship, and I had not been wrong. Someone was practising on the organ, badly, and in the end the discordant notes drove me away.

I got my driver, Roberts, to take me to Petticoat Lane and I told him to meet me at the other end of the road. There were the same stalls selling the same assortment of wares, and although many of the stall-holders were Jewish, there were also many who were East Enders, who shouted the merits of their goods in their loud, raucous voices. I used to enjoy walking down the road with Mary, greeting some of the stall-holders, taking time to look at the displays and feeling the quality of the materials, but this day I felt uncomfortable and a little wary. I realised, for the first time, that it was perhaps not the most sensible thing to come to a place like this alone.

I went to where Salome's shop used to be, but it was now a jeweller's and the shop-keeper did not know where she had gone. I then walked down the streets where we had visited "our" families but the barrenness of the place depressed me and the air was thick with the smell of cabbage and something else, quite repugnant. I was appalled that Mother Nature seemed to have given up, as had the miserable inhabitants.

I went back to the carriage and asked to be taken straight home, where I straightway had a bath to wash away the smells and the feeling of hopelessness that were engrained in my pores. I had wanted to re-live some of my happier times with Mary but instead had only made myself miserable and angry. No-one deserved to live in such a bleak place, and an idea began to take shape in the recess of my mind.

The next afternoon I visited my solicitor. Mr Wilkes was by now an elderly gentleman although he seemed to have all his faculties. I noticed that he still had a bowl of humbugs, but he didn't offer me any. Instead we shared a cup of tea and some plain biscuits before any kind of business was discussed. When we had exchanged pleasantries and the tea things had been taken away, he got a thick file from the shelf and untied the ribbon that held it all together.

"Now then, Miss Russell. You have some plans you wish to discuss?"

"Yes, I am planning to go back to Egypt for good, so I wanted to sell the houses. But then I thought, maybe, it would be more beneficial to turn the house in Kent into some sort of reformatory. What do you think?"

"A reformatory? For criminals? May I ask why?"

"Because I worked in one in Egypt and the youngsters were not criminals, Mr Wilkes, they were just unlucky to be born poor. Russell Hall would make a marvellous reformatory. Or perhaps a place where families can go for a few weeks as a holiday away from the poverty of the East End? I went back there yesterday. Mary, Miss de Morgan and I used to go visiting there. It hasn't improved; in fact it's worse than I remember. I don't need all the money, Mr Wilkes. I would like to do something useful with it."

He looked sternly at me over his glasses.

"Well, is it to be a reformatory, or a holiday home? Perhaps Miss Russell, you need some time to consider what you really want to do. It might be better to continue renting out the London house, rather than selling. It brings in a princely sum each year. You don't have to decide immediately. Go home to Kent and think about what you really want to do. Something will happen that helps you decide. Come back in, say, a month? We can then formulate a plan."

With that he re-tied the ribbon firmly around the file and put it back on the shelf. He shook my hand gently, patted my arm and advised me again to go home.

The next day I took his advice and by late afternoon I was walking through the front door of Russell Hall. I had warned the staff that I might visit so the rooms were aired and the first thing was to take tea under the embrace of the old oak tree. Its permanency comforted me and I felt my own roots bury themselves back into the Kentish soil. I then went into every room of the house, re-discovering my home. Nothing had changed, of course, and I realised that whether I converted or sold, then some of the rooms would need redecorating. My own bedroom particularly was in dire need of a refurbishment. I had slept in the same room from birth until I had left for London at twenty years old; the wallpaper had never been changed and still showed my immature artistic endeavours. The original design was simple, a cream background with a repeating pattern of five different flower heads positioned in the shape of a diamond: a rose, an iris, a bluebell, a daffodil and a tulip. I remembered one morning, when I was young and my passion for drawing had just started, a thrush outside in the garden had imposed itself into my reverie with its high-pitched warble. Inspired, I had leapt out of bed and without a moment's hesitation drew a rather primitive bird inside one of the diamonds, then quickly got back under the blankets to get warm again. No-one seemed to notice my artistic effort and so the next morning I added a rabbit, then a dog, then a horse to fill other gaps. As time went on and my skills improved, I added fairies, imps, dragons and princesses, who peeped around the flower heads, smiling winningly at whosoever discovered them. Bessy once commented that I perhaps shouldn't draw on the walls, but my father never went into my bedroom, so instead of chastising me she joined in the game of trying to find what I had added since the last time she had looked. After a few years there was hardly an inch of wallpaper that I had not somehow incorporated into a picture that ranged from a farmyard, to fairy-tale castle, to a ship's cabin, to an exotic jungle. It all looked so childish now; whatever happened I would need to redecorate.

I finished the tour in my father's study. I sat behind his overly large desk and read a letter from Sarah that had been waiting for me. It was long and chatty and full of details of the family's life. Antonia was recovering nicely and they were all looking forward to Georgie's wedding and I would still be there, wouldn't I?

My mother watched me as I read, as she had watched over my father as he worked each day. She had the gentlest smile that I have ever seen and her eyes brimmed with compassion. My father always said that it was a very life-like portrait. Bessy had once told me that Mama, despite being very weak, had been able to hold me after I was born. I closed my eyes and felt her arms around me holding me tight, the drop of a tear falling from her cheek onto mine, the feel of her warm breath, her dying breath, as she whispered my name, Hannah. I have never felt closer to Mama than I did then.

"What would you do, Mama?" Mama merely smiled at me and gave no clue as to what she thought.

Over the next few days I pushed my dilemma to the back of my mind and visited every cottage on the estate, making sure everything was in order and that the tenants wanted for nothing. Mr Black, the estate manager, had done a good job and had managed the estate efficiently and productively in my absence. The tenants had few complaints, and none that could not be sorted with a smile and a promise. One morning I awoke to the rain hammering against the window panes. It was not the gentle rain of my dream and I had no desire to go outside and sing and dance under the oak tree. Instead, I decided to finish my unpacking. I had filled the carpet bag with my own odds and ends in Florence. Once empty it looked a rather sorry thing; there was no sunshine to bring it alive and I have to say that it looked shabby and a slightly incongruous item in my very English bedroom.

I saw that the stitching inside was coming undone so I decided to repair it. I started to unpick the remainder of the old thread along the side of the base, which I noticed was of a different colour to the rest, and as I did so a corner of a piece of paper peeped out. I could see that it had writing on, so I continued to unpick until the whole of one side of the lining on the base of the bag was undone. I slid my fingers in and pulled out a wad of papers. I was quite excited as I had no idea what they could be or who would have put them there. There was a bundle of letters in a tight, neat hand that I did not recognise, tied in an emerald green satin ribbon, and some folded sheets of typewritten paper. I restrained my curiosity and, having put the bag in the bottom of the wardrobe, I went downstairs to the living room, where a fire had been lit to ward off the chill that pervaded the house.

I spread open the sheets of paper first and as I did so a newspaper cutting fluttered to the floor. I recognised it immediately as being the notice of the deaths of the men at the gold mine at Um Garaiart. So, Mary must have made this hide-away, but why? What could the other papers contain that warranted secreting them away? The title on the first type-written page was "The Witch and Egg." An alarm bell rang in the back of my head but I could not think why, so I settled down to read a hitherto unknown De Morgan fairy tale.

The Witch and Egg

Quite a long time ago now, there lived a witch. She wasn't a wicked witch, oh no! But she wasn't a particularly good one either. She did her very best and often, indeed, the warts disappeared or the hair grew or the boys fell in love as they were supposed to do. But sometimes they didn't. The people kept coming, though, for she was a kindly soul and she would tell the children fairy stories in which the witches were really terribly wicked and did the most despicable things that made the children scream in horror and delight, so much so that they forgot what spells their mothers had sent them to get in the first place.

They called her the Demogorgon, as they had her mother and her mother's mother. No-one could remember why, but she didn't mind the name as it made her sound a bit sinister, which was no bad thing for a witch. She lived in a cottage in a wood where she had been born, as had her mother and her mother's mother before her. She was sorry that she wouldn't be able to pass her spells and the house onto her own little witch-daughter, but she had never met one of her own kind, or indeed of any kind, whom she could bear for more than a few minutes, no matter for a life time. She did try casting some spells to snare a man but to no avail, unless the cat who wandered into her door one day can be considered a success. He wasn't a black cat nor did he have one particle of magic in his whole body; he was, in fact, one of the tabby cats from the nearby farm, but the witch loved him.

The witch had a good life and had lots of friends, both witches and non-witches. One non-witch was a particular friend and was called Hannabarbarose, Hanna for short. Hanna would pop round most days and they would go walking in the woods and pick the healing flowers that the witch used to make her spells. The witch thought Hanna was a bit silly and could do more with her life but she liked her nonetheless, but at the end of each day the witch was happy to close the door on the world and snuggle down with just Tabby. They would sit in front of the fire on a winter's night and tell each other stories. Well, the cat purred and could have been telling her a story if she only knew his language.

One day a man knocked on her door. It was unusual for a stranger to come to her and she felt a little shy but the man soon put her at ease with his smile and his pleasant manner. She offered him tea and cake - she made very tasty cakes with absolutely no magic, well hardly any. He introduced himself as E. G. Grenville but asked her to call him Egg. "All my friends do and I would be very happy if you did too."

They talked and talked, of this and that, and spent a very congenial few hours. He was just getting up to go when she remembered to ask him what he had wanted in the first place. He gave one of his wry smiles and said, "Riches. I have come to the conclusion that if I am to get any respect then I have to be rich. No matter that I am a good, nay an excellent engineer, and I can make all sorts of useful things. But no-one will listen to me or give me a job because I have no money. I don't suppose you have a spell do you?"

The witch shook her head. "I am so sorry, but there are no spells to make people rich, well, none that I know of. And we certainly couldn't use magic to make ourselves rich. That is against the law, the witches' and wizards' law, that is."

"Yes, otherwise I suppose you would live in a finer house."

"Oh no! I love my cottage. This is my home, as it was my mother's and my mother's mother's before. Why would I want to change it? What's wrong with it?"

And she looked around with the man's eyes and saw that the furniture was old and falling apart, the carpet was faded and threadbare and everything did look just plain old and tired. "I suppose things are getting a little old. But I do love it here."

"Of course you do. Please forgive me, I meant no disrespect. Perhaps I could come and help you by mending some of these things. I may call again?"

And so started a friendship that went on for many years. She sometimes gave him spells to ease his aching knees or to get rid of a bad headache, and he would mend her tables and chairs or fix a picture or a broken window frame. He even built her a contraption to wake her up every morning. As soon as the sun rose and the first sunbeams fell onto a certain spot, a lever swung around and hit a silver bell that never failed to wake her even from the deepest sleep. It didn't work if the sun didn't shine though!

The witch didn't tell Hanna or anyone about her friend. She was worried that they would laugh at her because she was quite old by now and he was quite a bit younger. One day the man came looking excited and told her that he had a job in a faraway land where the sun shone always and they needed him to build something to dig up gold. He would be gone for quite a while but when he was rich, and he was sure that he would be very, very rich, then he would send for her and perhaps, would she, might she, consider marrying him, maybe? She said "yes" and he was so excited that he hugged her and didn't see how sad she was. She didn't care that he wasn't rich and if he had asked her to marry him now and live in a pig sty, she would have said "yes."

So the man went, waving goodbye and promising to send for her as soon as he was rich. It took him a long while and although he sent news often, the years passed and the witch got older and sadder. She kept making her spells and telling her stories, but her heart was no longer in it and she pined for her Egg.

Then one day, as she sat dozing in the garden, it being a beautiful, warm summer's afternoon, a large white bird landed beside her and pecked her gently to wake her.

"Goodness! What sort of bird are you?"

"I am an ibis and I come from the land where the sun shines always. I have come to take you there."

Ever practical, the witch asked, "How?"

The ibis bird smiled and told her to sit on his back and somehow, either the bird grew or she shrank, but she was able to sit astride the bird. He was just stretching his wings when she remembered Tabby. "Wait! My cat. I can't go without him." So she slid off the bird's back and rushed into the cottage, picked up the sleeping cat that was curled on her bed and rushed back and sat on the bird's back again, all in the twinkling of an eye. "Alright Mr Ibis. Now we can go!"

And the bird spread his wings and effortlessly soared up into the blue sky and glided over all the countries until he came to the land where the sun shines always. He landed on top of a huge golden pyramid so that she could see the whole world spread out below, then he swooped down and down and gently came to a halt in the garden of a beautiful house. It was not made of gold but of white marble and there standing waiting for her was her Egg; older but still her Egg.

At first she was shy and all she could say was, "Hullo. I hope you don't mind that I have brought Tabby?"

The man soon put her at ease with his smile and his pleasant manner. And they were married and yes, Mr and Mrs Eusebius Gerald Grenville (now you see why he was called Egg) lived happily ever after, although not for as long as in most fairy tales for they were both quite old by now. Theirs was a happy home and filled with laughter, their own and that of other people, who came to listen to her fairy tales, eat her cakes and be amazed at his wonderful, often useful, inventions. Even Hanna came to visit them and did not begrudge them their happiness one little bit.

The end

I had to read it twice to be sure. Only then did the realisation hit me like a physical blow to the stomach. It was as if I had spent my whole adult life building an ornate sand-castle with intricate walls, moats and turrets, decorations of different shells and flags of seaweed, only

362

for it to be devastated by the onslaught of one huge tidal wave. Images from my life floated before my eyes like playing cards and then built themselves into a fragile pyramid. But the hand of reality pulled away a card from the bottom causing all the others to come tumbling down, like those that flew down upon Alice at the end of her adventures in Wonderland.

My head reeled and I couldn't even start to think which parts of my life were true and which were not.

How I hated that fairy tale!

How I hated Mary!

How I hated Egg!

I screwed the paper up suddenly and threw it onto the fire.

Who was Egg? It was then I noticed the newspaper cutting that had advised of her nephew's death. But it was not the name of Augustus De Morgan that she had ringed in black, but that of Eusebius G. Grenville. E.G.G.

I then picked up the letters and knew they would be love letters from Mr Grenville to Mary. I glanced at the first page of the top letter and saw that it was dated 1883. I looked at the newspaper cutting again: Eusebius G. Grenville (38). So in 1883 he would have been twenty six and Mary would have been thirty three. I started to read the letter, but I could not get beyond "My darling Mary," before the bile rose in my throat and I threw it, along with all the other letters, into the fire. I had no desire to read them for their words would forever be inside my head, tormenting me, mocking me, reminding me of my stupidity. The ribbon caught first and for a brief moment the letters were bound in a bow of multi-hued flame. Then the paper was devoured and quickly turned into blackened, crisp parchment, then into grey ashes, just like Mary's dreams of the future and my own dreams of what had never been. Watching the letters burn I remembered Mary's unfinished letter to me. What a fool I was! She had not wanted to tell me about her love for me, but for Mr Grenville. The different type of love she referred to was not a woman for a woman, but an older woman for a younger man. I sat watching the fire until there was nothing left, and although it was still alive, I felt chilled.

My first thought then was that Mary had thought me silly and my second, which made me laugh bitterly, was that William had been right about her having a lover who had something to do with eggs. I looked at the cutting again and Grenville's name leapt out, as it must have done to Mary when I had handed it to her. I remembered how absolutely devastated she had been at what we had all assumed to be her nephew's death. It was all now so clear. On that day she had seen all her hopes of a future happiness dashed; all the years of waiting patiently, all the planning, all the deceit had been for nothing. No wonder she had collapsed and never really recovered. A vision of her kneeling by the grave came to me, her face pale and tear-stained, and with a dawning realisation I remembered moving the opal brooch she had left at her lover's grave to that of her nephew, assuming she had made a mistake. God forgive me, I was pleased that I had foiled her plan.

I felt as if someone was hurling stones as scenes from the last twenty or so years of my life with Mary bombarded me, one after the other in quick succession, demanding re-evaluation. But I did not have the energy and despite the heavy rain I put on my galoshes and went for a long walk along the country lanes around the estate. That perhaps was the worst thing to do, for there was nothing else to do other than to think. My memory lingered on the time when we had gone to visit the graves at Um Garaiart. I could not remember the site manager's name, but I could hear his broad Scottish accent as he told us that he suspected that Mr Grenville had a sweetheart back in England whom he had wanted to marry. How Mary had restrained herself, I cannot imagine; I remember her sitting ram-rod straight trying not to cry, doubtless trying not to scream "I am that woman, he wanted to marry me!"

I wish I knew who Mr Grenville was. I kept going back to the nervous man from the Fabian Society. I could not remember his name but he must have been about the right age. Mary had claimed not even to remember his name; what a wicked, wicked deceiver she had been. All those times in London she had said she couldn't see me because she was busy writing, was she meeting him instead? How could she have been such a liar and I not know? How could I have loved such a person?

With my insides turned to stone I remembered how she had persuaded me to go to Egypt, for her "health." She had gone out there for her own sordid purposes, so she could be near her lover. With a start I realised that her sojourns to Alexandria had not been to see her nephew but instead to be with Grenville. Had she ever even met with her nephew? Oh my God! Had she and Grenville shared a house? Had they acted like a married couple? Had they actually been married? How many lies had she told to how many people?

Suddenly I remembered my unexpected visit to Mary when she had moved into lodgings, purportedly to be "independent." Ha! She hadn't wanted to be independent, at all, but merely to build a love nest with her fledgling lover. I recalled there had been strange noises from the bedroom. She had blithely blamed the draught. Had it been him? Had he been there all the time, laughing at me? Laughing at my naïveté? The smell when I had hugged her on leaving! It had not been a woman's scent that had merely brought my own father's cologne to mind, it had actually been the smell of a man on her skin. The very thought of it made me retch over and over again, until I felt my whole inside was just an empty void.

How I hated Mary.

How I hated *him*.

By now I was back home, physically drenched and emotionally exhausted, so that all I wanted to do was to go to the sitting room and curl up in the armchair by the fire that was still burning. As I thought of more and more instances when I had misread the situation, when I had understood her words in a way that she had never intended, when I had believed that she had feelings for me that I now realised were never there, I curled myself into a smaller and smaller ball, wrapping my arms tightly around my knees, letting the tears fall heedlessly onto my skirt. When I eventually unwrapped myself I felt like a husk, empty of all hope, love, and life. All I wanted to do was to hide away like an injured animal and lick my wounds, so I went to bed and stayed there for a month.

I remember little of that time other than the face of the doctor floating in and out of my vision; bowls of soup that I left untouched; bottles of pills emptying and being refilled; the smell of sweat; the darkness of a room whose curtains I refused to have opened.

The doctor afterwards said I had caught a chill on my walk that had turned into a bad bout of rheumatic fever. I didn't correct his hypothesis. I knew that I was grieving, not for the love of my hitherto beloved Mary, but rather of love itself.

One morning, I woke earlier than normal. The curtains weren't drawn properly and a shaft of early morning sunlight pierced the gloom and lit up a patch of carpet so that the colours seemed to glow. I suddenly felt dirty and I kicked off my sheets, pulled off my night dress and went to run myself a hot bath. I lay in the steaming water, washed my greasy hair and scrubbed myself all over until my skin was red and sore. When I got out and wrapped myself in my dressing gown I felt like a butterfly which had just emerged from its dark cocoon. I was tired of grieving, of loss and despair; I wanted to live again, I was ready for a new start.

During my "illness" I had been in no condition to read any letters and so it was three weeks after it arrived that I eventually read one from Georgie, the now familiar black edging warning me, but not preparing me, of its content.

My dearest Hannah,

There is no easy way to say this. Dear Mama passed away earlier this week from a severe bout of food poisoning. The death of the baby had devastated her and she just didn't seem to have the energy to fight her illness. By the time you read this I will be married. There seemed little point in waiting so we had a very quiet ceremony. I think some people thought I should have waited, but James convinced me it would be better for me to start a new life with him.

I have moved out of the house we rented and we are living with James's parents for a while.

Dear, Hannah, you are still very welcome to come out, but you will need to live in your own house as there is no room here. It may be better if you stayed in England for a while?

I'm sorry.

Your ever affectionate Georgie

I sat in numbed silence. After Mary, or the Mary I had thought she was, I had loved Sarah the most. But I was tired of death so I briskly folded the letter, whispered a goodbye to Sarah and realised that this was the "something" that Mr Wilkes had said might happen to help me make my mind up about my future. To my surprise I actually felt relief that I didn't have to travel back to Egypt. Although my time at Russell Hall had not been particularly happy since I arrived, it still felt like home, and I wanted to remain there.

I wandered around the house, relishing the fact that I would not have to sell or rent it out. It was a very big house, though, and ought to be filled with a family with a large number of boisterous children rather than one old spinster. As I wandered down the hallways, listening to the laughter of phantom children running up and down the corridors, watched over by the portraits of all the ancient Russells, I remembered the seed of an idea that had planted itself a few weeks ago, after my visit to the East End. I knew then what I was going to do.

The very next day I travelled to London and was able to see Mr Wilkes that afternoon. I impatiently waited for the tea ritual to complete and then excitedly told him my plans. "I have made my decision. I want to turn Russell Hall into a holiday home, a holiday home for East End families. Different ones will come and stay for three weeks each summer; they will breathe the country air, eat good wholesome food and walk along the country lanes gathering fruit and berries. I can live in the little cottage at the edge of the grounds, it is totally run down but it will be delightful once it has been renovated and it will be big enough for me. What do you think, Mr Wilkes?"

Mr Wilkes smiled and said he was pleased I had made my mind up and that it was a noble plan.

It took less than a year to turn my plan into reality. During that year I learned of yet another death: that of William Morris. I was saddened by his demise, but I was done with death; I spent a few moments reminiscing then pushed it to the back of my mind. I was not going to spend the rest of my life looking backwards with regret, but rather forwards with hope.

I was in my cottage by Easter 1897 and the house was ready for the first families in the July. I had moved some of the finer furniture from the house into the cottage and sold the rest, replacing them with more functional and hard-wearing pieces. I left most of the portraits to look over the families, they were doing no harm and they helped cover the walls. One very stern female grew a moustache one summer, but other than that they were left unharmed. The only picture I took to the cottage was the one of Mama. I hung her in the room I had converted into a studio and she looked down on me benignly as I painted and tried my hand at pottery.

The house was quite transformed. Some of the bedrooms were enlarged so that whole families could sleep together, as they were used to doing, whilst other smaller ones were available for those who wanted some peace and quiet. My father's study became a games room for the men; how he would have hated that! The dining room remained as it was, being sufficiently large enough to seat all the families at long tables; the reception rooms became places of industry for sewing, basket-making, weaving, carpentry, bicycle maintenance and other useful activities. I also had one of the downstairs rooms turned into another kitchen so that the adults and the children could learn to cook basic country fare, make jams and chutneys and even to brew beer and wine.

I didn't get involved in the holiday home very much; there was a team of qualified people to care for the families and ensure that they had a fulfilling and enjoyable few weeks away from the city. The children in particular had tasks to do each day, which usually caused much consternation to begin with but after only a few days they fought over who should collect the eggs; who should nurse the motherless lambs and calves; who should pick the vegetables for dinner; who should exercise the horses. I always made a point of doing some painting with each group; we used a large shed so that no one was worried if any paint missed the paper, and there was always a substantial amount that did. After just a few years it was as if the shed had been laid with a wonderful multi-coloured carpet. It always warmed my heart to see the families leaving at the end of their holiday, ruddier, plumper and all singing together at the tops of their voices, just three weeks after having arrived as a gaggle of morose, pale and skinny individuals.

The century turned.

I was forty and had settled happily into my life.

In 1907 I went into London to visit Mr Wilkes junior, his father having died a few years previously. I was early for our appointment, so I decided go for a stroll in Hyde Park. It was only late August but some of the leaves were just beginning to turn. I didn't take my pad; I had accumulated a vast portfolio of sketches over the years and was content to just wander, breathe in the late summer air and absorb the atmosphere. As I turned a corner I saw a large number of people ahead of me, some wearing sashes, others waving flags, banners or placards. I was too far away to see any of the writing. They were chanting and at first I thought it might be the Salvation Army, but then I noticed that they were all women and as I got nearer I could hear their mantra of "Votes for women! Votes for women!"

I could see now that the banners were embroidered with the names of different London areas, such as Hammersmith, Westminster, Islington, Stepney and Finsbury, and these, as well as the placards, commanded "Deeds not Words!" "Votes for Women!" "Women have Rights too!" or "Women Demand the Vote!" One large placard, held by four women stated that "No self-respecting woman should wish or work for the success of a party that ignores her sex." I realised that this was a rally for women's suffrage. Some activists, so I read in my copy of *The Times* that was sent every week, had decided that years of moderation and patience had achieved nothing and that it was time for direct action, deeds not words. I supported women's rights; how ludicrous it seemed to me that women could have no say in how their own country was run, no say in their own future, and yet such despicable men as Mr Edwardson and Lord Bradshaw could. How could someone such as I, Sarah or Georgie be deemed to be insufficiently competent enough to be able to make our own minds up?

I had suddenly become part, then, of the crowd of militant women, who were marching their way along the path towards Hyde Park Corner. Their enthusiasm was catching and I wished I had a placard but instead I paid for a flag and waved that vigorously. I saw Lady Shackleton shouting at the top of her voice and decided that if she could, then so could I. "VOTES FOR WOMEN! VOTES FOR WOMEN!"

The crowd finally halted at the Corner and after just a few minutes there was an expectant hush, until a woman separated herself from the throng and clambered onto a small stage, where she could see over the heads that spread out before her. The crowd immediately burst out cheering and screaming her name, "Emmeline! Emmeline!"

She stood smiling and waving for a few moments and then held her hands up to plead for silence. Then she gave a most wonderful speech, which everyone could hear perfectly, so strong and resonant was her voice. We had all heard the arguments before, of course, it was a very similar speech to the one Annie Besant had given when I had attended the Fabian Society meeting. We listened, transfixed, nonetheless: how women paid the same rates and taxes as men; how women were expected to be deeply involved in education, housing and employment but were not allowed to have a say in how they were run; how the honour and security of our country was of as much interest to women as it was to men; how women were just as patriotic and public-spirited as men; how meetings had been held, petitions signed, politeness maintained, but nothing achieved; how *now* was the time for women to become more vigorous, to march, to protest, to make their voices heard.

Mary would have loved this; the thought came unbidden. I knew she would have been at the forefront of every march; she would have been one of the organisers; hers would have been one of the voices demanding to be heard. She had believed that women should fight against their oppression, should use their bodies as weapons. Then I pushed her out of my mind; the wound was slowly healing each year, but it was still sore.

After Mrs Pankhurst had spoken, other women told of what their branches were doing in the fight for women's suffrage. How we applauded each report of increased membership, of demonstrations held, of petitions signed, of MPs confronted, of articles published, even, in one instance, of prison sentences endured. By the end of the rally I was so inspired and impassioned that I wrote an extremely large cheque to the WSPU, in the hope that it would help them achieve their noble aims.

I let other women do the fighting and returned home, to my East End families.

It all ended, however, in 1915, just a year ago, when the fighting was being done by men with guns, not women with placards. The house was commandeered by the army as a convalescence home. It needed few modifications, the bedrooms becoming the wards and the utility rooms remaining as such for the use of the recuperating patients. I was allowed to stay in my little cottage and Elly and her husband Stephen came and helped me out each day, as they still do.

I still had painting classes in the shed, although they were slightly more sedate and most of the paint remained on the paper. I always went to the house every day and sat with some of the patients, either reading to them, talking with them or just holding their hands. There seemed no end to the soldiers and sailors who were brought here to recuperate from their most terrible wounds, physical, mental and spiritual. Some of them might even have been at the Hall as children, but they were not transformed after just three weeks as they were back then. There were many men who returned to their families, their visible wounds healed, but God knows about the ones that cannot be seen. There were many, of course, who left to make the short journey down the road to the small graveyard, to join my mother and father overlooking the hop fields of Kent.

***

After many emotional hours I found my sketches of the garden I did for Mary's birthday, more than thirty five years earlier. I don't know how but I had indeed painted the jewel garden that I had dreamed of the previous night. I remembered how rejuvenated I had felt, how all my aches and pains had disappeared; I remembered the sound of the bells that seemed to beckon me on; I remembered the touch of Mary's lips when she kissed my cheek.

I wanted to go back there. I longed for night to fall so that I may sleep, so that I may return to the jewel garden.

Epilogue – In the Jewel Garden

I am there again; everything is more intense than it was last night. I am bewitched as soap bubbles seem to pop out of the pores of my skin. They float away and burst into smaller bubbles that sparkle like diamonds and fall to the ground, where they continue to shimmer. The pain that troubles me by day is ebbing, as if each bubble is taking a little bit of it away, and indeed when the bubbles stop my pain is gone.

I feel remarkably refreshed and full of anticipation, but of what I do not know. I wander down the paths towards the sound of the laughter that I know I will never reach and laugh to myself as gold and silver swallows swoop over my head seemingly showing me the way. The laughter is getting louder but I am now not so sure whether it is indeed human laughter or the sound of a hundred tiny bells. I turn a corner and I see someone standing there, as if waiting for me. As I get nearer I see it is Mary. A wave of affection almost overwhelms me and I want so much to embrace her, to show that I forgive her, that I can now love her as a friend. Someone is standing behind her in the shadows; I cannot see him but I know who it is. She is smiling broadly; she shakes her head and indicates that I should continue towards a golden arch that spans the path.

"I will see you soon, Hannah. Very soon."

I am puzzled but I do as she asks and stop in wonder as a myriad of rainbow-coloured butterflies spill out of the arch, carrying the sound of the tinkling laughter on their wings. I can just discern a figure standing on the threshold, but it is surrounded by a haze and it is only when I am but a few feet away that I can see her features.

It is as if she has walked straight out of the picture in my studio, although she is even more beautiful. She opens her arms and before I know it I am being embraced as never before. Her smell is intoxicating and her touch so intense it almost burns. She rocks me gently and coos quietly into my ear. Her arms are wrapped around me, holding me tight, the drop of a tear falls from her cheek onto mine. I feel her warm breath, her living breath, as my mother whispers my name, "Hannah." I am swaddled in the love I have been searching for all my life.

We walk through the golden arch together.

I know this is not a dream.

Postscript

I came across Mary De Morgan (1850 – 1907) whilst researching Victorian fairy-tale writers and my interest turned into something of an obsession. I found out enough about De Morgan to write her biography (*Out of the Shadows: the Life and Works of Mary De Morgan*), but there were still some intriguing gaps in my knowledge, which I decided to fill from my imagination – the result being *The Jewel Garden*. Some of the people mentioned in the book are genuine: Mary's mathematician father and social reformer mother, her brother William whose tiles are now collectors' items and her sister-in-law, the artist Evelyn De Morgan; her nephew who died at a gold mine in Um Garaiart; William Morris, who was a good friend of Mary's; Annie Besant who Mary may well have heard at a meeting of the Fabian Society and last, but not least, George Bernard Shaw, who couldn't stand her and referred to her as the Demogorgon.

Mary wrote three collections of the most beautiful and often thought-provoking fairy tales, *On a Pincushion*, *The Necklace of Princess Fiorimonde* and *The Windfairies*, extracts from which I have started each chapter to whet the readers interest. I never found any evidence of what prompted Mary to go to live in Egypt, where she became a directress of a girls' reformatory in Helouan until she died of tuberculosis at the age of 57. Oh, and "Mary's walk in the jewel garden – Nov 14 1856" is the title of an entry in a notebook kept by Mary's spiritualist mother, in which she recorded her own visions and the dreams of six year old Mary.

I have invented the whole Russell family and all other characters in the book. My biggest creation of all is the relationship between Hannah and Mary, and Mary and Eusebius Grenville.

I would like to thank three people in particular who have supported me through the rather daunting task of writing a novel: first and foremost Ann Evans, whose writing group I attended in Nuneaton when the book was just a twinkle in my eye and who has encouraged and supported me every inch of the way; Ben Smith who reviewed the first draft and gave me some excellent advise, resulting in a much better book and Linda Claridge-Middup, a great friend and artist, whose interpretation of the jewel garden adorns the cover of this book.

Printed in Poland
by Amazon Fulfillment
Poland Sp. z o.o., Wrocław

49505170R00228